In the purple afternoon sh█ █████ ████████ ████ran-
ite looked hollow and ██ ████████ ████████ █████ the
cliff down the ce████ ████ ████████ ████████ ██he
crevice through t█ ████████ ████████ ████ █████ █n
into the stony roots ████ ████████ ████████ ██████s
delirious as he was █ ████████ ████████ ████ █████,
such as the husky f█████ ████████ ████████ █nd disappearing as it twined ████ ████████ boulder-strewn
glacier below. The fig████ ████████ ding its ribs and limping,
and it kept pitching f██ward onto its hands and knees.
Every now and then it glanced around behind itself, searching for a tail it no longer had, and sometimes it looked up to
check the progress of Atreus and his companions. . . .

FORGOTTEN REALMS
NOVELS

Lost Empires

The Lost Library of Cormanthyr
Mel Odom

Faces of Deception
Troy Denning

Star of Cursrah
Clayton Emery
(February, 1999)

Lost Empires

Faces of Deception

Troy Denning

FACES OF DECEPTION

Lost Empires
©1998 TSR, Inc.
All Rights Reserved.

TSR, Inc., a subsidiary of Wizards of the Coast, Inc.
Made in the U.S.A.

Cover art by Fred Fields
First Printing: November 1998
Library of Congress Catalog Card Number: 97-062381
9 8 7 6 5 4 3 2 1
ISBN: 0-7869-1183-2
8586XXX1501

U.S., CANADA,
ASIA, PACIFIC, & LATIN AMERICA
Wizards of the Coast, Inc.
P.O. Box 707
Renton, WA 98057-0707
800-324-6496

EUROPEAN HEADQUARTERS
Wizards of the Coast, Belgium
P.B. 34
2300 Turnhout
Belgium
+32-14-44-30-44

Visit our web site at **www.tsr.com**

For Dixie Courant

Acknowledgments

I would like to thank my editor, Phil Athans, for his support and insight; Dale Donovan and Steven Schend for their swift and courteous reviews; and most especially Andria Hayday for her patience, support, and everything else.

1

Perhaps they thought ugly ears could not hear.

The celebrants sat scattered throughout the half empty temple, men with cleft chins and women with doelike eyes, all strikingly handsome or ravishingly beautiful, dressed in silken elegance and bathed in exotic perfumes. They were reclining on velvet love couches and resting on marble settees, murmuring in soft distress as they waited for Atreus Eleint to walk the Aisle of the Adorer. Some thought it blasphemy to let him drink from the Pool of Dreams. Others claimed his presence had already ruined attendance. They all agreed that today would spell the end of the Church of Beauty in Duhlnarim.

"What you waitin' for?" whispered Yago, looming over Atreus from behind. "I thought you wanted this."

The ogre was dressed in his best ceremonial armor, filling the marble entryway with a ten-foot wall of burnished leather and gleaming bronze. He had a raw, heavy-boned face with the sloping forehead, jutting jaw, and wart-covered hide typical of his race, but even this brutish visage drew less comment than Atreus's.

"I do," said Atreus, "but I'm nervous."

"What's to be nervous about?" Yago thumped Atreus's back with a hand the size of a buckler. "Go on."

Atreus nodded and started up the aisle, his arms spread

wide to display the brocade inside his cape. The pattern depicted the tail of the sacred peacock, fanning out to either side of Atreus's body. Though a master weaver had embroidered the design from thread of gold, it drew no more ovation than his velvet doublet or silk leg cannons. Even the finest clothes could not mask Atreus's singular shape; the hunchbacked form with the lopsided hump and jutting neck, the oversized arms, the bowed legs and one pigeon-toed foot.

Atreus stopped at the Show Ring and executed a graceful pirouette, spinning as lightly upon his deformed toes as any dancer. The celebrants covered their mouths and fell to tittering. No one clapped, even when he folded his arms in front of his chest and brought the two edges of his cape together, displaying the golden likeness of Sune Firehair. After today, he would be a celebrant in the Church of Beauty, and they did not consider that worthy of applause.

Atreus swallowed his disappointment, pasted a shad-lipped grin on his mouth, then executed a deep bow. If most of the celebrants grimaced and turned away, he did not blame them. His face was a gruesome, misshapen thing covered with lumps and swellings, laced with red veins, so abhorrent to look upon that he could not pass a mirror without shuddering himself. But if his appearance offended the worshipers of Sune Firehair, his wealth did not. They had been happy enough to accept the new couches upon which they reclined and the gurgling fountains and marble statues that decorated their temple's new garden.

Atreus turned toward the silvery dais in the front of the chamber, where three heartwarders stood waiting. Like all of Sune's priests, they were incredibly attractive. Their faces had that balance of symmetry and proportion that was the foundation of human beauty, a certain natural harmony that did not strike the eye so much as simply please it. By comparison, Atreus's own features were grossly imbalanced, with some parts much too large and others not large enough and nothing quite where it belonged. Had someone divided a portrait of his face down the center (not that he had ever asked an artist to paint such a hideous work), it would have been impossible to tell that the two halves belonged together.

"Atreus Eleint, through your devotion you have earned the right to look into the Pool of Dreams," said Heartwarder Julienne, the founder of Duhlnarim's Church of Beauty. "Will you avail yourself?"

"I will."

From the seats behind Atreus came a chorus of disapproving groans that Yago quickly silenced with a muted growl. The three heartwarders pretended not to notice the exchange, flashing smiles as lustrous as they were practiced. Unlike the celebrants, who were guests of the temple and therefore free to behave however they wished, etiquette required the heartwarders to make every worshiper feel welcome. Of course, good manners had not prevented Julienne from broaching the subject of a nice silken hood, but Atreus had politely declined, citing Sune's sacred exhortation to "hide not away." Besides, if he had to have such a hideous face it did not seem unfair to ask others to look at it.

Julienne extended her hand. "Then come."

Her assistants, a hazel-eyed beauty and a handsome young man, descended the stairs to take Atreus's gangling arms. Though the lightness of their touch betrayed their revulsion, Atreus's grin broadened into a heartfelt smile. Julienne grimaced at the sight of so many gray, snaggled teeth.

Leaving Yago at the base of the stairs, the assistant heartwarders escorted Atreus up to the Pool of Dreams. It was a raised oval basin about twice as large as a bathing tub, with silver sides embossed in a tangled pattern of intertwined lovers. Atreus kneeled beside the basin and kept his gaze fixed on Julienne, reluctant to shatter the joy of the moment with a glimpse of his own reflection.

"Why are you looking at me, Atreus Eleint?" Julienne cast her emerald eyes upon the water. "What you seek is in the pool."

Atreus took a deep breath, then lowered his gaze and gasped in astonishment. There was no reflection, only still black water as deep and dark as a rainy night. Remembering Julienne's words, he kept his eyes fixed on the glassy surface. A scarlet halo appeared far down in the depths, growing brighter and larger as it rose toward the surface.

Behold, Adorer, the Face of Beauty. The voice was at once breathy and dulcet, and so soft that Atreus could not tell whether he heard it with his ears or his heart. *Hear, Worshiper, the Voice of Love.*

The halo became a flowing mane of flaming hair, and then a woman's face appeared inside the ring. She was impossibly beautiful, with sapphire eyes and a tiny nose and lips as red as fire.

"I—I hear, O Goddess!"

The face hovered just beneath the surface of the water, shimmering and staring up at Atreus with no sign of revulsion or distaste. The rest of the temple darkened around him, and he lost all sensation of place and time. To Atreus it seemed he was floating in the night sky, hovering face-to-face with Sune Firehair herself.

The goddess pursed her lips in an almost mortal way, then asked, "Atreus Eleint, what are we to do with you?"

Atreus's answer was quick, for he knew exactly what should be done. "Take away this face, Goddess. Make me handsome."

"Take away your face?" The goddess furrowed her brow, and even her scowl was radiant. "How can I make you handsome? Beauty comes from within."

4

Atreus's heart fell. He grew so dizzy with anger he thought he would fall into the pool. How many times had he heard that same cliché from some well-meaning matron or sanctimonious priest? He had expected more of a goddess, but he knew better than to say so.

"If beauty comes from within, then only a demon could look like this." Atreus ran a set of spindly fingers down his cheek. "What have I done to deserve such a face?"

"What have you done that you don't?" Sune asked. "From the time you were a child, all you have thought of is your face, of how fate cheated you. Perhaps you would have preferred your mother had let you die?"

Atreus fell silent, afraid to admit how many times he had wished just that. He knew little of his true family. According to Yago, his entire clan had perished during the Ten Days of Eleint, when the peasants of neighboring Tethyr had risen to massacre their nobility. Atreus had survived only because the family sorcerer had disguised him as a baby ogre and entrusted him to the care of his mother's loyal Shieldbreaker bodyguards. Yago, the captain of those guards, had taken the newborn back to Rivenshield to raise as best an ogre could, faithfully safeguarding the enormous inheritance sent along by the child's mother.

Unfortunately, the spell that had saved Atreus as an infant became a curse as he matured, altering his life essence so that he grew into the ugliest young nobleman in Faerûn. He had tried everything to change his appearance, using his wealth to seek out mighty wizards, famous miracle workers, theatrical make-up artists, even surgeons. Nothing worked, and in some cases the efforts left him uglier than before.

Nor could Atreus seek help from the wizard who had cast the spell in the first place. The entire Shieldbreaker tribe claimed to have forgotten the identity of Atreus's family. Considering the mental capacity of ogres, this seemed

just barely possible, but Atreus suspected they had other
reasons for their silence. Over the years he had tried hundreds of times to cajole Yago into telling him more. The
ogre always maintained that he could recall nothing except
the month of Atreus's birth, the month that had provided
Atreus with the only family name he'd ever known.

In the end, Atreus had no choice but to accept Yago's word
and continue his quest with no knowledge of the magic that
had made him ugly in the first place. Finally a perplexed
sage had suggested joining the Church of Beauty, in the
hope that the goddess would take pity on him and use her
divine powers to make him handsome.

Atreus had immediately rented a small villa in Duhlnarim
and dedicated himself to the worship of Sune Firehair, Goddess of Beauty and Love. Now he was kneeling before her
Pool of Dreams, hardly able to believe the platitudes with
which she was repaying nearly two years of faithful devotion.

"If I have felt sorry for myself," Atreus said, "it is with
good reason. My failings are no worse than those of most
men."

"Perhaps." Sune's face rose closer, breaking the surface
of the pool. "But only you can change what you are."

Her sapphire eyes grew bright and cold, and Atreus
sensed that she was waiting.

"Then tell me how to change, and I will do it."

A slight smile crept across the goddess's lips. It was a flir-
tatious smile, such as beautiful women have always used to
entice favors from willing men.

"There might be something you can do." Her sapphire
eyes darted to their corners, as though she had only at that
moment thought of what she would ask. "You could bring me
a vial of sparkling water from the Fountain of Infinite Grace."

"The Fountain of Infinite Grace?" Atreus echoed.

"In paradise," Sune explained. "A place called Langdarma."

Before Atreus could ask where Langdarma was, the goddess's face rose completely out of the water. The visage turned vertical and hung in the air before him, its fiery hair hissing and crackling. The celebrants gasped, and the heartwarders folded their hands over their hearts. Yago merely grunted, unimpressed by what seemed to him a face too dainty to be attractive.

"Remember," said Sune. Her beautiful face dissolved into smoke and flame. "The water must be sparkling."

The temple remained as still as a painting. Never before had the goddess manifested herself at the Rite of Dreams, and Atreus could feel the gazes of the astounded celebrants on his back. Whether they had heard what passed between him and Sune he did not know, but he could tell by their stunned silence that he had become something more to them than an unpleasant joke.

"Look!"

The male heartwarder pointed into the Pool of Dreams, where a ragged parchment had appeared, floating on top of the water. On the scrap were drawn hundreds of mountains and dozens of long, snaking valleys with exotic names such as Gyatse and Yamdruk. And on the eastern edge, lying at the foot of three mountains marked the "Sisters of Serenity," was a valley called Langdarma.

Yago, who was so tall he could see over Atreus's shoulder without stepping onto the dais, peered into the Pool of Dreams. "Don't tell me that's a—"

"Map!" Atreus confirmed.

Yago groaned. He could see what was coming next, and ogres were not ones to place their faith in a piece of parchment scratched with a few lizard tracks.

Atreus snatched the map from the water and started down the steps, forgetting in his excitement to bow to Julienne. "Come on, Yago," he said. "We're going to Langdarma!"

TROY DENNING

"Langdarma?" Yago grumbled. He turned to follow Atreus down the Aisle of the Adorer. "Never heard of such a place. It's probably clear up by Arabel or something."

"Or something," Atreus agreed. He glanced down at his map. "Ever hear of the Yehimals?"

The ogre shook his head, and the celebrants began to close in around them, babbling congratulations and trying to sneak a look at the map. A few of the less squeamish even slapped Atreus's disfigured back or squeezed his round shoulder. The pair soon found themselves being swept along by a jabbering swarm of well-wishers.

Once the crowd had carried them out of earshot the assistant heartwarders turned to Julienne.

"Do you think this will work?" asked the hazel-eyed beauty.

"Of course." Julienne's smile was small and a little heartless. "The Yehimals are far, far away, and Langdarma is difficult to find . . . very difficult to find."

2

Three days after leaving the ship, Atreus still felt the sea rolling beneath his feet. He and Yago were standing outside the Grand Audience Hall of the Paradise Mahal on a white marble floor as firm as the bedrock of the world, swaying gently as they awaited an audience with the queen of Edenvale. In the distance behind the palace loomed the jagged white wall of the great Yehimal Mountains, where—somewhere—the Sisters of Serenity stood watch over the valley of Langdarma.

By the way the door guards eyed them, Atreus knew that his and Yago's constant rocking made them appear drunk or worse, but they could not help themselves. They had passed most of the four-month journey from Duhlnarim to the Utter East aboard a square-rigged cog *Squall Duchess,* which rode the waves like a piece of flotsam. It would be some time before their legs grew accustomed to solid ground again. Atreus only hoped their unsteady stances would not prevent Queen Rosalind from providing the help they needed.

A small courtier in billowing silks emerged from the scalloped portal of the audience hall. With black hair, a thin build, and golden skin, he was obviously one of the Mar natives who had inhabited this hot and sultry land when Rosalind's Faerûnian ancestors arrived to claim it. He dismissed Yago's imposing bulk with a disdainful smirk, then turned to Atreus, his lip curling as he took in the polished boots, linen trousers, and silk tunic beneath a brocaded cape. When his gaze reached Atreus's disfigured face, he gasped and stepped back, speaking sharply to the guards in Maran—a strange, melodious tongue of short syllables and throaty clicks.

The guards answered in the same language, pointing across the courtyard to the gates where the hired elephant that had carried Atreus inland stood waiting with its driver. As *Squall Duchess*'s captain had promised, the mere fact that Atreus had an ogre bodyguard and traveled in such luxury marked him as a man of consequence.

"I have a letter of introduction from my own liege, King Korox of Erlkazar," Atreus said. From inside his cloak he withdrew a folded parchment that Heartwarder Julienne had procured from the king's sister, Princess Dijara. Atreus bowed, displaying the unbroken wax on its royal seal. "I am Atreus Eleint of Rivenshield, in Barony Ahlarkhem of Erlkazar."

Though the Mar showed no sign of understanding Atreus, he accepted the letter and examined the seal, narrowing his eyes at the royal crown pressed into the golden wax. He glanced at the golden brocades in Atreus's cape, then bowed.

"I am Jyotish, chamberlain to Queen Rosalind," said the Mar, now speaking an archaic form of Realmspeak known as Thorass. The language was so outdated and heavily accented that Atreus had to guess some words from the context of others. "I will arrange an audience with Her Radiance."

Jyotish returned the letter and stepped aside, waving Atreus toward a huge pair of mahogany doors. As they started up the stairs, the sentries quickly crossed their glaives in front of Yago. The ogre scowled, then jerked the weapons from the guards' hands and tossed them into the courtyard. The guards cried out and reached for the swords, and Jyotish whirled on Atreus.

"What is the meaning of this?"

"I go where Atreus goes," Yago said, paying no attention to the sword tips now pointed in his direction. "I'm his bodyguard."

"Bodyguards are not permitted in the Grand Audience Chamber." Jyotish spoke directly to Atreus, as though demanding that he bring his pet under control. "No man may take his own guards into the queen's presence."

Atreus nodded. "Of course. I should have thought of that myself." He turned to Yago and said, "Why don't you wait here?"

A growl of displeasure rumbled deep in Yago's throat, but he was too good a soldier to argue the matter in front of others. He stepped back into the courtyard. "Give a yell if you need me."

"I'm sure I'll be fine," said Atreus. "There's no reason to expect trouble."

"That's when it's most dangerous." Yago snarled down at Jyotish, displaying his orange fangs, then spread his feet and folded his arms. "I'll be listening."

Jyotish scowled at the ogre's not-so-subtle warning, then turned to lead the way into the palace. As he opened the mahogany doors he quietly asked, "Is your bodyguard always so unruly?"

"Unruly?" Atreus raised his brow, genuinely surprised. "That's not unruly. Not for an ogre."

He stepped through the doorway into a dark, many-pillared room full of droning voices and sweet-smelling smoke. The lower walls were decorated with floral patterns of gold filigree on deep red lacquer. The upper parts were covered with brilliant frescoes depicting charging war elephants and strange, golemlike warriors. Tiny, shaven-headed Mar priests sat in apses along the walls, rocking back and forth and chanting in gravelly voices while toothless old women squatted on the floor chattering incessantly and spinning yarn with their fingers. Children ran about

11

laughing and chasing each other, paying so little attention to where they were going that one of them crashed into Atreus at a dead sprint.

The little girl landed at Atreus's feet still yelling and giggling, then suddenly fell silent when she noticed how one set of the stranger's toes turned inward. As her eyes ran up his bowed legs to his thick midsection, she scowled and began to scoot backward across the floor. Her gaze continued to rise toward his gruesome visage, and Atreus knew what was about to happen. He could only stand and watch as the girl's mouth fell open.

"Ysdar!" she bawled, pointing at him. "Ysd*aaaaar*!"

The room fell instantly silent and all eyes turned in Atreus's direction. Knowing he would only make the situation worse by reaching out to comfort the child, Atreus spread his hands at his side and tried a smile.

The girl's wail became a shriek. She leaped to her feet and disappeared screaming into the chamber's dark recesses. Jyotish stared at Atreus in horror, then stepped aside and began to click and prattle in the strange language of his people. The other Mar backed away, clapping their hands and jabbering admonitions Atreus did not understand, save for the occasional reference to "Ysdar." He could only shake his head and smile.

After a moment, a handsome young Mar with satyrlike ears and a cultured bearing stepped out of the crowd. Attired in cotton trousers and a silk tunic, he was dressed more in the manner of Faerûn than that of the Utter East. He started chattering at his fellows and waving them back.

When the tumult finally began to subside, he turned to Atreus and said, "Honored Guest, it is better if you keep your teeth hidden." This Mar's Realmspeak was modern, tinged with a Sembian accent, and—unlike Jyotish's—easy to understand. "The Mar are a backward and superstitious people who already think you one of Ysdar's fiends. There is no need to encourage them in this silliness."

"Encourage them?"

"By implying you want to eat them." The Mar flashed a pearly grin and tapped his bright teeth. "This means you are hungry."

Atreus brought his lips together. "Please apologize for me. Tell them I am an ignorant foreigner who is not hungry at all."

The Mar spoke first to Jyotish, then to his jabbering fellows. Jyotish nodded, and the crowd stopped hissing and clapping, though they continued to warily eye the stranger's hideous face.

Atreus's savior bowed to him. "Honored sir, allow me to introduce myself. I am Rishi Saubhari, a *bahrana* only recently come to Edenvale myself."

A bahrana was a member of the Mar upper class. Atreus did not yet grasp the subtle differences of appearance between bahranas and the lower class *taroks,* but after coming ashore in the Utter East, he had quickly learned what a grave insult it was to ask a bahrana to do a tarok's work.

"In his wisdom, the esteemed Jyotish senses that you have need of a companion familiar with our customs," said Rishi. "He asks that I serve you in this capacity, if you will have me."

"What a relief that would be," Atreus said, then gestured at his face. "As you can see, it's hard enough for me to make a good impression."

Rishi's expression remained unreadable. "I do not see why that should be." He drew closer and spoke in a quieter tone. "But we do have need to discuss compensation."

"Have no fear," Atreus replied, jangling his heavy purse. "You'll be well paid."

Rishi's eyes lit up. "A blessing on you, sir!" He took Atreus's arm and started forward as he spoke. "Shall we attend to the queen?"

The sea of Mar divided before the procession, shaking tassels at the ugly foreigner and softly murmuring about Ysdar.

Atreus leaned down to speak quietly to Rishi. "What is this 'Ysdar'?"

"Pay no attention to those heathens!" Rishi lowered his voice and spoke in a confidential tone. "The Mar of Edenvale are superstitious fools who would not know a devil of Ysdar if they saw one."

"All the same, I would like to know why they fear me," insisted Atreus.

"Very well." Rishi cast a meaningful glance at Atreus's purse. "But you must remember I am only doing as you command."

"Your truthfulness will be rewarded."

"Then as you wish," said Rishi. "According to legend, Ysdar is a devil from another world, an ancient evil unleashed many ages ago when the Lords of the Five Kingdoms weakened his prison."

Rishi was speaking of the Bloodforge Wars, of course. No traveler to the Utter East could escape hearing about the ancient carnage, for the wars were more a part of the region's history than the Ten Days of Eleint were part of Tethyr's. Shortly after conquering the Utter East, the Lords of the Five Kingdoms discovered the bloodforges, ancient war machines capable of manufacturing whole armies of magic golems. Unrestrained by the expense of raising and maintaining armies, the lords went mad with battle-lust, nearly destroying their lands and their peoples. To make matters worse, the lords did not realize that a horde of antediluvian horrors had lain trapped beneath the land so long they had vanished from memory. Every use of the bloodforges weakened the mystical bonds of their prison, and the creatures soon began to overrun the Five Kingdoms. Eventually, the lords realized their folly and struck a bargain not to use the terrible war machines, but the damage had already been done. According to rumor, the land had been filled with slime-smeared monsters and slithering horrors ever since.

"Ysdar is one of the Forgotten Ones?"

Rishi nodded. "The King of the Forgotten Ones, if the myths are to be believed." He glanced away, then added more quietly, "It is said his face is so ugly that anyone who looks upon it goes mad . . . though this is in no way a reflection on your honored person."

"Of course it is," Atreus replied, trying to keep the bitterness out of his voice. "Edenvale is no different than my own home. When people see ugly, they think evil."

The golden faces and black hair of the Mar began to give way to the creamier visages of the Ffolk, who stood conversing quietly in small groups of three and four. In many ways, the Ffolk still resembled their conquering ancestors. They were larger than the Mar and lighter of complexion, with pale eyes and square, western jaws. Though they had long ago exchanged the heavy furs and dreary wool of the Moonshae Isles for the bright cotton and colorful silks more suited to the Utter East's sweltering climate, they still preferred tight trousers and snug tunics to the billowing fashions of the Mar.

At the far end of the chamber stood a large enclosure surrounded by red velvet drapes, through which the Royal Warden was ushering a sporadic stream of haughty-looking supplicants, Ffolk and Mar alike. More often than not, the petitioners looked content as they departed, a sign that the queen considered herself duty bound to serve her people as much as they served her. Atreus hoped her sense of fairness would extend to foreigners.

As they approached, the warden raised a hand and spoke quietly to Rishi and Jyotish in Thorass, all the while frowning and stealing glances at Atreus. Jyotish said something about a hired elephant and a royal letter, while Rishi spoke in rapid Maran and plucked at his own tunic.

Finally, the stony-eyed warden gave a reluctant nod, and Rishi removed his silk shirt and held it up before Atreus. Though such behavior would have scandalized any royal court in the west, no one in the Paradise Mahal paid the Mar's shirtless chest the slightest attention.

"If you would be so kind as to bow down," said Rishi. "No disrespect is meant, but Queen Rosalind is not well, and the Royal Warden fears your singular appearance might prove too much of a shock."

Atreus hesitated. "I understand, but covering my face is a sacrilege to my goddess."

"Which goddess?" Jyotish demanded, scowling.

Atreus steeled himself to answer. "Sune Firehair."

"The western Goddess of Beauty?" asked Jyotish.

When Atreus nodded, the chamberlain exchanged glances with the Royal Warden. They broke into fits of snickering, and even Rishi had to bite his cheeks and turn away.

Atreus felt the angry heat rising to his cheeks. "One need not be beautiful to worship beauty."

"That is so," said the Royal Warden, for the first time speaking directly to Atreus. "It is also so that Queen Rosalind is not well. She cannot be shocked."

Rishi opened his shirt again and held it up before Atreus. "This is the only way to see Queen Rosalind. If it is important, Sune will understand."

"Perhaps you are right," Atreus said. He would be the first to admit that the goddess had been thinking of someone else when she admonished her worshipers to display their faces. "I would not want to cause Queen Rosalind any discomfort."

Atreus allowed Rishi to drape the shirt over his head, then arranged the neck hole so that he could see his feet and spare himself the embarrassment of stumbling. The cloth smelled of curry and cinnamon, which Mar bodies seemed to exude the way westerners did sweat.

The Royal Warden pulled a curtain aside, and Jyotish led the way through the gap into the velvety enclosure. A soft droning drifted down from above. Rishi guided Atreus up the stairs of a huge dais, grasping his hand and locking fingers in a manner that would have seemed far too intimate in Erlkazar. A cool breeze wafted down from a window somewhere above, and a bright rectangle of light began to blush through Atreus's makeshift hood. When they reached the top of the dais they stopped and took their place at the end of a short line of supplicants. Through the neck hole of Rishi's shirt, Atreus saw half a dozen of the petitioners turn to gape at his makeshift hood and whisper hushed speculations about its purpose.

It took only a few moments before a woman said, "What is all this?" Though her voice was reedy and frail, the murmuring supplicants fell instantly silent. "Why is that man wearing a hood?"

Jyotish bowed contritely and started to apologize for the disruption, but he was quickly interrupted by Rishi.

"Honored Queen of Brilliance, the man you inquire after has journeyed from the other side of the world to bask in your radiance." Rishi pulled Atreus toward the head of the line. "He is a most unusual fellow, unfamiliar with our customs and therefore in need of my humble assistance."

Through his narrow view hole, Atreus saw that they were approaching a huge bed with mahogany corner posts and a silken canopy. Spread across the mattress was an embroidered spread depicting six golden cranes wading through a reed pool. In the bed lay a small woman with honey-colored hair, ice-blue eyes, and a gaunt face as jaundiced as that of any goblin. The hands folded across her lap were almost skeletal, and her heavy crown, studded with rubies and diamonds, rested on a satin pillow at her side.

The queen regarded Rishi coldly. "And you are?"

"Rishi Saubhari, Radiance, a bahrana ginger-prince from the Free Cities." Rishi stopped two paces from the bed, where a handsome Ffolk man in a plain golden crown stood flanked by six guards. "It was not so very long ago that I myself was presented to Your Brilliance and the Royal Husband."

Still clasping Atreus's hand, he bowed first to the bedridden queen, then to the man with the golden crown. Atreus was about to do likewise when Jyotish scurried up and hurled himself to the floor.

"This is not my doing!" The chamberlain spoke so rapidly that Atreus could barely decipher his thick accent. "I could not stop them!"

Rishi turned toward Jyotish. "We were meant to *wait*?" He allowed his jaw to drop in a purely artificial expression of surprise. "The queen did not summon us forward? Apologies! Apologies many and profuse! Then I was much mistaken in the impression that she wished to meet this man—this man who has journeyed many months across land and sea all the way from the parched wastes of the far side of the world, and only so he might bask in the divine radiance of Edenvale's queen."

Rishi tugged sharply on Atreus's hand.

Taking the hint, Atreus bowed first to the queen, then to her husband. "Please excuse the interruption," he said, feeling rather clownish with Rishi's shirt draped over his head. "It was not my intention to disturb your court."

Rishi finally released Atreus's hand. "Allow me to present Atreus Eleint, a noble prince of Erlkazar—"

"Loyal citizen!" Atreus corrected, horrified. In Erlkazar, such a gross misrepresentation could cost a man his tongue. "I am not even a lord."

Rishi continued without missing a beat. "Our honored traveler is a man of no small consequence, bearing a royal letter of introduction from the King of Erlkazar himself."

Queen Rosalind shifted her gaze to Atreus, then spoke to him in Realmspeak as modern as Rishi's. "Is this true?"

"I have it here, Your Majesty." Moving slowly so as not to alarm the queen's bodyguards, Atreus reached into his cape and withdrew the parchment. "It is from His Royal Highness, King Korox of Erlkazar."

Atreus held out the letter, expecting someone to take it from him and break the seal for Queen Rosalind, as was the custom in western lands. The action drew an astonished groan from Jyotish and stony silence from the queen's retinue. Atreus tipped his head back and saw that he was pushing the letter toward the Royal Husband.

"What are you doing?" Rishi hissed. "You must present the letter to Her Radiance, not her husband!"

"I beg your pardon." Atreus stepped to the edge of the queen's bed and offered the parchment to her. "In my own land, one does not approach the king—er, monarch—directly."

Rosalind's voice grew as icy as it was frail. "Yes, I am aware that customs differ in the west."

With great effort, she lifted her hand to accept the letter. Atreus placed the parchment in her shaking palm. She passed it to the Royal Husband, then let her arm fall to the bed before dragging her hand back to her lap. Atreus suddenly felt thankful to the warden for insisting that he cover his hideous face. The last thing he wanted was to scare the poor woman to death.

The Royal Husband broke King Korox's seal, then turned to Rosalind and read in a deep voice free of accent.

"Greetings and Good Tidings to Her Royal Majesty Rosalind, Most Radiant Queen of the Great Land of Edenvale.

"We hope that this missive finds you as well as we are in Erlkazar. Be it known that the explorer bearing this letter, Atreus Eleint, is a man of no small ability and a particular

friend of ours. We ask that you grant him every courtesy
due a man of high station and help him along his way. We
eagerly await our chance to repay you in good kind.

"With high regards, His Royal Majesty Korox."

No sooner had the Royal Husband finished reading than
Rosalind looked to Atreus. "Well, explorer, how can we help
you and make your king happy with us?"

Atreus could not help smiling behind his makeshift
hood, for it had not occurred to him that he was an explorer
until he heard Korox's letter. "I am planning a journey into
the Yehimal Mountains. Any assistance you can provide by
way of a guide and porters would be greatly appreciated. I
will, of course, pay all the necessary expenses."

"Then how very fortunate it is that I am standing here,"
said Rishi. "My affairs in the ginger business—"

"At the moment, Rishi, we are not interested in your ginger," said Rosalind, cutting off the Mar. "But we will be in a
better position to help our explorer if he cares to tell us
what he is seeking. Unless, of course, it is a secret."

The queen fixed her eyes on Atreus's view hole and
waited, leaving no doubt in his mind that the help he
received would come in direct proportion to his candor.

"I am happy to name my goal," Atreus said. "I am searching for three peaks called the Sisters of Serenity."

"My goodness, what a happy coincidence!" exclaimed
Rishi. "By a great good fortune, it happens I passed there
just last—"

Scowling, the queen filled the air with an angry torrent of
short syllables and guttural clicks, chastising the Mar in his
own language.

Rishi gasped at the rebuke. "Oh no, I would not want
that, Most Radiant Queen! I am so sorry of the mistake and
from this moment onward shall say nothing more. It is not
necessary to trouble the Royal Husband, as no harm was
meant or intended or expected, and I will be forever silent

until you again give me leave to speak. I was only trying to be helpful, as I have journeyed into those same mountains a hundred times and would happily spare your Brilliance the trouble of seeking a guide for our esteemed—"

Atreus heard the siss of a dagger blade clearing its sheath. The Royal Husband growled, "Rishi!"

The little Mar fell instantly silent.

Rosalind spoke to Atreus. "Tell me, explorer, are the Sisters of Serenity to be your final destination?"

Atreus could tell by the way she asked that the queen knew the answer. "No, I am seeking the Valley of Langdarma."

The answer drew a chorus of snickering from the Ffolk on the dais, though the Mar remained silent.

The queen looked past Atreus and said in perfect Thorass, "That's enough! I will not have an envoy from a foreign kingdom laughed at in my court!" The sniggering died away, then she spoke again to Atreus in modern Realmspeak. "I wonder, explorer, if you would be kind enough to take the shirt off your head."

Atreus hesitated, recalling how the simple effort of accepting a letter had caused the queen's hand to tremble. "I am happy to grant any request you make of me, but I must warn you, the Mar claim I have the face of Ysdar."

"Most certainly!" added Jyotish. "It would be better for all if you did not look on it, Most Radiant."

"There is no need for concern, Jyotish," said Rosalind. "If the explorer were truly as ugly as Ysdar, would you be here to warn me off?"

Jyotish nodded. "Of course, Most Radiant. Not even Ysdar could make me crazy enough to leave your service."

Rosalind laughed, then gestured to Atreus. "You may remove the shirt, explorer. Forewarned is fair-armed. I doubt the shock will kill me."

"As you wish."

Atreus bowed his head and pulled the shirt off, returning it Rishi. He gave the queen a moment to grow accustomed to the misshapen contours of his ungainly skull, then raised his chin slowly, allowing her ample time to brace herself as each disfigured feature grew visible. When his head had risen high enough for him to observe her mouth, he saw that she had pasted a charitable smile on her lips. The smile wavered occasionally as the rest of his face came into view, but it never vanished entirely, not even when she found herself struggling to gaze into both of his cocked eyes at once.

"There," she said, though Atreus knew she was speaking more to herself than him. "That isn't so bad."

"Majesty, it's better not to make light of it," said Atreus. "I know what I look like, and pretending otherwise only makes us both uncomfortable."

At once, a look of great weariness replaced Rosalind's smile. "I am so glad to hear you say that, Atreus. It makes it easier to tell you what I must."

Atreus nodded, well-accustomed to seeing doors close because of his looks. "I understand. If you can't help me, King Korox will take no offense."

"I can help you, explorer," said Rosalind. Atreus's head snapped up, and the queen's eyes grew soft. "But I fear it is not the aid you seek."

"I would be most grateful for whatever you can do."

"I hope that will be true when I have said what I must."

The queen turned away, looking out the window across the rooftops of her city. In the distance, floating on a cloud of hazy green hills, stood the soaring wall of white-capped peaks toward which Atreus had been traveling for more than four months.

"The Yehimal Mountains are a mysterious and vast place," said Queen Rosalind. "There are many legends about what can be found in them. Diamonds as large as mountains, rivers that run yellow with gold, valleys filled with heavenly beauty . . . perhaps those legends are even true, but it does not matter. Those who seek such places never return except as jabbering lunatics, too crippled and mad to make sense of what they say. The Mar claim it is because Ysdar still roams the wilderness, preying on those foolish enough to trek where they don't belong. We Ffolk have another explanation. We know that these places exist only in the minds of those who seek them."

Rosalind turned away from her window but could not quite bring herself to look upon Atreus again. "You see, there is only one way I can help you, and that is by sending you back to King Korox sane and sound."

"But Langdarma does exist," Atreus insisted, growing concerned. "I have it on the . . . highest authority."

The queen began to look impatient. "What authority could possibly be higher than my own?"

"Only that of a goddess . . . my goddess, Sune Firehair." Atreus's reply drew a gentle murmur of laughter, and this time Rosalind made no attempt to silence the mirth. "Sune herself commanded me to seek the valley. I am to return with a vial of—"

"Your goddess is not worshiped in the Yehimals," Rosalind said. "She is barely remembered here in Edenvale, and so it is impossible that she knows of Langdarma."

"Then who gave me this?"

Atreus reached into his cape and withdrew the map he had received in Duhlnarim, so worn from folding and unfolding that it was beginning to tear along the creases. He unfolded the map and laid it on the queen's lap.

"As you can see, it is a map to Langdarma," he said. "All I ask is a guide to help me find the Sisters of Serenity, or, failing that, the best instructions you can offer."

Rosalind studied the map, her eyes silently scanning the names of the mountains and valleys. After a few moments, she looked up and sadly shook her head.

"I am sorry. Someone has deceived you. I do not recognize any of the names on this map. The Sisters of Serenity are as much a myth as Langdarma itself."

"Begging your pardon, Most Radiant Majesty, but perhaps that is not so," interrupted Rishi. He turned to Atreus. "As I have said, I visited these Sisters only last year in the company of a—"

"Silence!" commanded the Royal Husband. "Were you not warned?"

The Royal Husband glanced at Rosalind. When she nodded, he signaled to two guards, who snatched up the Mar as quick as a snake and carried him to the windows beyond the queen's bed.

"Please, please—no!" Rishi flailed about madly, kicking and writhing like a cobra in the claws of a mongoose. "Have mercy, good sirs! Do you think I am a bird? I cannot fly!"

Without replying, the guards hefted Rishi through the window and stepped back. The Mar's loud scream quickly faded, then ceased altogether. Atreus found himself staring slack-jawed out the window, wondering at the harshness of the queen's punishment.

The Royal Husband grimaced at the sight of Atreus's gaping mouth. "There's a roof outside that slants down to the moat," he explained. "The Mar will be fine."

"Which is more than we shall be able to say for you, explorer, if you insist on this search," said Rosalind.

"Langdarma is real," Atreus replied. "I myself saw Sune's face in the Pool of Dreams, but it is clear you cannot help me. If you will return my map, I will trouble you no more."

He extended a hand, but Rosalind jerked the map away.

"I fear I cannot permit what you wish," she said. "What would King Korox say if I allowed any harm to come to a 'particular friend' of his?"

An angry knot formed in Atreus's stomach, but he forced

himself to answer in an even voice. "As I have said, he will take no offense if you can't help me."

"But as I have said, I can help you." Rosalind nodded and her guards seized Atreus by the arms. She turned to the Royal Husband and passed him the map. "Dispose of that and have an honor guard take this 'explorer' back to the Doegan Shores. They are to place him on the next ship to the Sword Coast."

"A wise decision." The Royal Husband wadded Sune's map into a ball and pitched it out the window. "The last thing we need is this Atreus Eleint sneaking around the Yehimals. The Mar will think he is Ysdar himself!"

3

The avenue was cramped and crooked and crowded. The smell of spice—ginger and cinnamon and curry—masked the stench of the refuse spoiling in the gutters, and the din of jabbering voices filled the air with a constant drone as loud as it was maddening. High tenement buildings loomed along both sides of the street, their battered awnings and rickety second-story verandahs grazing the elephant's flanks as it ambled past. On many of the balconies stood hissing Mar, hurling small sticks at the poor beast and clapping their hands to drive its passenger from the city.

Atreus feigned indifference to their insults and kept his gaze fixed to the front. He was sitting in the crowded howdah on the elephant's back, with two Ffolk guards kneeling on the floor behind him. There were also a dozen riders struggling to clear the street ahead and another dozen riders bringing up the rear with Yago. Although the soldiers were dressed in the ceremonial livery of an honor guard, their surly bearing and wary watchfulness made plain that the only thing they were guarding against was Atreus's escape.

Atreus fought to hold his growing anger in check. As betrayed and insulted as he felt by Queen Rosalind's decision, he would gain nothing by venting his rage now. Better to wait a few days, until his escorts' horses began to suffer in the hot muggy terrain of Doegan, then escape to another of the Five Kingdoms. Edenvale was not the only realm

26

bordering the Yehimals, and he had heard a person with money could buy anything in Konigheim.

A pair of teak window shutters slammed open beside the howdah, revealing the murky interior of a second-story apartment. Atreus glimpsed what looked like a curved yellow dagger whirling out of the darkness, then cried out and raised his arm. Something soft struck his wrist and fell to the floor.

The two guards in the howdah rose and turned toward the window, directing their fellows below into the building. Yago roared in alarm and began to bull his way past his escorts, raising a great clamor of clanging armor and whinnying horses. Atreus looked down and found a banana lying at his feet. Scratched into the peel was a brief message: "Be ready." He glanced into the window and saw a plump silhouette retreating into the darkness, then snatched the banana off the floor.

Atreus looked back to see Yago, separated from the elephant by four double ranks of riders, shoving a startled horse out of his way. "There's nothing to worry about," he shouted. Atreus displayed the banana, then quickly peeled it and tossed the skin out of the howdah.

"It's only a banana, Yago. Go back to your place."

Yago furrowed his heavy brow in puzzlement, then turned to scowl at the nearest rider. "You call that guardin'?" He pointed a dagger-length finger at the banana in Atreus's hand. "That coulda been a knife!"

"But it wasn't," Atreus said. "So let's not worry about it."

He turned forward again and passed the banana to his elephant driver. "For Sunreet."

"You are too kind, Sahib," the driver replied, eating the banana himself. "She thanks you very much."

The guards guffawed loudly and called their fellows off. The procession resumed its slow pace down the street. Atreus sat back and tried not to look obvious as he scanned

the verandahs and windows ahead. He could not imagine
who had sent the message. Even if Rishi Saubhari had
weathered his plunge into the moat, he hardly seemed
likely to have the means to overpower two dozen of the
queen's horsemen. That left only an unknown Ffolk nobleman, no doubt eager to use Atreus's hideous face in some
intrigue that had less to do with finding Langdarma than
unseating a sickly queen.

The procession twined its way through the streets for
another ten minutes until the remnants of a gatehouse and
wall appeared fifty paces ahead. Built entirely of white marble, the "Pearl Curtain" had once enclosed the entire city,
but the fortifications had been razed during the Bloodforge
Wars and never rebuilt. Now the ruins served only to mark
the official city limit. Beyond them, the tenement buildings
grew smaller and less closely packed, finally giving way to
crop fields, then grazing lands, and eventually a lush forest.

The forest would be an ideal place for an ambush, and
Atreus was debating the wisdom of using the confusion to
escape when a string of sharp cracks echoed through the
street. Atreus dropped his gaze and saw bursts of light
flashing around the hooves of the horses ahead. Several of
the beasts whinnied and reared, bringing the whole procession to a sudden halt and dumping their riders into the
clouds of smoke swirling about the street.

Sunreet raised her trunk and let out a shrill trumpet. The
Mar in the street began to jabber in unintelligible hysteria.
The two guards behind Atreus shouldered their way for-
ward and kneeled in the front of the howdah.

"Shou powder," observed one.

"Expensive," said the other. "Too expensive for this."

Atreus glanced to the side and found himself looking
across a dilapidated balcony, to where a shadowy Mar
stood waving at him from inside a dark doorway. Atreus
made no move to leave the howdah, preferring his own

plan of escape to becoming involved in some traitor's plot against Queen Rosalind.

The Mar stepped into the light, revealing himself to be Rishi Saubhari. "Good sir, what are you waiting for?" Rishi asked. "I thought you wanted to see the Sisters of Serenity!"

The two howdah guards spun around.

"Do you know what you're about, wog?" demanded one. "We're on the queen's business here."

The other placed a foot on the howdah's rail, gathering himself to leap onto the balcony. "You'll answer to Her Radiance's jailer for this!"

Rishi ignored them both and slipped a hand inside his cloak. "We can still find Langdarma," he said, withdrawing a wad of soggy parchment. "I have your map!"

Though Atreus had long ago memorized every feature of the map, seeing it again overcame any reservations he had about accepting Rishi's help. As a gift from Sune herself, the map possessed a worth far in excess of the symbols written on it. He stood and shoved the first guard out of the howdah onto the elephant's shoulders, then grabbed the other by the belt and jerked him back inside. The fellow landed heavily on the floor, and Atreus knocked him unconscious with a big-knuckled fist to the hinge of the jaw.

A clamorous uproar arose behind the elephant. Yago, looming a full head above the riders surrounding him, began to fight his way forward, shouldering men from their saddles and shoving horses off their feet. Seeing that the ogre was about to lose his temper, Atreus pointed into the tenement building where Rishi stood waiting.

"Yago, kill no one!" he ordered. "Meet me inside."

The ogre nodded, then punched a horse unconscious and stepped over its fallen bulk, heading for the nearest door. Atreus sighed in relief. The last thing he needed was to anger Queen Rosalind by killing one of her guards. He

29

grabbed the smallest cargo basket from the back of the howdah.

"What are you doing?" Rishi cried. "My profuse apologies, but we have no time for luggage!"

"We have time for one!" The basket was heavy, and Atreus groaned as he tossed it across the small chasm to the verandah. "Catch!"

The basket struck Rishi square in the chest, driving him back through the doorway and onto the floor of the darkened room. Atreus stepped onto the rail to follow his basket across, but by then the first guard had clambered back into the howdah and grabbed hold of his leg.

Atreus jumped anyway, dragging his attacker along and catching hold of the verandah's balustrade. The guard swung like a pendulum and smashed into one of the horsemen who had ridden forward to stop the escape. When the fellow did not immediately drop off, Atreus simply pulled him along onto the balcony. Atreus was as strong as he was ugly—anyone raised by ogres had to be—and he hardly noticed the extra weight.

As Atreus tumbled over the balustrade, he twisted around and landed on his back. He sat up and drew his fist back to strike, then realized he could not hit his attacker in the face. The man was ruggedly handsome, with a square jaw and flat high cheeks, and it would have been an affront to Sune to ruin his good looks.

Taking advantage of the delay, the guard pulled his dagger and pushed the tip under Atreus's chin. "Don't move!"

Atreus grabbed his foe's knife hand and twisted against the thumb. The guard screamed and dropped the dagger. Atreus continued to twist, rolling the man onto his back, then spun onto his knees and gathered the fellow up and pitched him back into the howdah. Behind the elephant, a tangle of soldiers and horses lay in Yago's wake, struggling to unsnarl itself. The ogre himself was nowhere in sight, but the muffled crashes coming from the floor below left no doubt that he had made his way into the building.

By now, three more guards had clambered onto the verandah. They were advancing from both sides, eyeing Atreus warily and reaching for their swords. He slipped toward the pair on his right, slapping down the leader's sword and simultaneously launching a side-thrust kick at the second man in line. The blow caught the guard square in the chest, launching him off the verandah and down into the tangle of men and horses below.

The rickety balcony shook as the third guard rushed to strike from behind. Atreus grabbed the leader's collar and dropped to the floor, swinging around behind him. The move catapulted his captive into his attacker and sent both men tumbling over the balustrade into the confusion below.

Atreus rolled to his knees in the doorway. Rishi was standing inside the murky chamber, staring gape-mouthed out onto the verandah. At his feet sat the heavy basket Atreus had thrown to him, and there were fresh scrape marks on the teak floor. Whether or not the Mar's intention had been to steal, he had clearly been trying to take the cargo basket and flee.

Rishi pointed at the empty balcony behind Atreus. "You . . . how did you do defeat so many, good sir?"

"An ugly man learns to fight," Atreus said, standing.

"It was a . . . a thing of beauty!" Rishi's mouth continued to hang open, then his arm shot up and pointed out the door. "Good sir, watch your back!"

Atreus twisted forward and away, then glimpsed the tip of a sword arcing toward his head from across the verandah. Behind it came the guard he had knocked unconscious earlier, hurling himself off the balustrade in an assault as wild as it was foolish. Before Atreus could raise his arm to block, a tiny dagger flashed past from Rishi's direction and sank deep into the guard's gullet. The sword

31

slipped from the man's grasp, as he let out a surprised gurgle and collapsed through the doorway.

Atreus kneeled beside the man and pulled the dagger free, unleashing a stream of bright red froth. He looked at Rishi in horror.

"Why did you do that?"

"Perhaps the good sir forgets he owes me money," said Rishi. "It would hardly do to let him get killed before he pays."

"I wasn't going to get killed," said Atreus. He glanced back to see several pairs of hands reaching up to grasp the verandah railing. "But now you've made a marked man of me. The queen's guards will take a poor view of having one of their own killed."

"Then I suggest we go." Rishi gestured at the basket on the floor. "I fear the good sir must carry his own cargo. The basket is too heavy for me."

Atreus pulled his purse from his belt and dropped it on the floor for the dying man's family, then he grabbed his basket and followed the Mar across the dingy room into a dark, cramped corridor. An angry outcry erupted behind him as the guards climbed onto the balcony and noticed their dying comrade. Rishi pulled the door closed and led the way toward a dingy stairwell at the end of the hall.

As they approached, Yago's heavy steps began to rumble up the stairs, then the ogre appeared in the doorway, doubled over and packed into the narrow passage. When he saw Rishi and Atreus, he dropped to his hands and knees and tried to squeeze through the doorway.

"Not this way," Rishi called. "We must go up the stairs. Quickly!"

Yago retreated through the door and scrambled up the stairs on all fours, the whole stairwell shaking beneath his pounding feet. Rishi followed close behind, shouting at the ogre to move faster. Atreus brought up the rear, his knees pumping furiously as he hauled the heavy basket up the steps.

A door slammed open behind him, then someone cried, "The stairs!"

The hammering footfalls of a half-a-dozen charging men began to echo up the stairwell. Upon reaching the next floor, Atreus saw how well Rishi had planned their escape. On the landing, a dozen oil casks lay stacked on their sides, held in place by a single wooden wedge lodged between the floor and first barrel. After Yago and Atreus squeezed past, Rishi turned to kick the wedge free.

It twisted sideways, but did not come out.

Rishi's eyes widened. The angry guards reached the bottom of the stairs and started up, nostrils flaring and swords waving. Again, the Mar kicked at the wedge. This time, his toe bounced off without budging it.

Atreus squatted down and dropped the heavy basket on the floor. Rishi spun around at the resulting jingle, but he did not step out of the way.

"Move!" Atreus shouted, pulling the Mar aside.

The first guard was only a dozen steps below, staring up at the casks and sneering in relief.

When Atreus reached down and grabbed the wedge, the man's smirk vanished. He cocked his arm to throw his sword, and Atreus jerked the wedge free. The casks tumbled loose with a deafening rumble, bouncing down the stairs to bowl the guards over backward. One keg split and spilled oil everywhere, turning the whole stairwell into a slimy avalanche of somersaulting men and flying casks.

"Well done!" Rishi exclaimed, once again eyeing Atreus's heavy cargo basket. "Very well done. Now escape is assured."

"I'll believe that," Atreus said, "once we've actually escaped."

Atreus picked up his cargo, and he and Rishi started up

33

the stairs after Yago. Although the basket was ungainly and difficult to carry, he did not even consider abandoning it. The coffer inside held many ten-thousands of gold lions, a full quarter of the fortune bequeathed to him by his unknown mother. This was the amount he had dedicated to finding Langdarma, and he had no intention of leaving it to Queen Rosalind's guards.

They ascended three more flights of stairs, then stepped into a long hallway leading toward the rear of the building. Yago stopped and pointed toward a window at the end of the corridor, where a long plank lay on the bottom sill, stretching across a narrow alley to a similar casement in another building.

"Am I supposed to fit through that?" the ogre demanded.

"Most definitely not," Rishi replied. "Your weight would snap the board like straw. You must continue up to the roof."

"The roof?" asked Atreus.

"I have seen how strong the ogre is," said Rishi. "I am sure he will not be troubled by such a small leap."

Yago squinted out the distant window. "How far is it?"

"Oh, it cannot be far," said Rishi. "The board itself is not five paces long."

"Five paces?" The ogre stretched his arms apart, trying to envision the distance. "That's got to be as long as a—"

"Five of our paces. It is no more than two of yours," Rishi said as he braced his hands on Yago's hips, struggling in vain to shove the ogre into the stairwell. "Now go up on the roof—and hurry! Can you not hear our enemies?"

Atreus cocked his head, listening to the sound of the pounding feet below, then nodded to Yago. "Go on. We'll see you on the other side."

Yago reluctantly squeezed back through the door and rumbled up the steps, leaving Rishi and Atreus to continue down the corridor alone. The Mar stopped at the window and turned to Atreus.

"No indignity is meant, but you are heavy enough without your basket, and the board is very old. Perhaps I should go first and drag your cargo along behind me."

Atreus shook his head. "I'd feel terrible if you fell. The basket is too heavy for you." He eyed the plank. As weathered and gray as the board was, it was also quite thick, with no sign of rotting. "You go ahead. I'll be fine."

Rishi sighed, then leaped onto the board and trotted across as lightly as a cat. Atreus followed more slowly, holding the heavy basket away from his body so he could look down and see his feet. By the time he had taken five steps, he almost wished he had let Rishi steal the gold. The plank was bowing severely under his weight, and every step caused it to bounce so harshly he could hardly keep his balance. Forty feet below, a constant stream of Mar scurried past, oblivious to the danger that Atreus might slip and drop the basket on their heads or fall off the board entirely and come crashing down himself.

Atreus was halfway across, on the bounciest part of the board, when heavy boots began to pound down the corridor behind him. He looked up to find Rishi staring across the alley, eyes as wide as coins.

"Perhaps the master could come more quickly," said Rishi.

"I'm coming as fast as I can!" Atreus's gaze dropped back to the plank, and he began to grow dizzy as he contemplated the distance between his feet and the ground. "This isn't as easy as it looks!"

"The master is to be extolled for his remarkable balance," said Rishi. "But Her Radiance's men are proving most persistent."

Atreus took a deep breath, then rushed ahead three quick steps. The plank jumped like a quarterdeck on a stormy sea, and his fourth step found the board coming up when his foot expected it to be going down. He stumbled forward and fell to one knee, slamming the heavy basket down in front of him.

The plank bucked so hard that the end bounced completely off the sill and came down an inch closer to the edge. Atreus squeezed his eyelids shut and did not move, afraid of what would happen if he allowed himself to look at the alley below.

"Come back here, you ugly devil!" growled an angry voice behind him. "The queen's executioner will be wanting a word with you."

A rasping noise sounded ahead, and Atreus felt the board moving backward. He opened his eyes again and saw the end of the plank slowly scraping toward the edge of the windowsill.

Rishi thrust out his arms. "Give me the basket!"

"So you can run off with it?"

Atreus crawled forward, pushing the basket ahead of him. The board jerked beneath his knees, and the end slipped to within two fingers of the window's edge.

"Have I not earned your trust by now?" Rishi continued to reach for the basket. "I am only trying to help!"

"If you want to help, grab the board!" Atreus commanded.

"But I am only a Mar," Rishi whined. Despite his objection, he grabbed the plank with both hands. "I am no match for the strength of the Ffolk!"

The board wobbled sideways, and the guard called, "Last chance! Surrender now, or I'll finish you here."

"And kill those people down there?" Atreus glanced at the alley floor, where a small crowd had finally gathered to stare up at the strange confrontation above their heads. "I doubt the queen would approve of that."

"They'll get out of the way." The guard gave the plank a mighty tug.

Rishi pulled back and kept the end from slipping off the

window sill, but Atreus's knee dropped off the side. The board tipped sideways, nearly flipped, and Atreus cried out in alarm.

Rishi grunted and braced his feet against the wall, leaning back against the guard's strength. The plank began to wobble and shudder. Atreus sat down and straddled the board, and only then did he hazard a glance over his shoulder.

At the other end of the plank, two guards stood side-by-side, both holding the board and straining to pull it out of Rishi's hands. There were more men behind them, but quarters were too cramped for additional hands. Atreus's heart began to pound. Even if his foes did not realize it yet, they had only to let go to send Rishi tumbling backward and Atreus plunging to his death.

The guards suddenly scowled and glanced up at the ceiling, then Yago appeared on the tenement roof, standing directly over their heads. When the ogre saw Atreus's predicament, he frowned and kneeled, cocking his fist to punch through the roof.

"Yago, wait!" Atreus yelled

The ogre was already bringing his fist down. A huge hand smashed through ceiling of the tenement and began feeling around. Atreus turned back to Rishi and pushed the basket forward, pulling himself along behind it as fast as he could.

Rishi let out a deep groan and slipped closer to the window. The Mar's knuckles were as pale as ivory. He kept his gaze locked on the treasure basket and did not blink. Atreus scooted another step forward. He was close enough to push the basket through the window, but Rishi was in the way.

A strangled cry sounded from the other end of the plank as Yago finally caught hold of a guard. Atreus shouted a warning to the people below, then shoved the basket into Rishi's startled face.

The Mar had no choice but to release the board and grab

the treasure basket. As it dropped away, Atreus flung himself forward and caught hold of the sill. His body swung down and smashed into the wall, leaving him dangling from the window like a rag hung out to dry. The plank tumbled into the alley below, demolishing two pairs of window shutters as it bounced off the tenement walls on the way down.

"Good sir?" Rishi's voice came from the other side of the window. "Are you there?"

"Of course." Atreus pulled himself up onto the sill. "You'll have to work harder than that if you want my treasure."

"How can you say such a thing?" Rishi demanded. He was sitting on the floor with both arms wrapped around the heavy basket. "I am only trying to help."

"And you've done so much. Being a hunted killer is bound to be a great help in finding Langdarma."

Atreus swung his feet into the corridor, then looked back to see Yago's hand hanging through a hole in the ceiling. The ogre was smashing a hapless guard about the hallway as though the man's body were a warhammer.

"Yago!" Atreus called. "Come on."

The ogre dropped his victim, then pulled his hand back through the ceiling and disappeared behind the roof line. An instant later he came hurtling across the alley, flailing his arms and legs as though he were trying to fly. Atreus took an instant to judge where Yago would land, then grabbed Rishi's ankle and jerked him back toward the window.

"Good sir!" Rishi screeched. "Good sir, I am not some sack of rice to be dragged—"

The ceiling exploded into a spray of splinters and plaster, then Yago crashed down where Rishi had been sitting a moment before. The floor bucked and shook from the impact of the ogre's ten-foot body, and Rishi's indignation turned to shock.

"In the name of the Forgotten Ones!" he gasped, peering over his shoulder.

Yago groaned, then rolled onto his back and began to look around the dusty corridor. "Hey," he said, "I made it. . . ."

Something struck the tenement wall behind Atreus. He looked back to see a guard standing in the window opposite, accepting a fresh dagger from one of his fellows.

"We're not out of the city yet," Atreus said, grabbing the basket from Rishi's hands and spinning around, holding it up before him. "Yago, will you get going?"

As the ogre rolled to his knees, Rishi slipped past and led the way down the hall. Atreus backed after them, holding the basket up like a shield. This did not prevent the angry guard from hurling several more daggers through the window. The knives were hardly balanced for throwing, but one managed to lodge itself in the basket and another tumbled past perilously close to Yago's back.

At last, Rishi turned a corner and ducked down a stairwell, and Atreus finally had time to take note of the foreign sounds and smells of the building. From behind every door came melodic Maran jabber. The upper floors, used primarily for residences, smelled—perhaps even stank—of exotic cooking spices. Every now and then the trio had to squeeze past a small group of Mar coming up the stairs. The men clapped at Yago and stared at Atreus's face with open hostility. The women retreated to the landing below and let them pass, blushing and averting their eyes. The children gasped in open awe of Yago's size, then hissed and clapped their hands to ward off Atreus and his "wickedness." By the time the trio reached the ground floor, Atreus felt happy to have grown up among the Shieldbreakers. At least Yago's sons and nephews had considered his unfortunate looks nothing worse than an excuse to start a good fight.

When they reached the ground floor, Rishi led the way through an open poultry market into a narrow lane. Atreus was so turned around that until a pair of Mar wandered past carrying a long plank, he did not recognize it as the same alley over which he had been hanging a few minutes earlier.

"Over here, my banana-loving friend!"

The call came from a short distance down the alley, where a round-faced Mar with a waxed mustache sat in the driver's seat of a large covered wagon. He was a plump man, about the same size and shape as the shadowy figure who had thrown the banana into the howdah. Hitched to the man's wagon were two of the strangest oxen Atreus had ever seen. They had narrow, cowlike faces with curved horns as long as a man's arm, and their bodies were hidden head-to-hoof beneath shaggy skirts of golden-black hair.

Rishi draped his hand around Atreus's elbow in the overly familiar way of the Mar and led him toward the cart.

"Bharat, my good friend! This is the unfortunate gentleman I was telling you about, and this is his large servant." Rishi gestured at Yago. "Is everything ready?"

"Yes, yes, just as you asked. Hide yourselves beneath my carpets, and we are on our way to Langdarma." Bharat smiled too eagerly, displaying teeth as white as snow, then nodded to Yago. "I brought my largest wagon, but even so, I fear you will have to fold your legs."

Rishi started toward the back of the cart, but Atreus made no move to follow.

"We're going to Langdarma in an oxcart?" he asked.

Rishi feigned a look of shock. "But of course! Surely, you did not think we could take your elephant?"

4

Bharat's carpet wagon had nearly crested the front range of the Yehimal Mountains when the Queen's Guard finally caught up to it. The riders, mounted on shaggy mountain ponies about the size of a good war dog, traveled lightly, with little more than sabers, haversacks, and long woolen hauberks that served as both coat and armor. Behind them, three days back and a thousand switchbacks down the wooded mountainside, lay the misty forests of Edenvale. The capital itself was still visible, a tiny dun-colored circle on the far horizon.

The guards, all rugged-faced Mar accustomed to the rigors of mountain travel, urged their ponies into a trot, surrounding the wagon on all sides. Bharat feigned surprise and reached for the axe beneath his seat, as though mistaking the riders for a company of road bandits.

"We are the Queen's Men, driver," said the leader. He spoke in Thorass to indicate he was on official business. "You have nothing to fear from us, unless you are the one hiding Ysdar's devil and his murderous servants—and if you are, you will not escape us anyway. Let us have a look in your cart."

Bharat glanced around at the riders, then sighed and reluctantly reined his strange oxen—the beasts were called "yaks"—to a halt. "I have no devils with me," he said plainly. "I will show you."

Bharat wrapped the reins around a seat brace and turned

41

to crawl into the cargo area, but the leader swung his lance down to block the way.

"We will look ourselves. This devil is very clever and dangerous. Perhaps he and his servants slipped into your cart when you were not looking. I would not want you injured."

Bharat turned his palms to the sky, shrugging, and sat back down. A dozen riders dismounted, passing their lances and reins to their fellows, then stepped to the rear of the wagon. Half of them drew their sabers and stood ready to attack. The others began to drag Bharat's carpets out of the cargo bed, unrolling each one and tossing it into the middle of the muddy road.

"What are you doing?" Bharat exclaimed. "That is my whole fortune!"

"A little dirt will do no harm to a good carpet," the leader replied.

"But why is it necessary to unroll them all?" Bharat demanded, growing genuinely angry. "If your devil and his servants had rolled themselves up inside my carpets, surely men as astute as yours would notice the bulges!"

"This is a very clever devil. We do not know what he can do," the leader said, and gave Bharat a cockeyed sneer, showing a single gold tooth. "Perhaps you are even this devil in disguise."

The implication was clear enough. Too much protesting could be taken the wrong way. Bharat watched in silence as the searchers spread his carpets across the road, then started on his provisions and personal belongings. They looked inside everything, even waterskins, and felt inside the pockets of his extra clothes. They opened his food bags and ran their filthy hands through his rice and barley, and they drained his oil jar into a cooking pot.

Bharat could only shake his head. "This devil's magic must be very powerful," he said, "if you think he can breathe cooking oil."

"Very powerful indeed," the leader assured him. "He can fight four men at once and command ogres to do his will, and several Ffolk have seen him walk on air. Queen Rosalind herself told me he knows things no man should know."

"Truly?" Bharat asked.

The leader nodded, and the corners of his mouth turned down in a self-impressed scowl. "She said we must catch him, or there will be Ysdar to pay."

When the searchers had finally emptied the wagon, they began to crawl around the cargo bed on their hands and knees, rapping the floor and walls with the hilts of their daggers. Bharat watched nervously.

"Are you not satisfied yet?" he demanded. "You have delayed me too long already, and I am expected in Borobodur."

The leader only grinned and waited, and it did not take long before one of the searchers located the hollow sound of the wagon's secret compartment.

The leader grinned. "A smuggler's hole?"

"A merchant's friend," Bharat countered. "Used only to protect honest profits from road thieves and not for any other purpose."

"Then, as you are only now on your way to market, I expect it would be empty."

"Not exactly."

"I see." The leader looked to the men at the back of the wagon. "Perhaps we should open it."

Three more guards clambered into the crowded wagon, their swords at the ready. When they could not figure out how to open the compartment, another soldier stepped around to retrieve the axe from under Bharat's seat.

Bharat placed a restraining hand on the fellow's arm. "Wait," he said. "I will open it for you."

The leader nodded his permission. Bharat slipped a hand

43

behind the seat and tripped a hidden lever, then reached back and motioned the guards to pry up the center of the floor. Underneath lay a foot-deep compartment just large enough to hold a man. At the moment, the space contained nothing but a leather rucksack, so new that its beeswax waterproofing was still shiny and slick. The searchers opened the top and turned it upside down, but nothing fell out.

"That is all?" the leader demanded. "Why would a carpet seller be hiding a new rucksack?"

Bharat shrugged. "It seemed a good place to store it."

The leader narrowed his eyes suspiciously, then rode around to the back of the wagon and peered inside. When it grew obvious that the cart held no more secrets, he shook his head in puzzlement. He motioned his men to their ponies and looked back to Bharat.

"Apologies for troubling an honest merchant such as yourself," the leader said, speaking from the back of the wagon. "We have not found this devil yet, but he is here in the mountains. If you happen across him, you must run the other way and report it to the first Queen's Man you see. He is a very wicked devil who will not hesitate to kill you in a horrible manner and eat your body."

Bharat's mouth fell as though frightened. "Truly?"

"Yes." The leader nodded officiously, then rode to the front of the wagon and spoke in a confidential voice. "I should not tell you this, but we have troubled you greatly, and you will have need of the knowledge."

"What you tell me, I will never repeat to a living soul."

"Good. Then I can be terribly candid with you." The leader leaned in close and said, "This is a very particular devil who delights in stealing the firstborn child. We have only been chasing him for three days, and already we have spoken to nine fathers who have lost their eldest in this manner."

44

"Nine?" Bharat gasped. "The gluttonous beast!"

The leader sat up straight in his saddle, then added, "Nine that we know of."

"Then I will seek out a Queen's Man the instant I see him," Bharat replied. "But if this devil can trick even you, how will I recognize him?"

"Oh, you will know him. He is an ugly monster, as terrible to look upon as Ysdar himself. He will be served by a sly bahrana and a western ogre whose skin has turned orange from bathing in blood." The leader glanced back and, seeing that his men were ready to ride, waved them forward. "Are you able to re-pack your goods without our help? We must be off."

"Yes, yes, I am grateful for your warning." Bharat shooed the man up the road. "After the devil!"

His consent was hardly necessary. The leader was already guiding his pony into line with the rest of the company. Bharat wearily climbed down, then selected two large stones from the side of the road and blocked the front wheels so his yaks could rest. He went to the rear of the wagon and carefully poured his cooking oil back into its jar, then wiped the pot clean with the sleeve of his tunic. Finally, when the last of the Queen's Men had disappeared around the switchback and he was sure they weren't coming back, Bharat walked a short distance down the road and looked up the steep mountainside. He could see nothing but the massive tree trunks and impenetrable rhododendron undergrowth of a lush fir forest.

"Perhaps my friends would care to come out now?" he asked. "We must hurry and re-pack, if we are to find a safe campsite before the evening rains start."

Atreus and his two companions sat up, plucking rhododendron branches out of their sleeves, collars, and pant legs.

"There is no need to camp," said Rishi, casting a sly grin

in Atreus's direction. "We will just ask Ysdar's devil to shrink us, then we will spend a dry and cozy night in an empty jar . . . or perhaps in a yak's ear. I am sure it is warm in there."

"A most excellent idea," agreed Bharat, "but I will be too afraid to sleep. Yago has not had his bath today!"

The ogre scowled. "I was born orange," he said, pulling the treasure basket from its hiding place. "And I don't take that many baths."

"Indeed," commented Bharat. "And yet you smell as sweet as a lily."

"You Mar," Atreus snapped, in no mood for joking. "Is there not one of you who isn't a born liar?"

Rishi and Bharat fell silent and sullen. Atreus did not care. He was accustomed to being thought slovenly, wicked, and even stupid because of how he looked, but this was the first time anyone had accused him of being a cannibal and a kidnapper. By the time they reached the Sisters of Serenity, that rumormongering patrol leader would have every traveler in the Yehimals ready to behead Atreus in his sleep.

Motioning Yago to follow, Atreus scrambled down to the road and returned to the wagon. When Bharat and Rishi came up behind him conversing softly in Maran, he whirled on them.

"You will do me the kindness of speaking in Realmspeak or not at all. I've enough to worry about without wondering what you two are plotting," Atreus said sternly, then snatched the rucksack off the road and turned to Bharat. "What is this for?"

"You will n-need it," the Mar explained. "You cannot reach the Sisters of Serenity in a carpet wagon. You will have to walk many days."

Atreus frowned. "Then why is there only one rucksack?"

Bharat's face paled from its normal golden bronze to

saffron. He looked to Rishi for help.

"Good sir, there is no reason for being angry," said Rishi. "It is only that there are no rucksacks large enough for Yago, and Bharat did not know how strong you are for one of the Ffolk. He assumed most naturally that I would be carrying your load."

"Yes, yes—very good! That is just so," said Bharat. "In the Utter East, wealthy Ffolk hire porters to carry their things."

He flashed his too-bright smile and waited for his employer to accept the explanation. Atreus simply climbed into the wagon and returned the rucksack to its cubby hole, then pushed the floor back into place. The porter's explanation made sense as far as it went, but he still did not understand why the carpet seller had hidden the sack in the first place. Certainly, the Queen's Men had not seemed terribly upset at finding it, and that left only him and Yago that Bharat could have been concealing it from. The two Mar would bear even more watching than he originally thought.

Atreus settled onto his haunches. "Why don't you pass the baggage in? I'll pack." He reached out to accept the first load. "And I'm sorry for that remark about born liars. If anyone should know better than to say such things, it's me. That patrol leader's lies made me angry."

Bharat's insincere smile remained on his face as he said, "No apology necessary. The captain was indeed a very big liar. He made me angry as well."

"Ignorant Mar like him are what made Queen Rosalind reluctant to help you," Rishi added as he hefted a sack of rice into the wagon. "Someday, I will give you his tongue."

"Thanks, but no thanks."

Atreus grimaced, then moved the rice to the front of the cargo bed. They finished re-packing the wagon quickly, leaving a place between the carpets so he and Yago could lie down and hide when they passed someone on the road.

That night, Atreus had Yago stay close to the treasure basket and politely refused to go to his bed inside the wagon until Bharat and Rishi had gone to theirs underneath it. His caution was somewhat unnecessary. Only he could open the coffer inside the treasure basket and it was too heavy for either Mar to carry off, but he wanted them to know he was thinking about the possibility as much as they were.

The next day dawned clear and cold, as did most in the Yehimals. After a breakfast of warm yak milk and cold barley, they traveled a few hours up to the end of the valley. There, much to Atreus's amazement, the road started up a mountainside longer and steeper than the one they had crested just the night before. As they ascended, the rhododendron undergrowth vanished, giving way to silver-barked bushes Atreus did not recognize. The trees grew smaller and closer together, and the breeze became cool and thin. The valley in which they had camped the night before seemed as distant and low as had the plains of Edenvale, and still they climbed. When the afternoon mists came, their breaths turned into billowing clouds of vapor, and a chill dampness sank into their bones.

They continued to climb for three more days, the forest eventually growing thin and patchy, sometimes vanishing altogether when the slope became too steep or rocky. The wind nipped at their ears, and their own breaths kept them swaddled in perpetual clouds of white steam. Gradually, Atreus pretended to let his guard down. He neglected to remind Yago to keep a close watch on the basket, then started to go to bed first. He paid less attention to his treasure and complained more often about fatigue and cold. He even had Yago forget to take the basket with him when he went to sleep at night, and still the Mar made no attempt to steal his gold.

Eventually, they crested this mountainside too, and began to cross an endless succession of ridges and valleys. Often, they traveled miles through alpine meadows far above the timberline, then descended into deep valleys full of mist and mountain bamboo. Several times a day, they met yak caravans coming in the opposite direction. Atreus and Yago would hide beneath the carpets while Rishi and Bharat stopped to gossip, for travelers in the Yehimals had long ago learned the wisdom of pausing to hear what lay ahead.

The news was always of Ysdar's ugly devil, and the accounts grew increasingly exaggerated. Tales such as his ogre having slaughtered a herd of yaks, his Mar servant maiming all the children in a village, and the devil himself murdering an entire company of the Queen's Men were common. Of course, no one could name the places where any of this had occurred. Rishi and Bharat seemed to find these stories a great amusement. After hearing one, their moods grew as jocular as Atreus's did foul. Eventually, the two Mar stopped translating the reports for their master, knowing that the latest accounts of his outrages would make their "good sir" even angrier than their refusal to repeat what was being said about him.

Twice after hearing that the Queen's Men were approaching, Atreus, Rishi, and Yago had to hide in the rocks while a patrol searched the wagon. The inspections went much the same as before, save that Bharat now accepted them as a matter of course and insisted on having his rugs neatly stacked instead of strewn all over the road. The rucksack continued to draw comment, as the soldiers could not imagine a merchant abandoning his goods to go trekking through the mountains.

Finally, the morning came when Atreus opened his treasure basket to check the coffer inside and saw scratch marks on the brass latch. He was less surprised to discover his companions had tried to break into the chest than that Yago had not heard the attempt. The ogre had slept beside the basket all night without noticing a thing.

Atreus closed the lid and said nothing, though now he began to worry. So far, they had not reached any of the valleys or mountains named on Sune's map, and the thought occurred to him that Rishi might not know how to find the Sisters of Serenity after all. Perhaps the two Mar were simply leading him about blindly, waiting for their chance to rob and abandon him—or worse. Given the hideous rumors coursing through the mountains, they could murder him and be hailed as heroes. Atreus and Yago began to sleep in shifts, napping in the wagon and closing their eyes at night only after they were certain the two Mar had slumbered off.

They had been traveling little more than a tenday when Bharat, preparing their usual supper of fried vegetables over rice, turned the oil jar over and nothing came out. He cursed and hurled the vessel against a rock. As it shattered, he turned to Rishi and spoke in rapid Maran. Rishi shook his head and made an angry reply, then glanced across the fire to where Atreus was sitting.

Atreus signaled Yago with a glance, then gathered his legs beneath himself and reluctantly shifted his weight to the balls of his feet. They were camped well above the timberline, huddled on the lee side of a boulder with a snowstorm blowing in, wrapped tight in their cloaks and burning dried yak dung they had gathered along the road. At the moment, the last thing Atreus felt like doing was fighting off a robbery attempt.

The two Mar continued to argue in their strange tongue of melodic syllables and guttural clicks, now entirely oblivious to their companion.

"Use Realmspeak," Atreus said. "I don't like being left out of arguments . . . particularly when they're about me."

Bharat turned at once, his ever-ready smile plastered across his face, and said, "Oh no, the good sir is not to be deceived. We are not arguing about you . . . we are not arguing at all."

"We were only discussing a small matter, which is of no importance to you," added Rishi.

Atreus scowled at the shards of the broken oil jar and said, "We are four companions traveling together. What is important to one is important to all."

Rishi shrugged, then glanced at Bharat and said, "Very well. I suppose it must be said. We are running out of food. This is why Bharat is upset."

Atreus studied Bharat until the Mar's counterfeit grin began to twitch, then asked, "Why should we be running out of food? You knew we would be going to the Sisters of Serenity."

"Just so, but I knew also that the Queen's Men would be searching for you," Bharat replied. "What would they think if they found food for three men and an ogre in a wagon with only one driver? I did the best I could."

"And you made no plans to replenish our supplies?"

Bharat fell silent and glanced away, flustered.

"It is the soldiers," said Rishi, coming to his rescue. "They are making things difficult."

"Ah yes, the soldiers," Bharat said, his gaze swinging back to Atreus. "With all the rumors they are spreading, it is too dangerous to buy anything from the villages. These mountain Mar are terrible gossips, always asking questions and looking under other people's carpets."

"Bharat is very discouraged by this," Rishi said. He gestured at his companion's ample stomach. "He is not accustomed to missing meals. No doubt, it would help if he had something else to think about. Perhaps you could pay him what he has earned so far through his loyal services?"

Thinking the request a reasonable one, Atreus reached

for his belt purse—then remembered where he had left it and pulled his hand away.

"Very clever, Rishi," he said.

"Good sir?"

"What happens when I open the coffer?" Atreus asked. "Do you plant one of your little throwing daggers in Yago's throat, and Bharat another in my back?"

Rishi's eyes went wide. "Never!"

"Why not?" Atreus glanced from Rishi to Bharat. "You know you can't slip the lock. I've seen the scratch marks where you tried."

Bharat's jaw fell, and he turned to gape at Rishi in feigned outrage. "You? A robber?"

"Bharat, don't play the innocent," Atreus said, shaking his head. "It would be a mistake to assume that because I am ugly, I am also stupid. You're in on his plan."

"Plan?" Bharat tried to look indignant. "What plan?"

"You aren't taking me to the Sisters of Serenity at all." Atreus did not try to keep the bitterness out of his voice, and Yago rose, curling his big hands into fists. "You brought me up here to rob me."

"Not true!" Bharat protested. "We are only two days from where your map starts."

Without quite realizing what he was doing, Atreus stepped around the fire and snatched Bharat up by the collar. "Don't take me for a fool!"

Rishi was up instantly, pushing himself between his friend and Atreus. "Oh, Bharat would never do that," he insisted. "Never in a thousand lifetimes!"

Atreus released the Mar and stepped back, surprised by the depth of his rage. He had to clench his fists to keep his hands from trembling, and his face and ears were so full of hot anger that he no longer felt the cold bite of the wind.

"I'm sorry if I frightened you," Atreus said, "but I

warned you. Nothing makes me angrier than being treated as though I'm stupid."

Bharat glared at him from the opposite side of the fire. "We do not need you!" he spat. "It is you who need us! How would you find your Langdarma without us? What would happen if we told the Queen's Men about you?"

"You don't want to find out," growled Yago.

Atreus met the Mar's angry stare, and neither of them said anything.

It was Rishi who finally spoke. "Perhaps this is my fault to some small degree. Perhaps I have, most inadvertently and only through the best of intentions, misled the good sir in a manner most trivial and unimportant."

Atreus scowled. "How would that be?"

"In a tiny way that will have no impact whatsoever on the ultimate outcome of our endeavor, as is evidenced by the heavy presence in this part of the Yehimals of the Queen's Men, who are most assuredly here only because the Sisters of Serenity must be somewhere nearby."

"Rishi, are you telling me you don't know where the Sisters are?"

"Not at all! I have a very good idea where they might be," Rishi said, then took a step backward. "It is only that I have never actually . . . seen them myself. But I have traveled to one of the valleys on your map, by means of a secret caravan route used by certain, uh . . . traders from Konigheim. If we can find this trail, I am confident we will eventually find the Sisters of Serenity. As I have said, the Queen's Men would not be gathering in this area if our destination was not near."

Atreus groaned and fell silent, pondering his slim chances of reaching the peaks without the help of his two companions. Given his ignorance of the Yehimals and the unlikelihood of "Ysdar's devil" receiving help from the superstitious mountain people, he realized that Bharat had been right. He needed the Mar more than they wanted his gold.

Atreus turned to Bharat. "You can take me to the valley at the edge of this map?"

"Did I not say so?" Bharat's voice was still filled with disdain. "The closest is only two days away."

"Then you will have your payment in two days."

Atreus went to the cart and pulled his treasure basket out, placing it on the ground beside the fire. He lifted the lid, then reached inside and touched the wooden coffer, placing his palm over the magic ward that sealed the chest. He did not bother to hide this from the two Mar, as only his touch would release the enchanted lock.

Atreus opened the coffer, revealing the mass of golden coins inside. He grabbed a handful and passed them to Bharat. "This gold means nothing to me, and it will only prove a burden in trying to reach Langdarma. After I am certain that you have led me to the edge of my map, you can take your third and leave."

"My *third*?" Bharat gasped.

"That does not seem fair?"

"Very fair!" Bharat gasped again. Despite his words, his gaze remained locked on the chest. "It is far in excess of what I expected, but a third?" He glanced in Rishi's direction. "Why not half? After all, it is my cart we are using . . . and my yaks."

"Rishi will accompany me to Langdarma." Atreus withdrew a second handful of coins and passed them to Rishi. "Save for the small portion I save for the passage home, the rest of the coins will be his."

"The good sir is too generous," said Rishi. Like Bharat, he could not take his eyes off the coffer's contents. "I hope you will make your passage home a comfortable one."

"I'm glad you're both pleased." Atreus closed the coffer, then listened to the telltale hiss of the magic lock reactivating itself. "But if you don't like my terms, you are free to leave with what I've given you already."

"Leave?" gasped Rishi. "Oh no, I am most happy to go with you as far as you wish."

"And you will take one of my yaks with you," offered Bharat, "to carry your load and provide milk and warmth in the high places where there is none."

"Good. Let us hope we'll all be happy men in two days." Atreus said as he closed the lid of the cargo basket. "Until then, we can put this unpleasantness behind us and sleep well."

It did not escape Atreus's notice that as he spoke, the eyes of the two Mar remained fixed on the basket. He shook his head, then took the pot and went off to milk the yaks. It was someone else's turn to worry about his gold.

5

Atreus's first sound sleep in many days ended with a clap of thunder, then a flash so bright he saw it inside his eyelids. He threw aside the carpets he had been using as blankets and sat up, looking out the back of the wagon toward the fire pit. It was that gray time just before dawn when first light started to kindle a pearly sheen in the previous night's snow. Yago was nowhere to be seen, having risen early to hunt for something furry or feathered to supplement his inadequate diet. In the ogre's empty bed kneeled a pudgy silhouette, hunched over the open treasure basket and pressing palms to eyes. The figure took its hands away, then swiveled its head around aimlessly.

"Blind!" The voice was Bharat's. "The devil has blinded me!"

Rishi scrambled out from beneath the wagon and ran over to the treasure basket, barefooted and uncloaked despite the deep snow. When he saw the lid lying open, he pushed Bharat into the smoldering fire pit and began shrieking in angry Maran.

"In Realmspeak, Rishi," ordered Atreus. He dug out a boot and began to pull it on. "How many times must I remind you?"

Rishi switched instantly to Realmspeak shrieking, "Thief!" He kicked Bharat in the ribs.

Bharat rolled into the snow and curled into a ball. "Have mercy, my friend. You are kicking a blind man!"

"You were stealing my gold," Rishi accused, and kicked him again, this time in the back.

"That's enough, Rishi," Atreus ordered. "He's no good to us injured."

Rishi kicked Bharat one more time, then turned toward Atreus. "What good is he to us now?" he asked. "Who can trust a thief?"

Bharat remained curled into a ball. "It is not what you think," he pleaded. "I was only looking. . . ."

"Only looking?" Rishi reached behind the treasure chest, plucked the rucksack out of the snow, and asked, "What is this for?"

He hurled the bag at Bharat, who flinched, then raised his chin defiantly.

"Our split was supposed to be even . . ." Bharat said, "and now you are ready to take two thirds!"

"Of course! Now I must go with this fool into the High Yehimals," Rishi said, then paused, seeming to realize what he had said, and spun toward Atreus. "Pay him no heed. Bharat has always been a thief and a—"

"Yes," Atreus interrupted, "one is known by the company he keeps." He pointed at Rishi's bare feet and added, "You'd better get dressed. You won't be any good to me with frost-bitten feet."

Rishi glanced down at his toes, then ducked beneath the wagon and began to dig for his clothes.

Atreus finished lacing his boots, then slipped his heavy woolen cloak over his shoulders and stepped out into the morning. The air was calm and clear, with the last stars fading from sight and the orange dawn spreading across the frigid sky. The yaks stood a short distance down the hill, tied nose to tail for easy leading. The one in the rear had a pair of canvas bags secured to its shaggy back. Over the shoulders of the other lay a blanket and ropes, ready to secure a rucksack full of gold.

Yago came pounding out of the morning dimness, a half-eaten marmot dangling from one hand. "What . . .

TROY DENNING

happened?" he huffed. "I heard a bang."

"The trap on my treasure coffer." Atreus gestured at the open basket. "Bharat didn't think a third was fair."

"I meant no harm!" Bharat protested. "I was only going to take my half—"

"Bharat, this is the last time I'll warn you about taking me for a fool," Atreus said. When the Mar fell silent, he turned to Yago. "Keep an eye on him while you finish your breakfast. I'll get us ready to go."

Leaving Bharat to Yago's watchful eye, Atreus retrieved the yaks and unpacked the beast in the rear. He found Bharat's belongings in the first bag and what remained of the food in the second.

"What a disgraceful thief," Rishi commented, now fully dressed. "He meant us to starve. I will cut his throat, and then we can be on our way."

Bharat swung toward the sound. "Two thirds of the gold is not enough for you? Now you must kill me for the rest?"

"It is better than you deserve," Rishi said, "but we have no time for a proper punishment." He pulled one of his small knives and started toward Bharat.

Atreus caught Rishi by the arm. "I thought Bharat was your friend," he said.

"A friend does not steal his friend's gold," Rishi snarled.

"It's not yours yet," Atreus reminded him. "The gold does not belong to you until we reach Langdarma."

Rishi's golden face darkened to the color of mahogany and he said, "Oh, begging your pardon, here I go getting ahead of myself again." He held his dagger out toward Atreus. "Of course, the good sir wishes to punish the thief himself."

"The good sir does not." Atreus replied, pushing the dagger away. "As a matter of fact, I'm quite happy with how things turned out."

Rishi frowned and asked, "You would let a man steal from you?"

58

"If it is the only way to learn the truth, yes." Atreus took Bharat's arm and pulled the Mar to his feet but continued to speak to Rishi. "Had you tried to open the coffer, I would have known you have no idea where we are going. But since you're willing to wait for a larger share of the gold, I know we're near the edge of my map."

"This was a test?" shrieked Bharat. "You blinded me to find if I was telling the truth?"

"He didn't do nothing," said Yago, crunching a bone. "You're the one who tried to open the coffer. You deserve what you got."

"Which isn't as terrible as it could have been," said Atreus, guiding Bharat to the front of the wagon. "Your blindness will pass."

Bharat sighed in relief, then furrowed his brow and clutched Atreus's arm. "And what of our bargain?" he asked. "Was that only to see if we were telling the truth?"

"If you will honor it, then I will." Atreus said as he helped the Mar into the wagon's passenger seat.

Bharat did not release Atreus's arm. "But the split will be even, of course."

"Even?" Rishi asked. He was beside them in an instant. "Are you going to Langdarma? I am the one taking more risk."

"Our agreement is already more than fair, Bharat" agreed Atreus. He peeled the Mar's hand off his arm. "Be happy with the gold you're receiving now. It's enough to make you wealthy many times over."

Bharat shook his head stubbornly. "But I am a bahrana, just as Rishi. My share should be half. Anything less is to call me a tarok."

"Only by the backward customs of Edenvale," countered Rishi. "The good sir and his gold come from the far realm of Erlkazar. We should honor the custom of that land, where it is the habit to honor a man's value and not his position."

"But we met in Edenvale," Bharat said, turning his head

away. "I will abide by its customs, or by none at all."

"If that's your choice, I'll rekindle the fire." Atreus reached up to take the Mar's arm. "By tomorrow or the next day, you'll see well enough to start back with the gold I've already given you."

Bharat's unseeing eyes grew wide. "And now you are trying to cheat me out of even my miserable third!" he shouted. "I am coming with you, whether you like it or not."

Bharat folded his arms and let Atreus and the others pack the wagon and harness the yaks. Then the small company set off on a cold and solemn ride. They spent much of the morning angling up a windblasted mountainside, until their route joined several others and rounded the shoulder into a steep alpine gorge. The distant roar of a mighty river began to rumble up from a tiny ribbon of water thousands of feet below, and the road became little more than a perilously tilted track.

Rishi stopped the wagon so they could look across the river. On the opposite side of the gorge lay an immense plateau of snowy hummocks and leafy green willow bushes. In the untold distance beyond stood a remote wall of ice-draped mountains, as jagged as orc's teeth and so high they were scratching tiny furrows of white cloud into the belly of the passing sky.

"The Spine of the World Dragon," Rishi announced, pointing at the peaks. "The valleys on your map lie there."

Without any trees or animals for scale, Atreus could not quite comprehend the magnitude of the mountains. To him the range looked like the brink of the world, a sheer barrier of ice-coated spires as high as it was impassable.

"Men can live there?" asked Yago, incredulous.

"If it is the wish of the mountain gods," said Bharat. He was facing the peaks, though his sightless eyes were fixed on the sky above. "But more often, it is their wish that men die there."

"And how could a cowardly rug seller who has never ventured beyond the safety of the roads know such a thing?" demanded Rishi. He glanced over his shoulder at Atreus. "Pay Bharat no mind. It is said the Mar were born there, and of course that is where we shall find Langdarma . . . if we are strong enough."

For the first time Atreus wondered if he was strong enough. On his map, the peaks were little more than circles of fanning lines, with the names of the valleys written along serpentine spaces below. There was nothing to suggest the staggering height of the mountains or the sheer ruggedness of their ice-caked flanks. That a paradise could be hidden in such a place seemed impossible, and yet the sight made Atreus believe in Langdarma all the more strongly. Sune taught that beauty had to be guarded, and he could think of no better protection than those mountains.

"Perhaps the good sir and his servant would hide now?" asked Rishi. "Several roads pass along here, and we are certain to meet many foolish Mar who would be most alarmed to see Ysdar's devil riding in a yak wagon."

Atreus and Yago ducked down between the carpet rolls, half-covering themselves beneath the cotton tarp Bharat used as a dust shroud. Rishi slapped the reins, urging the yaks forward onto the precarious canyon trail. The listing track turned out to be more heavily traveled than any of the roads they had been on so far. Several times an hour, Atreus and Yago had to pull the dust shroud over their heads as Rishi eased to the side of the road to let pass another wagon or a caravan of yaks. Twice, after hearing of an approaching patrol, he and Yago hid in the rocks below the road bank.

As it happened, both patrols were heading back to the comforts of Edenvale and paid little attention to Rishi or the wagon. The leaders paused only long enough to brag about how close they had come to catching Ysdar's devil, assuring the two carpet sellers that they themselves had chased the fiend deep into the mountains and made the Yehimals once again safe for travel. Rishi and Bharat thanked them profusely for their efforts, and when a passing salt caravan mentioned yet a third company down in the willows, no one thought it necessary for Atreus and Yago to leave the cart. The two westerners simply remained in back, peering out between their guides, ready to pull the dust shroud over their heads at an instant's notice.

After a time they rounded a bend and felt cold vapor in the air. Perhaps a mile ahead the shoulder of the mountain curved away, exposing yet more of the snow-hummocked plateau and revealing the head of the canyon, where a lazy river came twining out of the willows to plunge into the gorge. The result was a beautiful horsetail waterfall, so long it turned to mist before reaching the rocks below.

The road left the mountainside just past the waterfall, then began branching off through the willows. One of the less traveled offshoots turned toward the sky-scratching peaks Rishi had pointed out as their destination, crossing the river via a suspension bridge of woven vines and swaying planks. They were halfway across when the third patrol emerged from the willows on the other side. The company had only two dozen warriors, but riding beside the leader was a small man in a cloak and sable hat. His face was paler and more fine-boned than those of his Mar companions, and in the crook of his arm he carried an elaborately carved staff decorated with mystic symbols.

"Now look what your greed has brought on us, Bharat," hissed Rishi. "A *wu-jen!*"

"Wu-jen?" rumbled Yago.

"From Shou Lung," Bharat explained.

"They are sorcerers of great skill. The equals of Ysdar himself, it is said," Rishi said, speaking so softly that Atreus could barely hear him. "But I have dealt with their kind before. Cover yourselves and have no fear."

Atreus and Yago slipped down between the carpet rolls and pulled the dust shroud over their heads, then listened to the wagon rumble the rest of the way across the bridge. At the far end Rishi pulled far enough ahead so that he was not blocking the way, then stopped.

"A pleasant afternoon to you and your men, sir," said Rishi. "What news of Ysdar's devil?"

"Many rumors, but no news," came the leader's unusually frank reply. The hollow clop of hooves on wood sounded behind the wagon as the patrol started across the bridge. "For all the havoc he is spreading, he has proven a most elusive devil."

"Then you will certainly be pleased to hear that he has fled," said Rishi. "Already this morning I have spoken to two different patrols who chased the devil deep into the Yehimals and were forced to turn back only because of enormous avalanches."

The leader's good-natured laugh was cut short by the angry wu-jen. "In Shou Lung, we find little humor in failure. Naraka, it is your people's barbaric love of lying that causes us to return without success. Had we not spent fifteen days chasing wild Mar rumors, I would have this devil hanging outside the Paradise Mahal already."

"That is most certainly true, honored wu-jen." Rishi's tone, at once sardonic and patronizing, managed to convey how sorry he felt that Naraka and his men had to endure such a pretentious wu-jen. "I will not detain you further from your terribly important duties."

Rishi slapped the reins, and the yaks started forward.

"Did I say you are free to go, driver?" asked the wu-jen. "Wait one moment."

"Oh, begging the wu-jen's pardon!"

Rishi took his time halting the yaks, and the wagon traveled more than a dozen paces before coming to a stop.

"It was my impression that he had no interest in the words of a lying Mar," Rishi explained.

"I find it wiser to pay more interest to what Mar do not say than to what they do," retorted the wu-jen. Atreus heard two ponies pass back along his side of the cart, but the rest of the patrol seemed to be continuing across the bridge. "Where do you come from?"

"Last night, we camped—"

"Not you, driver," said the wu-jen. "Let your master tell me."

The two Mar were silent. For a moment, Atreus feared they were waiting for him to speak. Then the cart rocked as Bharat turned sideways.

"M-me?"

"Is there another master on the cart?" retorted the wu-jen.

Atreus clutched his dagger. Not for the first time, he wished that he had grabbed his sword instead of his gold when he jumped off the elephant.

When Bharat did not answer the wu-jen, Rishi said, "I hope the wu-jen will forgive my boldness, but he is terribly mistaken. I am the master here."

"Truly?" asked the wu-jen. "That is most surprising. I would have thought a blind master needs a seeing driver. Tell me, Blind Helper, why does a seeing master need you?"

"I am not a helper." Bharat's voice was indignant. "We are both bahrana carpet sellers. We are equals."

"Ah, then why does the driver call himself master?"

"Because he is a liar and a thief who thinks he can cheat a blind man out of his due," answered Bharat. "Tell me, good wu-jen, is it fair that one man who is the equal of another should receive only a third of the profits?"

Atreus bit his lip to keep from snarling aloud at the veiled threat, but Rishi took it in stride.

64

"Pay the blind fool no attention," said the Mar. "Certainly, the wu-jen will agree that when one man does two-thirds of the work, he should have two-thirds of the reward?"

"The wu-jen will agree that it is none of his concern," replied the wu-jen. "But a blind man's senses are very sharp. Perhaps he hears this devil or smells him somewhere along the way?"

"No, I heard nothing unusual." Bharat's answer came quickly—too quickly, Atreus thought. "And it is impossible in this cart to smell anything but my greedy partner."

"Ah, most unfortunate for us. But we are grateful for your candidness. It is very unusual for a Mar not to make up a story." The wu-jen's voice grew less suspicious, though the irony in his words was not lost on Atreus. "By what road did you come?"

"By the Thanza road." Rishi answered quickly, robbing Bharat of the chance to malign him further. "From Edenvale."

"Of course . . . the Thanza road," said the wu-jen. "Strange, I do not recall anyone mentioning a blind merchant. You Mar are so full of gossip, and selling beautiful carpets is an uncommon occupation for a blind man."

"That is easy to explain," Rishi said. "The old fool cannot tell whether his eyelids are up or down. It often looks like he is napping. And now, if the great wu-jen permits, we must be on our way. We have far to go before dark."

"And where are you bound, Blind Man?"

Bharat hesitated. "I am not sure."

"Not sure?" asked the wu-jen.

"I am never certain where my lying partner is taking me." Bharat shifted in his seat. "Since he does not consider me his equal, he does not often tell me."

"You know this time," Rishi said. "We have already agreed, and it is too late to change now."

Bharat remained silent, and Atreus grew so angry that

his hand began to hurt from squeezing his dagger. After this was over, he would let the pudgy Mar know what he thought of blackmail.

"I am waiting," said the wu-jen. "What is your destination?"

"Oh, begging the wu-jen's forgiveness," said Bharat. "My friend is right. I recall now that we are going to Gyatse."

Rishi groaned.

"To Gyatse?" scoffed Naraka, the patrol leader. "You cannot sell carpets in Gyatse."

"If the patrol leader has stayed in Gyatse, perhaps he has noticed that they have only stone floors," said Rishi. "There is not one carpet in the whole village . . . and a very cold village it is! They have a great need for our carpets."

"Need, yes, but they are paupers in Gyatse," said the wu-jen. "The whole village together could not buy a single carpet. Perhaps we should look at these carpets."

Atreus braced himself, ready to spring the instant the dust shroud was pulled back. Suddenly the wagon rocked, and Bharat cried, "Save me!"

Atreus flung off the dust shroud and saw Rishi holding Bharat by the shoulder of his cloak.

"Help! Ysdar's devil has blinded me!" Bharat screamed and tried to fling himself off the wagon, but Rishi jerked him back to his seat.

Yago sat up facing the rear of the cart, and Atreus rolled to his knees facing the front. Outside the cart, the wu-jen was twisting around to reach into his saddlebags while Naraka, on the far side of the sorcerer, was awkwardly trying to bring his lance to bear. Yago started to push himself out the back of the wagon, but Atreus caught the ogre by the shoulder and shook his head. The last thing he wanted was to fight it out with Naraka's patrol here.

Bharat continued to struggle, crying, "They're after my gold!"

66

Rishi's free hand flashed up and struck Bharat in the gullet, then whipped back, launching something small and silver in the opposite direction. The wu-jen screeched and clutched at a tiny dagger protruding from his throat, and Bharat tumbled back into Atreus's lap, coating everything in the cargo bed with gouts of warm, coppery blood.

As Atreus struggled with Bharat's gurgling form, Rishi ducked Naraka's awkward lance thrust, then slapped the yaks with the reins. The wagon lurched forward and the leader began to shout at his patrol. Atreus pushed aside Bharat's gurgling form and spun toward the rear of the wagon, expecting to find Yago struggling to block half a dozen flying lances.

Instead most of the patrol was on the other side of the river struggling to organize itself. Only the last three riders in line were able to answer their commander's call, and even they were just backing their ponies off the bridge.

"I could go wreck that bridge," suggested Yago. As he spoke, the ogre struggled in the cramped space to gather his legs beneath him. "Wouldn't take much to get past them three riders."

Atreus shook his head. "If it did, you'd be trapped and alone," he said. "Better to stay together."

"Help!" screamed Rishi. "Help—he will kill me!"

Atreus turned to find Rishi trying to duck Naraka's lance and steer at the same time. He caught the weapon by the shaft and shoved it away, then peered around the front edge of the canopy.

When Naraka saw Atreus's hideous, blood-covered face, he shrieked and released his end of the lance to reach for his sword. Atreus jammed the butt into the patrol leader's chest and pushed hard. Naraka fell, dragging his pony down on top of himself, then tumbled away into the snowy willows.

"Hah! Well done, good sir!" Rishi said, then dragged himself back onto the bench and slapped the reins, somehow urging more speed from the trotting yaks. "That will delay them!"

Atreus glanced back and saw that the three pursuers from the bridge had indeed seized on their leader's fall as an excuse to stop. One of the riders was kneeling on the road, holding the limp wu-jen in his lap while another man pressed his ear to the sorcerer's chest. The third was dismounting near where Naraka had tumbled into the willows, calling down over the road bank to see if he needed any help.

Now that the immediate danger was past, Atreus's ears began to pound with anger. He used his sleeve to wipe Bharat's blood from his face, then slapped Rishi's head with the shaft of Naraka's lance.

"What's wrong with you?"

"Wrong with me?" Rishi asked. He leaned away, rubbing the side of his head. "I am not the one beating my poor servant for no good reason."

"Murder is not a reason?" Atreus asked. He ducked into the wagon and touched his fingers to Bharat's slit throat. There was no pulse. "This wasn't necessary."

"Many profuse apologies for any mistake the good sir thinks I have made, but Bharat betrayed us. He deserved to die."

"He was your friend," Atreus retorted. "Losing his third of the gold would have been punishment enough. You could have let him jump, and it would have been the same to us."

"And what of the wu-jen?" Rishi asked indignantly. "Should I have spared his life as well? Or does killing only bother you when it is someone you know?"

"Unnecessary killing bothers me," Atreus said. "The wu-jen's death was necessary to avoid capture."

"I see," said Rishi. "A very convenient distinction. I will try to keep it in mind so as not to offend the good sir in the future."

"Uh—forget that wu-jen," said Yago. "Tell me what you want done about them."

Thirty paces down the road, Naraka's men were reluctantly urging their mounts into a charge. With the riders' stirrups nearly dragging the ground and the necks of the little ponies stretched forward in a fierce gallop, the sight seemed almost comical save for the sharp points of their lances and how rapidly they were to coming up behind the wagon.

"Can you make this cart go any faster?"

"Certainly . . . if I find a long hill and cut the yaks free," Rishi replied. "Until then, perhaps you would consider our pursuers? If you delay them for only five minutes, we can flee into the willows and escape to our secret caravan road. After that, the gods themselves will not find us."

Atreus thought for a moment, then shoved Bharat's body toward Yago. "Get him out of the way."

The ogre pitched the stout Mar out onto the road.

Atreus grabbed the dust cover and fed it over the rearmost canopy brace, draping it down to prevent Naraka's riders from hurling their lances into the wagon. He cut a tiny square out of one corner so he could see, then had Yago pick up the heaviest carpet in the cargo bed. By the time they finished, Naraka and his leading riders were only a few paces away, with the rest of the patrol hard on their heels.

Naraka barked an order, and the riders in front grasped their lances like spears. Watching through his viewing hole, Atreus realized that the Edenvale Mar were not quite as foolish as Rishi made them sound. Naraka rode up beside the wagon and reached out to jerk down the improvised curtain.

"Now, Yago!" Atreus shouted.

Yago shoved the carpet out under the dustcover, giving it a sideways spin so that it turned across the road. The six closest riders barely had time to curse before the heavy roll caught their mounts across the front legs. The ponies went down in a screeching mass, filling the air with a cacophony of panicked whinnies and clanging equipment. An instant later, the second rank of riders crashed into the mess and tumbled over their fallen comrades, stretching the mayhem another dozen paces up the road. The men at the end of the column avoided the snarl of legs and lances by swerving into the willows, then returned to the road with their weapons ready to hurl.

Yago grabbed a second carpet roll. Naraka's hand grabbed the edge of the dustcover.

"Duck!" Atreus yelled.

The wagon swerved as Rishi obeyed. Naraka jerked the curtain down, and the riders launched their lances. Atreus hunched down behind the wagon's tailgate and heard three quick thuds and a wet thwack as one of the missiles sank into Yago's shoulder. The remaining lances hissed through the length of the cargo bed to clatter off the driver's bench.

"Not to complain, but are you doing anything back there?" Rishi demanded.

Yago shoved the carpet onto the road. The roll caught two of the galloping ponies across the breast and slid down to their legs. The beasts and their riders went screeching and tumbling in four different directions, tripping three more ponies and leaving only one of Naraka's men in pursuit.

"Here!" Yago plucked the lance out of his shoulder and passed it over.

Atreus wasted no time hurling it at the rider's chest. The man threw himself out his saddle and barely escaped being impaled. Naraka himself came swinging around the corner of the cargo canopy, sword blade flashing. Atreus caught the assault at the wrist almost casually, grabbed his attacker by the throat, and jerked him into the wagon.

Naraka landed on his back beside Yago, his sword arm pinned to the floor. He brought a knee up and slammed it into Atreus's side, then tried to jerk his weapon free. Atreus merely grunted, having suffered a thousand blows far more powerful at the hands of his ogre siblings. He began to squeeze Naraka's throat.

"I'll have the sword whether you release it or not," Atreus warned. "The only thing you control is whether or not I crush your windpipe to get it."

For the first time, Naraka really seemed to look at Atreus's bloody face. His eyes grew as round as coins, and his lips trembled and glistened with sweat. Yago sat up and ripped the cloak off Naraka's shoulders, using it to start bandaging his wound. The patrol leader released his sword and began to babble wildly in Maran.

Rishi laughed. "He is calling upon the Old Gods to accept his death on the queen's behalf and smite down Ysdar's devil."

Atreus's heart filled with dismay. The reaction was little different than the one his appearance usually evoked. An ugly face could not be human. He tossed Naraka's sword to the other side of the cart, then released the Mar.

"I am no monster," he said. "Leave me alone, and you have nothing to fear."

Naraka swallowed and glanced nervously away, then found himself staring into Yago's purple eyes. He screamed and reached for his belt dagger. Atreus slapped the hand down, gently removed the knife, and tossed it over beside the sword. Naraka spit in his face and cursed him in Maran.

"Oh, now you are in trouble," chuckled Rishi. He was alternating between steering the wagon and glancing back over his shoulder. "That stupid Mar thinks you will not kill him because you fear the vengeance of the Old Gods. It would be wise to prove him wrong."

"I won't kill him in cold blood." Atreus glared at Naraka.

71

"I mean no harm to you or your queen, so I have nothing to fear from your gods. Do you understand?"

Naraka's face remained wild with fear, and his eyes began to search the wagon for a weapon.

Atreus looked to Rishi. "Does he understand?"

"Who can tell?" Rishi shrugged. "He is mad with fear. If you do not wish to kill him, then at least let Yago break an arm or a leg. Otherwise he will hound us all the way to Langdarma."

"Rishi, enough!" Atreus looked back to his prisoner and spoke in a calm voice. "I know you understand me. I mean no harm to you or Queen Rosalind."

"Lying devil!" Naraka hissed. "You have done much harm already! You have killed the queen's wu-jen!"

"It was not my intent, nor was it my fault," Atreus replied. "Had Queen Rosalind shown me the courtesy she would have shown any handsome man, there would never have been trouble between us."

Atreus glanced back and saw Naraka's warriors beginning to mount and draw swords. Reluctant as they had been to attack earlier, they were not about to abandon their leader to Ysdar's devil. Atreus swung his prisoner to the rear of the wagon.

"Leave me alone, and there will be no more trouble between us. Tell your queen that."

With that, he hefted Naraka over the tailgate and dropped him to the road.

Naraka rolled once, then came up screaming in Maran.

Rishi slapped the reins, shaking his head. "Oh, my, what a curse!" he said. "The good sir is certainly going to wish he had broken something on that stupid Mar. . . ."

6

They pulled the wagon down into the willows, into two feet of cold, clear water, and when Atreus jumped in, his legs went instantly numb. He took Naraka's sword and the hastily loaded rucksack from Yago, then waded forward to where Rishi was freeing the yaks from their harnesses.

"I d-don't think this will w-work," Atreus chattered. "We'll f-freeze to death."

"The good s-sir may have f-faith in his servant." Rishi's hands were shaking so badly he could barely work. "It is our p-pursuers who will freeze, not us. We have yaks."

A loud splash sounded from the rear of the wagon, then Yago said, "Ch-chilly!"

The ogre stooped down and began to bathe his wounded shoulder in the cold water, moving his arm back and forth to work the stiffness out.

"What about Yago?" Atreus kept his voice low. "He's too big for a yak."

"He will find plenty to eat in the swamp. That will keep him warm." Rishi motioned for the rucksack. "The only other choice is to confront our pursuers, and then there will certainly be much killing, which I know the good sir finds so distasteful."

Seeing that the Mar was right, Atreus hoisted the rucksack onto a yak's back. Rishi slipped a rope through the shoulder straps and pulled it toward the beast's withers, then frowned and hefted its weight.

"My goodness, this is light," Rishi remarked. "What does it contain?"

"Our bedrolls and extra cloaks, the last of our food, the cooking pot and waterskins—"

"And what of your treasure coffer?" Rishi broke in.

"My treasure coffer? Even if we had a way to carry it, we don't have time—"

"If you don't bring the coffer, how can you pay me?" demanded Rishi. "You have your own reasons for seeking Langdarma. I am doing it for the gold."

"But Naraka's patrol is—"

"Had the good sir listened to his guide and killed Naraka, the patrol would undoubtedly have turned back by now," Rishi said as he stepped away from the yak. He stood with arms folded, leaving the rucksack to hang half secured. "You may spare your enemies if you wish, but your kindness will not cost me my fortune."

Atreus sighed and glanced through the willows back toward the road. When he saw no sign of Naraka's patrol, he nodded reluctantly. "If we can carry it," he said. "Yago's in no condition—"

"Yaks can carry anything," Rishi said, resuming his work. "You will see."

Atreus laid his sword on the rucksack, securing it in place beneath the cinch rope, then waded over to the front of the wagon. His numb feet were little more than frozen weights, and they slipped twice as he pulled himself onto the driver's footboard. He kneeled on the bench and leaned into the back, reaching for his treasure basket.

The sound of approaching hooves began to drum down the road. Atreus peered out through the back of the cargo bed, looking through the long tunnel of smashed willows the wagon had left in its wake. The leaves were too thick to see up onto the road, but he had little doubt about whom he was hearing. He threw open the treasure basket, then groaned as he hefted the heavy coffer out.

"Here," said Yago. "I'll take that."

74

Atreus turned to find his friend standing beside the driver's bench, both arms extended to take the coffer. Though the ogre's face betrayed no hint of his pain, he could not quite lift his wounded arm high enough to accept the box.

Atreus shook his head. "You rest your arm," he said. "We might need it later."

The sound of the drumming hooves grew louder. Rishi came over with the yaks and gently shouldered Yago aside. The Mar was sitting sidesaddle on the lead mount, holding a willow switch in one hand and the second beast's tether in the other.

"Perhaps you will hold the coffer until we have time to secure it," said Rishi. "It should not be long. Most likely, our pursuers will not even notice where we left the road."

Up on the road, Naraka chattered several commands in Maran, and the galloping hooves suddenly slowed.

"They noticed," Yago growled.

"It means nothing." Rishi waved Atreus toward the yak. "If you will be so kind as to mount, they cannot follow us into the swamp."

Atreus threw a leg over the yak and settled down behind its humped shoulders. He saw at once why Rishi had chosen to sit sidesaddle. Straddling the creature's broad back was incredibly uncomfortable, but with both hands holding the coffer, the only way to keep his balance was to squeeze the beast between his knees.

The rattle of falling stones sounded from the road bank. A single pony whinnied as it stepped into the icy water.

Rishi tapped his yak on the neck. The beast turned away from the wagon and started into the swamp, drawing Atreus's mount along. The creatures had an awkward, rolling gait, and Atreus found himself instantly in danger of falling off. He braced the heavy coffer on the yak's hump and pressed his heels into its belly and tried not to think of the icy water below. Yago followed along close behind, his splashing feet masking the softer babble of the yaks' hooves. If the ogre found the frigid water more than merely uncomfortable, he betrayed no sign.

A few moments later, Naraka's scout gave the alarm cry. The patrol leader started barking orders, and the rest of his men clattered down into the willows, their ponies whinnying at the freezing water.

"They will certainly turn back soon," Rishi whispered. "These Edenvale Mar have no determination."

Rishi steered the yaks down a meandering labyrinth of narrow tunnel-like passages, always working to keep a screen of thickets between them and their pursuers. They passed a snow-covered hummock, and the yaks stopped and started to nose for grass. Rishi cursed the lead animal softly and slapped its neck. The reluctant beast finally turned away and continued forward.

Naraka's patrol stayed close behind, splashing through the swamp in a long, evenly spaced line. Rishi kept looking back over his shoulder and scowling, then turning to Atreus to reassure him that their pursuers would soon give up. Instead, the ponies drew ever nearer, whinnying and snorting with every step. Atreus could well understand their displeasure. He could not keep his own feet from dragging in the frigid swamp, and they had become little more than frozen weights. Only Yago, with his thick layer of ogre fat, seemed as unaffected by the cold as the shaggy yaks.

After a time, the sky started to gray with oncoming dusk. A chill breeze rose from the east and wafted across the swamp. Atreus and Rishi fell to shivering, and even Yago commented once or twice on the cold. Behind them, the ponies grew quiet, save for an occasional splash when one stumbled and spilled its rider into the water.

At last, Naraka began to shout orders in Maran, his voice echoing through the swamp first in one direction, then the other. Rishi sighed in relief, as he guided the yaks into the heart of the willow thicket and stopped.

"Naraka is calling his men to him," the Mar explained. "They will certainly turn back now."

As the ponies splashed toward Naraka's voice, Atreus allowed himself the luxury of lifting his sodden boots out of the water. Though his feet felt as heavy and dead as stones, his lower legs were throbbing stumps of cold pain. His thighs ached from squeezing his mount, and the effort of balancing the heavy coffer had numbed his shoulders with fatigue. He could not imagine passing the night in this cold swamp, and yet he did not see how they could spend it anywhere else.

The splashing slowly faded as the last of Naraka's men rejoined the patrol, and the swamp fell ominously silent. After a few moments, the sound of murmuring voices began to filter through the willows, occasionally punctuated by the soft crackle of snapping sticks.

"The fiend," Rishi hissed. "Does he care nothing for his men and his ponies?"

"What's he doing?" Yago asked.

"Preparing a camp." Rishi shook his head sadly, then cast an accusatory glance in Atreus's direction. "How unfortunate the good sir did not kill him when he had the chance. His mercy will cost us many hours of cold misery and perhaps a few toes as well."

Rishi urged the yaks onto a small hummock in the heart of the thicket. The hungry beasts immediately pawed through the snow and began to tear at the mossy grass beneath. The Mar slid off his mount, freeing the rucksack with a single tug on the rope.

"Hurry. We must make camp before dark." Rishi turned to Yago. "The marsh is full of good things to eat. If you go down by the water, I am sure you will catch something."

"Eels?" Yago licked his lips. Whole raw eels were an ogre

77

delicacy, second only to bear brains. "I could swallow a dozen of them at once!"

"Fish," Rishi said. "I fear the water is too cold for eels."

The ogre's face fell, but he went to kneel at the water's edge. Atreus dropped his treasure coffer into the snow, then swung an aching leg over the yak's shoulders and slid to the ground. The impact sent waves of agony shooting up his cold legs, but he felt no sensation at all in his feet.

"There is no need for concern," Rishi said, eyeing Atreus's clumsy limp. "The feeling will come back when you start to move."

Rishi passed him an extra cloak from the rucksack and set to work stomping down a place to sleep. Atreus took the sword and began to cut willows for insulation. As promised, the feeling soon returned to Atreus's feet, and he wished it had not. The flesh felt as if it were on fire, and the bones underneath ached with the cold. He hacked all the harder.

The light was just starting to fade when a sporadic series of screeches and agonized whinnies echoed across the swamp. Hardly able to believe the awful sound was being made by ponies, Atreus stopped work and looked up. In the twilight sky, he could barely make out three distant columns of smoke.

"In the name of Sune," Atreus gasped. "What's Naraka doing? Burning his ponies alive?"

"That is no doubt what the poor beasts fear, but we are not to be so lucky," said Rishi. "The ponies must be warmed and dried before the night turns cold, or ice will form on their legs and perhaps cripple them before morning."

Atreus glanced at the grazing yaks, who seemed quite content with the snowy ice balls hanging from their shaggy legs.

"Oh no, do not worry about the yaks," laughed Rishi. "For them, cold is better. If not for us, they could keep going all night."

This turned Atreus's thoughts to his own soggy feet. He cleared a place for a fire and gathered several handfuls of brown grass from under the hummock's heavy thatch. Rishi looked increasingly distressed as Atreus began to stack dead willow stalks next to the fire pit. When he withdrew his flint and steel from the rucksack, the Mar could contain his alarm no longer.

"Excuse me, but surely the good sir is not thinking of making a fire."

"He is doing more than thinking of it," Atreus replied. "His feet are wet and cold, and he wants to be able walk when he gets out of this swamp."

Rishi paled. "Perhaps the good sir is unaccustomed to the trials of being a fugitive. Even if the patrol cannot see the fire's light, we are upwind. They will smell the smoke and follow it to us."

Atreus turned toward the frigid channel, where Yago was kneeling on the shore with his arm thrust into the swamp up to the elbow. "Through that water? Impossible!"

Rishi calmly removed his boots and trousers, stepped past Yago, and waded out into the icy swamp. He turned to face Atreus. "How l-long would you like me to stay?"

Yago raised his brow at the Mar's strange behavior, then gasped and looked back into the water. There was a brief splash, and he flipped an odd two-foot fish up onto the hummock. With a bulldog jaw and a long round body striped with brown and yellow scales, the thing looked like a hybrid of catfish and grayling. As soon as it hit the snow, it began to flop about, working its way back toward the water.

Yago lunged up the hill to pin down his catch, and Atreus turned back to Rishi.

"All right, no fire." He waved the Mar out of the water. "But I thought you said Edenvale Mar had no determination?"

"I do not think Naraka is from Edenvale." Rishi climbed ashore and began drying his legs with grass. "But he will certainly turn back in the morning. He is only hoping we will be foolish enough to make a fire tonight and lead him to us."

Yago looked at his catch. "No fire?"

Atreus put the flint and steel away. "Afraid not."

"Great," the ogre grumbled. "As if eatin' fish wasn't bad enough."

He killed the swamp fish with a bite to the back of the neck, then began to devour it, scales and all. Atreus and Rishi made do with a dinner of raw barley in warm yak milk, and the sun vanished, plunging the camp into chilling darkness. Rishi brought the yaks over to the bed he had prepared, forcing them to lie down about three feet apart, with their backs toward each other and their heads at opposite ends. He tethered them in place by tying each beast's lead to the tail of the other one.

Atreus removed his boots and put on a dry pair of socks. He and Rishi wrapped themselves in their extra cloaks and settled down between the yaks, each clutching the other one's feet to his chest. Yago laid down on the outside of the makeshift shelter, curling up beside one of the shaggy beasts.

They did not really sleep. The temperature plunged, and they spent most of the night shivering. Atreus's feet ached terribly, and Rishi assured him this was a good sign. When his toes started to sting a few hours later, the Mar said this was even better. Yago fidgeted relentlessly, rocking his yak back and forth, and at one point cursed the beast for not being still. At first, Atreus watched the constellations, trying to mark the time by their progress. Later, he tried to avoid looking at them. The minutes were passing like hours, and what movement he did notice only made him think of the dropping temperature.

After what felt like a hundred frozen hours, Rishi suddenly sat up and pulled on his boots, declaring the time had come to rise. While the Mar untethered and milked the yaks, Yago went down to the channel and punched through the ice crust that had formed during the night, returning with two more big swamp fish. Confident they would be gone before Naraka's men could find their campsite, they started a fire and gorged themselves on a warm meal.

The hot food rejuvenated Atreus. He soon found himself optimistic enough to remove his tattered map from inside his tunic and examine it in the firelight. Gyatse was the first valley on the chart, and from what he had heard the people there would welcome a few gold coins. Perhaps that would be a good place to replenish their supplies. Of course, Rishi would have to do the buying. One look at Atreus's face and the Mar would flee for their lives.

Yago peered over Atreus's shoulder, squinting at the meaningless squiggles. "That thing say how far is it to Rishi's secret caravan road?"

"If it did, the road would not be much of a secret," said Rishi.

Yago frowned, then reached down to tap the map with a big greasy finger. "But this is a map. It tells us how to find stuff."

"Not Rishi's road." Atreus did not attempt to explain further. He had tried a dozen times to help Yago understand the mystery of map reading, but the ogre still found the lines and symbols impossible to decipher. Consequently, the ogre regarded maps as some sort of divining magic. "We'll just have to be patient."

Atreus folded the map and returned it to his tunic, then helped Rishi load the yaks while Yago cleaned and rebandaged his wound. They transferred half the gold to the rucksack so Rishi could lash a balanced load onto shoulders of the lead yak, and by the time they finished, the gray glow of first light was showing in the eastern sky. Naturally, Rishi insisted on riding with the treasure, but Atreus did not worry about being abandoned. Half the gold remained safely locked in its inviolable coffer, and he knew the Mar would never settle for half when he could have all.

The yaks plunged into the swamp without hesitation, their hooves crashing through the thick ice and leaving an easy path to follow. Atreus hardly cared. Without the coffer, he could sit sidesaddle on his yak and hold his feet out of the water, and that alone was a good start to the day.

The sky had just brightened to the color of blue steel when Naraka's patrol began to splash up from behind. They were moving fast and in a large group, eager to catch up before the sun melted the ice away.

"I guess Naraka didn't turn back after all," Atreus noted.

"Naraka is a terrible bully who is driving his men beyond all endurance," Rishi said. "The good sir may rest assured that they will certainly rebel against—"

"I don't think we'd better count on that," Atreus interrupted. "And we can't outrun their ponies, not when we're so easy to track."

Rishi glanced toward the eastern horizon, where the sun had not yet risen high enough to show itself over the tall willows. "The sun will melt this ice very soon, and then—"

"I need no hollow assurances, Rishi. We all know they'll catch up long before this ice melts," Atreus said as he urged his mount up beside the Mar's. "Do you have any of your throwing daggers left?"

Rishi lifted his brow. "Has the master decided it is necessary to kill our pursuers?"

Atreus shook his head. "No, but the time has come to chase them off. How many daggers do you have?"

"Enough." Rishi opened his cloak, revealing two long lines of small silver hilts.

Atreus turned to Yago. "How does your shoulder feel?"

The ogre reached over and used his injured arm to pluck a willow bush out by its roots. "A little stiff, but ready enough to swing a club."

Atreus grinned and said, "Follow me."

He urged his yak ahead of Rishi's and led the way through the winding channels, all the time listening to the splashing of Naraka's ponies grow louder. After a time, the channel curled around the head of a small, willow-screened hummock. Atreus and Rishi tethered their yaks on the far side, then the three companions sneaked back across the little island and crouched behind the willows on the other side. In front of them lay the passage through which they had just ridden, their path clearly marked by the channel of broken ice.

The patrol was so close that Atreus could hear murmuring voices and snorting ponies, but it seemed to take forever to arrive. He felt himself growing numb in the cold air and began to squeeze the hilt of his stolen sword, trying to keep his arm from growing stiff. Finally, Naraka came trotting into sight, his eyes fixed on the channel of broken ice. As soon as he saw the hairpin curve ahead, the captain slowed and began to scan the willows along the banks.

Atreus cursed silently and laid down in the snow, motioning for Yago and Rishi to do likewise. Naraka continued cautiously ahead, his eyes working the shore methodically, looking first high then low, low then high, then finally moving on to the next thicket.

Atreus held his hand palm up, signaling his companions to remain still. "Catch-and-club" had been a favorite game among his ogre siblings, and he had learned early that motion attracts attention. As long as they remained as still as the willows screening them, they would not be noticed.

Naraka's gaze reached their thicket, and Rishi gasped almost audibly. Atreus frowned at the Mar, silently willing him to hold his breath. Naraka glanced the base of the willow screen, then ran his eyes up the length of the stalks and back down again. He paused for a moment, then finally moved on.

Atreus let his breath out, waiting as the rest of the patrol followed Naraka into the channel. He did not move until Naraka was halfway to the bend and there were a half-dozen riders in the water in front of them.

"Remember, don't kill them," Atreus whispered. "What we need is a panic, not an angry mob."

"I understand." Rishi rose to a crouch. "Your plan is very wise and clear."

Rishi pulled three little knives from inside his cloak. Yago rose to his knees and cupped his hands, holding them about two feet apart. Atreus gathered his legs beneath him, ready to jump to the Mar's defense if matters did not go as planned, then nodded.

Rishi leaped into the willows, splashing through the ice at the edge of the thicket. Several riders cried out in alarm and jerked their mounts around just as the Mar hurled his first dagger. Yago brought his hands together, creating a deep booming clap at about the same time the blade sank into the shoulder of the closest pony.

The beast whinnied and reared wildly, hurling its astonished rider from the saddle. He bounced off the pony behind him and splashed face first into the icy water, then surfaced an instant later, shrieking as though he were the one who had been wounded.

Naraka spun on his saddle, screaming orders and reaching for his sword. Several riders lowered their lances, and Rishi hurled another dagger. Yago clapped his hands, and again the blade caught a pony in the shoulder. The creature shrieked and shied away, then touched the ice crust behind it and bolted down the channel. A trio of riders managed to retain control of their mounts, urging them into a stiff, chill-legged charge.

"One more!" Atreus called.

Rishi hurled his third dagger, and again Yago clapped. This time, several ponies flinched noticeably. The beast leading the charge turned its head as though to wheel around, but it was the middle pony that caught the dagger—in the shoulder, as before—and went down.

The lead rider jerked his mount back into the charge, closing to within two paces of the willows where Rishi stood fumbling for another throwing dagger. Atreus jumped into the thicket and shoved the Mar aside, raising his sword even as he cursed the icy water pouring into his frozen boots. The rider's eyes widened. He cried out something about "Ysdar's devil" and turned his lance toward Atreus.

Atreus tapped the lance aside with his sword, as he stepped forward and caught the man across the chest with the flat of the blade. The rider splashed into the water, and Rishi was on him in a second, jerking the weapons from his scabbard belt. Yago unseated the third guard with even less trouble, jerking a willow out by the roots and hurling the muddy mess into the fellow's chest. The man tumbled backward off his pony.

A voice hissed, "You dare assail a bahrana?"

Atreus looked down to find Rishi pressing the edge of a dagger to the first rider's gullet.

"I will teach you better than to attack above your class," Rishi threatened.

"No!" Atreus caught Rishi's hand, planting a foot on the rider's chest and pushing him underwater, shouting, "Go!"

Atreus shoved Rishi up the hummock, then glanced back at the patrol. Naraka's pony was splashing down the channel in a slow, awkward gallop, while most of his men were struggling to bring their panicked mounts under control. Only the riders at the rear of the patrol were still in command of their ponies, but they were making only a token effort to get past the confusion and attack.

When one warrior raised his lance to throw, Naraka barked an order in Maran and pointed at Atreus's foot, where the submerged captive's arms were still flailing in the water. An idea flashed through Atreus's mind. He smiled and reached down, pulling his prisoner's head up by the long hair.

"Tonight, this man serves me in Ysdar's hell!" Atreus called. He hacked off a handful of hair and shook it in Naraka's direction. "Before this is done, you will all serve me in Ysdar's hell!"

The patrol gave a collective gasp. Even Naraka turned pale, but that did not keep him from kicking his mount until the poor creature stumbled on the silty bottom and fell. Atreus allowed himself a throaty laugh, then tucked the lock of stolen hair into his belt and clambered out of the willows.

On the other side of the hummock, Rishi had already untethered their mounts. The pony of the unhorsed man was standing at the end of their little caravan, its reins tied to the tail of Atreus's yak.

"What's the pony for?" Atreus snapped off a fresh willow to use as a riding crop, then climbed onto his yak. "You said they were no good in the swamp."

"The good sir is correct. Ponies are terrible in the swamp," Rishi agreed, urging his yak into the water. "But taking it will cause our enemies great trouble, as no pony can carry two men. Without it, they will certainly have to turn back."

"Certainly?" scoffed Yago. "I've heard that before. . . ."

"Well, it can't hurt," said Atreus. "Besides, we may need a pack animal when we reach this secret caravan road." He turned to Rishi. "How soon will that be?"

"Oh, very soon," replied the Mar. "By highsun at the latest, and certainly much before that if we were successful in frightening off Naraka."

They traveled for nearly a quarter hour, then began to hear distant splashes behind them. Rishi cursed their pursuers for demons, and Atreus began to fear they would not be rid of the patrol until they killed Naraka. This was something Atreus was loathe to do, as he admired the man's determination. Fortunately, the patrol was moving far more cautiously. By the time it had drawn close enough to worry about, the sun had risen well into the sky, though the ice had not yet melted off the channels.

Atreus and his companions attacked the patrol again. This time, they wounded only Naraka's mount, though several nervous ponies threw their riders at the sound of Yago's thunderous clapping. The riders, better prepared than last time, managed to launch a counterattack of flying lances, driving the ambushers away before Rishi could unleash a second dagger.

And so the morning went, with Yago clapping every time Rishi hurled one of his daggers. The number of pursuers dropped steadily as those on wounded mounts fell behind. The ponies grew increasingly skittish as their fellows were wounded, to the point that they sometimes fled at the mere sound of the ogre's big hands. Once Rishi was grabbed from behind and had to stab a man in the thigh. Another time Yago punched a pony unconscious, and Atreus had to save its trapped rider from drowning.

This mercy only served to convince the patrol that he intended to enslave them all in Ysdar's hell. Those who had already lost tresses to him grew desperate and attacked rashly, while those who had lost no hair grew more cautious than ever. Atreus stopped cutting off their locks, though he took pains to make it appear he was still trying.

There were only a dozen riders left when Naraka finally anticipated an ambush and laid a trap of his own. The trio was rushing across a hummock toward the sound of splashing when Naraka and eight men took them from the side. Yago, ten paces in the lead, was quickly separated from Atreus and Rishi.

Rishi managed to fling a dagger into Naraka's arm. The patrol leader responded in kind, catching Atreus just under the collarbone with a hurled lance. Atreus took the blow without falling, then yanked the weapon out and slammed its shaft across Naraka's throat. The patrol leader tumbled from his saddle, and the battle became a blur.

On the other side of the hummock, Yago was being driven toward the water, wielding a lance with his wounded arm and holding a screaming man in the other. One of Rishi's daggers flashed past and took a pony behind the jaw, dropping beast and rider in a cacophony of screeching and crashing. Another pony leaped its fallen fellow and landed only paces away.

Atreus hurled himself at its feet and came up holding his sword. He blocked a lance, slamming his blade into the rider's flank and felt warm blood spatter his face. He stepped away and found three men advancing on him cautiously, their lances low and ready. Yago was nowhere in sight, but there was a lot of splashing on the far side of the hummock.

"Yago!" Atreus yelled. "Come back!"

"Can't!" came the reply. "Got myself walled off!"

Atreus cursed, and the three riders kicked their ponies, urging them into a charge.

"Yago, break off!" Atreus yelled. "Run!"

Atreus turned and hurled himself out of the ponies' path, rolled, and came up sprinting. He saw Rishi already at the yaks, just climbing onto the lead beast's back.

"Rishi! If you leave me, I swear you'll wish—"

"Leave you?" Rishi called, as though the thought had not even occurred to him. "I would never do that!"

The little Mar spun, already flinging one of his daggers. Atreus ducked, then heard a pained cry behind him.

"You see, I am very faithful!"

Rishi raised another knife, but did not throw it, his eyes darting back and forth between the riders behind Atreus. Having witnessed the Mar's accuracy many times, neither man felt like risking an attack, and Atreus raced the last few steps to his mount in relative safety. He jumped on his yak, slapped its neck with the flat of his blade, and they were quickly splashing through the water at a trot.

When Atreus heard no sign of pursuers, he paused to look back. Naraka's man were scurrying over the hummock, tending to their wounded and struggling to calm their panicked mounts. Atreus saw no sign of Yago, but neither did he hear any hint that the battle was continuing on the far side of the hummock.

"Did you see what happened to Yago?" Atreus asked. "Did he get away?"

Rishi furrowed his brow. "I saw no more than you, but did you not hear him?"

Atreus shook his head. "Things were too confused," he said.

"Yago told us to go," Rishi said, glancing up the channel. "I suggest we obey, before they recover their wits and realize what an advantage they have."

Atreus narrowed his eyes, far from certain that he believed the sly Mar. "What were his words, exactly?"

Rishi frowned. "I cannot be sure I heard him right. It sounded like, 'Both eyes, front and back!'"

Atreus sighed in relief. "Okay, let's go."

"You are not worried about your friend?" Despite his question, Rishi wasted no time starting up the channel.

" 'Both eyes' is an old ogre saying. It means he's whole," Atreus explained as he scooped a shard of broken ice out of the water and pressed it to his wound to stop the bleeding. "And I think 'front and back' means he's going to follow the patrol. If there's trouble again, he'll attack from behind."

Rishi nodded. "Very sensible, but what happens when Naraka turns around?"

"That's not going to happen. Not now," Atreus replied, glancing back. Naraka's patrol was already lost in the willows. "Not until one of us is dead."

"You see?" asked Rishi. "Is that not what I told you back in Bharat's wagon?"

The Mar looked forward again, leaving Atreus to tend to his wound. His shoulder felt stiff and throbbing, but there were no broken bones, and he could still move his arm. As these things went, he had been lucky. Though he felt terribly weak and would certainly suffer a fever later, he could keep traveling.

Of more immediate concern was his guide's loyalty. "Rishi, you do know what will happen if you try to open that coffer without me?"

Rishi twisted around. "Why would I ever try such a thing?" he asked. "Until we reach Langdarma, the gold is not even mine."

"I'm glad to hear you have not forgotten," Atreus said. "You were in an awful hurry to leave back there."

"Not at all! No, never!" said Rishi. "It was only that someone had to untether the yaks if we were to make a swift escape, and you were doing so well. Did I not come to your aid when you called?"

Though Atreus was not entirely sure the Mar's knife had been meant for the man behind him, he reluctantly nodded. "You may have saved my life. Allow me to repay you by mentioning that there are many traps on my coffer, the least of which is the one that blinded Bharat."

Rishi's eyes grew unreadable. "It is very considerate of you to mention this, but it hardly matters to me."

"Of course," said Atreus.

"The gold will be mine soon enough," Rishi added. "Now that Naraka is wounded, the patrol will certainly leave us to continue our journey in peace."

"Certainly."

But Naraka did not turn back. Within minutes they heard the patrol splashing through the water behind them, though somewhat more slowly than before. As the sun neared its zenith, the ice finally vanished from the channels. Rishi doubled back, guiding them down a tunnel-like passage so shallow that at times they were passing over new growth, then struck off in a new direction.

The splashing of the patrol grew abruptly distant, and Atreus began to worry about finding Yago again. The swamp was turning out to be vastly larger than it looked from the other side of the gorge. If they were lucky enough to lose Naraka, it seemed all too possible that they would also lose Yago.

The pony began to nicker and snort more often, lamenting the growing separation from its mates. Atreus cut the beast loose. There was every chance the poor creature would lose its way and freeze to death that night, but he could not afford to be compassionate. After the wounds the two sides had inflicted on each other during the last ambush, the chase had taken on a new intensity, and Atreus knew the next fight would be to the death.

They continued deeper into the swamp. The high willows blocked their view of the mighty peaks to the east, but every now and then the view opened up as they passed an intersecting channel or an expanse of open water. It did not escape Atreus's notice that in these places Rishi stopped to study the sky-scraping mountains for ever-increasing periods of time.

Highsun came and went, and still they saw no sign of the road. If anything, the swamp seemed to close in around them. Sightings of the mountains became less frequent, and when they did occur, Rishi frowned and sometimes muttered to himself. They began to hear Naraka's patrol shouting in the distance. The hummocks grew uncommon, and the willows thickened to the point that the two fugitives had to plow through, leaving a furrow of broken and bent stalks in their wake.

The sun lost its warmth and sank lower in the sky, and the same icy breeze Atreus had felt the evening before started to rise. His wound began to throb and burn, while the rest of him grew so cold he started to shiver. His feet ached with a wet chill, and no amount of swinging seemed to warm them. Though the pain was safer, he longed for yesterday's numbness.

A tiny shout went up in the distance behind them. It was quickly answered by several others, and the flurry of voices that followed left no doubt that one of Naraka's men had stumbled across their trail. Atreus tried to console himself with the thought that Yago would not be far behind.

Rishi stopped his yak and stood, balancing himself precariously on its shoulder hump. He did not look back in the direction of the shouts, but eastward toward the hidden mountains.

"What a relief!" Despite his words, he did not sound relieved. "We are certainly almost there."

"Certainly?" Atreus scoffed. "You have no idea where we are, do you?"

"The good sir may certain—ah—he may have every faith in his guide," said Rishi. "The road is very near. I have seen it."

Scowling, Atreus swung his numb feet up, then stood wobbling on the yak's back and looked toward the massive mountains in the distance. He saw nothing ahead but a ribbon of open water.

"There's no road out there!" he snapped. "There isn't even a dry place to spend the night."

Before Rishi could reply, a distant voice cried out behind them. Atreus looked back to see a tiny pony rider in the bend of a channel, pointing a lance in his direction. The man turned his mount toward Atreus and disappeared into the willows, and a moment later the whole thicket began to quiver.

Atreus cursed, then squatted down and swung his legs over the yak's side. "The man is a bloodhound," he said. "Naraka and his patrol are about half a mile behind. They saw me."

"No matter. We can easily lose them again." Rishi turned his yak toward the ribbon of open water.

They had no choice except to plow straight through the willows, leaving an easy trail to follow. This did not concern Atreus nearly as much as the apparent impossibility of finding a dry place to spend the night. Though he and Rishi had more or less dried out after their morning ambushes, they were both hungry and far from warm. After the sun went down, the bitter cold would be a steady drain on their strength—strength that in Atreus's case was already being tested by a throbbing wound.

Soon, the yaks' feet began to plunge deeper into the water. Small, arrow-shaped ripples appeared at the base of the willow stalks, and it grew clear they were approaching a river. Rishi continued to plow forward until the water rose above the yaks' knees. Finally, he turned upstream, ducking in and out of a network of narrow passages that ran parallel to the main channel. Every now and then they crossed a broader clearing that opened into the river itself, framing a picturelike panorama of water, willows, and sky-scraping peaks.

Naraka's patrol made good use of the passages and the now obvious bearing of their quarry. It was not long before Atreus began to hear the occasional shouted order.

Even with Yago behind the patrol, Atreus did not want to risk a battle this close to dark. Without a dry place to start a fire, the winners would escape death for only as long as it took to freeze.

"We're going to have to cross," Atreus said.

Rishi shook his head. "The river is very deep."

"Yaks can't swim?"

"Of course they can," Rishi replied. "And we will be soaked, with no place to camp."

"We can't camp on this side either."

Rishi shrugged and said, "Who can say, but at least we will not be wet."

They continued along the shore, and the sky grew steadily grayer. Naraka's patrol closed the distance, until their voices became a steady murmur creeping up from behind. Atreus began to roll his shoulder and gently swing his arm back and forth, preparing his wound for a battle that now seemed inevitable.

The willows were just beginning to stripe the water with late afternoon shadows when more murmuring voices sounded ahead. Atreus's first fear was that some of Naraka's men had circled around to cut them off, but then he also noticed a faint, sporadic clanking. Rishi cursed quietly in Maran and peered back toward Naraka's patrol.

"What's wrong?" Even as he asked the question, Atreus fathomed the source of the clanking. "Have we reached the road?"

"Some time ago," Rishi whispered. "And now we must leave it."

"What?" Atreus peered through the willows and saw nothing but river. "Do you mean—"

"The good sir understands very well. And soon, so will Naraka." Rishi started to turn away from the river. "We must lead him away from the river before he sees the boats."

"Boats!" Atreus nearly shouted the word, and the willows fell silent as Naraka's patrol stopped to listen. "We have no boats. How are we to use a river with no—"

"Sssssh!" Rishi held his finger to his lips, then hissed, "The Swamp Way is like any road. There are inns spread

along its course, and at those inns boats can often be pur-
chased."

Atreus listened a moment, then groaned. The clanking
and voices upstream were growing louder.

"We're going the wrong direction."

Rishi scowled and glanced nervously upstream and
down. "Certainly the good sir has sound reason for claiming
to know more than his guide?" he said. "Perhaps he has
been in this swamp before, or perhaps he has a divine map
from his goddess such as the one that shows him how to
reach the fabled valley, but not the mountains where it lies?"

"The boat is coming downstream," Atreus replied, "so,
unless these rivermen make a habit of running in the dark,
the nearest inn is not far behind us . . . on the other side of
Naraka."

Rishi's face fell, and Naraka's voice began shouting
orders. It did not sound nearly distant enough to please
Atreus.

"He's found our trail." Atreus turned his yak toward the
river and urged it forward. "Maybe we can catch a ride."

"No! Wait!" Rishi cried. "What about Yago? Surely you do
not mean to leave him alone with Naraka?"

"Yago is behind Naraka," Atreus said, continuing toward
the river. "That means he's downstream. We'll pick him up
on the way past."

Ponies began to splash through the water, moving fast
and coming straight toward them. The murmur on the
boats was almost as loud as that of Naraka's patrol, the
clanking so sharp that Atreus could distinctly identify it as
chains.

"You do not understand!" Rishi cried, riding after Atreus.
"We must go to the inn. These boats are not for sale!"

"Anything is for sale if you have enough gold," Atreus
insisted, pointing to the rucksack hanging from Rishi's yak.
"And we have enough gold."

Atreus emerged from the willows and found himself staring upstream at a sharp bend in the river. As he watched, a long wooden dugout floated around the corner, guided by a single man in the rear. In front of the pilot stood several burly guards, looming over a dozen people—men, women, and children—chained to the bottom of the boat.

"Slaves?" Atreus gasped. He turned to Rishi, too stunned to be outraged. "I'm following a slaver?"

7

A second boat floated around the bend, also holding a dozen slaves. The captives sat three abreast, with a single chain running through their wrist manacles from one side of the boat to the other. They had the dark hair and golden skin of the Mar, but their faces were rounder and their eyes narrower. Their cheeks and black eyes were bulging, most had a crust of dried blood beneath their nostrils, lips so swollen they could barely close their mouths. Their clothes were filthy, ripped, and too flimsy for a journey through the cold swamp. Most were shivering. All were staring into the water with hopeless, unseeing eyes.

At the rear of the boat stood a pair of guards, larger and of lighter complexion than their captives. They dressed in warm furs and held furled whips in their hands. At their sides hung long padded clubs, no doubt used to beat slaves senseless without damaging their market value. The two men were frowning and looking past Atreus and Rishi into the willows, where Naraka's patrol was rustling toward shore.

A wave of revulsion rose in Atreus. The thought of buying help from slavers sickened him, but their boats seemed his only hope of survival. Whether or not he defeated Naraka, he would need plenty of warm food and a dry place to sleep if he wanted to see the dawn.

"Perhaps now the good sir sees why we may not ask for a ride," said Rishi. "It is death to anyone who reveals the Swamp Road to the Queen's Men. We must lead the patrol away and circle back to the inn, or the rivermen will kill us as surely as our pursuers."

Rishi turned away from the shore, suddenly crying out and pressing himself flat to his mount's back. A pair of wooden lances flew out of the willows, one striking the gold-filled rucksack on his yak and the other sailing over his head into the river.

A grunt sounded downstream from Atreus. He ducked, then heard a lance hiss past and splash into the water. He twisted toward his unseen attacker, automatically bringing his sword around in an inverted guard, and deflected a second lance coming at his ribs. He urged his mount deeper into the willows, not because he cared whether Naraka's men saw the slave boats, but because it was death to be trapped against the river.

He was too late. There were two riders lurking in the willows ahead. On the other side of Rishi, another pair—these still armed with lances—were easing through the thicket upstream. Naraka and four more men were coming from downstream, ready to sweep in from behind the instant Atreus and Rishi engaged either pair of riders.

"Yago!" Atreus called. "Need help! Where are you?"

Yago did not answer, and Atreus's heart fell. He could only guess at Naraka's casualties in their last clash, but it seemed to him the patrol should have been larger by three or four riders. Whether Naraka had lost those men slaying Yago or simply left them behind to delay the ogre Atreus had no way to know. But had Yago been in earshot, he would have answered.

A cold fury rose inside Atreus, and he turned his yak downstream toward Naraka. Whatever had happened to Yago, the patrol leader's prejudice was to blame—the patrol leader's and that of his queen.

"This way, Rishi!"

Hoping to make good use of the yaks' size, Atreus eased his mount into deeper water. Ten paces ahead, Naraka and his group mirrored the movement, two men holding lances and two holding swords.

Rishi came up from the rear, stationing himself a pace back and just inshore of Atreus. Behind them, the other four riders began to splash through the water, slowly tightening the noose.

"Will the good sir have any objection to killing?" Rishi asked quietly.

"The choice is no longer ours," said Atreus. "Take the two with the lances."

No sooner had Atreus spoken than a silver blade hissed past his head, flashing toward Naraka's. The lancer on the end cried out and tried to duck away, but the knife caught him at the base of the skull. He went limp instantly and splashed into the water.

As the other lancer raised his weapon Rishi suddenly cursed and cried out in pain. Atreus glanced back to see the Mar leaning down, groaning and tugging at a lance lodged in the calf of his leg. The rider who had thrown it was moving up from behind with his three companions, their ponies half swimming in the deep water.

A grunt sounded from Naraka's group, and Atreus looked forward to see the second lancer hurling a wooden shaft in Rishi's direction. He flicked his sword up, hitting the weapon in mid flight and sending it arcing out into the river. Oblivious, Rishi was still tugging at the lance lodged in his calf.

"Leave that for later!" Atreus yelled.

"Later?" Rishi gasped. "It is stuck through my leg!"

"Forget it," Atreus said as he urged his yak forward. "Stop the men behind us. I'll clear the way."

He angled toward the river as if he were trying to squeeze past his foes. Naraka moved to cut him off, guiding his mount into water so deep that it began to lap at his saddle. On the patrol leader's arm was a red stain where Rishi's knife had found its mark earlier, and he held his elbow close to his ribs. His eyes were filled with doubt, and his face was pale with the fear any man would feel when riding out to battle a devil, but his gaze never faltered.

The other two riders swung around toward Atreus's flank, their legs splashing as they frantically kicked at their mounts. The ponies snorted and whinnied, but they were moving as fast as they could in the deep water. The whole battle seemed to be taking shape in slow motion.

There was a startled cry behind Atreus, then a splash. Three more splashes quickly followed. He looked back to see a wounded rider flailing about in the water, clasping at the shiny hilt protruding from just under his collarbone. One of his fellows was beside him, trying to keep the wounded man's head above the surface. The other two were swimming alongside their ponies, ready to dive the instant Rishi raised another throwing dagger.

Curious voices began to roll across the water from the slave boats, and the rattle of chains grew louder and more agitated. The first two dugouts had already passed well downstream, and three more were floating around the bend. The passengers—captives and guards alike—were staring at the shore in bewilderment.

The sound of rippling water drew Atreus's gaze back to his foes. Naraka and his men were only two paces away now, almost within reach of a wild thrust.

"I am sorry for what has passed between us," Atreus said, "and for what is about to."

He raised his sword and kissed the blade, then drew the locks of hair he had collected from his belt and cast them into the river. The eyes of the Mar widened. Then his soldiers hurled themselves into the battle with wild abandon. Naraka came in from the front, standing in his stirrups to lean between the yak's horns and thrust at Atreus's ribs.

Atreus twisted away, at the same time leaning back to escape the second rider's wild head slash. When the third attacker came in with a low thrust, he blocked with his weapon's cutting edge, then circled over the top and brought the blade down on his foe's wrist. The hand came free with a sickening pop and sank into the river still holding its sword.

As the man screamed, Atreus twisted back toward Naraka and slashed at the second rider's midsection. The man managed an awkward inverted block that left his head utterly exposed, and Atreus switched attacks smoothly, smashing his sword pommel into the fellow's face. The rider's nose shattered, and he tumbled out of his saddle.

Naraka's sword caught Atreus in the flank, passing entirely through that little roll of flesh just above the belt. Atreus yelled and lashed out with his sore arm, grabbing the patrol leader by the wrist and jerking him forward onto the yak's head.

Naraka's other hand arced around, a shiny dagger flashing in his grasp. Atreus released his foe and jerked back and the blade came down on the fleshy hump between the yak's shoulders. The beast bellowed and whipped its head sideways, flinging the patrol leader into the willows.

Naraka's sword tore free with a ghastly slurping sound, as Atreus's waist erupted into molten anguish. He heard himself scream in pain, then felt himself touching a huge flap of skin without quite realizing that he had reached down to probe the sticky mess above his belt.

A roar went up from the slave boats, which had come closer to watch the battle. The guards were facing him as they drifted past, grinning and shaking their fists in approval. The slaves were staring in wide-eyed horror.

"Help!"

The cry came from Rishi and was followed by an unintelligible scream.

Atreus spun around to find three riders swimming up behind them. One grabbed the lance in Rishi's leg and was

101

trying to drag the Mar off his yak. The other two were circling out to approach from the sides. All three had blue lips
and chattering teeth, and they were shaking so hard they
could barely hold their weapons.

Atreus grabbed Rishi's yak by the horn and pulled the
beast alongside his, dragging along the man holding the
lance. The Mar screamed and flung himself flat on the
beast's back, his fingers digging deep into its shaggy fur.

"Lift your leg!" Atreus ordered.

"Lift it?" There were tears streaming from Rishi's eyes as
he said, "It is not possible. They have me by . . . lance. . . ."

"Lift it!" Atreus shouted, then raised his sword and
leaned around behind his guide. "Lift it or lose it."

Rishi buried his face in his mount's fur and tried to obey.
The lance came out of the water just enough to see, and
Atreus brought his sword down. The blow severed the
shaft a foot behind the Mar's calf, leaving the man at the
other end to fall back into the water.

The other two riders continued forward, wading through
water up to their chests. Rishi kept his face buried and
screamed as though Atreus had struck his leg instead of
the lance. Naraka began to work his way back through the
willows, barking orders and pulling along the rider with the
smashed nose. Atreus grabbed the lead of Rishi's yak and
turned away from shore.

"You cannot do this!" Rishi yelled. The water was already
lapping at his thighs. "The rivermen will kill us."

"So will Naraka," Atreus said, nodding back toward the
willows where the patrol's survivors were gathering their
ponies. "And if they don't, the cold will. We can't let these
boats past."

Rishi raised his voice to protest but lost his breath to the
cold when the yaks stepped into deep water and began to
swim. Atreus's muscles stiffened, and the strength began
to seep from his body. He glanced back and saw Naraka

leading four riders into the river. The one who had lost his hand to Atreus was in no condition to fight, but the fellow with the smashed nose had found the strength to continue, and of course Naraka would not stop until he was dead.

The guards on the slave boats began to call back and forth, and the dugouts started to angle toward Atreus and Rishi.

"You see? Does that look like they mean to kill us?"

When Rishi did not make the expected disparaging reply, Atreus glanced back and saw the Mar's poor yak swimming along with little more than its nose above water. Even that slipped beneath the surface sporadically, only to pop back up spewing water and mucus.

"Rishi, what's wrong with you?"

"Me? It is my yak that is too dumb to swim."

"It's not dumb, it's drowning!" Atreus said. Behind Rishi, Naraka and his men were swimming along beside their ponies, holding their saddle horns and coming up fast. "Cut the gold free!"

Rishi looked as though Atreus had uttered a sacrilege. "You would sacrifice all this gold to spare a yak?"

"If you lose the yak, you lose the gold."

Atreus pulled hard on the beast's lead, drawing it alongside his own. The poor creature's eyes were as big as saucers, and it was breathing so hard that it sprayed his face with water. Behind the yak, Naraka and his men had closed to within five paces of its tail. Atreus plunged a hand into the icy water and managed to locate the rucksack, then slipped his sword under the cargo rope and began to saw.

"No! You are mistaken in this," Rishi begged, clutching Atreus by the elbow, but the Mar's grasp was too weak to pull his arm away. "I am as heavy as the gold. If I swim—"

"You float. Gold doesn't."

Atreus's blade bit through the rope, and the rucksack slipped into the muddy depths. The yak's head bobbed out of the water at once, but its neck and shoulders remained submerged. It was breathing harder than ever. Atreus slipped his sword under the coffer's rope, but Rishi leaned down and clutched the chest in his arms.

"The yak can carry this much!"

Atreus's yak gave a sudden jerk, and he looked back to see one of Naraka's men holding its tail. Two more riders were coming up behind Rishi. Atreus cut the rope. When Rishi continued to hold the coffer, he slammed the Mar in the shoulder and shoved him off the struggling yak.

"Forget the gold! Fight!"

The Mar vanished under the waves, still clutching the heavy coffer to his chest. Atreus spun on his mount's back, drawing his sword tip across the faces of two men behind him. They screamed and clutched at their wounds, and the current carried them off.

Rishi surfaced behind a third rider, taking him completely by surprise and planting a dagger in his ribs. The man shrieked and began to flail about in anguish. Rishi shoved the fellow's head underwater, then grabbed hold of his pony's saddle.

A deep, unearthly voice rasped across the water. Atreus glanced upstream to see a huge, bargelike boat coming around the bend. Twice as wide as the dugouts, it had a flat profile packed with slaves, a square bow manned by four guards, and a double set of oars being worked by two rowers. On the stern, a gaunt manlike figure with sloping shoulders and a pointy head stood in front of a crude cabin watching the battle.

That was all Atreus could see before a fourth rider splashed up behind Rishi, his sword scribing an arc toward the Mar's head. Rishi rolled into the assault, leaving the blow to slice harmlessly into the river, and dived. The rider began to slash madly at the water, cried out, and sank from sight.

Naraka swam up alongside Atreus, dagger flashing in one hand and sword flailing in the other. Atreus rolled off the far side of his mount and let his sword sink into the river, pulling himself under the beast's shaggy belly. He could see Naraka's legs in front of him, kicking madly as the patrol leader pulled himself onto the yak's back. One foot nearly caught Atreus in the head. He ducked out of the way, then kicked hard and came up behind his foe.

Naraka realized his mistake as soon as he heard Atreus's head break the surface. He pushed off the yak, turning to face his attacker. Atreus cupped both hands and slapped the patrol leader's ears. Naraka's eyes lit with pain. He began to sink, too dazed to keep himself afloat. Atreus caught him by the arm and knocked the dagger loose, and by then Naraka had recovered enough to raise his sword.

Atreus knuckle-punched him in the throat, but even that did not stop the determined patrol leader. The sword flashed down. Atreus shoved a hand up and caught hold of the wrist. In the next instant, the fingers of Naraka's other hand were ripping at his waist, gouging into his wound and tearing at the flap of loose skin. Atreus screamed and felt his chest fill with cold water, and he began to sink.

He reached up and caught Naraka by the throat, trying desperately to crush his attacker's windpipe, but the cold water had sapped his strength. It was all he could do to keep squeezing. Naraka tried to jerk his sword arm free, but the patrol leader was growing weak too. He followed Atreus beneath the surface, and they hung in the icy current for a long time, clutching and tearing at each other with cold-numbed fingers.

Something crackled in Naraka's throat. His eyes bulged, and a filmy white bubble slipped from his lips. The sword tumbled from his hand, but Atreus continued to squeeze, even after he saw water fill the dead man's open throat. He wanted to shake the patrol leader alive, to rebuke him for the prejudice and ignorance that had made them enemies in the first place. Of course, Naraka would not have listened. He was too good a soldier; he did as his queen commanded, whether that meant hunting down innocuous explorers or hurling himself into battle against ghastly devils.

Feeling no regrets for killing him, Atreus pushed Naraka's body away. The patrol leader might not have deserved to die because of his ignorance, but neither had Atreus, nor Yago, if that was what had become of the ogre.

Atreus broke the surface coughing and gasping for air. He felt more weak than cold, though he could sense the river sucking more heat from his body with every passing moment. His yak was gone, swimming for the far shore, and the small slave boats were well downstream, zigzagging back and forth after the surviving members of Naraka's patrol.

Atreus thrust an arm up. "Here!" His voice was a mere croak, his legs so stiff he could barely tread water. "Help!"

The distant dugouts paid him no attention. One of the little boats slowed, as a slaver pulled a limp rider half out of the river and slit the man's throat. Atreus was too exhausted to be shocked. He merely hoped he would not meet the same fate.

Upstream, Rishi cried out, "I have g-gold!" The Mar sounded as weak as Atreus felt. "Help me, and you shall be r-rewarded."

Atreus turned and saw Rishi splashing toward the big slave barge where half a dozen men stood just forward of the ramshackle cabin with the gaunt figure he had glimpsed earlier. There were no more boats coming around the bend, and all the others were well downstream, murdering the last of Naraka's wounded riders.

Rishi raised his hand, holding the small purse of gold Atreus had given him earlier. "I have gold," he said. "It is yours!"

The gaunt figure turned toward the center of the boat and barked a command. At once, the two oarsmen began to row against the current, holding the vessel in place. Rishi tucked his gold away and began to swim. Atreus followed, determined to find a place on the boat.

As he neared the barge, Atreus saw that the gaunt figure looked more like a demon than any sort of human. His slimy, snakelike torso was covered in green-glistening scales, while his spindly fingers ended in filthy-looking claws long enough to disembowel a yak. To protect him from the frigid weather, he wore nothing more than a loin-cloth and a soiled yellow cape, and a long barbed tail flicked back and forth over his shoulder.

His face was even more hideous than his body. He had a narrow, pointed head with a bony brow ridge, a pair of beady black eyes set deep in dark hollow sockets, and a huge nose dribbling mucus and shaped vaguely like an arrowhead. His flaky-lipped mouth stretched a full handspan across his face, exhibiting a row of jagged fangs that rose up from his lower jaw like saw teeth. Hanging from his chin was a greasy black beard braided into long spikes and teeming with white lice.

When Rishi reached the boat, the hideous figure—Atreus supposed he was the slavemaster—dropped to his belly and thrust an arm over the side. "Pay up!" the demon called.

To Atreus's surprise, Rishi did not insist on being pulled aboard before yielding his gold. He simply withdrew the purse from inside his tunic and placed it in the fellow's hand. "I c-can get you more . . . much more. . . ."

Leaving Rishi to kick against the slow current, the slave-master tore open the purse and pulled out a gold piece. He tested it on his teeth, then glared down at the Mar.

"How much more?"

"Enough to drown a yak!" Rishi reached up. "And it is all

yours, for no more than sparing my life."

The slave master's eyes narrowed to tiny slits. "You try to peel me, sod, and you'll wish you drowned."

With that, he plucked Rishi out of the river and tossed him onto the deck like some half-dead fish. Atreus reached the boat, then began to scratch at the slimy hull, too sore and exhausted to call out for help. A scaly hand reached down and caught him by his wounded shoulder. Recalling the fate of Naraka's men, Atreus raised his good arm to block the expected dagger, already starting to explain why his life should be spared.

There was no need. The slavemaster jerked him out of the water and dropped him on the deck beside Rishi, then kneeled down and brought his face close to Atreus's. His breath stank of rotten fish.

"You don't smell like no Walker!"

"Walker?"

"If you got to ask, you ain't," said the slave master. "So what in the Thousand Darknesses are you?"

"A m-man, of course," Atreus said indignantly. "A human being."

The slave master's lip curled into a sneer, revealing a stringy mass of rotten gum. "You're a funny one, bubber. Could be worth something in Baator." He faced the ramshackle cabin in the stern. "Seema! Gather up your brews and come out here. I got something for you."

The slave master turned to Rishi, who was lying beside Atreus shaking. "Now, where's this gold you were jabbering about?"

Rishi paled and said, "Just up the river." He cast an angry glance in Atreus's direction. "In the river."

"What do you mean, in the river?" The slave master asked angrily, jerking Rishi up by the collar. "Like on the bottom?"

"It is his fault, Terrible One," Rishi said, pointing at Atreus. "He sank it!"

The Terrible One's barbed tail began to twitch. He rose, casually lifting Rishi with one hand. "It don't matter who sank it, addlepate," he said. "You tried to bob me. All the gold in this squalid little world does me no good on the bottom of a river!"

"The river is not deep," Rishi offered, pointing upstream. "Take me back to that bend tomorrow, and I can dive down and find it for you!"

The slave master considered this, his fangs scratching his upper lip. Finally, he tucked Rishi under one arm and started forward. Rishi's feet clipped the heads of some of the captives as the fiend stepped over rows of neatly chained slaves. The two oarsmen heard him coming and scrambled out of the way, allowing the boat to drift as the Terrible One passed. Even the bow guards scurried away to give him a wide berth.

The slave master draped Rishi over the side. "Prove it," he said.

The slaver opened his hand, and Rishi splashed back into the river.

Atreus gasped and started to rise, but stopped when a stinging whip wrapped itself around his throat.

"Sit down," said a gruff voice behind him. The guard at the other end of the whip jerked the handle, and the coil grew so tight that Atreus began to gasp. "Tarch didn't say you could watch."

"And yet, did he say you were allowed to harm this man?" The question came from the shack on the stern. Though heavily accented with a strange dialect of Maran, the woman's voice was as pure and lyrical as a lyre. "This man should not be strangled."

The guard continued to hold the whip taut, choking Atreus. "What?" he asked, then turned to the door. "You think you're giving orders now?"

"It is an observation, not an order. This man will die if you keep strangling him."

Atreus grasped the whip cord and managed to loosen the coil enough to breathe, then twisted around to see a dark-haired woman emerging from the shack. In her hands, she held a wooden tray.

"Did Tarch not say that this one is meant for Baator?"

"Tarch says a lot of things." Despite his words, the guard flicked his whip, loosening the coil. He kicked Atreus in the thigh, then said, "We're watching you. Try anything, and we'll whip you skinless."

The woman kneeled on the deck beside Atreus and said to the guard, "I am sure he will be very cooperative."

She was dressed simply, in a heavy tabard of dark yak-hair over an equally heavy tunic, and she wore her black hair twisted into silky braids. Her face was round and gentle, with a small nose and almond eyes as deeply brown as mahogany. There was a peacefulness in her bearing that seemed to well up from inside and envelop her in a halo of grace, and when she smiled at Atreus she was more beautiful than any priestess of Sune.

"I am Seema. I will look to your wounds, yes?" the woman said. She looked straight into Atreus's eyes and betrayed no sign of revulsion or abhorrence, or even that she had noticed the hideousness of his face. "How do you feel?"

"Yes . . . er, fine." Atreus was so stunned by her beauty and her reaction to his ugliness—or rather, her lack of reaction—that he could hardly follow her questions. "Perhaps a little cold, Atreus—uh, I mean I am Atreus . . . Atreus Eleint."

Seema nodded, pulled his arm away from his waist, and examined the wound there. Her hand on his skin felt as warm as the sun. "Do you feel weak, Atreus?"

Atreus nodded, unable to take his eyes off her face. "Tired."

Seema smiled again, displaying a set of teeth as white as

snow, and pulled off his sopping cloak. She tossed it aside, then started to unlace Atreus's tunic. He found himself wondering how such a beautiful and kindly woman could be working with a crew of slavers. Certainly, it was not unusual for attractive women to associate with evil men, but such women were never truly beautiful. They lacked the grace and serenity that Seema radiated so clearly.

"This man is very wet and tired," Seema said, glancing at the guard who had lashed Atreus earlier. "There is danger of the cold sleep."

The slaver scowled, then hung his whip on his belt and disappeared into the cabin. A moment later, he tossed a pair of dry blankets out on the deck, calling, "I'll find some clothes."

Seema smiled to herself and pulled Atreus's tunic over his head. When she saw the festering wound beneath his collarbone she raised her brow and poked around the edges until a stream of yellow ichor poured out. She grimaced and started to unfasten his empty sword belt.

Atreus caught her hands between his. "I, uh . . . I can manage."

Seema glanced down at his shivering fingers and looked confused, but she shrugged and said, "As you wish."

As Atreus struggled to remove the last of his clothes, Seema began to take cloth satchels from inside her tabard and drop pinches of pungent, brightly colored powders into an earthenware bowl. Atreus wrapped a blanket around himself and became so caught up in watching her lithe fingers that he did not remember Rishi until one of Tarch's men called out.

"There he is! He's got a rock or something." An instant later, the guard added, "He's going under again. . . . I think he's drowning."

The rest of the guards rushed over to the side where the lookout was pointing behind the boat. Tarch roared a command, and the oarsmen began to row against the current. The slave master came rushing back, kicking the heads of helpless captives in his mad scramble to step over them.

"I've lost him," the guard reported.

"Get in there and find him, berk!"

The slaver glanced down at the river. "You mean jump in?" he asked, surely knowing the answer.

Atreus started to rise, but Seema caught him by the arm and shook her head. "Leave it to the guards," she told him. "You are too weak."

Tarch cleared the last row of slaves and bounded toward the side of the boat, his tail whipping back and forth so fiercely that it swept the feet from beneath one of the men guarding Atreus. The slaver at the side peeled off his weapon belt and reluctantly hopped into the water.

Seeing the attention of the guards fixed on the river, Seema leaned in closer and whispered, "Your friend is safe enough for tonight, but I think he should not show Tarch where to find the gold. Tarch says he must die for what he did."

"Leading the queen's men to the river?" Atreus asked.

"Tarch did not say what angered him," Seema answered. She put away her pouches and poured water over the pungent mixture she had prepared. "I suppose leading those men here may be the offense."

"You don't know?"

"Why should I?"

Atreus raised his brow, then glanced at the slavers lined up along the side of the boat. "I thought you were one of them," he said.

"By the lotus, no!" The anger in her eyes vanished as quickly as it had appeared. She pointed her chin at the rows of slaves ahead and said, "I am one of them."

Atreus did not know whether to despair or rejoice. Enslaving someone as beautiful as Seema was a terrible outrage against Sune, and it would have been an equal blasphemy for her to be one of the slavers.

"Forgive my witless tongue," he said. "I am as stupid as I am ugly." Atreus felt himself blushing and turned away, knowing that the color only served to emphasize his motley complexion. Hoping to excuse his affront with an explanation, he gestured at her feet. "When I saw no chains, I thought you were one of them."

"You are no more stupid than you are ugly," Seema said. "Tarch wants no scars on me. He says his buyers will pay a hundred times more for the chance to 'paint their own canvas.'"

Atreus did not know what to say, so he said nothing.

Seema began to stir her mixture with a finger, at the same time speaking in a soft Maran dialect that sounded more ancient and delicate than any Atreus had heard so far. Wisps of steam began to rise from the bowl. She continued to stir and avoided looking into Atreus's eyes.

"I am not sure I understand what kind of buyer Tarch is thinking of," she said. "Do you know, Atreus?"

"I can only guess." Atreus reached out but stopped short of actually clasping her shoulder. He had long ago learned that few women found comfort in his touch. "Don't let it worry you," he said. "Whatever Tarch has in mind, I'll stop him."

Seema raised her gaze. "Now you *are* sounding foolish," she said simply. "No one can stop Tarch."

8

Atreus stopped shivering after the third swallow of Seema's steaming elixir, and by the fifth swallow his strength was returning. The concoction tasted of flower pollen and pine needles, yet it sat in the stomach like a good hearty stew, fueling the furnace inside and chasing the cold ache from his muscles.

With warmth came pain. His festering shoulder wound started to throb again, and the gash in his waist kept sending fingers of agony through his abdomen. Even with his strength returning, Atreus was in no condition to escape or free Seema, yet he feared the situation would only grow worse after his captors finally plucked Rishi from the river.

Atreus allowed himself three more swallows of the restorative, drinking slowly and carefully so he did not dishonor Sune by dribbling down his long chin. After lowering the bowl, he glanced around the deck. The guard who had gone to fetch him dry clothes was still inside the cabin, but the other slavers were all gathered along the side of the boat, jeering at the man Tarch had chased into the river after Rishi. No one was paying attention to Atreus or Seema.

"The guards aren't very watchful," Atreus observed. He glanced at the dimming sky. "What happens after dark?"

Seema shrugged and said, "It is difficult to say. This will be our first night on the river, but in the mountains the guards chained the other slaves to boulders and took turns watching them."

"And you?" Atreus asked.

114

"Tarch kept me with him." Seema looked away. "He said it was to protect me from his men, and perhaps it was. Certainly no night passed without screams."

"Rishi said they have inns along the river," Atreus said.

"You must let me look to your wounds." Seema pushed Atreus down to an elbow. "I may not see you after tonight. If the guards can have a fire, they will bring out their anvil and put on your manacles. After that, you will sit with the others until we reach Konigheim."

"Where we are to be sold?"

Seema nodded. "There is a market there," she said, then sprinkled yellow powder over Atreus's mangled waist. The wound began to go numb. "Tarch says 'bashers from all across the Multiverse' will be waiting to buy from him."

A cry went up from the side of the boat, and the guards began to point into the water where Rishi had again broken the surface. Atreus sat up, gathering himself to spring. He hardly felt ready for a fight, but short of Yago's sudden return—and he knew he could not trust in that—he would never have a better chance to free himself or his fellow captives.

The slavers let out a collective curse as Rishi vanished again. Someone began yelling instructions, and Tarch tossed the direction-giver into the water to help. Atreus held himself in check, hoping the unpredictable slave master would throw a few more men overboard.

Seema pushed Atreus back down. "You can do nothing our captors will not do," she assured him. "Now that he thinks your friend can recover the gold, Tarch will stop at nothing to see him back alive."

Though Atreus was concerned for Rishi, his thoughts had already leaped to his own fate, and Seema's. "What's this 'Multiverse' of Tarch's? And who are the 'bashers'?"

Seema shrugged, then removed a curved needle from one of her pouches and threaded it with coarse black thread. "Tarch is a devil. He says many things I do not understand."

Atreus raised his brow. "A devil?" he asked. "One of Ysdar's?"

Seema's brown eyes lit in brief distress. She laughed nervously. "It is possible, but Ysdar has been locked away for a very long time." She pushed the needle through a flap of Atreus's skin and said, "Ysdar is only a myth now."

"Myths can be dangerous, too," Atreus replied. "He certainly caused me enough trouble."

Seema raised her brow but said nothing and began to sew. There was a faint tugging at the edge of the gash, but the yellow powder had left the wound too numb to feel more. Atreus sipped at the elixir and glanced around the barge casually, taking stock of the situation. He counted thirty slaves chained in the center of the boat, with only eight slavers still aboard to guard them; four in the bow and four in the stern. There were also the two burly oarsmen and Tarch himself, who was a great unknown, but with surprise the odds would clearly favor the slaves. In fact, Atreus found it difficult to understand why they had not rebelled already.

He leaned closer to Seema and whispered, "What can you tell me about Tarch in a fight?"

Seema scowled and said, "You mustn't ask such things. Blood draws blood—"

A rousing cry went up from the edge of the barge and Atreus knew one of the slavers in the water had come up with Rishi. Tarch growled an order at the oarsmen, and the boat began to move upstream with surprising speed.

Leaving his wound half stitched, Atreus pushed Seema's hand away and started to rise. The slaver who had gone to fetch his dry clothes emerged from the cabin carrying an armload of grimy cloaks and trousers.

"What's all the noise?" he demanded, looking to Seema.

Atreus settled back to his elbow. "They've got Rishi back. It looks like you're going to be rich men."

"Tarch will be rich," the slaver corrected, dumping the clothes on the deck. "He isn't much for sharing."

As the slaver turned to join the others, Atreus flung his blanket aside. He grabbed the back of the guard's belt and pulled himself up, at the same time driving the heel of his palm into the base of the man's skull. Something popped in the slaver's neck, then he collapsed into his killer's arms.

Atreus jerked the padded club off the man's belt and sprang across the deck, raising the weapon to strike even as Seema cried out in shock. A pair of guards spun toward her voice, but Atreus ignored them and went straight for Tarch. The club caught the devil across the side of the head and knocked him into the water.

Atreus continued the swing, smashing the club into a guard's head. The impact knocked the man unconscious and sent him sprawling across the deck toward Seema. Atreus crippled a second slaver with a stomp kick to the knee, then found himself standing on the outside edge of the deck, facing two guards with their own clubs.

He pressed the assault, sliding forward to feint at the one standing on the inside of the deck. As Inside tried to block, Outside took the bait, slipping around to attack from the rear. Atreus performed a quick reverse-spin, catching the fool in the chest with a back-thrust kick that launched Outside into the river.

Suddenly alone, Inside screamed for help and backed away. Atreus moved in fast, beating the slaver's guard down in three quick blows and finishing him off with an elbow to the temple. So powerful was the strike that the man's eye popped free of its socket. He screamed and reached for his head, then fell silent and collapsed.

Atreus returned to the side and kicked the slaver with the mangled knee over the edge, and only then did he pause to peer into the river. His victims lay in a line trailing downstream from the boat, with Tarch floating facedown at the far end, his scaly arms and tail lashing the water as though instinctively trying to right himself. Rishi was a short distance upstream, bobbing in the grasp of the first guard Tarch had sent to rescue him. Both the Mar and his captor were shivering, coughing, and looking as astonished as they did exhausted.

"In the name of the Forgotten Ones, good sir!" called Rishi, coughing up water. "What are you doing?"

"Escaping," Atreus replied. A confused uproar rose forward. He glanced toward the bow to see the four bow guards rushing back, clambering over slaves with whips and clubs in hand. He waved at Rishi. "If you want to live, get over here and help!"

Rishi's hand disappeared beneath his cloak. In the next instant, his rescuer cried out and released him, then floated away grasping his ribs. The Mar swam for the boat.

When Atreus turned back to the forward guards, he found Seema standing before him. Her hands were covered with blood, and she had such a look of confusion on her face that he feared the worst.

"Seema, are you injured?" Atreus reached out to grasp her shoulder, but she quickly shook his hand off and pulled away. He lowered his arm and wondered what he could have been thinking. "I'm sorry. I shouldn't have presumed—"

"Two men!" she cried. "You killed two men!"

Atreus shrugged, unable to understand why she seemed so surprised. "It was nothing," he said humbly. "I had the advantage of surprise."

The barge lurched, then began to travel in the opposite direction as the oarsmen began rowing downstream. Atreus stepped around Seema, gesturing toward the rear of the boat.

"Rishi will need help getting aboard."

Atreus grabbed a second club off the second dead guard, then leaped a row of slaves and started forward. The bow guards swarmed past the oarsmen on both sides, determined to meet their foe en masse.

Atreus angled off toward the starboard oarlock. The four slavers seemed confused for a moment, then saw that smashing the oarlock would prevent the barge from going after Tarch. They rushed to cut Atreus off, spreading themselves out in a line. He cut back toward the middle, leaping two rows of screaming slaves to attack the guard on the end.

The slaver lashed out with his whip and wrapped up one of Atreus's arms, then brought his club around in a wild attack. Atreus deflected the blow with the shaft of one of his own weapons, then stepped forward and smashed the hard butt into the slaver's brow. The man's eyes were still turning glassy as Atreus turned to meet his next pair of foes.

The two guards split up, leaping slave rows in opposite directions so they could approach from both flanks. The last slaver advanced to take their place, and Atreus suddenly found himself facing three foes. He pulled his arm free of his last victim's whip and began to whirl his clubs through the air, weaving an impenetrable curtain of defense around his body. The effort pained his sore shoulder, but he did not dare give his enemies a static opening.

The three slavers cracked their whips and advanced, their padded clubs held at the high ready. Atreus eased back, his breath coming hard and ragged. The slaves cringed and covered their heads, filling the boat with the eerie rattle of chains.

"Stand and fight for yourselves!" Atreus yelled. "What's wrong with you?"

The slaves did nothing except wail and rattle their chains more loudly. The guards smirked and struck with their whips. Atreus caught two attacks in his defensive curtain, then dropped his clubs before his foes could use them to draw him off balance. The third whip got through and twined itself around his forearm. He circled his hand over the cord and caught hold, giving it a mighty jerk.

When the slaver came stumbling forward, Atreus pivoted sideways and planted a stomp-kick square in the fellow's chest. The sternum broke with a loud pop, then the guard dropped to the deck gasping and groaning. Hoping to catch their foe weaponless, the last two slavers charged.

Atreus turned and sprinted for the rowing platform behind him. The two oarsmen abandoned their duties to meet him, but they were hardly a match for one who had grown up brawling with ogres. Atreus grabbed the first by the shirt and slammed him into the second, then brought the first one forward again and head butted him.

The man's nose exploded across his face, spewing blood and cartilage in every direction. Atreus flung his victim into the guards behind him, stepping forward to kick the second oarsman's feet from beneath him. The fellow landed flat on his back, and Atreus finished him with a stomp to the throat. He turned to find his last two attackers trying to claw their way out from beneath the oarsman with the smashed nose.

Atreus grinned and leaped into the fray, biting an ear off and gouging two eyes out with his naked fingers, both favorite ogre brawling tricks. By the time he finished, he was painted in blood, and the two slavers were clutching their mutilated faces, screaming miserably and lying at the feet of their horrified charges.

Atreus rose, braced his hands on his knees, and tried to ignore the pain racking his body. His wounds were taking their toll, even after Seema's elixir. Normally, a little wrestling match would hardly be enough to tire him.

"B-by the Forgotten Ones, look what you have done! Eight men and T-Tarch!" cried Rishi. The Mar was kneeling on the aft deck, soaked and shivering as Seema tugged at his wet clothes. "You *are* Ysdar's devil!"

The words caused the slaves to cringe away from Atreus. He cursed under his breath and held out his hands to reassure the frightened captives, but this only caused them to cry out in their native tongue and fling themselves away.

"I am not a devil!" Even as Atreus said this, he glanced down at his naked, blood-smeared body and realized how deceiving appearances could be. "Rishi, tell them! I'm just a man."

Atreus started toward the dry clothes awaiting him on the rear deck, then saw a scaly hand rise up behind the stern and grasp the barge. He snatched the nearest club and started aft, the slaves straining against their chains to lean out of his way. Rishi's jaw dropped, and what little color he had vanished.

"There is no need for temper, good sir! I will tell them!"

Rishi began to speak to the slaves in Maran, somehow staggering to his feet despite the stump of the severed lance still protruding from his calf. Seema frowned and draped a dry blanket over his shoulders, scolding him in her version of the same language. A second scaly hand appeared beside the first, and still neither of them noticed.

Atreus leaped another row of slaves, and Rishi reached into his cloak for a throwing knife.

"No! Behind you," Atreus shouted, pointing with his club.

The sound of cascading water murmured up from the river, and Tarch's pointed head appeared just above the deck. Rishi spun and flung his knife in one motion, striking the slave master square between the eyes.

The tip scattered a few scales, then clattered to the deck, unable to penetrate Tarch's thick brow.

"I knew you was trying to peel me," Tarch growled.

The devil pulled himself up over the edge of the deck.

Rishi cursed and grabbed Seema, hobbling around to put her between himself and the slave master.

"This is not my doing!" Rishi produced a throwing knife and pressed it to Seema's cheek, saying, "Touch me, and I will mark her!"

Atreus hit the rear deck at a sprint and, ignoring his urge to club Rishi senseless on the way past, rushed to meet the slave master. Tarch sprang onto his feet as nimbly as a lynx. Atreus charged in swinging.

This time, Tarch was ready. He caught the attack on his wrist, then counterpunched to the body. Atreus tried to leap clear, and only his backward momentum kept the slave master's fist from driving a shattered rib through his lungs. As it was, the impact forced the air from his chest and knocked him three full paces backward.

Atreus staggered and barely managed to keep his feet, allowing Tarch to step securely onto the deck. Rishi backed away slowly, still holding his knife to Seema's face, and the slaves murmured in fear.

"You can take a punch." Tarch stepped toward Atreus. "That's good. There'll be a lot of punches in Baator."

Atreus did not reply—his aching lungs did not contain the air. He simply launched himself at the slave master, club held high. When Tarch raised his arm to block, Atreus leaped into the air and planted both feet square in the slave master's chest. Tarch stumbled backward and slipped overboard, catching the edge of the deck as he dropped into the water. Atreus landed on his side and began to slam his heels down on the slave master's scaly fingers. Two digits came loose, but then Tarch's second hand caught him by the ankle.

A strange tingling stung Atreus's flesh. His leg grew numb and weak, and his whole body started to quiver. An unreasoning fear welled up inside him, chasing from his mind all he had ever learned about fighting. He dropped his club and clawed at the deck. He could think only of escaping the terror that had him, of freeing himself of this inhuman thing and hurling himself into the icy river and swimming for the shore. Any shore.

Tarch's pointy head peered over the side, his grasp still firm on Atreus's ankle. "Leatherhead! Now you've driven me berkers," the slave master swore. "Gold or no gold, I'll make bloodmeal of you and your—"

A whip cracked, coiling itself around Tarch's throat and cutting short his threat. As the slave master choked out his rage, Atreus looked across the deck and was astonished to find Rishi standing at the other end, feet braced and pulling hard to keep the line taut.

"Good sir, you m-must take up your club and hit him!"

In his mindless panic, Atreus came near to not understanding. He turned away and clawed at the deck, still trying to kick his leg free. He felt shamed by his behavior but could not help himself. This fear was unlike anything he had ever known. It was the overwhelming terror of indestructible evil.

A strangled chortle rose from Tarch's throat, and Atreus realized, dimly, that the devil was laughing at him. The slave master let go of the deck and grabbed the whip. A stream of flame shot up the strand, moving so fast that Rishi barely had time to drop the weapon before a brilliant flash consumed the handle and arced down to touch off a small deck fire.

As all this occurred, Tarch started to sink back into the river, dragging Atreus with him. This was too much. Clutching for anything he could grab, Atreus found only the club, which would do nothing to keep his captor from dragging him down into a watery hell. He grasped the weapon in both hands and twisted around, slamming the shaft into the slave master's skull.

The impact rocked Tarch's head sideways but did not

cause him to open his hand. The slave master sank to his neck in the river, continuing to drag his captive with him. Atreus brought the club around again, this time connecting just behind the devil's pointed ear.

Tarch's beady eyes rolled back in their hollow sockets. His hand came free of Atreus's ankle, and he splashed into the river. His legs and torso bobbed up beside him, so that he was floating spread-eagled beside the barge. Atreus used the club to shove the slave master away, then kneeled on the edge of the deck watching him twitch and tremble. When the devil had finally drifted a safe distance off, Atreus rose and turned forward.

Seema and Rishi were busy smothering the deck fire with blankets, while the slaves were craning their necks to see what was happening on the rear deck. Still suffering the strange effects of Tarch's grasp, Atreus pointed at the rowing platform in the center of the boat.

"What's wrong with you?" he screamed. "Start rowing!"

The slaves only cowered and looked as though they feared he would kill them. Atreus glanced over the side and saw Tarch still drifting back toward the boat, his chest rising and falling with shallow breath.

Atreus turned back to the slaves and screamed again, "I said row, damn you!"

Seema dropped her blanket over the smoldering fire and came over to him. "Breathe deeply, Atreus. Compose yourself," she said, touching his arm. He immediately began to feel more calm. "Tarch has used his power on you. If you think, you will recall that the slaves are chained. You will know they cannot do what you ask."

Atreus's terror began to subside. After a moment, he nodded. "You are right, of course." Now that his panic was fading, he was beginning to feel embarrassed by his behavior. "Forgive me. I promised to protect you from Tarch, and now here I am, so terrified that I cannot even think clearly."

124

Atreus selected a cloak and a pair of trousers from the dingy pile of clothes still lying on the deck, then turned toward the rowing station. "I'll start us upstream," he told her. "See if you can unchain someone and get him to take my place."

"Whatever you wish."

Seema surprised him with a bow, then turned toward the cabin, leaving a shivering and staggering Rishi to put out the remains of the deck fire. Atreus pulled on his new clothes and went forward to the rowing station. All that remained of the day's light was a gray glow in the western sky, and he could barely see the willows stretching away into the vastness. Yago was out there somewhere, either lost or dead, and Atreus had no idea how he would find out which.

He started to call out for his friend, then looked downstream and thought better of it. The last two dugouts were just rounding the bend below, about two hundred paces distant. Calling for Yago would only alert them to his presence and place him in more danger. It would be better to trust the ogre to figure things out on his own. He was a capable hunter and would know how to read the signs when he came to the shore where they had battled Naraka.

Atreus grabbed the monstrous oars and swung the boat around, and soon he was working too hard to notice the growing chill. Seema emerged from the cabin with a hammer and cold chisel that she tried to give to one of the larger slaves. At first, the astonished fellow kept looking in Atreus's direction and refused to take the tools, but when Seema pointed at the empty rowing station, he finally seemed to understand and began pounding at his shackles.

By the time the slave freed himself, dusk had fallen completely, leaving the boat illuminated only by the light of the full moon. The man approached Atreus warily and carefully laid the hammer and chisel at his feet, then grabbed the second set of oars and began to row.

Too exhausted to puzzle over the peculiar behavior,

125

Atreus gave the tools to the nearest slave and instructed him to free everyone. This occasioned a great deal of confused murmuring, but eventually Atreus managed to communicate what he wanted and went aft to join Seema and Rishi. He pulled a spare blanket over his shoulders and sank down on the deck beside them.

"What's wrong with them?" he asked. "They don't seem very eager to escape."

"They are afraid," said Seema. She was working by the light of a small oil lamp, poking and prodding at the lance in Rishi's leg. "They think you will kill them if they try."

"Me?" Atreus exclaimed. "We're all in this together!"

Seema looked up. "What do you mean, *together*?"

"They do not understand you, Atreus," Rishi laughed. "They think you are one thieving devil stealing from another."

Atreus sighed and looked at Seema. "Is that what you think?"

"I think being a thief is only a small wickedness," Seema said, avoiding Atreus's gaze as she continued to examine Rishi's leg. "There are greater evils in this world."

"I am no thief," Atreus declared, "and I am no devil. When we reach the head of the river, they are free to return to their homes. Tell them."

Seema looked up. "Truly?"

It was Rishi who answered, "Oh yes, truly. The good sir is a silly fool who cares nothing for wealth." The Mar cast a wistful glance downriver, toward Atreus's sunken gold. "He will throw it away on the merest pretext."

"Human beings are not wealth," Atreus said. He nodded to Seema. "Tell them. They will row faster knowing they are free men."

"Oh, I see." Seema's eyes grew sad, but she rose and spoke rapidly in Maran.

The slaves began to murmur even louder and cast wary

glances at the aft deck. Atreus huddled in his blanket and tried not to look quite so much like a blood-smeared devil.

"Rishi, how do I say she is telling the truth?"

"Ekc'kta reeto."

Atreus repeated the phrase, though he did not come even close to imitating the Mar's strange throat click.

The slaves gasped and looked confused, until someone began jabbering in Maran. The others began to laugh, and suddenly the boat broke into a swirl of frenzied activity, with men rushing forward to serve as pilots while others jumped up to help at the oars.

"What did I say?" Atreus asked.

"That yaks are very honest," said Rishi, "but I think they understand what you meant."

"It would have been simpler to say it in Realmspeak," Seema added. "Mountain Mar are not ignorant savages, you know."

"No, you are not savages at all," said Rishi, pointedly leaving out the word "ignorant."

Seema scowled, then knelt down and placed her knees on Rishi's leg to either side of the broken lance.

"Will you remove the shaft?" she asked, looking to Atreus. "Pull it straight out, the quicker the better."

Rishi twisted around, his eyes wide with fear. "Quicker? Wait one—"

Atreus grabbed the shaft and pulled, removing it in one smooth motion. Rishi howled in pain, and dark blood began to bubble from the wound. Seema stuffed a rolled bandage into the hole, causing the Mar so much pain that he pounded the deck and twisted around to glare at her.

"You are a depraved mountain witch!" he screamed, "to inflict such pain and enjoy it!"

"The lance had to come out." Seema sprinkled white dust on the hole, drawing another sharp hiss from Rishi. "This will prevent the wound from festering."

"Succubus!"

Recalling the numbing powder Seema had used on his wound, Atreus said to Rishi, "Perhaps it would hurt less if you showed more gratitude."

The Mar whirled toward Atreus. "You dare speak to me of gratitude? You, whose promise is not worth a yak?"

"I won't argue this again," said Atreus. "Gold means nothing to a drowned man."

"You are a liar and thief! Had you wanted to keep your word, you could have waited to escape until after Tarch pulled the gold up tomorrow."

Atreus shook his head. "I would have been in shackles by tomorrow, and you would have been killed the instant Tarch had the gold. I did what was best for all of us. Now, I am done discussing this."

"And I am done with you. I have seen the way you repay those who serve you!" Rishi would not hold still for Seema to bandage his leg as he continued to rant, "You would rather let Yago lose himself in the swamp than spend a single night in shackles!"

"Watch your tongue," Atreus warned. "If Yago is alive, he'll find us. If he isn't . . . I want to hear nothing about it from you."

"Oh, you cannot hide behind the memory of Yago," Rishi sneered. "It is no secret to me what happens when a pretty slave girl smiles at someone like you."

Atreus raised his brow. "Someone like me?" he asked, insulted. Atreus was trembling with anger, perhaps because there was more than a little truth in Rishi's venom. "What, exactly, do you think someone like me feels when a beautiful woman smiles at him?"

Without awaiting a reply, Atreus rose and started forward.

"Do not come tomorrow and beg me to be your guide," Rishi called after him. "I do not take fools on fable-chases for free, you know!"

Atreus bit back a furious reply, slipped past the rowers

who were working two men to an oar and propelling the barge along at a surprisingly brisk pace and went up to the bow. The Mar lookouts greeted him with nervous smiles and gave him a wide berth, which was just as well in his current mood. He laid down on the edge of the deck and cupped the dark river water in his hands and began to wash the blood from his devil's face.

When he finished, he found Seema waiting with her lamp and tray of potions. "We were not finished," she said. "I must tend your wounds, or you will be in no condition to flee Tarch tomorrow."

Atreus laid down on his side. "I'm sorry for the things Rishi said," he told her. "I can see for myself that your people are not ignorant."

"They are only words," Seema replied, then knelt beside him and pulled aside his cloak. The needle and thread she had been using earlier still dangled from his wound. "Was he telling the truth? Am I the reason you killed the slavers?"

Atreus looked away, but said, "Part of the reason. I couldn't bear to think what Tarch had in store for you."

"I see."

Seema shoved the needle through a flap of skin, drawing a sharp hiss of pain from Atreus.

"I, uh, can feel that," he said. "I think the numbing powder has worn off."

"I know," Seema said, pulling the thread through. Atreus's side felt like it was burning. "I give you strength and tend your wounds, and you repay me with killing?"

She shoved the needle in again, and this time Atreus managed not to hiss.

9

Atreus woke to the murmur of voices and to the roar of a nearby waterfall. When he opened his eyes he found himself lying on the bow deck, buried beneath an avalanche of yak-hair blankets, staring at a stony mountainside looming up behind the barge's stern cabin. The slope was grassy, steep, and strewn with massive crags of folded rock. Over the largest of these outcroppings hung the terminus of a glacier, a dirty curtain of ice with a silver ribbon of meltwater arcing out from beneath it. Above the glacier, a low pall of snow clouds cloaked the mountain heights in a veil of gray vapor.

The voices continued to murmur, rippling out of the willow swamp alongside the barge. Atreus stayed beneath his blankets, thinking it wiser not to draw attention to himself until he gathered his groggy wits. He did not recall falling asleep, only wrapping himself in a blanket and sitting down to sip another of Seema's potions. If the concoction had knocked him out, it had also rejuvenated him. He felt strong and rested, with no sign of fever. His wounds itched more than they ached, and when he ran his fingers over the lance puncture in his breast he was surprised to find it already closed. Seema's healing magic was more powerful than he had thought.

As Atreus's head cleared, he saw that he had been abandoned. Save for vacant slave chains snaking across the decks and two sets of oars still resting in their locks, the barge was empty, beached stern-first so everyone could sneak ashore without disturbing him on the bow. A familiar

130

cold hollowness arose inside Atreus. This was hardly the first time someone had taken pains to avoid him, but it was certainly the most callous. Having saved the Mar from a life of bondage he had thought they might return his kindness by helping him find his way to Langdarma, but he should have known better than to think any act of kindness would blind people to his humped back and disfigured face.

The willows beside the barge shook briefly, and the nose of a dugout emerged to gently bump the hull. A pair of slavers jumped aboard and rushed aft, not bothering to glance forward or even to tie their boat to an eye hook. Atreus frowned, but made no move to attack. The two men carried swords instead of whips and padded clubs, and he heard more voices murmuring out in the swamp. Fighting seemed less wise than simply trying to slip away once the slavers entered the barge's ramshackle cabin.

But the pair did not go to the cabin. Instead, they divided and circled around it from both sides.

"Tarch!" yelled one. "Over here!"

"We've got her!"

A slender figure emerged from behind the cabin and began to flee up the mountainside, her black braids and dark tabard leaving no doubt that it was Seema. Atreus threw off his blankets and pulled on his frozen boots, then grabbed Sune's map from his belongings and ran aft. As the slavers disappeared around behind the cabin, Rishi emerged from the front door, blurry-eyed and wrapped in blankets.

"What is all this noise?" Rishi asked. "What has become of everyone?"

"They left us," Atreus told him as he crossed the rear deck in two strides and pushed his way into the cabin. "Are there any weapons in here?"

The interior was murky and rank, with no bed except a pallet of filthy straw. A cask of foul-smelling grog sat in one corner, and a tangled mound of shackles and chains lay heaped against the back wall. There were no true weapons in sight, but several sets of smithy's tools sat by the door.

"The barge is ours?" Rishi gasped, still trying to comprehend what Atreus had told him. "Then we can recover the gold!"

"I'm afraid not." Atreus went to the back wall and rummaged through the chain heap. "Tarch is after Seema. There are a pair of slavers chasing her now."

"All the better. While they are pursuing her, we can slip away."

Atreus whirled on the Mar, pulling a six-foot length of chain from the heap. "How can you say such a thing? She saved our lives."

Rishi eyed the chain nervously, backing toward the door. "I am only thinking of the good sir," he lied.

"I thought you were done with me," Atreus replied. He stepped over to the pile of smithy tools. "I recall something about what happens when a pretty slave girl smiles at me."

Rishi's face darkened. "Many harsh words are spoken when people are tired and cold, but there is no reason for us to be angry with each other. After we recover the gold, everything will be as before. We can resume our journey and find Langdarma, certainly in a very short time."

"Certainly?" Atreus scoffed. He picked up a heavy forge hammer and stepped toward the door. "You know where to find the gold if you want it. I'm going after Seema."

Outside, the swamp was filled with calling voices, but the two slavers were not answering. The pair needed all their breath to keep pace with Seema. She was racing up the mountainside toward the waterfall beneath the glacier, holding her long skirt with both hands, bounding from rocks to grass tufts as lightly as a gazelle.

Atreus leaped off the barge and rushed across a grassy flat to the base of the mountain. After so much time in the swamp, the ground felt solid and good beneath his feet, but he found himself gasping for breath as soon as he started to climb. His legs grew weighty and slow, and they burned with fatigue. The chain and hammer became as heavy as boulders, and his wounds began to throb miserably. No matter how quickly he pumped his knees, he fell farther behind, and it took an effort of will to launch himself from each grass tuft up to the next one.

Seema continued to dance effortlessly up the slope, the two slavers clambering at her heels. Excited cries began to rise from below, and Atreus knew she had climbed high enough to be seen from the swamp. Tarch and his men would be swarming toward the barge now, but Atreus did not look back to see them. With his lungs burning and a ferocious headache pounding at his temples, it was all he could do to keep running. Seema did not stray from her course until the mist of the waterfall began to spray her, and even then she turned only toward a drier section of cliff.

As shallow as the angle was, the two slavers made good use of it, closing to within half a dozen steps of her. Atreus's knees began to tremble with exhaustion, and his aching chest filled with phlegm, but he forced himself to go on. What was a monster good for, if not to save beautiful damsels cornered by bestial slavers?

But Seema had other ideas. She hit the cliff at a run, leaping up to thrust her hands into a crevice so narrow it seemed a mere line. Pulling herself up with her arms, she swung her feet onto a pair of nubby toeholds and began to clamber up the rocks like a spider.

So astonished was Atreus that he almost stopped running, but the slavers were not surprised at all. Reaching the cliff only a few seconds behind Seema, they dropped their swords and began to jump, grabbing for her feet. When this did not work, the heavier one cupped his hands and boosted the lighter one up. The man caught Seema by the ankle and began to tug.

"Come along . . . girl," he puffed. "Don't bruise yourself. You don't want to do that, or Tarch'll start getting ideas about . . . keeping you."

Seema began to kick, trying to free her ankle.

"Just pull her down!" urged the bottom man.

"N-no!" Atreus gasped, now only five paces below.

Both slavers glanced down and their eyes grew wide. Leaving his partner to hang from Seema's ankle, the bottom man snatched his sword and stepped down to attack. With the blow arcing down from above, Atreus had no choice but to twist out of the way and fling his chain up in a wild, backhand block. The steel links struck with a metallic clatter and wrapped themselves around the blade. Atreus jerked the sword from his attacker's grasp.

In the next instant, a booted heel crashed into Atreus's jaw. He saw stars, then his knees went limp, and he found himself rolling down the mountainside with no memory of having fallen. He rotated onto his back, swinging his feet around to kick his heels into a tuft of soft grass. He lurched to a stop and heard his foe clattering down the slope above. Atreus rolled over to find the slaver almost upon him, now holding the smithy's hammer he did not remember dropping.

Atreus staggered to his feet, head spinning and spent muscles trembling. Somewhere along the way the sword came untangled from the chain and scattered itself down the slope in three broken pieces. Atreus whirled the chain above his head. The slaver slowed, circling around to approach from the side.

Head still spinning, Atreus lurched across the hill. The astonished slaver stumbled back, eyes darting toward the chain still whistling above his foe's head. Finally, he seemed to collect himself and stopped. He cocked his arm and planted his forward foot, then hurled the heavy hammer.

There was no time to duck or dodge. Atreus sprang into a charge, snapping his arm up to protect his head. The hammer glanced off his wrist and tumbled away. Then Atreus was on the slaver, swinging the heavy chain into the man's head.

The fellow's eyes went dull and gray, but somehow he kept his feet and came up with a belt dagger. He attacked low, shooting the knife in toward Atreus's groin.

Atreus skipped backward and slapped the weapon down, bringing his blocking hand up in a vicious back-fisted strike. The slaver's jaw clacked shut. He spit out the tip of his tongue and stumbled back, blind with pain and slashing his dagger about madly. Atreus whirled the chain down across his attacker's wrist, entangling the fellow's arm and knocking his knife loose. The slaver howled and tried to jerk free but succeeded only in drawing Atreus closer.

Atreus grabbed him behind the neck and pulled, at the same time slamming a knee to his foe's chest. There were two muffled cracks, and the man groaned and dropped to the ground, wheezing and clutching at his side.

Atreus kicked the slaver down the slope and saw Rishi scrambling up the mountainside, moving quickly despite his limp and the large bundle slung over his shoulder. Farther below, Tarch and a dozen men were just starting across the narrow flat that separated the mountains from the swamp. Staggering along in front of them, covering six feet a step despite a numb-footed limp, was Yago.

The ogre's face and cloak were caked with ice and mud, and a veritable copse of broken willow stalks jutted up from inside his belt and collar. He looked as if he had passed the night wallowing in the swamp, but Atreus knew better. Yago understood the value of concealment as well as any good hunter, and his camouflage suggested he had spent the night trailing Tarch and his slavers. They had probably not even realized he was there until he broke from the willows and started across the flat.

Too breathless to call out to his friend, Atreus merely waved, then scrambled up the mountainside, his lungs burning so badly he feared he had bruised them tumbling down the hill. On the cliff above, the slaver finally released Seema's ankle and dropped to the ground. She started to climb higher, looked down at Atreus, and stopped where she was.

The slaver retrieved his sword and met Atreus five paces below the cliff, using his uphill advantage to attack with a vicious overhand strike. Too exhausted to dodge or feint, Atreus simply dropped to the ground and swung his chain around in an overhand strike.

The surprised slaver stumbled forward off-balance, and the chain caught him across the wrist, twining itself around his forearm. Atreus spun downhill, whipping his foe overhead like a stone in a sling. The chain reached the end of its length and untwined, hurtling the fellow down the slope like a catapult. The slaver hit a dozen paces below, crashing headlong into a boulder and tumbling down the mountainside in a limp heap. Atreus retrieved his dropped sword and rushed up the slope to Seema.

"Are you . . ." he started to say, but was too out of breath to finish.

"I am fine," Seema replied, sounding rather aloof. "Have you injured yourself again?"

"I don't think so. Unless you count . . . being out of breath."

Atreus turned to see Rishi taking the dagger from the second slaver's weapon belt. Instead of slitting the man's throat, he surprised Atreus by simply adding the knife to his bundle of goods. Fifty paces below, Yago was climbing up the slope, steadily opening the distance between himself and the rest of the slavers.

"I'm sorry for the trouble waiting with us caused you," Atreus said, motioning to the barge.

"Yes, so am I," Seema said, glancing toward the two slavers lying motionless below. "Be quiet now and rest. When your friend gets here we will have to move quickly, or there will be more bloodshed."

Atreus braced his hands on his knees and struggled to catch his breath between fits of coughing. His wounds were throbbing, but the pain was nothing compared to the agony in his pounding head and burning chest. He silently thanked Vaprak, god of the ogres, for looking after his bodyguard. Without Yago, he could not imagine where he would find the strength to defeat Tarch and his men.

Rishi arrived gasping and trembling, hardly able to hold the blanket bundled over his shoulder.

"So you decided to forget about the gold after all," Atreus observed.

"It was . . . decided for me," Rishi wheezed. "But perhaps . . . the gods will see fit to . . . leave it there until we return."

"Which will not be until your next life, if we do not leave before Tarch's giant catches us," said Seema.

"Tarch's giant?" Atreus turned toward Yago, who was only twenty paces below. "That's no giant, that's Yago . . . my bodyguard."

Seema raised her brow at this, but seemed to take no comfort in the fact that they had an ogre on their side. She simply turned away, eyed the cliff above their heads, and said, "I suppose you two and your ogre friend cannot climb."

"Not that!" Atreus exclaimed, astonished she would even suggest such a thing. "It must be five hundred feet high."

"I suppose we must go around," Seema said, taking the bundle from Rishi. "What is in here?"

"Blankets and food," the Mar replied. "Other things we might need."

Seema fished through the bundle, then withdrew the

dagger he had taken from the second slaver and pitched it down the mountainside.

"We will not need that," she said, motioning to the sword and chain in Atreus's hands. "Or those."

Atreus glanced down the slope at Tarch and his warriors. He shoved the sword into his belt and draped the chain over his shoulders. "It will do me no harm to carry it," he told her.

"If you must."

Yago arrived stinking of swamp mud and sweat. Too exhausted to offer greetings, the ogre simply braced his hands on his knees and filled the cold air with clouds of white breath.

"It's good to see you again," Atreus said, and clasped his friend's big shoulder. "It's about time."

The ogre's head snapped up, then he saw Atreus's grin, gave him the evil eye, and said, "You could of left a boat for me!"

"Oh, you have no business blaming us for that." Rishi grinned, then added, "We had to get our own. Certainly, a big fellow like you should have had no trouble doing the same thing."

Yago snarled and looked as though he would bite the Mar. Seema grabbed Rishi's supply bundle and shoved it into the ogre's waist.

"Now that you are here, make yourself useful," she said. "It is going to be difficult enough to save all of you without wasting any more time."

With that, she whirled away and started along the base of the cliff, moving so swiftly and gracefully that Atreus felt as if he was stumbling along after her. Rishi was almost skipping, and even Yago had to scurry to keep pace.

When Tarch and his slavers saw where the four were going, they began to angle toward the edge of the cliff and close the distance. Seema gathered her skirt and broke into a trot, and Atreus, Rishi, and Yago were soon puffing as hard as before.

They rounded the cliff with their pursuers less than fifty paces behind, then started to pick their way up a boulder-strewn *couloir*—a narrow rock chute so steep that Atreus and Rishi began to grab for handholds. Seema simply leaned a little forward and sprang up the gully as though hopping stones across a stream. Atreus tried to imitate her gait and only found himself tiring more rapidly. Behind him, Yago's heavy breath sounded like a forge bellows, and Rishi's wheezing left no doubt that he found the climb just as difficult as his companions.

Atreus looked up and wished he had not. The couloir continued to climb at the same steep angle for at least a thousand paces, then vanished into the clouds.

Rishi groaned. "My lungs will burst," he complained. "I cannot keep running!"

Seema did not look back, only said, "Just a little farther."

A boulder wobbled beneath her feet, and she sprang up the gully all the more quickly.

Atreus stopped beside the rock and looked back. When he saw Tarch and his men clambering into the bottom of the narrow gully, he stepped around to the upper side of the boulder.

"Rishi! Out of . . . the way."

When he began to push, Seema finally stopped climbing.

"Wait!" She looked down toward Tarch, then yelled, "You must take shelter! We are going to start pushing boulders down."

The slavers looked up, confused, then suddenly seemed to realize what Seema was saying. They rushed back down the couloir and disappeared around the corner. Tarch merely scowled and started up the gully at his best sprint.

Atreus shoved the boulder.

The rock toppled free and rumbled down the couloir,

TROY DENNING

gathering speed and cracking into other boulders. Each
time it struck, another huge stone came loose and tumbled down the chute, until the whole lower gully seemed
to be crashing down on the slavers. Tarch flung himself at
the gulch wall and scrambled up the rocky face like a
huge lizard, then clung there watching stones pass
beneath him.

Rishi whirled on Seema, panting, "Why did you warn
them? We could have . . . had them all!"

"Not Tarch, and he is the only one that matters," said
Seema. "Now you have had your rest. We must go again."

With the rockslide still rumbling, she turned and
bounded up the gully.

Atreus and the others followed as best they could, but
none of them could match Seema's pace. She would bound
ahead, then stop to urge them on, never seeming more
than a little winded. Atreus grew so exhausted that he
became dizzy and had to steady himself with every step,
and he noticed Rishi and Yago doing the same. Their
trembling knees started to give out at unpredictable
moments, and Rishi's wounded leg knotted itself into such
a tight ball that he cried out in agony with every step. Not
once did Seema lose her balance, and soon she started to
hang back and pull the Mar along by his arm.

Behind them, Tarch scrambled up the couloir alone, his
men having decided they were more likely to survive his
wrath than the sporadic volleys of boulders Atreus kept
launching. Although the rockslides caused the slave master to keep falling farther behind, they were never a danger
to him. Every time Atreus laid his shoulder to a loose rock,
Seema would shout a warning.

They had almost reached the clouds when Rishi dropped
to a knee, then collapsed again as he tried to get up. Tarch
started to sprint up the couloir, sensing he had finally run
his quarry to ground.

"Come along." Seema tugged at the Mar's arm. "We are almost in the clouds."

Rishi tried to stand, but fell as soon as he put weight on his wounded leg. "It is no good," he admitted. "I can go no farther."

Tarch continued to sprint up the gully. Atreus pressed against a boulder, but the stone would not budge.

"You must get up!" Seema said, then clasped her hand around Rishi's wrist and started to drag him up the couloir. "I do not want it on my soul if Tarch kills you."

"You should have . . . thought of that before you warned him about the rocks," Rishi said as he tried to jerk his hand free and failed. He was too tired. "You are a disloyal and ungrateful woman."

"Ungrateful!" Seema exclaimed, but she continued up the slope, dragging Rishi along. Atreus grabbed the Mar by the other arm and did his best to help. Yago brought up the rear, breathing harder than any of them, using one hand to steady himself and the other to hold the supply bundle.

"Why should I be grateful for what you have done?" Seema demanded. "I did not ask you to free me. I did not ask you to kill those men."

"You were . . . running," Atreus panted. He glanced back, then kicked a loose rock down the gully. The stone, too small to start a slide, bounced past Tarch harmlessly. "You must not want to be a slave."

"No one wants to be slave," Seema said, her gaze remaining fixed on the clouds above them. "That does not mean you can kill the slavers."

"They was going to sell you," Yago wheezed. His chest was heaving from the exertion, and his orange skin had paled to a sickly ivory. "They deserved to get killed."

"The man who passes judgment on another also judges himself," Seema said. She tore her eyes away from the clouds and gave the ogre a hard stare. "I saw the slavers do many terrible things, but they did not kill anyone."

Atreus remained silent, stung by her disapproving tone. Until now, he had simply assumed that Seema wanted to be rescued, thinking her aversion to killing nothing more than a healer's natural distaste for death. It had not occurred to him that she might regard the slaying of her captors as an evil greater than being enslaved in the first place.

When Atreus said nothing to defend him, Yago scowled and said, "A person fights for himself. A person does not let others make him a slave."

"A person does not kill," Seema hissed. "It is a terrible stain on the soul, and I will not have it done in my name."

The words struck Atreus like a blow to the chest. He forgot to watch his footing and slipped on a tuft of grass, barely noticing as Yago caught him and stopped him from sliding down the slope. Though Sune did not prohibit her worshipers from fighting—especially in defense of beauty, love, or their own lives—she did regard both war-mongering and unprovoked murder as terrible scars upon a worshiper's soul. To Seema, apparently, any kind of killing was an ugliness of spirit.

Atreus scrambled to his feet and grasped Rishi's arm again. A few moments later they reached the clouds and entered a misty world of white air and damp rock. Seema dragged them another fifty paces up the couloir, then suddenly stopped on a large boulder. Though he was only an arm's length away, the fog made her look ghostly and ethereal.

"You will not kill again," she told them all. It was neither a question nor a command, only a statement. "No more deaths."

"Now is certainly not the best time . . . to debate this," gasped Rishi. "We must keep going, or there will undoubtedly be at least three more when we are caught. . . ."

Seema made no move to continue up the couloir. "No,"

she insisted. "I must know before we carry on."

Yago growled softly, and Atreus glanced back to see his friend glaring down the gulch. It was impossible to see anything in the mist, but this was the ogre's way of making plain what he thought about taking orders from strangers, though, of course, he would do whatever Atreus wanted.

Atreus drew the sword from his belt and swung it flat against the boulder. The blade snapped with a sharp chime, and Yago groaned miserably.

"By the gods!" Rishi cried. "Have you lost your mind?"

Atreus ignored him, looked to Seema, and said, "No more deaths."

Seema looked to Yago. "And you?" she asked.

The ogre glanced at Atreus, then growled, "If Atreus wants."

"Good," she said. As she turned to Rishi, the sound of clattering stones began to echo up through the mist. "Do you also promise?"

The Mar glanced toward the sound and said, "Surely it is better for Tarch to die than all of us."

Seema's eyes grew sad, and she stepped down off the boulder. "I must leave you," she said. "I am the one he is looking for, and there will be no more killing if I go to him."

"Wait." Atreus caught her by the arm, turned to Rishi, and said, "Make the promise. I can't let Seema go by herself, even if there is to be no more killing."

Rishi's eyes narrowed. "Good sir, you are a very bad liar," he said. "It is only Seema that Tarch wishes alive. He will be most happy to kill you . . . and Yago."

"He will try," said Atreus, "but now that Yago's here, perhaps we can subdue him without killing him. Are you sure you want to be the only one trying to kill him—or the only one left, if we fail?"

Rishi considered this a moment, grew pale, and licked his lips. He turned to Seema. "I promise."

She studied the Mar for several moments. The clattering below continued to grow louder, but it was impossible to tell how close Tarch was. Atreus had learned during his sea crossing that everything sounded different in fog, and the only thing he could see below was Yago's heavy breath swirling the vapor.

After a time, Seema nodded to Rishi and said, "I will take you at your word, but if you are lying to me. . . ."

"I'll be responsible for him," Atreus assured her, casting a warning glance at the Mar. "I'm sure he won't give me reason to regret it."

"Never! I am being most honest and truthful," Rishi said, turning up the couloir. "Now may we please hurry?"

Seema caught the Mar by the arm and said, "Not that way."

She motioned toward the couloir's rocky wall, then looked down the slope. "Tarch," she called, "you must take shelter again. We have found a loose boulder!"

She caught Yago's eye and pointed to the boulder upon which she had been standing. The ogre grinned and passed the supply bundle to Atreus. Wrapping his gangling arms around the stone, he heaved it into the fog. The rock landed with a resounding crash and began to bound down the slope. Soon the rumble of a massive rockslide was reverberating up the couloir.

"Follow me."

Seema's voice was barely audible over the clamor of the falling rocks. She turned to the couloir wall and slipped her hands into a crevice, then scrambled up the twenty-foot cliff in a few quick moves. Atreus could not help feeling sheepish. Seema was the rescuer now. She probably knew a thousand ways to evade Tarch, and none of them involved fighting.

With the clatter of the rockslide still masking their escape, Yago boosted Rishi up, then scrambled up the wall himself. Atreus tossed the supply bundle to the ogre and brought up the rear. Soon they were crossing the face of a rocky crag. Although the outcropping was not much steeper than the couloir, it felt immeasurably more dangerous, with the mist-slickened rock dropping away into bottomless fog and nothing but white cloud at their backs.

Seema sauntered along the crag as though it were a balcony walkway, barely touching its stony face with her uphill hand. Rishi and Atreus faced the rock and inched along sideways, keeping both hands on the stone at all times. Yago turned away from the outcropping and leaned back against it, crawling along like a back-jointed spider and holding the supply bundle in one hand. It was not long before a nervous rumble began to reverberate from his chest.

"Yago, do you think it would be easier if you turned around?" Atreus asked softly. "That way you can see the rock."

"I can feel the rock." Yago's deep whisper cut through the fog like a hissing wind. Fortunately, the rockslide was still clattering to a halt back in the couloir, so it seemed unlikely Tarch would hear. "If I fall, I want to see where I'm going."

Atreus sighed and reached out. Knowing it would do no good to argue, he said, "Let me carry the supplies. We don't want to lose them if you fall."

Yago refused to yield the bundle. "Keep your hands on the rock!" the ogre said too loudly. "You'll fall."

"Our lives depend on our silence," Seema hissed. She stretched a hand past Rishi, then added, "I will not fall. Pass me the supplies."

Yago scowled but quietly passed the bundle forward. They continued across the outcropping and the sound of the rockslide died away behind them. A short time later, they heard Tarch in the couloir, his feet kicking stones and gravel down the gully as he climbed past. They all breathed a little easier, and it was not long before they began to hear a steady roar echoing up through the fog. Guessing that this would be the waterfall he had seen that morning, Atreus began to keep a watch for the hanging glacier.

He almost didn't recognize it when they reached it. The rocky crag simply ended, as though they had come to the edge of the mountain itself. Seeing nothing but gray haze beyond, Atreus expected Seema to climb around the corner and continue on. Instead, she stepped down off the out-cropping and seemed to simply hover in the fog.

Rishi stopped and peered over the edge, his mouth gaping in astonishment. "What are you standing on?"

"Snow, of course. Come along." Seema reached out with her free hand and warned, "Be very careful of your footing. This glacier is more dangerous than the hillside we have been crossing. It is very steep, and you do not want to slide off the bottom. It is a long plunge down to the swamp."

Rishi allowed her to help him down, and to Atreus they appeared to be floating in the fog. She turned and started to angle up the glacier. It looked as though she were climbing the cloud into the heavens themselves.

"Be careful to step only where I step," Seema said, looking back over her shoulder. "Glaciers are full of hidden perils. It is easy to fall into a crevasse or drop into the melt water underneath."

Yago peered over the edge of the cliff into the gray haze, then looked back to Atreus and said, "I don't see no snow. Let's go another way."

Atreus gave Yago a gentle push. "One foot at a time," he whispered, mindful of the ogre's pride. "We're going in the right direction. These are the High Yehimals, and Lang-darma is somewhere up there."

"According to those bird scratches on your map?" sneered Yago dubiously.

Despite his doubts, the ogre gingerly lowered himself over the edge. When his foot finally touched the snow, he smiled and stepped away from the crag. In the flat light, Atreus still could not tell the snow from the fog. It looked as though even an ogre could walk on air.

Atreus lowered himself over the edge and started up the glacier after his companions. The climbing quickly grew steep and fatiguing, with Seema zigzagging back and forth so sharply that they seemed to take four steps to advance one pace uphill. Sometimes, Atreus could see her reason for swerving. From time to time they would encounter a looming tower of ice—what Seema called a serac—that seemed ready to topple over, or an abyssal crevasse so narrow and snow-choked it was almost invisible. Other times, it was more difficult to tell what she was avoiding. Here and there a small furrow marked a buried crevasse, or a faint gurgling showed only her where a snow-covered pit opened into the river of melt water beneath the glacier. She gave any rock a wide berth, for stones collected heat when the sun was out and melted treacherous holes around themselves, and she always avoided exposed ice. On such a sheer slope, even a tiny slip could mean plunging into a deep crevasse or slamming into a serac.

The steep climb aggravated Rishi's leg wound. He fell back to the end of the line, and soon Yago was hauling the Mar on his back. Atreus followed close behind Seema, carrying the supply bundle over his shoulder so her hands would be free in case she ran into trouble route-finding. After a time they came to a high ice cliff and began to traverse along the base, looking for a way around. Atreus finally caught his breath enough to start a conversation.

"There hasn't been time to thank you for staying with Rishi and me."

"You and your servant were in poor health when Tarch pulled you from the river." As she spoke, Seema continued along the ice cliff, peering into the white fog ahead. "I wanted to be certain you would recover."

"Still, it was kind of you not to leave with your people," said Atreus. "At the moment, my resources are limited, but if there is anything I can do to repay you . . ."

Seema stopped and turned, looking up into Atreus's pouchy eyes. "If you keep your promise," she said, "that will be enough. Besides, the others were not 'my people.' They are from Gyatse and Yamdruk. I come from much higher."

The names caused Atreus's heart to leap into his throat. Both places were on his map, and Yamdruk was no more than six valleys from Langdarma.

Seema started forward again, casting a wary eye on the cliff above their heads. Atreus followed along, trying to quell his growing excitement and avoid alarming his beautiful guide. Given her anger over the dead slavers, he was far from certain she would be eager to help him find Langdarma, especially if that happened to be the high place from which she came.

Atreus took a deep breath, then tried to sound casual as he asked, "If you aren't from Yamdruk or Gyatse, how did you come to be captured with their people?"

"I needed yellow man's beard," she explained. "They do not grow in my home, so I came down to search for it."

Atreus frowned and, confused, asked, "Do you mean you have no men in your home?" Perhaps she came from some sort of devotional order that allowed only women. "Or that your men have no beards?"

"We have men! What kind of place has no men?" she laughed. It was a light, happy sound that chimed off the ice cliff and sang away into the fog. "We do not have hemlock trees, and they are where yellow man's beard grows. It is a moss good for curing black-belly fever."

"So Tarch captured you in Yamdruk?"

It was a hopeful guess. On his map, Yamdruk was closer to Langdarma than Gyatse.

Seema grew quiet, then said, "He caught me near Yamdruk, yes. But my people do not make a habit of visiting others."

"Perhaps you will allow me to repay your kindness by going to Yamdruk and collecting some yellow man's beard for you?"

Seema glanced over her shoulder warily, then shook her head saying, "The child is long dead. Black-belly fever kills quickly, and I have been gone for weeks."

Atreus could not tell whether her tone was suspicious or sad. "I am sorry to hear that," he said.

Seema was careful not to turn around.

"Yes, so am I."

They reached the edge of the ice cliff and began to pick their way up a jumble of toppled seracs, pausing every now and then to offer Yago a steadying hand. As they climbed, the fog began to thin. The wind came up, the temperature dropped, and the glacier came alive with silver light and blue shadows. They cut holes in their extra blankets and wore them over their shoulders like tunics, but this did nothing to protect their fingers and noses from the biting cold.

At last they crested the slope and found themselves looking across a vast crinkled plain of ice, bulging with pressure ridges and furrowed with concentric rings of crevasses. Here and there, pyramids of granite jutted up through the ice in the interior, while long curving glaciers swept like spider arms down into the canyons along the edges. Scattered along the rim, scratching at a cobalt sky with pinnacles as sharp and gleaming as sword tips, were the impossibly high peaks Atreus had seen from the far side of the swamp. And there, almost directly across the ice field, were three bell-shaped spires. The Sisters of Serenity.

The crash of a tumbling serac rumbled up the glacier

behind them. Atreus cast a wary look down the slope but saw only the billowing white clouds through which they had just ascended.

"Probably just an avalanche," he said.

"Just an avalanche," agreed Yago.

Rishi rolled his eyes and shook his head, and neither Atreus nor Yago looked away until Seema pointed toward a small glacier on the left.

"That leads to Gyatse. I will see you safely down to the valley, then return to my own home."

Atreus shook his head and told her, "We're not going to Gyatse."

He could feel that it was a bad time to broach the subject, but he did not want to waste any steps going in the wrong direction, especially not with the Sisters of Serenity in plain sight and Tarch on their trail.

He pointed across the ice field toward the three mountains and said, "That is where we're going."

Seema did not look as surprised as Atreus expected. "The Sisters?" she asked. "There is nothing but ice and rock there. Why would you want to go there?"

Atreus's reply was frank. "To find Langdarma."

Seema regarded him with a combination of wariness and pity, then pursed her lips and took his forearm. "What is it you are looking for in Langdarma?" she asked quietly.

A sense of profound relief filled Atreus. "Beauty," he answered. "I have been told I will become handsome there."

Seema's eyes grew glassy. "You have journeyed all this way for nothing," she said simply. "You cannot find beauty in Langdarma. It is a myth, just as is Ysdar."

She touched his heart, "It exists here," then reached up to touch his face, "not here."

Atreus caught her hand. "Don't. I know what you're doing. I've seen it all my life. You think an ugly man has no

150

business in Langdarma." He withdrew Sune's map, unfolded it, and pointed at the valley beneath the Sisters of Serenity and said, "I know about Langdarma. There's no use lying to me, so please don't."

A clatter echoed up from the clouds below.

Rishi shifted uncomfortably on Yago's back and glanced down the glacier. "That was no avalanche!" he called.

Seema ignored him and examined Atreus's map. "Someone is lying to you, but it is not me," she said, shaking her head sadly. "You cannot go to Langdarma. It is a state of being, not a place, and no man with a murderous heart may find it. I am sorry. More sorry than you can know."

"This was given to me by Sune herself!" Atreus insisted and shook the map in her face. "Who do you expect me to believe . . . my goddess, or you?"

Seema's gaze grew stony.

"I do not know this Sune of yours, but I do know the Yehimals. There is no Langdarma. I will take you to the Sisters of Serenity, and you will see for yourself that there is no valley there."

10

A two-day crust of ice clung to Atreus's bushy eyebrows, numbing cold and so heavy it pushed his lids down over his eyes. He was half blind with snow glare anyway, so it hardly mattered. Even with wide open eyes, the Sisters of Serenity would have looked much the same. They were three craggy white bells silhouetted against an azure sky, so high they loomed over Atreus and his companions, even miles away, standing at the precipitous brink of the vast plain of ice they had just crossed.

A hundred feet below, a snow-blanketed glacier swept away almost vertically, spilling into the broad valley that separated them from their destination. There it joined a jumbled blue cascade of ice blocks curving down from a second glacier beneath the Sisters of Serenity. The two flows became one and continued down the valley, creating yet another glacier, this one more than a mile wide and as long as a river.

Seema pointed at the huge glacier and said, "There is your Langdarma."

Atreus stared down at the ice without responding. Unlike the smaller glaciers feeding it, this one looked almost smooth, with a long stripe of rock and gravel running down its center. The line marked the seam between the smaller glaciers where the two edges came together full of rock and gravel torn from mountainsides. The dark stripe looked almost painted on, as if some god had thought a dirty streak just the thing to bring out the pearly crispness of the ice and snow.

After a time, Yago said, "It's not what I expected." The ogre rubbed his stubbled chin and added, "But there's beauty in it. I can see that."

"Maybe, but not the kind of beauty we're looking for," said Atreus. "Sune is no fan of starkness."

He opened his map and studied the area around the Sisters of Serenity. According to the chart, Langdarma lay in the broad valley directly below, but a ladder symbol beneath the three Sisters suggested the entrance might lie at the base of the middle one.

"You see?" said Seema. "There is nothing but ice here."

"I am so sorry for the good sir. To come all this way, and for nothing," said Rishi. He packed a snowball and hurled it off the icy cliff. The orb fell far short of the valley and disappeared onto the glacier below. "Langdarma is only a fable after all."

"Fables are as real as mountains," Seema said, "but you must look for them in your heart."

"That is certainly a small consolation to a man who has journeyed so far in such desperate hope," Rishi replied, squinting back across the ice field, scanning the white glare for the dark, distant figure that had been hounding their trail across the ice field. "At least we are fortunate in our timing. Tarch is nowhere in sight. If we hurry, we can certainly circle around him and be on our way before that tailed devil realizes we have turned around."

"Yamdruk is only a day's walk from here," said Seema. "I will take you there before continuing home."

When Atreus said nothing, Rishi laid a comforting hand on his shoulder. "I will help you sneak back down the river and perhaps recover the gold, so that this journey will not ruin your fortune as well."

Atreus shook the Mar's hand off. "And perhaps Yago and I will meet an unfortunate accident," he said harshly, "leaving you with enough gold to drown a yak?"

Rishi put on a hurt face and stepped back. "I am only thinking of the good sir," he said. "I would certainly be content with any reward he might generously grant for my humble services."

"Your reward will have to wait." Atreus raised his map, shook it gently in the air, and said, "This came from Sune herself. She would not have given it to me if there is nothing here."

"This Sune is your goddess?" asked Seema.

"The goddess of love and beauty," Atreus said, nodding.

Seema's eyes lit with sudden comprehension. "Then you are a blessed man who has already found Langdarma," She told him, stepping back to look Atreus up and down, seeming to regard him in a new light. "Is it not said that the gods appear only to those who already see them? Surely, she gave you the map to show you that you have been looking in the wrong place."

"Sune?" Yago scoffed. "That fickle bitch?"

"Yago!"

"I say what I see," the ogre grumbled. "That's my duty. Likely as not she gave you the map just to get you out of the temple. You know how them celebrants were always complaining about that ugly face of yours."

"Yes." Atreus could not keep the pain out of his voice. "I do."

"Oh, by the Blood Queen! You don't have to be so touchy." Despite his words, Yago's orange face darkened to crimson. "It's not like how you look is your fault . . . and I'd fight with you on my left any day."

This was the highest compliment a Shieldbreaker could pay. Atreus grasped his friend's huge arm.

"I know you would, Yago, and I'd be honored." Atreus glanced across the valley toward the jumbled glacier beneath the Sisters of Serenity and said, "That's why I must ask you to cross one last valley with me."

154

The ogre nodded. "I'd smash your head if we didn't. We've come this far, so we'd better see it through to the end."

"What?" Seema's objection came too quickly. "I mean to say, what about Tarch? He will follow us. . . ."

Atreus turned to her with a raised brow. "Why should that matter? There's nothing but ice and snow down there." He paused a moment, then added, "Or is . . . ?"

"No, no . . . only ice and snow." Again, Seema's response came too quickly. "What else could there be? We are in the Wild Lands now. I am only afraid that the devil will force us to flee down the valley. We will be lost."

"Really?" Atreus smirked, more convinced than ever that the key to finding Langdarma lay in the glaciers below. "You *are* trying to protect something, but I don't think it is us."

"Perhaps the good sir should consider the evidence before his eyes!" Rishi sounded almost panicked. "Even Yago thinks your friends were only playing a trick, and it will be much safer for everyone to turn back now."

"You and Seema are free to go. You can take the gold with my blessings, if you can find it, but Yago and I will see our journey through to the end."

Atreus and Yago began to work their way along the brink of the ice field, searching for a route down onto the glacier. Rishi looked hopefully in Seema's direction, but she only shook her head and started after the two westerners. The group moved quickly. Over the past few days, Seema had used her healing magic on her companions many times, and their wounds seldom troubled them now. They soon came to a blocky ravine where a wedge of ice had been squeezed out of the rim, creating a narrow corridor that wind and day-melt had eroded into a steep but passable gully.

Seema circled around to the sunny side and led the way down a drift of wind-packed snow. The bottom of the shadowed gully was as icy as it was steep, and they had to descend half walking and half sliding. By the time they emerged from the mouth of the ravine, they were all nervous, shivering, and glad for the relative safety of the glacier's sun-softened surface.

Seema descended a few yards, kicking her heels into the wind-crusted snow to make flat, safe steps. Abruptly she stopped and warily glanced across the glacier. Motioning for the others to stay where they were, she drew her knife and dropped to her knees, then began hacking blocks out of the snow pack. A foot down, the snow suddenly grew soft and sugary. She put her knife away and continued to dig, eventually climbing into the hole and disappearing to her waist.

"This is very bad." Seema peered out of the hole. "It is not safe."

Atreus rolled his eyes and started down the slope. "You're only convincing me that you're trying to hide something."

"No, come and look." Seema waved him over and pointed at the icy layer in the bottom of the hole. "Do you see how it is slick below and hard on top, with a layer of soft sugar in between?"

"Yes."

"It is very dangerous on a steep slope like this," Seema said. "It is like a carpet over marbles. The whole mountainside can break loose and slide down in a big avalanche."

The thought occurred to Atreus that Seema was just finding another excuse to keep him away from the Sisters of Serenity, but he could see for himself that what she said was true. He pulled a handful of the sugary snow from the hole and let it run between his fingers, glancing over at Yago.

The ogre merely shrugged. "I told you it was dangerous when we started."

Atreus stood, facing Seema. "What can we do to protect ourselves?" he asked her.

"We can turn around."

"Aside from that," Atreus replied.

Seema sighed, then led them back into the mouth of the gully. She instructed Yago to start yelling across the valley, hoping to set off any impending avalanches with his booming voice. While the ogre bellowed, she took the supply bundle and began to unravel the long threads of a yak-hair blanket, knotting them together to create four dark strands, each twenty or thirty paces long. By the time she finished, Yago had managed to start a small slide on the opposite wall of the valley, but the snow on the glacier below remained ominously inert.

Seema tied one of the long strands around her own waist and had each of her companions do the same, leaving the ends to drag in the snow. If an avalanche buried someone, the dark cord would float to the top so the others could find the victim—or so she said. They began to zigzag down the glacier, keeping themselves well spaced and crossing dangerous areas one person at a time, so there would always be three people to dig out a victim. Atreus found himself worrying less about avalanches than hidden crevasses, but Seema seemed to have an uncanny sense for avoiding such pitfalls.

They were about a quarter of the way down when Yago, bringing up the rear of the line, plunged through the wind-crusted snow and sank to his chest. Unable to feel anything beneath his feet, he could not tell whether he was buried in a particularly deep snowbank or hanging over a hidden crevasse, and he did not want to call out for fear of touching off an avalanche. He simply stretched his long arms across the snow to spread his weight and waited. Eventually, the others noticed that he was missing and returned to pull him free. After that, Atreus brought up the end of the line.

As they descended, the snow grew more unstable. Small slabs began to break off beneath their feet and slide down the wind crust. The farther they descended, the larger the slabs grew, and Atreus began to feel an avalanche was imminent. He suggested having Yago yell again. Seema rejected the idea, saying the danger was no greater than before, as long as the slabs did not start coming from above. Atreus was not sure he believed her, especially when she grew even more cautious and insisted that they start crossing the entire glacier one person at a time.

They were about halfway down when Atreus heard a brief hissing noise above, then saw a raft-sized slab of snow shoot past and drop into the dark mouth of a crevasse. In the next instant, he was sprinting across the snow toward his friends, who stood waiting beneath the shelter of a rocky outcropping. There was no decision or thinking; he simply found himself running, hoping to reach safety before the avalanche swept him away.

But the roaring never came. No billowing clouds of snow swept down to swallow him up, nor did his world suddenly turn white and cold. He simply found himself standing at the outcropping with his companions, trembling and breathing hard.

"What's your hurry?" asked Yago. "He ain't that close."

"Close?" Atreus panted, hands braced on his knees. "Who?"

Yago looked up toward the narrow gap through which they had descended onto the glacier. A single dark figure was coming straight down the slope, taking long plunging steps that kicked loose huge slabs of wind-crusted snow.

"Tarch!"

"He is a fool to come down like that," said Seema. "He will bring the whole slope down."

"Then perhaps we should run," Rishi offered, prodding Seema toward the glacier. "The time for caution is past."

Seema did not move. "No," she said. "Now we must be more cautious than before." She turned to look at them. "Do not make the mistake of thinking Tarch is the danger. The Yehimals have claimed a hundred times more lives than he has."

"Yes, but the Yehimals are not hunting us," said Atreus. "Maybe we should hurry things along."

"You cannot hurry in these mountains. That is the fool's way." Seema pointed at the dark line of a crevasse lying perpendicular across Tarch's path and said, "The tailed devil is being careless, and a thousand hazards lie before him. We will do far better to look to ourselves and let the mountain take care of our pursuer."

"I suppose you're right," said Atreus. "We'll have plenty of time to worry if he catches up."

Seema nodded. "Good," she said. "We will continue as before."

She started across the glacier, choosing an angle much steeper than before. Atreus took the frozen chain from around his neck and tapped it against the rock wall, knocking the ice out of the links. Rishi quietly beseeched the gods to blind the "tailed devil" and send him plunging into a bottomless abyss and close it as promptly as possible. The Mar's supplications went unheeded. Tarch descended the glacier at a near run, twisting and turning his way through the labyrinth of crevasses, sometimes leaping narrow ones and other times trotting across snow bridges as thin as sails. His plunging steps sent a steady stream of snow slabs hissing down the slope. Several times those speeding cakes seemed destined to sweep Seema off the mountain. Atreus and his companions could only watch, afraid that a warning shout would bring the whole slope crashing down on her.

The nearer Tarch drew, the more nervous Rishi became. He began to complain bitterly about his forced promise not to kill the tailed devil, and he chastised Atreus several

times for breaking his sword back in the couloir. Yago grew
tired of Rishi's griping and quietly noted that no one had
promised Seema anything about *his* safety. This was
enough to quiet the Mar.

Finally, Seema reached a rocky alcove on the opposite
wall, perhaps one more traverse from the bottom of the
dangerous area. Even before she turned to signal, Rishi
was bounding along in her footsteps, his dark avalanche
cord trailing in his wake.

Above, Tarch had descended nearly half the glacier's
length. Unless he met with one of the hazards Seema had
spoken of, he would catch the company long before they
completed the final traverse. The thought of fighting him
again sent a chill down Atreus's spine. He could not forget
the fear he had experienced when Tarch touched him, nor
the tongue of flame that had nearly engulfed Rishi.
Perhaps "tailed devil" was not an exaggeration at all. The
slave master certainly had the magic of a creature from the
Thousand Hells.

Atreus's thoughts were interrupted by Yago's deep
voice. "I suppose you meant what you told the girl?" The
ogre's gaze was fixed on Tarch. "About not killing that devil
thing, I mean."

"You know I did."

"I was afraid of that." Yago glared down at Atreus with
one big bloodshot eye, then shook his head, saying, "You
humans and your mating games. It'd be simpler for everyone if you just claimed her."

Atreus felt the heat rise to his cheeks. "What are you
talking about?"

"The girl," Yago said, gesturing vaguely in Seema's direction. "She looks a good prize, from what I've seen of how
humans judge."

"She is a good prize," Atreus admitted, "but you've been
around people. You know we can't just wrestle a female

down and expect her to start keeping the cave."

"Too bad," said Yago. "She'd let you win."

Atreus rolled his eyes.

"You don't think so?" Yago asked. "She don't want us killing that devil that's after her, and if she's just trying to outrun it, we sure ain't speeding her up any. So what's she doing here, if she ain't waiting for you to claim her?"

Yago's question was a good one, though Atreus suspected the answer had less to do with him than what lay beneath the Sisters of Serenity. "Trust me, Seema isn't here because she wants to wrestle me. No woman would. I'm too ugly."

Yago considered this a moment, then shrugged. "You're a good enough fighter," he said, as though that should account for more than appearance, "but I don't see why you made her that promise."

"You know why," Atreus said. "You were there."

"Oh yeah, I forgot. So a woman who won't have you doesn't let herself get caught by a slaver she won't let us kill." For an ogre, the irony in Yago's deep voice was a rare show of wit. He shook his head, then added, "If someone's missing something here, it ain't me."

Yago glanced up the glacier. Three hundred paces above, Tarch was just leaping a crevasse, arms flailing and tail whipping. He landed in a billowing puff of snow and crashed through the wind crust, launching a ship-sized circle of broken slabs down the slope. Why the whole mountainside did not break free and sweep him away, Atreus did not know. Either the snow was more stable than Seema claimed, or the slave master was the luckiest devil this side of the Abyss.

Rishi reached the far side of the glacier, and Seema waved.

Yago nudged Atreus forward and said, "Go on."

Atreus shook his head. "If you break through again, you won't have a chance against Tarch."

"But I'm the bodyguard." When this did not work, Yago growled, "We'll go together."

"And let him bury us both in an avalanche? We're better off spread out," Atreus said, shoving the ogre forward. "Now stop wasting time and go."

Reluctantly, Yago started across the slope. He could not run for fear of plunging through the wind crust, but his long strides covered ground rapidly. He was soon scurrying along the top of a serac field on the far side of the glacier, just a dozen paces from the sheltered alcove where Rishi and Seema stood waiting.

Tarch rounded a crevasse only twenty paces above, turned away, and continued straight down the slope. Atreus was so astonished that he merely stood there collecting his wits. Tarch could hardly have missed seeing him—Atreus was standing in plain sight—so the only conceivable explanation was that the slave master did not think him worthy of attacking.

Atreus charged out onto the glacier, as angry at being ignored as he was apprehensive about the coming battle. He whirled the chain over his head, filling the air with a metallic thrum. Tarch continued to angle down the glacier toward the alcove where Seema stood waiting.

"Up here!" Atreus's voice echoed across the canyon.

A snow slab broke loose beneath him and started down the slope, nearly sweeping him off his feet. Tarch continued to ignore him. Atreus pumped his knees furiously, his footsteps reverberating off the wind crust as he closed with the devil to a little more than arm's reach. They circled below a crevasse and started to pass above another one, then Tarch pulled up short, stopping so suddenly that Atreus crashed headlong into his back.

Tarch's tail lashed out, trying to sweep Atreus's feet from under him. Atreus jumped, avoiding the attack, and whipped his chain at his foe's head. He never saw the devil's foot come up, only felt the big heel sink into his stomach and double him over. He sensed himself flying backward and saw Tarch leaping after him, then felt himself crashing down on the wind crust and the slave master slamming down on top of him.

The mountain sighed, a deep silent rumble that Atreus sensed down in the hollow of his stomach. Tarch felt it too and sat up, startled, taking his weight off Atreus's chest. The devil looked up the slope.

Atreus noticed the glacier wall sliding past, remembered the crevasse below, brought his chain up and slammed it into Tarch's head. The devil roared, lashed out, and gouged at Atreus's throat. A snow slab the size of an elephant caught them from above and hurled them backward through the churning air, still battling. Atreus whipped his chain up again and felt it catch around the slave master's neck. White sugar snow poured down around him, falling from above, rising from below, pouring in from all sides. Tarch clawed at Atreus's face and caught the corner of an eye.

They tumbled again. Atreus's head exploded into pain as the claw slipped free. He could not tell whether or not he had been blinded. Everything was white. A deep, breathless cold rose up to swallow him. The chain tugged at his hand, snapped his arm out full length, and strained the socket. He clenched his fist until the nails bit into his palm, felt the crushing pain of the chain tightening around his hand.

The avalanche rolled Atreus, slower, twisting his arm around behind him until he thought the chain would rip it off. He began to sting with cold and sensed the world dropping away. The chain went slack. Whether Tarch was tumbling closer or slipping free, he could not tell. Everything was cold, churning whiteness, sugary and soft.

The tumbling stopped, and Atreus had the sensation of floating. The snow cradled him, closing in around him. He remained frozen in the same awkward position, one arm twisted around behind him, dimly aware by his queasy stomach that he was sliding. He tried to pull his arm forward but found it too packed in snow to move. He tried to twist around to dig, found his body as caught as his arm. Tried to pull his hand free, could not retract his elbow. Circle his wrist, clench his fist, wiggle a single fingertip . . . all stuck fast, stuck fast as a beetle in amber.

The sliding sensation vanished. The snow pressed in from all sides. He felt it in his ears, against his eyes, in his nostrils, growing heavier and colder with each heartbeat. His pulse began to roar, and he knew he was panicking, but panic in these helpless circumstances was a mere cruel joke. Could he flail about madly? Run blindly to his death? He could do nothing but lie motionless and stare into the unimaginable whiteness of the snow.

Funny that it should still be so white, with him buried so deep. His bones ached from being crushed, his ears rang from the pressure, his lungs burned for air. He pushed his lips apart and tried to suck in a breath through the snow, but he could not expand his ribs, could not move all those tons with only his chest.

The white never vanished. The pain faded, the pressure diminished, the roar of his pulse ebbed away, the yearning for breath became a distant memory, and the white remained.

Atreus found himself standing beneath a pearly sky in a valley of white marble, facing an alabaster palace surrounded by snowy ponds filled with white lotus. At his side stood a white-caped figure with a long, translucent tail and silvery-white scales.

The form turned, and Atreus saw that it was Tarch, now with a flowing white beard and blond eyes. All the brutality had left his jagged features, and his face radiated the same serenity and contentment as did Seema's. He saluted

Atreus with a clawed hand, then climbed the palace steps and disappeared through a door. Atreus was alone.

He stood before the palace, studying its asymmetric majesty. It had an ancient, guileless beauty, with a large open rotunda on one end and a square balcony room on the other. Connecting the two was a long gallery of scalloped arches and slender columns, with a Y-shaped staircase that descended down to the lower porch. The bottom story was painted in bright horizontal stripes, while the upper was decorated with swirling, ornately carved reliefs. The architecture could hardly be called balanced, and no part of the building seemed to belong with the rest, yet it was the most stunning palace he had ever seen, casual and warmly unpretentious and all the more magnificent.

Atreus climbed the stairs to the gallery and found himself standing in an icy wind, staring into the rotunda where a brilliant silver flame flickered in a bronze brazier.

"All is not harmony and balance." The voice was Seema's. "If you see beauty in yourself, so everyone will see it."

Still staring into the silvery fire, Atreus walked into the rotunda. Now that he was inside, he could see a cowled silhouette standing behind the brazier, its identity, even its gender, masked by the brilliant glow of the flame. The figure placed its hands over the brazier and slowly spread them. The flame broadened into a shimmering silver square.

"Look."

Atreus stooped down to obey, then cried out in shock.

There was a face in the silver square, as unbalanced and misshapen as his own, with the same beetling brow and sunken eyes, the same oversized nose and twisted mouth, but this face was handsome, rugged and happy and utterly at peace with itself.

"What would you do for this?" Now the voice was Tarch's, deep and raspy and rough. "What would you give

165

to have this face?"

Atreus looked up at the cowled figure. "Anything," was his answer. "I would give anything . . . my fortune, my life . . . anything."

"Wrong answer."

The figure brought its hands together and the shimmering square shrank to a single tongue of guttering flame.

"Your fortune means nothing to me, and I do not want your life."

Atreus stared at the fading flame and asked, "What then? Tell me, and you shall have it!"

The cowled figure lowered its hands and the last wisp of flame winked out, revealing the face beneath the hood.

"You know what I want." The voice remained Tarch's, but the face was Seema's. "Give it to me, and you shall have what you want."

Now the voice as well became Seema's. "Give it to me," she said, "and you shall have Langdarma."

She reached out and leaned across the brazier as though to embrace him. A sense of serenity and contentment flooded over Atreus and he understood at last what the figure wanted from him. He stretched out his arms and stepped forward to accept the embrace, then suddenly grew dizzy and pitched forward and found himself hovering over the brazier, staring down at a single white ember still shining in the dead charcoal.

"Too late," the voice, now distant and sexless, said. "He's for the dead book now."

Atreus craned his neck around to look up beneath the hood and found himself staring into the empty stone eyes of a statue. The statue reached down, grasped the edge of the brazier, and the brazier turned into a thousand-spoked wheel, the white ember its burning hub.

"The Seraph spins the wheel round and round." The statue twirled the wheel as it spoke and the white ember

FACES OF DECEPTION

became a six-pointed snowflake, feathery and beautiful and cold, motionless in the heart of the spinning circle. "Round and round and nobody knows where falls the dead man's soul."

Atreus's stomach became light and empty and he began to fall, whirling down toward the white crystal brilliance.

167

11

The fall took . . . how long? To Atreus, it seemed the mere
flash of an instant and the endless drag of forever. Beneath
him rose the thousand-spoked wheel, still spinning, as vast
and as flat as a dead calm sea. The feathery snowflake in
the center hovered motionless, growing neither larger nor
smaller, but growing more brilliant with each passing
moment. The long plummet made his stomach qualmish
and hollow, and the brightening snowflake filled his eyes
with a cold, scratchy ache. The chill air whipped past his
face, tickling his flesh, drawing the heat from his body. His
joints stiffened and his bones grew as heavy as ice. He
plunged toward the frigid oblivion of the dead, blinded by
the glare of that feathery, six-pointed star.

An eternity later, the snowflake melted into a dark-
hearted halo. Something pressed itself against Atreus's
frozen lips. His numb flesh sensed only the weight, not the
touch. Warm air swirled down through his throat and
flooded his lungs. His pulse boomed to life. Blood rushed
in his ears. The halo grew dim, and he saw Seema's smooth
cheek pressed close, her brown eyes staring down at him,
her dark hair making a tent around their faces. Her soft lips
were pressed against his and her mouth was working, her
hot breath mingling with his. A sense of joyous wonder
welled up inside him, and something more primal stirred
lower down. He reached up, twined his fingers into her
silky hair, and returned the kiss.

Seema pulled away, her brow arching in surprise.

Atreus took his hand out of Seema's hair, dimly aware

that he had made a terrible mistake. "I, uh . . . I thought. . . ." he trailed off, fearing he would only make matters worse. "I didn't mean to—"

"It certainly felt like you meant to!" Seema's cheeks darkened, then she laughed lightly and called over her shoulder, "Have no fear for your friend. He only lured me down here to steal a kiss."

"Not at all!" said Atreus, mortified and struggling to identify where "here" was. "We were in Langdarma—"

"You have seen Langdarma?" Seema gasped.

"Yes," Atreus said, thankful to talk about anything but the kiss. "It is . . . white . . . and beautiful . . . and we were inside a . . ."

The image faded even as he tried to describe it. He recalled only the peace, the feeling of falling, and a handsome face in a shimmering mirror. He closed his eyes, trying to recreate the memory through sheer will, but it was lost, wiped away when he kissed Seema.

Seema clasped his forearm. "You cannot describe Langdarma," she told him, her voice warm and understanding. "Is bliss not different for everyone?"

"I . . . I don't know," Atreus answered, still confused by his surroundings.

He seemed to be lying in the bottom of a small white well, with Seema crammed in beside him. About six feet above her, Rishi and Yago were kneeling atop the wall, silhouetted against a brilliant blue sky, furiously dragging armfuls of snow away from the edge.

As soon as Atreus remembered the snow, comprehension came crashing in like the avalanche itself. He tried to sit up and found he could not. He remained entombed in snow from the waist down, one arm still twisted around beneath him. The air in the bottom of the hole was shadowy and frigid, and the pressure on his legs made his muscles ache.

Atreus was seized by the overwhelming fear that the pit's walls were about to come crashing down. He began to claw madly at the snow, trying to dig out his waist so he could sit up and pull his arm free.

"Yago! Get me out of here!"

Atreus had hardly closed his mouth before the ogre's long arms stretched down to pluck Seema out of the hole. She cried out in surprise, but Yago paid her no attention and set her aside without apology. He lowered his legs over the edge and planted one immense foot on each side of Atreus's chest, then squeezed down into the hole and grabbed him under his arms.

Yago began to pull, slowly and steadily, but the snow held fast. Atreus felt as though he would be torn in two. The ogre twisted him back and forth ever so slightly, and there was a loud slurping sound. The pressure on Atreus's legs vanished, and he began to rise, until the chain tightened around his buried hand, bringing him to an abrupt halt.

"Wait!" Atreus commanded.

Yago stopped pulling, and Seema leaned over the pit, peering down over the ogre's shoulder.

"Did he hurt you?" she asked. "Dragging a person out of an avalanche is not a good way to rescue him."

"No, I'm fine," said Atreus. "It's Tarch."

"Tarch?" echoed Rishi. "That tailed devil is still alive?"

"I don't know," Atreus said, "but if he is, he might be buried under me. I still have the chain, and it was wrapped around his neck when the avalanche started."

"And you are not thinking you should let go?" Rishi asked, incredulous.

Atreus glanced up at Seema and said, "I'm willing, but the decision isn't mine. We all promised not to kill Tarch."

"Tarch started the avalanche," said Yago. "I don't see why we have to dig him out."

"Because if we don't, it will cost Seema her magic . . .

right?" Atreus glanced at the healer, hoping she would correct him.

Instead, she nodded and said, "We must do what we can for him, and not only because failing to do so will harm my magic. It would injure all our souls."

"That particular peril I am most happy to brave," said Rishi. "Whereas no good at all can come of freeing an angry devil like Tarch."

"Had Tarch not pulled you from the river, you would be frozen or drowned. You would not be here to say such things," countered Seema. "It is not for you to turn the wheel of life."

"But I am not turning it," Rishi said, addressing his argument to Atreus. "Tarch did this to himself. We are only turning the wheel if we save him."

Seema's counter was swift and confident. "To let someone die when you can save him is the same as killing him . . . and to kill is to turn the wheel."

"What's so wrong with that?" Yago demanded. "Seems to me wheels is made for turning."

"We are not made to turn them. Not the wheel of life," said Seema. "It is not for us to kill."

Yago scowled. "Been killing all my life. Can't live without killing." He held up his thick fingers and began to tick them off, saying, "Kill to eat, to earn my pay, and 'specially to keep stuff from killing me."

Seema listened to the ogre's confession with an expression of horror, then turned to Atreus and said, "We have no time to argue. You promised not to kill, so the only question is whether you are a man of his word."

"If I weren't, would I have said anything in the first place?"

Atreus did not understand Seema's reluctance to let Tarch die. To him, there was a big difference between taking the life of an innocent victim and killing in self-defense, but he held his word as sacred as Seema did life. He looked up at Yago and said, "A promise is a promise."

"I didn't promise to *save* him!" the ogre grumbled. Nevertheless, he let Atreus back down. "If this ain't the dumbest thing since Orna tried to milk a beehive!"

Rishi exhaled in frustration, then took the cooking pot and began to scoop out the edges of the pit. "We are going to need a bigger hole."

"With plenty of room for a fight," added Yago.

While Atreus lay in the snow clinging to the chain, Yago and Rishi spent the next two hours grumbling as they excavated a huge hole around him. Once the pit grew large enough for the sun to shine into, he began to warm up. By the time they had dug down to the end of the chain, he was feeling strong enough to fight.

As matters turned out, there was no need. They found nothing at the other end of the chain but more snow. Atreus took his turn with the cooking pot and dug down another two feet to a solid crust of ice. After he had cleared a circle as wide as he was tall, Seema shook her head.

"It is hopeless to keep digging." She sounded disappointed, though hardly sorrowful. "Tarch could be anywhere. Come out of there."

"Yes, it is time we gave up the search." Rishi did not bother to disguise his eagerness. "After spending all this time buried beneath so many tons of snow, Tarch has certainly met his death by now."

"Nothing is ever certain, Rishi," said Atreus, tossing the cooking pot up. "Tarch strikes me as a lot harder to kill than you think."

"All the more reason to leave him down there," said Yago, extending an arm to Atreus.

After being pulled from the hole, Atreus was astonished to find how far he had been swept. Just a few hundred paces away stood the jumbled icefall leading up to the

Sisters of Serenity. The valley around him lay buried beneath untold acres of avalanche run out: mountainous piles of compacted snow, with slabs of wind crust jutting up at all angles. The little glacier behind them had been scraped clean down to its shimmering silver surface, and its crevasses were now filled with milky bands of sugar snow.

Seema passed Atreus a bowl filled with one of her elixirs. She spoke a few words of magic, and the potion began to steam.

"Drink it quickly. It will help renew your vigor."

Atreus quaffed the contents down and felt some of his strength return, but the effect was hardly as noticeable as before. He washed the bowl out with snow and tried not to show his disappointment, but Seema was too perceptive to be fooled.

"Tarch's loss has affected my magic?" she asked.

"A little, perhaps. But I do feel better."

Seema's face fell.

"I'm sorry," said Atreus. "I wasn't trying to kill him."

"It is not your fault," Seema reassured him. She touched his arm, and Atreus's thoughts flashed to the warmth of her lips against his. "You were very brave to try to subdue such a dangerous foe and not resort to killing. It is my own anger that has caused my magic to grow weak. In truth, I am as happy as Rishi and Yago that we did not find the devil. This has stained my soul as darkly as a death."

Atreus glanced at the sun, then said, "We still have a few hours of light. Perhaps if we found him—"

"That is most unlikely," Seema interrupted, waving her hand at the surrounding acres of avalanche run out. "There is no telling where Tarch is buried. We found you only by following the cord tied around your waist."

Atreus could not help feeling relieved. Tarch did not strike him as the type to repay a kind act with gratitude, and the last thing he wanted was to try subduing the tailed devil again.

"Next time, we'll have to give a cord to Tarch," mocked Yago. The ogre rolled the bowl and cooking pot into the supply bundle, then slung it over his shoulder and turned toward the icefall. "No use worrying about it now. We got places to go, sights to see."

Seema frowned. "Atreus has been through a terrible experience," she said. "He needs food and rest."

"I'll rest better up there." Atreus looked up toward the shadowy cliffs beneath the Sisters of Serenity and said, "I couldn't possibly eat."

Now that he was so close to his goal, he could not bear the thought of stopping. His stomach was full of butterflies, his head spinning in anticipation. Whatever they found beneath the Sisters, it would not be what he expected. He had seen enough already to realize that Langdarma was not the verdant paradise he had imagined. He felt more confident than ever that they would find the Fountain of Infinite Grace. Sune had not sent him across half the world for nothing. He remembered that much from his avalanche dream.

They spent the rest of the afternoon working their way around the looming seracs and gaping crevasses of the long icefall. Seema picked their route with extra care, at times using her dagger to chip footholds on steep or particularly slick sections. Unlike any of the glaciers they had crossed so far, this one seemed to be moving perceptibly. There was an almost constant trembling beneath their feet, and at times the crevasses actually appeared to open and close before their eyes. Once, Yago was nearly crushed when a serac crashed down between him and Rishi, and another time they waited for one to topple over and fill a crevasse they were trying to cross.

By the time they crested the fall, the sun was sinking

behind the three Sisters, streaking the sky with golden veins. Seema hurried across the shadowy snow toward the edge of the glacier, leaving Atreus little opportunity to study the vale he had come so far to visit. From what he could see, the basin was filled with ice, as was every valley in the high Yehimals, and shaped like a ceramic bowl gone bad on the throwing wheel. On three sides, a dark semicircle of cliffs soared up to form the separate peaks of the Sisters of Serenity. On the fourth side, the icefall they had just ascended tumbled down into the great valley below. In that stark Yehimal way, the dale was as beautiful as any he had ever seen, but there was no sign of the Fountain of Infinite Grace or of any water not already frozen.

They reached the gentle ridge of rocks that marked the edge of the glacier, and Atreus had no more time to ponder the vale. After several nights on the snow together, they no longer needed Seema's direction to perform their chores. While Yago set to work digging a snow cave, Rishi scurried along the mountainside, scouring the rocky crags for dwarf pines and snapping off dried stems to supplement their meager supply of dried yak dung. Seema busied herself lighting the butter lamps and preparing the food. Atreus retraced their steps, filling in their tracks. After dark, the wind would cover everything with a light dusting of snow and render their trail utterly invisible. Given the avalanche, he was no longer sure that such precautions were necessary, but he took them anyway. Until he knew for certain what had happened to Tarch, it would be safer to assume that the devil was still out there.

By the time Atreus returned to camp, the sun had vanished behind the Sisters and the sky had turned to purple velvet. They ate a twilight dinner of lukewarm barley soup, then climbed into the snow cave and arranged themselves on the thin mattress of pine boughs. The little den was surprisingly warm. Despite Yago's thunderous snoring, the others quickly drifted into a slumber.

Atreus was too anxious to sleep. He spent the first part of the night wide awake, keeping the vent hole clear of blowing snow and worrying that Langdarma might be the myth everyone claimed. The second part he spent listening to the glaciers rumble, convincing himself he would find the valley in the morning, if he just looked carefully enough. Sune was every bit as fickle and flighty as Yago claimed, but she was not cruel, nor given to abusing her faithful worshipers. Sometime before dawn, Atreus's racing mind finally yielded to his weariness, and he drifted off into an unsettled sleep.

When morning finally came, he woke to find himself alone, the snow cave dimly illuminated by the pale blue rays spilling through the ventilation hole. He pulled on his cloak and crawled out through the entrance tunnel, emerging into a world of golden dawn. The sun was just peeking up from behind the glacier they had descended the previous day, painting the snow-blanketed heights of the Sisters of Serenity in brilliant hues of orange and yellow. Yago and the others stood a few paces away, peering over the icefall. Atreus joined them and found himself looking down at a puff of blue mist hanging over the avalanche run out.

"That's a funny-looking cloud," he said.

"We were just observing the same thing," said Rishi. "Strange how it hangs over the debris of yesterday's avalanche, is it not?"

"It is too cold for a ground fog," added Seema. "It can only have something to do with Tarch."

Atreus recalled the tongue of flame the slave master had used on the barge. "Could he be melting his way out of the avalanche?"

No one answered, and Atreus knew they were all thinking the same thing. The basin beneath the Sisters of Serenity was both small and a dead end. If Tarch caught them there escape would be impossible.

Finally, Yago turned to Seema. "At least you don't have to feel guilty about him being dead," he half joked.

Seema shook her head. "We do not know that he is alive," she said. "Who can say what happens to a devil's body when he dies? Perhaps it burns up."

"Well?" Atreus asked Rishi. "You've traveled the slave road before."

Rishi shrugged. "In my experience, the devils from beyond never die," he said heavily, "only those who cross them."

Atreus stared down at the avalanche run out, recalling how swiftly his utter helplessness had been transformed into unconsciousness. He faced Seema and said, "Even if Tarch survived, he hasn't melted his way out yet. There may still be time for you and Rishi to reach the other side of the valley."

"And you?" she asked.

Atreus looked back toward the barren cliffs beneath the Sisters, then shook his head. "I've come too far," he said. "If Tarch kills me, he kills me, but I'm not leaving."

"Then I will stay, too." Seema smiled, then added, "Do you think I am the kind of girl you can kiss and send away?"

Atreus felt the heat rise to his cheeks. He turned away before the blush could further mottle his blotchy complexion, disguising the maneuver by drawing Sune's map from within his cloak and pretending to study features he already knew by heart. According to the chart, the little basin before him was a hanging meadow at the upper end of Langdarma, surrounded on three sides by the sheer cliffs of the Sisters of Serenity. In the back of the basin, almost directly beneath the peak of the middle Sister, was the ladder symbol, leading to a narrow switchback trail that was the only route into the meadow from the surrounding mountains.

As far as Atreus could see, the only semblance between the map and the area before him were the sheer cliffs and the general shape of the basin. The meadow, of course, was buried under the small glacier that spilled down the icefall, and the main valley of Langdarma was supposed to start about where the avalanche run out lay. It occurred to Atreus that perhaps Langdarma had been scoured away by glaciers hundreds of years before, but he quickly chased the thought from his mind. Surely, a goddess could not be guilty of such a terrible mistake.

Atreus pointed across the valley toward the base of the middle Sister. There, the glacier sloped up to a dark line that marked the chasm where the ice pulled away from the mountain. "That is where we need to go."

Seema arched her delicate eyebrows. "The clefting?" She snatched the map from Atreus's hands, studied it warily, and said, "What are we to do there?"

Atreus shrugged. "I don't know." he said. "Look around ... see what we find. None of this is what I expected."

Atreus's confusion seemed to relieve Seema. She returned his map, and they gathered their things and set off. Although the glacier was relatively flat across most of the basin, they had to wind their way through a labyrinth of newly opened crevasses and listing boulders, all the while watching their back trail for Tarch. The short journey seemed to take forever, and by the time they reached the head of the glacier, Atreus could no longer bear Seema's slow, deliberate pace. He slipped past Yago and Rishi and would have taken the lead himself had Seema not increased her own pace and left him panting for breath. When they finally reached the clefting, he collapsed gasping on the steep slope, his arms draped over the brink of the chasm and his eyes staring down into its frigid depths.

He saw nothing but a rubble-choked fissure fifty feet deep, crammed with drifting snow and jagged boulders fallen from the soaring cliffs above. He continued to stare, panting for breath, trying to see paradise in the debris below. Seema sat on the brink beside him and rested her hand on his shoulder. Atreus's heart grew as heavy as stone. The healer's touch was the only hint of Langdarma to be found in this basin.

"I am sorry," she said.

Atreus felt himself starting to sink into despair, but shook his head against the feeling and stood. "No," he said, "there is no need for sorrow. This is the place. I just have to look harder."

He removed the map from his cloak and craned his neck to look up, trying locate himself in relation to the summit of the middle Sister. It was a futile task, as it was impossible to see the top of any peak from so close to its bottom. Atreus did notice a band of dark granite that he recalled being almost directly below the pinnacle. He began to work his way along the brink of the clefting, glancing back and forth between the map and the cliff face. Seema followed along, struggling to peer over his shoulder and see what he was looking for.

Rishi and Yago clambered up the slope behind them and peered down into the clefting. The ogre grunted derisively.

"You call that beautiful? Give me a good cave any day."

Atreus ignored him and stopped when he came to the dark granite a dozen paces later. The clefting here was narrow and drifted over, so it was impossible to tell where the glacier ended and the chasm began. Atreus put his map away, then dropped to his hands and knees and began to dig away the wind-packed snow. An exhausting half-hour later, he finally located the edge of the glacier and started to tunnel down into the clefting.

Yago kneeled beside him and began to rip jagged blocks of snow from the hole. "What's the plan?" the ogre asked. "To dig our way into Langdarma?"

TROY DENNING

"If we have to," answered Atreus. "There's supposed to be a trail somewhere under here. If we can find it—"

A hole suddenly opened under Yago's hands. He bellowed and tumbled forward, flailing his arms in an effort to catch himself, but the drift collapsed beneath his weight and fell into the clefting, carrying the ogre along with it.

Atreus started to plummet after his friend but was saved when Rishi caught hold of his collar. For an instant, no one reacted, stunned by the reminder of just how quickly disaster could come in the Yehimals.

An angry voice bellowed out of the clefting, "What are . . . you waiting for?" Yago sounded as though he were having trouble breathing. "If you think this is fun . . . think again!"

Atreus clawed his way back to the chasm brink and peered over the edge. Like the rest of the clefting, this part was choked with boulders, many wedged at various heights down the fissure. Twenty-five feet below, the bottom lay hidden under the heaped remnants of the collapsed snowdrift. It took a few moments to find Yago's head protruding out of the snow in the shadow of a huge rock. The rest of the ogre remained completely buried. He was working his chin back and forth, trying to scrape himself out of the snow, but it would clearly be a long time before he could dig himself free.

"Are you hurt?" Seema called.

"Hurt? Of course not!" he said indignantly. The ogre began to chin the snow more furiously. Like most proud Shieldbreaker warriors, Yago considered pain a sign of weakness. "I'm just stuck!"

"Stop whining, or we'll leave you there!" called Atreus, relieved.

"Whining?" Yago boomed. "Who's whining?"

"Who do you think?"

Atreus took a moment to pick a route, swung his legs over the brink of the chasm, and dropped eight feet down

180

to the first snow-capped boulder. When his boots slipped on the landing, he simply jumped to the next one, then bounced down to a third and dropped into the soft snow a few paces from his friend's head.

"Whining!" growled Yago. "When I get out of here, I'll show you who's a whiner!"

"Yeah?" Atreus lifted his foot as though to kick snow in the ogre's face and said, "Not too bright to tell me now, is it?"

Yago's purple eyes grew as large as saucers.

"You wouldn't!"

"What do you think?" Atreus asked and brought his foot down, blanketing the ogre's head with snow.

The ogre's orange cheeks darkened to fiery crimson. "That's a fine thing to do when you can't even pay my wages," he said.

Atreus laughed, then kneeled beside the ogre, began to dig, and said, "That's what you get for scaring me half to death,"

"You think you're scared now . . ." Yago warned as he tried to hold a straight face but could not keep from grinning. "When I get out of here, I'm gonna . . ." He began to guffaw so hard that his head rocked back and forth. "I'm gonna knock you . . . from one end of this gully to the other!"

"Be quiet down there!" cried Seema. "What is wrong with you? You'll bring the whole mountain down on your heads."

Atreus craned his neck around. Far above, he saw two little heads peering over the icy side of the chasm, with nothing above but blue sky on one side and looming granite on the other. Before he could answer, the ogre's arm came bursting up out of the snow and caught him square in the chest, sending him tumbling head over heels down the clefting.

"By Vaprak's ears, it's a good day to be a Shieldbreaker!"

chortled Yago. He began to dig himself free. "It's a good day not to be dead!"

This drew another round of laughter from Atreus, who was so relieved to find his friend uninjured that he could barely control himself. Yago joined in the mirth, and Rishi and Seema looked to one another in puzzlement.

"My goodness, the air down there must be bad," said Rishi. "They have lost their wits!"

"Is that it?" called Seema. "Are you dizzy?"

Atreus could only shake his head and hold his ribs, trying to avoid laughing too hard and starting a rockfall. Ogre humor could not be explained, especially to someone who would certainly see nothing funny in taking advantage of a helpless friend. The mirth slowly faded as Yago dug himself out, and by the time he finished, the hysterics were completely gone.

"Atreus, I don't see no signs of this trail of yours," Yago said, glancing along the clefting in both directions. "Where's it supposed to be?"

Atreus led the way across a dozen snowy boulders to the dark band in the mountain's craggy face, then looked at his map. It was difficult to relate the symbols on the map to their location in the clefting, but the ladder did seem to lie directly under the peak, which ought to be more or less straight up the dark band above them.

"I think it starts somewhere around here," he answered. Not bothering to show the map to the ogre, Atreus pointed down the chasm. "You look down there. I'll go the other way."

Leaving Rishi and Seema on the glacier to watch for Tarch, Atreus and Yago began their search. It took Atreus a full hour to scramble over the rubble to the far end of the clefting. He found nothing but more boulders and deeper snowdrifts, sometimes so powdery that he practically had to swim. In places, where the wind had bridged the abyss with wind crust, the chasm became a narrow, winding tunnel. In other places it became more of a gully than a gorge, with gently sloping sides and a bed of jumbled boulders. Atreus saw no sign of a ladder or trail, though he was acutely aware that it might lie buried under all the tons of snow and rubble under his feet.

By the time Atreus turned around, the frigid air in the bottom of the shadowed chasm had chilled him to the bone. He grew more and more convinced that the ladder was not a literal one. After all, he had seen for himself that the valley on his map contained only ice and snow. On the way back, he tried to look at everything in a new light. He searched for patterns in the rock that resembled the trail on his map, sang Sune's praises and offered her prayers as he went, and once he even stopped to meditate in a rare ray of reflected sunshine.

When Atreus returned to the dark band, he was no closer to Langdarma than before. Yago was in the bottom of a deep hole, surrounded by a low wall of snow and struggling to tear a man-sized boulder out of the ice. Seema was peering down from above, watching the ogre work and looking puzzled. Atreus kneeled at the edge of the excavation, his heart pounding with the faint hope that Yago had a good reason for his work.

"What's all this?" Atreus asked.

Instead of answering, Yago gave a hearty grunt and finally tore the boulder from its icy moorings. He took a deep breath, then turned and pushed the stone up toward his friend. Atreus leaped aside and helped the ogre roll the heavy rock safely away from the edge of the hole.

"Did you find something?" he asked.

"The same as you I imagine," panted the ogre. "Ice and rock."

Atreus's stomach grew hollow.

"What's this hole for?"

"Just getting a jump on things," said Yago. "You said—"

"I know what I said! Do you think we're going to dig the whole glacier out?" Atreus gestured at the looming wall of ice beside them and added, "In the name of beauty . . . I thought I knew how stupid ogres could be."

Yago furrowed his jutting brow and turned back to his digging, this time pulling a dog-sized chunk of ice from the hole.

"Atreus, why are you yelling at your friend?" demanded Seema. "It is yourself you are angry with."

Atreus scowled up at the healer, and the soft beauty of her eyes withered his angry rebuke.

"Yago has risked much to help you," Seema said. "Do you not think he deserves an apology?"

So gentle and soothing was Seema's tone that Atreus saw at once how right she was. The longer he searched for the elusive path to Langdarma, the more he feared he would not find it. Perhaps his stubborn devotion had touched a cruel corner of Sune's heart. Perhaps she had answered his constant prayers not with the gift he sought so earnestly, but by making him the butt of the most vicious joke he had yet suffered .

Atreus whirled on Yago. "I've had enough of this," he said. "I'm getting out of here."

"Glad to be rid of you!" came the reply.

Yago went back to his hole, and Atreus stormed off down the clefting. No doubt, the exchange was not the apology Seema had expected, but it was what passed for reconciliation among ogres.

This end of the chasm was much the same as the first, except that Yago had already broken trail and the going was faster than before. As Atreus moved, he tried to see his surroundings not so much in a literal sense, as an ogre might, but in the more symbolic manner Seema suggested. The journey to a distant land would be the physical expression of his desire for change, the high mountains the measure of the difficulty of the task, the snow and ice the purity of heart required to succeed. And what of his companions? Rishi could only be greed and temptation, Seema the beauty he came to pursue, Tarch—cruel and indestructible—the lurking monster that would destroy the prize to possess it, and Yago, an ogre, was his savage past, the brutish aspect of himself he had to forsake in order to win his prize.

The sun finally rose high enough to peer over the brink of the clefting, pouring its golden warmth down into the shadowed chasm. Atreus stopped, struck by the harmony of it all. Every element had its place, every part its meaning. The scheme was so neat and symmetrical that only Sune could have arranged it; or his own mind, fabricating interpretations for what were really random events.

Atreus pulled the map from inside his cloak and studied it in light of his newfound insight. It looked the same as before, but now he saw only names stenciled into empty valleys, nothing to suggest the untold acres of ice he had crossed, nor the verdant paradises he had imagined. Seema was right. Langdarma was a myth, and myths existed only within the heart. He tore the map into tiny pieces, then looked up into the sky.

"This is the best you can do, Goddess?" He dropped the shredded map into the snow. "You expect me to desert Yago to be beautiful inside?"

The sun vanished behind the looming mountain, once again plunging Atreus into the frozen shadows of the clefting.

12

"You're what?" growled Yago. The ogre stood shoulder-deep in his trench, glaring up at Atreus in slack-jawed disbelief.

"I'm going home," Atreus replied, squatting down to help his friend out of the hole. It was less than an hour after his revelation in the sun, and already the bottom of the clefting was as cold as night. "Come on."

Yago did not take the offered hand. "Already?" the ogre asked.

Atreus shrugged. "Seema was right," he said. "Langdarma is a myth."

The ogre eyed Atreus warily.

"They've been telling you that since Edenvale. Why believe them now?"

Atreus gestured at the icy wall behind them and said, "The glacier. If Langdarma ever existed, it's gone now."

Yago shook his head. "You said yourself there was a trick to it," he reminded Atreus. The ogre stooped down and returned to his digging, his voice becoming hollow and tinny. "This isn't like you, giving up so easy."

"Don't!" Atreus leaped into the trench, grabbed the ogre's arm, and said, "Do you want me to say it? You were right. Sune never meant to make me handsome. She just wanted me out of her church."

Yago frowned, pondering Atreus's words, then grew sad and covered his friend's shoulder with his big hand. "We'll pay a visit to that fickle sow's temple when we get back," he promised, "and teach her a thing or two about making promises she don't keep."

"You'd do that for me, I know, but this thing's ugly enough," Atreus said, pointing at his own face. "I don't want it known as the face that started a war."

Yago sighed and boosted Atreus up to the lowest of the boulders above their heads, then they clambered out of the clefting. Even in the shadow of the middle Sister's looming cliffs, the air was much warmer than down in the chasm. This did little to cheer Atreus, who merely motioned for the others to follow and started down the slope. The glacier below was still blinding white with the sun's afternoon reflection. With any luck, they could cross it and be well past the icefall before the evening shadows came.

Seema quickly caught up to him. "What did you find?" she asked.

"What you said I would," replied Atreus. "Nothing."

She frowned and said, "I said that you would find Langdarma inside. Did you not say you had after the avalanche?"

"I said a lot of things," Atreus replied. "I was half dead."

Seema shook her head. "No," she said. "I saw it in your eyes. You had seen it."

"Is it there now?" Atreus stopped and glared down at her and pressed, "Do you still see it?"

"No," Seema said as she backed away, her face growing pale. "I see only that you are angry with me."

The sight of Seema's alarm shamed Atreus. Her kindness had lulled him into forgetting that he was a monster, that on his face any sign of ire took on the appearance of a mortal threat. He willed his face to relax and started down the slope again.

"I am angry, yes, but not with you," he said gently. "Without you, I would have gotten myself and my friends killed a dozen times. My anger is with my goddess and with myself for being fool enough to believe her."

"There is no reason to be angry with either," said Seema.

187

"You have seen Langdarma. If you look inside, you will find it again."

"I'm not interested in what's inside." Atreus could not keep the bitterness out of his voice. "I came to change what is on the outside."

Seema shook her head sadly and said, "You have forgotten everything."

"What have I forgotten? That I must change inside before I can change outside? I have heard that a thousand times, but I am done playing Sune's fool. I'll always have this face . . . no matter how I feel about it."

"That is true," said Seema.

"It is not what Sune promised. She deceived me."

Seema fell silent and looked away. They reached the bottom of the slope, stepped out onto the sunny part of the glacier, and began to wind their way through a labyrinth of boulders and crevasses toward the icefall. With the full sun beating down on their backs, the four companions soon grew so hot that they removed their cloaks and made poor Yago carry them in the supply bundle. The glare was unbearable. Even squinting, it made their eyes burn and sent daggers of pain shooting through their heads.

After a time, Seema returned to walk at Atreus's side. "It is not always cruel, you know," she told him.

"What isn't?"

"Deceiving," Seema answered. "Sometimes it is done for a person's own good."

"This wasn't. Sune didn't have to send me across the world to prove I would always be ugly. I was pretty sure of that already."

"Perhaps that is not why she sent you," suggested Seema. "Perhaps she sent you to learn that you are not ugly."

Atreus glared down at her. "Thanks for trying," he said, "but I'm done with fables . . . and you're only making things worse."

Seema's head snapped away as though struck, and Atreus instantly regretted his words. He had not intended to hurt the healer's feelings, and he was not quite sure how he had. Most of the time, people were relieved to hear him acknowledge his hideousness. It freed them of the uncomfortable burden of pretending to find him attractive. Seema, on the other hand, had reacted as though he had called *her* ugly. Atreus thought the matter over a while longer, then shrugged. Perhaps she had just seen something particularly unpleasant in his face.

Seema did not speak again until they reached the edge of the icefall, where the little glacier filled the air with groans and crackles as it spilled down to the main valley.

"The afternoon can be a treacherous time to descend the fall," she said. "We could just as easily wait until morning, if you want to have a last look around the basin."

"Oh no, there is nothing to be gained by that," said Rishi. When the others frowned at his outburst, he cringed and added, "I mean to say, are we not running low on food? It will be difficult enough to retrace our steps with the little we have."

"There's always you," suggested Yago.

Rishi's eyes widened, and then he showed his teeth in an uneasy grin. "You are making a joke," Rishi said hopefully. "Very funny."

The ogre looked toward Atreus, his brow furrowed as though confused, and asked, "What's he mean?"

Rishi paled and began to back away, and Seema regarded the ogre with a look previously reserved only for Tarch. Atreus chuckled, the only one to realize that Yago was still mocking the little Mar.

"Relax, Rishi, we'll be back in the Five Kingdoms long before Yago gets that hungry."

Atreus studied the avalanche run out at the base of the icefall. There was no longer a cloud of vapor hanging over its surface, and he could see an icy, funnel-shaped hole where Tarch had melted his way out of the snow. "The sooner we get down from here, the better," Atreus added. "I fear I've put us at risk already."

Atreus pointed down at Tarch's escape hole.

Seema gasped and Rishi moaned. Yago simply removed Atreus's chain from the supply bundle and passed it forward. They spent a few minutes searching for their foe in the maze of seracs and crevasses below and finally gave up. Seema led them over to the edge of the glacier and started to pick a direct route down, reasoning that since they had not seen the tailed devil yet, he must be following their old trail up the middle of the icefall.

A day in the sun had made slush of much of the ice. Although it was easy to kick steps in the steep sections, their feet were soon numb from the wet cold. They began to stumble and slip, even on relatively steady footing. Once, they nearly lost Yago when he slid fifty paces and slammed into a serac, toppling it over in the opposite direction. Both Rishi and Atreus had close calls when the slush gave way beneath their boots and sent them gliding toward deep crevasses. As frightening as these mishaps were, none of them were as unnerving as the all-too-frequent boom of a falling ice block. Several times, they felt the glacier jump with the impact of a nearby monolith, and once they were showered with ice chips from behind. It did not take long before they began to worry less about Tarch than thawing seracs.

They were a thousand paces from the bottom, working their way down a steep ledge between a mountainous ice slab and a narrow lateral crevasse, when Atreus glimpsed movement out of the corner of his eye. He tapped Seema on the shoulder and whirled around. He found himself staring across an icy abyss deep into a bluish maze of horizontal crevasses and cockeyed seracs. It looked like some sort of crazy cemetery, full of open graves and monolithic tomb-stones.

"What is it?" Seema whispered.

"It can only be that tailed devil," Rishi hissed, leaping to conclusions. He glanced up and down the steep ledge, then started to push his way forward. "Hurry! We are doomed if he traps us here."

Yago grabbed the Mar from behind. "Stay put, or I push you in. And be quiet!" His deep voice rumbled across the icefall twice as loud as Rishi's.

Atreus eyed the crevasse beside them, peering down into its blue depths. At close to four paces, it was wider than he felt comfortable jumping from a standstill, but there was another way.

"Yago, remember that game your nephews used to play with me?"

The ogre scowled, thinking, then glanced at the crevasse and raised his heavy brow.

His answer was a cautious, "Yeah. . . ."

"Can you make it?"

The ogre scratched his head and closed one eye, mea-suring the distance. "Probably," he said, "but you know it don't work unless there's someone on the other side."

"There will be," Atreus promised.

Yago grinned and passed the supply bundle to Rishi.

Atreus looked across the crevasse into the maze of cock-eyed seracs. He could feel the tailed devil out there watch-ing them, nursing his cold anger. The Sisters of Serenity seemed a long way to come for retribution, but Tarch was after more than simple vengeance. He was after Seema, and Atreus suspected the slave master would be willing to travel a lot farther than this to capture such a prize.

Atreus turned toward Rishi and Seema. "When Tarch comes," he told them, "flee uphill and circle around. He'll be expecting you to run downhill."

Seema frowned and asked, "Where will you be?"

"We'll meet you down in the valley," he said, "but don't wait for us. If we're not there before you, it means something went wrong."

Seema shook her head. "I can't let you do this," she said. "Tarch will kill you."

"He'll try." As Atreus spoke, a muffled splash sounded somewhere in the serac field. "There's going to be a fight, Seema. The only thing you can control is whether it means anything."

Seema closed her eyes, then nodded. "No killing," she insisted again. "Not on my behalf."

"No killing?" Yago grumbled. "This fight's going to be hard enough—"

Atreus raised his hand to silence his friend.

"We've given our word, Yago. No killing. If you can't abide by that pledge, then you'll have to stay—"

"Not on your life!" The ogre glowered down at Seema, then nodded and said, "You have my word."

"And you mean to leave me here with the woman?" demanded Rishi. To Atreus's surprise, the Mar actually sounded insulted. "I am as much a man as you. Have I not proven my skill in battle many times?"

"Too many times," Atreus said, "but someone has to stay—"

Atreus was cut off by an angry snarl and the sound of feet splashing through slush. He turned to see Tarch charging out from the seracs, his reptilian scales reflecting rainbows in the brilliant sun. Though the tailed devil carried no weapons, the claws at the ends of his fingertips looked more dangerous than any sword, and of course he had plenty of other surprises.

Atreus stretched the chain between his hands, calling, "Now, Yago!"

In the next instant, he was dangling upside down by his ankles, swinging backward as Yago cocked him to throw.

The wall of ice behind them was coming up perilously fast.

"Throw, Yago! Throw!"

Atreus turned away just as his shoulder slammed into the ice, suddenly whipping forward and seeing the icy depths of the crevasse spin past beneath him. He caught a glimpse of Tarch's sharp-toothed mouth hanging agape, as he slammed into the devil broadside and bowled him over backward.

Atreus came down flat, driving the wind out of his foe's lungs and winning himself a much needed instant to secure his advantage. He sank his teeth into Tarch's ear and tasted something awful, like rotten fish. They began to slide down the slushy slope, and Atreus smashed an elbow into the devil's flank.

The blow would have broken the ribs of a man, but it merely irritated Tarch. The devil growled once and hurled his attacker off. Atreus kept his jaw clenched, nearly snapping his own neck as the devil's ear came off in his teeth. Tarch roared in pain and slapped at his wound, then rolled to his knees. Atreus was already on him, whipping the chain into the slave master's skull time after time. He did not worry about his promise to Seema. It would take more than a few blows to kill the devil.

In his confusion, Tarch actually brought his arms up to cover his head. Atreus switched his chain to the body and heard a rib snap. If he could break five or six more, the agony just might make the devil flee.

As it was, the pain only brought Tarch to his senses. The devil lashed out with a hammer-hard fist and caught his attacker in the shin.

Atreus felt something snap and fell screaming. He landed head down on his back and started a long slide toward a nearby crevasse, but Tarch saw no delight in such simple death. The devil caught him by his injured leg and reeled him back.

"Slag *my* boys, will you?" the devil growled. He twisted

Atreus's leg around like a wheel as Atreus wailed in pain and rolled to his stomach, still holding the chain. "Peel my best girl, will you?"

Tarch twisted again. Atreus spun to his back and found himself looking up into his foe's sunken black eyes. Yago was sliding down the hill behind the devil, having just leaped across the crevasse.

"Before I'm done with you," said Tarch, "you'll be beggin' me to kill you nice and slow-like!"

"I doubt it," Atreus groaned.

He whipped the chain forward. Tarch hopped it with a quick one-two step and gave Atreus's leg a savage twist, then abruptly let go as a pair of huge hands caught hold of his tail. His eyes flashed crimson, and he started to turn. Yago yanked him off his feet and spun him around, slamming the astonished devil into a serac.

There was a tremendous clatter, and the frozen monolith rained jagged shards of ice down on all three fighters. Tarch whirled on his attacker with slashing claws, but he was no match for the strength of an ogre. Yago cocked his arms back for another smash, flinging the devil out to the end of his tail, then swung again, stepping into the blow like a woodsmasher clubbing down a tree.

Tarch hit with a resounding crash. Something deep inside the serac cracked, and the monolith slumped forward. The devil let out a low groan and started to go limp, shook himself back to consciousness, and managed to fix on angry glare on his foe.

"One more time!" he hissed.

Yago brought his arms back for a smash Atreus prayed would finish their foe when a loud pop echoed across the ice. Tarch went sailing down the icefall, leaving his tail in Yago's hands and trailing an arc of rust-colored blood. The slaver crashed through an ice slab and landed ten paces below Atreus.

Yago scowled at the writhing appendage in his hands, staring at the meaty stump as though he could not quite figure out what had happened. There was not as much blood as Atreus would have expected, and he had the sinking feeling that the injury was not enfeebling. He drew his knee up beneath him, and even this little bit of effort sent daggers of pain shooting through his leg.

Yago tossed Tarch's tail into a crevasse and went crashing and sliding down the slope after the battered devil. On the other side of the chasm, Seema was reluctantly fleeing up the ledge as instructed. Rishi was nowhere to be seen, but there was no time to worry about what had become of the Mar. Tarch was gathering himself up to meet Yago, and the ogre was chortling with overconfidence.

"Careful, Yago!" Atreus called, pushing himself up on his good leg. "Don't let him touch—"

Even as Atreus spoke, Yago launched himself into the air and landed on top of Tarch. They tumbled down the slope locked in a death clench. The devil was all but invisible inside the ogre's grasp, and Atreus could well imagine those hairy arms crushing the slave master's battered ribs.

The pair bounced off a serac and slid toward a smile-shaped crevasse lying across the slope below. Atreus started after them, then howled in pain as he put weight on his injured leg. He managed two hopping steps before he fell on his back and started to slide. Instead of trying to stop, he steered himself in the general direction of the combat.

Whether Yago saw the crevasse below him was impossible to say, but Tarch managed to free a scaly arm and start scratching at the ice. Slowly, the sharp claws arrested the pair's descent, bringing them to a halt only five paces above the icy chasm. Yago rolled on top of his foe and sank his jagged yellow teeth into the devil's neck.

Atreus's heart leaped into his throat. Among ogres, this particular trick always brought the fight to a quick end.

Unable to free himself without ripping open his own neck, the victim either submitted or died. Atreus wanted to shout a reminder about not killing, but held his tongue. It would be too much of an advantage to let Tarch know they did not mean to slay him.

Atreus hit a shady spot and picked up speed. He rolled back into the sun, causing his leg no end of agony, and began to claw at the slush trying to slow his descent before he smashed into the brawl and sent both combatants over the edge of the crevasse.

A muffled bellow sounded from the battle. Yago released his death hold and raised his head. His eyes were wide with panic, his mouth was smeared with scales and blood, and Atreus knew instantly that Tarch had used his fear touch. The ogre slammed a huge palm into the devil's chest, then jumped up and began to back away, oblivious to the danger of losing his footing or stepping into a crevasse.

"Yago, stop!" Atreus shouted, steering himself toward Tarch. "Look behind you!"

The ogre stopped, but could not bring himself to glance away from his scaly enemy. Tarch rolled to his knees. Atreus brought his good leg up, aiming a soggy boot at his enemy's face. The devil scowled; then Atreus was there, feeling the satisfying jolt of his heel smashing into the slave master's arrow-shaped nose.

The impact stopped Atreus dead and launched Tarch over backward. The devil landed on his back and slid headlong toward the crevasse below. As he was about to plummet into its grinning mouth, he whipped his legs over his head and somersaulted in the air and landed on his belly, his legs dangling over the brink of the icy chasm and his talons dug deep into its rim.

"Hurry Yago!" cried Rishi's voice. "Go and finish him!"

Atreus glanced over to see Rishi rushing up behind Yago, having done exactly the opposite of what Atreus instructed. The little Mar tried to shove the terrified ogre into battle and succeeded only in convincing him to retreat farther up the hill. Atreus cocked his knee back and pushed off, launching himself at Tarch.

The devil pulled one set of claws from the ice and pointed up the slope. A roiling orange cloud erupted from his fingers Atreus smelled brimstone and scorched flesh and heard someone screaming.

He remained fully alert, gagging on the stench of his own burning flesh, watching the fire lick across his body, feeling his skin melt in the heat. He saw Rishi dash across the slope to Tarch and start kicking at the claws still fastened in the ice. He heard Yago bellow, heard him come crashing across the glacier, felt the ogre's big hands rolling him through the sizzling slush, felt the icy coolness against his stinging flesh, and smelled, at last, the flames hissing into steam.

Yago pulled him into his lap and cradled him against his chest. Atreus saw Rishi at the edge of the crevasse, peering down into its blue depths. All that remained of Tarch were a few rust-colored streaks on the brink of the chasm.

"I was afraid!" Yago moaned. "You needed me, and I couldn't move."

Not your fault.

The words echoed emptily inside Atreus's head. He could not make his lips work.

He did the same thing to me.

"I am so . . . sor-ry!" Yago had trouble forming this last word, which was as foreign to the ogre tongue as the term for children won in a game of knucklebones was to humans. "What happened to me?"

The ogre smashed his fist into the side of his own face. The blow struck so sharply that Rishi gave a start and nearly plummeted into the crevasse.

Yago spit an orange tooth out onto the ice, shouting, "Coward!"

Atreus fought through his pain and managed to grasp the ogre's arm. He shook his head.

Yago's eyes grew glassy. "Am so!" the ogre insisted. "You saw me . . . just standing there!"

"Atreus does not blame you, my friend," said Rishi. The Mar backed away from the crevasse and came up to join them, grimacing at Atreus's condition. "The same thing happened to him on the slave boat. It is the devil's touch."

"It don't matter," growled Yago. "I made the Vow. Shield-breakers aren't scared of nothing!"

"That is an impossible vow to keep. Every man fears something." Rishi grasped the ogre's elbow and urged him up the hill, saying, "And now let us go. What became of Tarch I cannot tell, but it is too much to hope that a fall of only a few hundred feet would kill him."

Yago started to rise, then caught himself and sat back down. "Let him come," he said. "I'm not running."

Atreus squeezed Yago's forearm and tried to nod. The effort sent waves of agony surging through his body, but he was terrified that the stubborn ogre would let his pride get them all killed. He could feel his own strength oozing out through his scalded pores, but just as importantly, he could tell by the nervous edge in his friend's voice that Yago was not ready to face Tarch again.

"There, do you see?" Rishi asked, motioning to Atreus's nodding head. "The good sir wants us to go. He needs Seema's help."

Yago scowled in thought, then reluctantly nodded. "We'll go," he said "but not because I'm scared."

"Oh no, there has never been any question of that," agreed Rishi. "I am frightened enough for us all. You are thinking only of the good sir's welfare."

Still scowling, Yago started up the hill. Atreus's burns began to ache in earnest. He could not keep from moaning as the ogre's clothes rubbed against his raw flesh. His broken leg became a distant throbbing, and he slipped into a murky world of pain and delirium. He grew desperately thirsty and started to shiver. Yago's voice became a nightmarish roar, alternately trying to comfort Atreus and cursing himself for a coward. Amazingly enough, Rishi proved the staunch one, continually reassuring Atreus that he really looked no worse than before, perhaps even better. It was a terrible lie, of course, but exactly what Atreus needed to hear.

Sometime later—it seemed hours, but could not have been more than three or four minutes—Seema came bounding and sliding down the slope. "How bad?" she demanded, dropping the supply bundle at Yago's feet. "Put him down where I can see him. Get those rags off him. Pack him in snow. Rishi, talk to him! Keep talking. . . ."

Atreus's companions rushed to obey the healer's orders. His body roared with pain. When the tattered remnants of his clothes were pulled free, he could not help screaming. As much as it hurt to be touched, the cold slush had a numbing effect on his burns, and his anguish dulled to a raw ache.

Soon, he felt Seema's hands on him, rubbing his wounds with some minty-smelling potion. The sting faded completely, leaving him to a deeper anguish inside his seared muscles. Seema uttered a spell in the exotic language of her magic, then pressed her lips to Atreus's. He remembered the kiss of the day before and tried to steal another, but she only wet his lips with one of her potions, using her own tongue to dribble it into his mouth.

A languid fog rose up to engulf him, and he prayed he would fall into insensible sleep. Instead, he slipped into a terrible waking dream, aware of his anguish but apart from it, conscious of what was happening but unable to do anything about it.

"What's wrong with him?" demanded Yago. "He's going to live, ain't he?"

"I have taken away his pain," answered Seema. "The rest is not for me to control."

"Don't you say that! You're a healer. Heal!"

"I have done what I can, but my magic is weak," Seema said. "What happened to Tarch? Was there killing?"

"There *will* be if you don't do something . . . and fast!"

Don't threaten her! Atreus wanted to shout the command, but he could not even whisper it, could not even shake his head. He was a spectator in his own body.

"I am sure Seema is certainly doing her best," said Rishi. "She is as fond of Atreus in her way as you are in yours."

"She has a bad way of showing it," snapped Yago. "If she would have let us kill Tarch in the first place . . ."

"I could not have done even this much for Atreus," said Seema. "Now tell me what happened. If you did not kill Tarch—"

"He is most certainly alive!" said Rishi. "I saw him moving in the bottom of the crevasse."

This was not what the Mar had told Yago, but Atreus was hardly in a position to correct him.

"I will try another time."

Again, Seema uttered one of her spells, then pressed her lips to Atreus's and dribbled more of her potion into his mouth. He slipped further into his dreamworld, so that events alternately rushed by in a blur or crept past in excruciating slowness. He did not feel any stronger.

"Wellllll?" Yago's voice was deep and torpid.

"I don't know," Seema replied.

"You mean it isn't working!" Yago was silent for a moment, then asked, "What happens to your precious magic if Atreus dies? You might as well have flamed him yourself, for all your high talk about not killing."

Seema recoiled from the anger in the ogre's voice.

"That is hardly fair."

"Is too!" growled Yago. "He should've never made you

that promise. But how could the boy think straight, with you batting them pretty eyes and flashing them white teeth? If he dies, it's on your head, not mine."

The conversation came to Atreus as though he were listening to a trio of ghosts. Seema fell silent. Some dim part of him realized he should be speaking in her defense, that he should be telling Yago he knew exactly what he was doing, but Atreus could barely gather his thoughts, much less make them known.

After a moment, Rishi said, "Nobody is to blame for what happened to Atreus except Tarch. Perhaps my friend Yago, feeling that he may have in some way failed his master, is putting the blame he feels—"

"What blame?" Yago snarled.

"Then again, perhaps not," said Rishi.

But Yago was not done yet.

"If not for Seema and her promise, we'd have been rid of Tarch a long time ago. He wouldn't never have touched me!" the ogre bellowed, shaking his head angrily. "The blame here don't belong to me. You can't go fighting devils unless you mean to kill them."

"You are right, of course," interrupted Seema. "This is all my fault."

"You bet it is!" said Yago. "What are you going to do about it?"

Seema was silent for several moments, then said, "I have caused many deaths and much pain, and that is why my magic has grown weak." She laid a cloak over Atreus, and he could not help groaning at even its light touch. "We have no choice but to take him to my valley."

"I doubt he can survive such a long journey," said Rishi. "Surely, it would be better to let him rest and take our chances that he will recover."

"What about Tarch? If he is alive, as you told me, he will come after us."

Seema stood and started up the icefall. "Besides," she said, "my home is closer than you think, and we will be safe there."

Yago scooped Atreus up, but made no move to follow the healer.

"Where you going? I didn't see nothing but snow up there."

"Of course not," Seema answered, pausing to look over her shoulder. "It is not so easy to see Langdarma."

13

In the purple afternoon shadows, the band of dark granite looked hollow and empty, like a giant fissure splitting the cliff down the center. Atreus could imagine following the crevice through to the other side of the mountain, or down into the stony roots of the Sisters of Serenity themselves. As delirious as he was, Atreus could imagine a lot of things, such as the husky form behind them, appearing and disappearing as it twined its way across the boulder-strewn glacier below. The figure was holding its ribs and limping, and it kept pitching forward onto its hands and knees. Every now and then it glanced around behind itself, searching for a tail it no longer had, and sometimes it looked up to check the progress of Atreus and his companions.

Atreus tried to point and found his arm pinned against Yago's chest. He groaned as the effort brought him back into his pain-racked body. Until now, he had passed the trip across the glacier a pleasant distance above himself, somewhere outside the seared and hideous form in Yago's arms, a spirit connected to his body by only a thin strand of memory. Time itself had ebbed and flowed, swirling past in slow eddies as his companions scrambled up the icefall, then rushing ahead madly as they crossed the snowy flats. Atreus had floated along, vaguely aware that Seema had promised to take them to Langdarma and wondering how she could offer such a thing. She herself had called it a myth, and he could not believe she would deceive him. Not about something so important.

Seema reached the clefting and stopped directly across

from the dark band of granite. With the sun hidden behind the middle Sister, this part of the glacier was a sheet of hard ice, so she had to stand in the tracks they had made that morning. Rishi stopped a pace below her, both feet planted comfortably in one of Yago's frozen footprints, and Yago stopped behind the Mar. Atreus found himself looking back down into the basin. Their pursuer had vanished again, leaving Atreus to wonder whether he had been imagining the dark figure all along.

"This isn't Langdarma," said Yago. The ogre leaned past Rishi and peered down into the frigid blue murk of the clefting. "We been here before."

"You searched, but you did not examine," said Seema. "This is the way to Langdarma. Rishi and I will go first. Then you can pass Atreus down to us."

The healer lowered herself into the clefting, dropping onto the first of the boulders wedged between the cliff and the glacier wall. Rishi followed, and Yago stepped to the brink of the chasm. As the ogre turned to straddle the edge, Atreus glimpsed a dark figure below, angling up the slope along the course of their frozen tracks. The form was hazy and indistinct, no more than a darker blue in the indigo shadow of the mountain, but it looked solid enough to set Atreus's heart pounding.

Look!

The word echoed around inside Atreus's mind, but could not quite find his lips. He had a little more luck trying to point. As Yago bent down to lower him into the clefting, his arm came free of the ogre's grasp and swung toward the dark figure. A surge of anguish rushed through his body, but he kept his hand raised.

"Don't worry," Yago said. "They know what'll happen if they drop you."

Atreus forced himself to keep pointing as he heard an agonized groan escape his lips.

"I do not think it is us he fears," said Rishi. "Is he not pointing down the slope?"

Atreus sighed in relief and let his arm drop. Yago scowled and passed him into the waiting arms of Seema and Rishi, then turned to look down toward the glacier.

"He must've seen our friend back there," said Yago. "Tarch is coming up fast now."

Atreus nearly choked on his astonishment. If his companions knew about Tarch, what were they doing here? They would be trapped in the clefting, with no room to flee and even less to maneuver.

"We must hurry," said Seema. Leaving Atreus to Rishi's care, she squatted at the edge of the boulder, then jumped down to the next one, landing as lightly as a feather. "Come along."

Yago lowered himself into the clefting, took Atreus from Rishi, and descended to the bottom of the trench in two quick hops. Seema and Rishi followed close behind, and soon Atreus's companions were standing together in the bottom of abyss. The murk was thick and frozen, as dense as resin and as cold as death. Atreus started to shiver and felt, absurdly, a ring of goose bumps surrounding his burns. A fiery nettling sank deep into his bones. His broken leg began to throb, and he sensed himself slipping away, aware of his pain yet apart from it.

Yago said something about losing him, and Rishi began to worry about Tarch catching them in the trench. Seema spoke to them both in calm assurance and took their hands, leading the way to the dark band of granite. Atreus's perceptions must have grown hazy and unreliable, for it seemed to him that she simply pressed herself against the face of the cliff and melted inside.

Yago and Rishi followed and gasped, and Atreus's stomach floated up toward his chest, as though he were falling. Seema walked ahead and became the only thing visible in the darkness. Yago and Rishi followed, and the falling sensation continued.

After a time, a golden wheel appeared far below their feet, its scarlet spokes slowing revolving around the glimmering six-pointed star of a snowflake. As they traveled deeper into the murk, the wheel stayed beneath them, growing larger with each step. The snowflake began to pulse. As it grew larger, it became apparent that the different triangles inside its star were pulsing randomly, flashing first sapphire, then emerald, ruby, diamond . . . all the colors of the gems.

Seema continued to walk, and the falling sensation persisted. The wheel grew ever larger, its golden rim spreading outward until it became large enough to encircle them all. The scarlet spokes ceased their spinning, and Atreus grew dizzy, as though he were twirling around. The snowflake seemed to dissolve, to become nothing but pulsing arrows, each pointing down a different spoke of the wheel.

The wheel became as the basin beneath the Sisters of Serenity. The scarlet spokes grew as long and wide as roads, each pointing off toward a different corner of the compass, and the pulsing triangles became the size of ship decks.

At last Seema stopped walking, and the triangles rejoined, becoming a snowflake as large as the glacier basin. The wheel's golden rim disappeared somewhere over the horizon, and the scarlet spokes vanished. The dizziness and the falling sensation faded. The air grew tepid and moist, and Atreus stopped shivering. Seema turned toward one of the snowflake's distant points and spoke a few words in the archaic tongue of her people.

A blue light appeared above the point. Yago and Rishi cried out as their knees buckled. A warm wind began to whip past, and though there was no sensation of movement, the light slowly began to expand, becoming a tiny blue square. What little sense of time Atreus still had vanished completely. They seemed to stand there forever watching the square grow larger, the breeze whipping through their hair, and the musty smell of a cave growing ever stronger in their nostrils. When the square had expanded to the size of a man and they found themselves standing before a shining blue portal, it seemed that only an instant had passed.

Again Seema took the hands of Yago and Rishi. "You will see many strange things," she told them. "Do not release my hand, or you will be lost."

Seema stepped through the portal. The blue light began to swirl and eddy around her, and her movements grew smooth and slow. Rishi gulped down a deep breath and followed, but Yago stopped at the door and stared wide into the whirling radiance.

Seema said something that did not pass the portal, then opened her mouth wide and drew in a deep breath. A moment later, she exhaled, sending little eddies of current swirling away from her face. She smiled and pulled the ogre's hand. Yago took a deep breath and allowed himself to be drawn forward. As they passed through the door, Atreus felt liquid pressure all around him. The watery warmth made his burns itch, and he watched from somewhere outside himself as his mouth opened to groan. His heart began to pound in fear, but the strange fluid that rushed down into his lungs could not have been water. Instead of coughing or choking, he merely moaned. It was a strange, gurgling sound that reminded him of the chortling call of flying cranes.

They seemed to be in some sort of strange underwater labyrinth made of undulating weeds and rocky ledges, with no surface that Atreus could see. Seema started forward, leading the way across the sandy bottom as though she had

walked the maze a thousand times. Atreus did not even try
to keep track of their route. The agony caused by the warm
water more than bridged the gap between his body and
spirit. He could think of nothing but his anguish, so it was
enough for him that they seemed to be heading uphill.

After a time, they climbed high enough that they began to
see the crests of the maze walls looming above their heads.
There were fish up there, swimming back and forth and
gobbling each other up as only fish can do, but none of them
ever seemed to drift down into the corridors of the watery
labyrinth. Atreus thought this strange, until Yago finally
broke the surface and emerged into the scorching hot air.

Atreus's body erupted into such anguish that he could no
longer tell whether he was above it or in it. He simply
opened his mouth and let out a bellow that sent the air-
swimming fish wiggling off into the distant corners of the
atmosphere. After that, he lost all track of his surroundings. He barely noticed the pools of burning water in which
Seema cooled his wounds, or the billowing thunderclouds
that rolled along the floor and stabbed up into the darkness
with bolts of lightning, or the constant tolling of the wind
chimes in the still hot air. All these, Atreus dismissed as
fever delirium, so when they stepped through a dark portal
and found themselves standing on a rocky ledge two miles
above the floor of a broad, verdant basin, his first thought
was that he was still hallucinating.

A gentle drizzle was wafting down from a mottled blue sky
that might have been ice as easily as clouds. The first shadows of purple twilight were stealing down the sheer faces of
the basin's granite walls. Here and there, a tongue of blue ice
hung high on a cliff, creeping out from beneath the edges of
the blotchy sky to send a long horsetail waterfall cascading
toward the valley floor. The silvery ribbons turned to mist
after a thousand feet or so, vanishing into the empty air long
before they reached the slopes at the base of the cliffs.

The slopes themselves were mottled in deep woods and emerald meadows, flecked with thatch-roofed hamlets and crude stock sheds. A glistening web of narrow streams spilled down into the center of the valley, where a broad clear river meandered through several miles of neat green barley fields, disappearing over the edge of the basin into a deep, vast valley beyond.

"Welcome to my home," Seema said, at last releasing the hands of her companions. "Welcome to Langdarma."

This was too much for Atreus. Too weary and pained to rejoice, he simply allowed himself to believe what he saw, to accept the truth of Seema's words and not consider their implications, to embrace the lushness and the warmth of the place and not question whether it was real or hallucination.

He experienced a strange calm then, a peace that flowed up and through him, connecting him to the beauty below in some enigmatic way he could never understand. He felt himself return to his anguished body. His pain washed over him like running water, sank into his flesh like the bright warmth of the sun and filled his chest like salty sea air. This time he did not fight it. He embraced his agony as a part of himself, welcomed it as the scream of life still raging strong inside him, and then he felt the fear leave. His body released its hold on his spirit, now confident that he would not allow the pain to chase him away, and he saw the clouds of oblivion rise up to carry him into the world of numbness and rest.

Later, Atreus's slumber was invaded by a male voice much too dulcet to belong to his companions. For a time, he dreamed that he was back in the Church of Beauty, listening to a perfectly pitched tenor sing the goddess's praises. Never had he heard such a pure sound, untainted by the slightest tinge of coarseness or the faintest hint of hollowness. It was as lyrical as silk and smooth as a poem, and Atreus felt blessed just to hear it in a dream.

As Atreus grew aware of the bitter reek of a butter lamp, he began to realize he was not dreaming. The voice was real, coming from someplace down beyond his feet. Seema was answering, apprehensive and apologetic, her own sweet voice sounding twittery and flutey by comparison. As Atreus struggled to wakefulness, his pain began to return, though not as terrible as before. He could feel a piece of chiffon covering the burns on his upper body, and Seema's warm hand was smearing a watery ointment over his raw and naked legs.

An embarrassing thought flashed through Atreus's mind, snapping him instantly to full consciousness. His eyes popped open, and he found himself staring at the ceiling planks of a small stone hut. He was lying on a straw-covered pallet, with a flickering butter lamp resting on a rough-hewn table beside him. The room was remarkably warm, at least compared to the snow caves in which they had been sleeping the last few nights, and he could hear a fire crackling in a hearth somewhere nearby.

Atreus raised his head and glanced down the length of his body, discovering that his worst fears were true. He lay hideously naked from the waist down, with his scorched flesh and broken leg, crooked hips and ugly ogrelike loins fully exposed. Nor did he have any illusions about who had removed the remnants of his trousers, as Seema was rubbing her ointment onto a burn higher on his thigh than any female hand had ever touched before. He found himself suddenly thankful for his pain. It was probably the only thing that saved him from an even greater embarrassment.

Seema turned to look at him and said softly, "You are awake." If his grotesque nakedness caused her any discomfort, she did not show it. "I hope it is not because I am hurting you."

Atreus shook his head and started to say, "I heard a . . ." He did not want to call what he had heard a mere voice. He shook his head, then finally said, "I guess it was a song. I must have been dreaming."

"It was not a song, or a dream," said a male voice, the same dulcet voice that Atreus had heard earlier. "Though I thank you for thinking so."

A milky-skinned man with a slender build and the appearance of youthful vigor stepped into view. Wearing nothing but a white cotton sarong draped around his hips, he was dressed almost as immodestly as Atreus, though he was immeasurably more handsome, with cascading silver hair and piercing silver eyes that riveted the observer in place. Nor were his stunning good looks the most striking thing about him, for a huge pair of feathery white wings arched up behind his shoulders, creating a sort of pearly halo that followed him wherever he went.

Atreus let his head drop back to the pallet, convinced that he was looking at one of Sune's divine seraphs.

"I must be dead."

"Do not say such things!" said Seema. She stood and stared at Atreus as though he had uttered a blasphemy. "Not in front of the *sannyasi!*"

"Atreus is not to blame. He is only speaking what he believes to be so," said the sannyasi, who motioned Seema not to be angry, then came to the sleeping pallet and lowered his hand as though to touch Atreus's sloping forehead. "May I?"

Atreus nodded, and the sannyasi placed a milky palm on his brow. At first, it felt cool and soothing. Then Atreus's scorched flesh began to sting again. His broken leg started to throb, and the throbbing worked its way up his leg into his hip. The tingling in his burns seeped deep down through his muscles into his blood and turned his veins into channels of boiling fire, and the searing heat began to rush up through his body toward the sannyasi's hand.

All of Atreus's pain reached his neck at once, filling him

211

with such a fiery agony that he thought his throat would open like a boiled sausage. He screamed and thrashed at the sides of his pallet and reached up to tear the hand from his brow.

The sannyasi's palm remained in place, holding Atreus down as firmly as it did gently, and even all of Atreus's anguish-borne strength could not tear the milky hand from his brow. For a moment, his head hurt as it had never hurt before. His ears ached with the roar of a thousand thunderclaps, his nostrils burned with lava, and his eyes felt like they were melting. His brains boiled inside his skull, and his ears roared with the hiss of escaping steam, then the pain vanished, evaporating through the thick bone of his brow.

Without being aware that he had closed them, Atreus opened his eyes and found himself looking up at the sannyasi. Now, the milky face looked as old as the mountains themselves. His lips were drawn tight and his brow was furrowed, and Atreus saw in his expression all the pain that had been drawn from his own body.

Before Atreus could thank the sannyasi, Yago and Rishi rushed through the door, the ogre's broad shoulders tearing out the door jambs and a fair section of stone wall. As soon as they saw the white-winged figure standing over Atreus, their mouths fell open in astonishment. Rishi stopped to stare in gape-mouthed wonder. Yago crossed the floor in a single thundering step and grabbed a feathery wing.

"What you doing?" he said. The ogre drew himself up to his full height, knocking two ceiling planks out of the roof, and tried to pull the sannyasi off the floor.

He might as well have tried to lift a mountain. The sannyasi remained firmly planted on the rough-hewn planks, and nothing, not so much as a wing feather, yielded to the ogre's strength.

Yago scowled, then responded as ogres do to unexplained things, by trying to smash it with his fist.

The blow would have caved in the head of any normal man, but the sannyasi did not even flinch. Yago howled in pain and clutched the offending hand. Rishi's eyes grew wide and round, and he rushed from the room making occult signs and jabbering in Maran.

Atreus scowled at his friend. "Yago!" he shouted. "What are you doing?"

"Me?" the ogre boomed. "The way you screamed, I thought he was tearing your guts out."

The sannyasi turned to Yago. "Do not be angry with your son," he said. "He was in terrible pain."

Yago looked horrified. "Son?"

The sannyasi motioned at Atreus and said, "Your son Atreus. He will recover soon." Oblivious to the insult he had just inflicted on the ogre, the sannyasi turned to Seema. "Now you see what comes with strangers. You have brought violence and anger into our midst."

"It's not Seema's fault," Atreus said, propping himself up. "She was only trying to save—"

"Of course," interrupted the sannyasi, "but it is not permitted to bring strangers into Langdarma."

Atreus's jaw fell, and he wondered if he remained in the grip of his fever delirium. Certainly, the sannyasi looked more like a hallucination than a real being, and he refused to believe that Seema had lied to him about Langdarma being a myth.

After a moment, Seema said in a quiet voice, "I had no choice but to bring them. They were in terrible danger, and to leave them behind would have been murder."

The sannyasi considered this, then reluctantly nodded. "If that is true, letting them die would have been a terrible stain on your soul, but you are still to blame." His white wings began to flutter ever so slightly. He gestured at Atreus and Yago and said, "This is what comes of visiting the outside world. You cannot escape its taint."

Seema lifted her chin. "Would my soul have been any less tainted had I not tried to save Jalil?" she asked.

The sannyasi's milky face grew sad. "Even here," he replied, "death is the inevitable consequence of life."

"Jalil was a child!" Seema protested, shaking her head. "His time should not have come for many years."

"And you know this how?"

"By the pain in my heart."

"Ahh . . . then your heart has misled you." The sannyasi's pure voice grew sterner as he continued, "It is not for you to say who will live any more than it is for you to say who will die. You left the valley to find a cure, and Jalil died anyway. The wisdom of a healer lies in knowing what can be changed and what cannot. To claim more is to usurp the powers of the Serene Ones."

Seema's expression grew apprehensive. "That was not my intention," she said.

"But that was the result," the sannyasi said, then took Seema's shoulders and pulled her close, folding her inside his wings. "Seema Indrani, your vanity has cast a shadow on your soul and brought anger and violence into Langdarma. Your magic has become a burden you can no longer bear. I free you of it."

When the sannyasi opened his wings, Seema looked weary and dejected. Without raising her gaze, she nodded and stepped back.

"As you will have it, Sannyasi," she said.

"No!" Atreus exclaimed, sitting up and facing the sannyasi. "She did nothing wrong. You can't punish Seema for saving us."

The sannyasi gently pushed Atreus back down and said, "I am not punishing her. Until Seema lifts the shadow on her soul, her magic is only a trap. It will poison her thoughts with vanity and folly, and she will bring more wickedness down on us all." The sannyasi turned to Seema.

"You will watch over Atreus and his companions during their stay in Langdarma. If they do no harm and come to none themselves, your magic will return."

Seema bowed her head.

"Your wisdom shines like the sky, Sannyasi."

The sannyasi smiled benignly, turned to Atreus, and said, "You and your friends may rest in Langdarma until you are well enough to travel. I ask only that you observe our customs, and that you speak no angry words inside Langdarma."

Atreus nodded.

The sannyasi folded his wings tightly behind his shoulders. "This will be difficult for you, but I know you will try." His silver eyes softened. He leaned down to touch Atreus's shoulders and continued, "And I am sorry for the grief you will feel after you leave."

"What grief?" Yago demanded from the corner.

"You will be tormented by the memory of paradise," the sannyasi answered, continuing to look at Atreus. "There is nothing I can do to ease this burden."

"I wouldn't want you to," said Atreus. "Better to have the memory than nothing at all."

"You will come to think differently." The sannyasi shook his head sadly, then laid his milky palm over Atreus's eyes. "Now sleep. You must rest if you are to heal."

Atreus could not have disobeyed if he wanted to. Even before the sentence was finished, the sannyasi's dulcet voice had lulled him into a dreamless trance. Atreus's eyelids fell, his breathing slowed, and he sank into a deep, vitalizing slumber.

Atreus passed the next three days on that same sleeping pallet, staring up at the plank ceiling or gazing out through the window at an unchanging panorama of looming cliffs and forested hills. Every morning he was awakened by the sound of groaning yaks and clanging bells as the herders drove their beasts out to pasture, and every evening he was lulled to sleep by laughing voices as they returned. During the day, he occasionally heard someone talking out in the street, though his window faced the wrong way for him to see who they were. Seema came five times a day to feed him and change his bandages. Though she often lingered longer than necessary, Atreus found it difficult to make conversation, feeling at once guilty about her sacrifices on his behalf and angry with her for deceiving him about Langdarma's existence.

At Atreus's insistence, Yago and Rishi spent most of their time touring the wonders of the valley, returning each evening so weary they barely had the energy to describe their adventures. The explorations seemed to take a heavy toll on Yago especially, as Langdarma's customary fare of grains, legumes, and yak cheese were poor substitutes for charred meat and sour mead. Although the ogre could easily have supplemented his diet with a few rabbits or deer, he observed his promise to the sannyasi and refrained from hunting anything more lively than blackberries. Rishi also seemed to honor the hospitality of their hosts, if only because the people of Langdarma lived very simply and had nothing to steal.

On the fourth day, Atreus was strong enough to move out onto a small wooden balcony overlooking the tiny hamlet where Seema made her home. From his chair, he could look out across the stone huts down to the meadows where the villagers grazed their yaks and the terraced slopes where they grew their peas and beans. A small gully curled around below the terraces, marking the boundary between the village lands and the forested slope that led down to the stone-walled fields in the basin's fertile bottomland.

Late in the afternoon, Atreus was staring out across the fields, trying to imagine where he might find the Fountain of Infinite Grace, when Seema came out and sat beside him

216

She was carrying no food or bandages, and her manner was unusually reserved. For a long time she simply sat there and followed his gaze across the valley until he grew nervous and began to imagine she had somehow sensed what he was searching for.

When she finally spoke, it was without looking at him.

"Truly it is a miracle how just sitting and gazing out at Langdarma can heal one's soul. I was hoping it might also heal what has come between us."

The comment itself did not surprise Atreus nearly so much as his reaction to it. He suddenly felt bitter and resentful, and he heard himself say, "That is a strange thing to hear from someone who tried to convince me Langdarma does not exist."

Seema recoiled from the acid in his voice, and said, "Did you not promise the sannyasi you would speak no angry words here?"

Atreus felt another rush of anger well up inside him but managed to bite his tongue and say nothing until it passed.

"I'm sorry," he said finally, "that's true, but you did tell me that Langdarma was only a myth."

Seema's golden cheeks darkened to a tarnished bronze.

"Yes, I lied to you. I had hoped by now you would understand why."

"I understand." Despite his promise to the sannyasi, Atreus could not keep the bitterness out of his voice. He touched a finger to his hideous cheek and said, "I have understood my whole life. My mistake was in thinking you were different than people elsewhere."

Seema looked at her hands. "I do not know how people are elsewhere," she said, "but I did not lie to you because of how you look."

"Don't insult me," Atreus told her, then waved his hand at the lush forest below. "Everything is beautiful in Langdarma, and I am ugly. I know why you didn't want me here."

Now Seema's voice took on an angry edge. "That is not so. You saw the sannyasi's anger for yourself."

Atreus shrugged and said, "What's the difference? Whether you found me too ugly or simply knew the sannyasi would, the result was the same."

"You are not ugly. It is only that you do not belong here. The sannyasi's concern is for your welfare and Langdarma's."

Atreus rolled his eyes and looked toward a swarm of scarlet butterflies dancing among the white blossoms of a plum tree.

Seema stood and came to his chair. "If you were ugly," she asked, "would I do this?"

Taking Atreus's cheeks in her hands, she leaned down and pressed her lips to his, and this time she was not trying to breathe for him. There was nothing friendly or modest in the kiss. Her mouth was warm and liquid and charged with ardor, and Atreus began to feel stirrings he had only dreamed of. His hands rose of their own accord and grasped her shoulders, drawing her down onto his lap. She did not resist. He pulled her close, mashing her body close to his, feeling her wonderful softness against his lumpy brawn, so lost in passion that when he heard a sudden peculiar hissing sound, he did not even recognize it as his own voice. Seema cried out and jumped out of the chair.

"Your burns!" she cried, staring down at his bandaged thighs.

Atreus blushed, realizing there was more to notice in his lap than burns. Seema paid no attention to his embarrassment. She pulled the bandages back, then winced at his torn and oozing scabs.

"We should continue this later," she said, kissing Atreus on the cheek. "The sannyasi would be most displeased if I interfered with your recovery."

"You won't," Atreus said. His sour mood of a few minutes

earlier had vanished, vanquished by the giddy astonishment Seema's kiss had stirred within his breast. "And even if you do, I don't particularly care what the sannyasi thinks."

Seema's jaw started to drop in shock, then she smiled. "*I* do." She wagged a finger at Atreus and drew her chair closer, adding, "There will be plenty of time later for Devotions."

"Devotions?"

Now it was Seema who blushed. "You know. . . ."

But Atreus did not know, having learned as a young man that any sort of amorous advance would send a woman scurrying for the safety of her father's counting room.

Seema took his hand, drawing Atreus's thoughts back to the balcony. "Perhaps it is better to wait anyway. It seems a lifetime since Tarch pulled you onto the slave barge, but it has been less than a tenday. In truth, I hardly know you."

"What do you want to know?"

Seema thought for a moment, then said, "Why you are so angry with yourself."

"Angry? I don't believe I am."

Seema nodded and said, "You are. I see it in this 'ugliness' you talk about. Why would you call yourself such names if you were not angry with yourself?"

Atreus scowled. "Perhaps because that is what I learned from others."

"Ah . . . so you are angry because you do not look the way they think you should, and so you cross the world, hoping that this penance will put you at peace with yourself."

"Not exactly," Atreus said, unsure as to whether or not she was mocking him. "I came to find Langdarma."

"Because someone told you it would make you handsome." Seema smiled, faced him, and tapped his chest. "And it will, if you let it."

"I know, I know . . . beauty comes from within," Atreus

219

said. "But to tell you the truth, I'm hoping for something more external."

He gazed directly into Seema's brown eyes, quietly praying that she would say something about the Fountain of Infinite Grace. Instead, she only touched her fingers to his cheek.

"I am afraid you will have to look inside first. Until you change the way you look at yourself, nothing in Langdarma will change how others see you."

"Really?" Atreus started to ask her about the Fountain, then recalled how she had deceived him about Langdarma's existence and felt his eyes grow hard. Not wanting her to see that he knew she was lying, he withdrew his hand from hers and looked away. "Then I have just crossed half the world for nothing."

"No, not for nothing," said Seema. "Inside every ugliness lies a greater beauty. Before you leave, I will make you understand this. I promise."

Not trusting himself to make a civil answer, Atreus merely grunted.

"Perhaps I should prepare you something to eat," Seema said, standing. "Your hunger is making you cross."

As she turned to go, the door downstairs banged open. "Atreus!" Yago's deep voice reverberated up through the house.

"Out here," Atreus called, his heart jumping at the ogre's excitement. "On the balcony . . . with Seema."

He emphasized these last two words as a warning. The last thing he wanted was for Yago to burst through the door and blurt out that they had finally found the Fountain of Infinite Grace. If Seema was not willing to tell him about it, he suspected the sannyasi would take a dim view of them knowing its location.

Yago came pounding up the stairs so hard that he shook the entire hut, stomping across Atreus's room toward the balcony. Seema met him at the door, her eyes wide with alarm, her hand raised to stop him.

"Stay inside," she warned, "or you will tear my poor balcony off my house."

Yago dropped to his hands and knees, then thrust his head and shoulders out through the door.

Before the ogre could speak, Atreus said, "Yago, calm down. I'm sure your news can wait until you gather your thoughts."

"A moment, yes, but perhaps not longer," panted Rishi. The Mar squeezed past the ogre. "We have just come from Phari, where there is most disturbing news."

"Phari?" Atreus asked.

"A hamlet on the other side of the basin," explained Seema. "What is wrong in Phari?"

"Tarch!" boomed Yago.

Seema's face paled to sickly yellow. "That is not possible!" she said. "He could not follow us through the Passing."

"He did," insisted Yago. "A man's daughter is missing."

Seema frowned. "You saw Tarch take her?" she asked.

"No, thank the Forgotten Ones," answered Rishi. "She did not come home last night. They were searching for her when we arrived."

Seema took a moment to gather her wits, then asked, "What did you tell them?"

"Tell them?" echoed Rishi. "That we had not seen the girl. Then we left. They kept looking at Yago and his big teeth and saying absurd things about the yeti, and I could see at once there was no use trying to reason with them."

"You said nothing about Tarch?" Seema asked.

Yago shook his head. "They were edgy enough without us starting rumors about scaly devils," he explained.

Seema closed her eyes in relief. "You were right to hold your tongues," she said. "I am sure this has nothing to do with Tarch."

"How?" Atreus asked, perched on the edge of his chair. "How do you know that?"

Seema said, "Even if he could have tracked us into the mountain—which he could not do—he does not know the Passing magic. He would be trapped inside forever."

"All the same, Tarch has a nasty way of surprising us," said Atreus. He stood, biting back a hiss of pain as his mending leg objected. "We'd better go have a look."

"There is no need." Seema pushed Atreus into his chair and added, "Even if there was, you are in no condition to go anywhere."

"But Tarch—"

"Could not have followed us," Seema insisted. There was just enough doubt in her voice to make Atreus wonder whom she was trying to convince. "Even in Langdarma, we have the normal sorts of tragedy. Children drown or hit their heads or get lost just like anyplace else, and you will only add to the family's anguish with senseless talk of devils."

14

Atreus sat alone at the rough-hewn table, sipping buttered tea from a wooden mug while Seema cleaned the iron breakfast pot. He would have helped, but her cooking area was more an apothecary than a kitchen, and no one was permitted to invade that spicy-smelling realm of earthenware jars and stoppered vials. Yago and Rishi were clumping around upstairs, gathering bedrolls and extra cloaks in preparation for an overnight foray. Having found no sign of the Fountain of Infinite Grace in the basin, Atreus had prevailed upon them to begin exploring the main valley.

"There is no need to be envious," said Seema. "We will be joining your friends soon. Your leg is growing stronger every day."

Atreus nodded slowly. "That's just what I was thinking," he said, "and soon after that I'll be well enough to leave."

"Perhaps not so soon. The sannyasi will not ask you to go until you are strong enough to cross the High Yehimals without help, and by then the weather may well have turned." Seema feigned a look of pity and added, "I am sorry to tell you this, but it is possible you will still be here next spring."

"I can think of worse fates," Atreus said, half grinning. "This place has a way of growing on you."

Seema pouted and asked, "And what of the company?"

"I liked the company from the start. The company is what I'll miss most when I go." Atreus paused, then asked, "I will have to go, won't I?"

"I am afraid Yago has nothing to worry about," Seema

said, referring to the ogre's obvious eagerness to be on his way home. Any place that frowned on head-bashing and banned hunting was hardly a Shieldbreaker's idea of paradise. "The sannyasi has never allowed an outsider to remain in Langdarma. When it is safe for you to leave, he will insist that you do."

Atreus could only nod. Having fallen under the spell of what little of Langdarma he had seen, he would gladly have traded all his wealth back in Erlkazar for a simple stone hut on the Sisters' verdant slopes.

Seema's brown eyes grew sad, and she began to coat her iron pot with flower oil.

"Today, shall we walk down to the play yard and see the children again? I think they would like that."

"So would I," he said. When Atreus had limped by the day before, several little girls had surprised him by bringing him a garland of wildflowers to help him heal. "Do you know, that's the first time a child ever ran *toward* me?"

Seema laughed. "Yes, I could see that. You were so surprised, I thought *you* would run."

"I would have, if my leg had been stronger."

Atreus smiled and took a drink from his wooden mug. The brew tasted more like a salty bouillon than tea. It was thick and greasy and probably the one thing he did not really love about Langdarma.

From the street outside came the thump-thump of running feet. A dark streak raced past the open window, and the door banged open. An adolescent boy rushed inside, panting for breath and filling the hut with the smell of sweat.

"There has been a rockslide!" He gulped down a breath, then continued, "My father needs help."

Seema grabbed a woolen satchel off the wall and began to stuff it with herbs and vials. "I will do what I can Timin, but you know the sannyasi has taken away my—"

"Oh no, not *your* help!" interrupted Timin. "Kumara is already there, but the rocks are very large and we need the orange man to move them."

Seema let her satchel drop, her face falling as though she had been slapped. "Of course," she said.

Atreus limped to the stairs and hollered, "Yago!"

"Yeah?"

"Come quick!"

The ceiling shook as the ogre pounded across the floor above.

Seema handed Timin the last of Atreus's buttered tea. "Drink," she told him. "You will need strength for the run back. Where is your father trapped?"

"Beneath the Caves of Blue."

The youth began to gulp down the greasy tea.

"The Caves of Blue?" Seema frowned. "What was he doing there?"

Timin lowered the mug and passed it back to Atreus. "Searching for my sister," he said.

Atreus and Seema exchanged alarmed glances. Before they could ask any more questions, Yago squeezed down the stairs, his orange fangs bared in alarm.

"What is it?"

"Come quickly!" Paying no attention to Yago's expression, Timin grasped the ogre by the wrist and tugged him toward the door, saying, "You are needed."

Yago scowled and glanced toward Atreus.

Atreus nodded and said, "Do as he asks."

The ogre shrugged, then ducked through the door behind Timin. Atreus glanced at Rishi, who was coming down the stairs to investigate the uproar.

"Go with them," Atreus said to the Mar, pointing out the door. "Hurry . . . and keep an eye out for Tarch."

Rishi paled. "Tarch? I thought there was no way—"

"There isn't," said Seema, and Atreus finished for her,

"But this is a strange coincidence."

"And if it is more than a coincidence?" Rishi demanded. "What do you expect me to do about it?"

"The same thing you did at the icefall," Atreus said as he shoved the little Mar out the door. "We'll be along as fast as I can run."

"Run?" Seema asked, shaking her head. "You are not even ready to walk, and the Caves of Blue are at the far end of the basin, very high up the slope."

Atreus started out the door after his friends. "I'll crawl if I have to," he promised.

In the end, Seema borrowed a yak and led the way toward the Caves of Blue. Had Atreus's thoughts not been consumed by visions of Tarch abducting the beautiful girls of the valley, the journey would have been an enchanting one. The trails were lined with soaring birch and fir, many so large that even Yago could not have closed his long arms around the trunks. The ground itself was blanketed with a bounteous undergrowth of blossoming rhododendron that arched out over the trail sprinkling pink petals on their heads as they passed. Every now and then, they would come to a golden stream snaking its way down to the big river in the center of the basin, or cross an open meadow of long green grass where a small herd of yaks grazed contentedly.

After a time, they reached the terraced slopes surrounding a small hamlet similar to the one where Seema lived. Here, they were besieged by distressed women who began to fill in the troubling details of the rockslide. Timin's father had awakened that morning to discover his eldest daughter, a young woman of seventeen, missing. Discovering two set of footprints leading away from his hut, he had set off at once to catch the pair. Not long afterward, the rumble of a nearby landslide had shaken the hamlet. Timin had followed the dust plume to a slope of *talus*—a jumbled scarp of loose rock—beneath the Caves of Blue. There he found his father trapped under a huge boulder. There was no sign of his sister or the mysterious man with whom she had left.

Atreus was astonished by the utter innocence of the villagers. Had a similar event occurred in Erlkazar, the father would have assumed the worst and set off with a company of armed men to hunt down the abductor. Here, the girl's disappearance seemed more confusing than alarming, as though they could not imagine why she would leave without saying good-bye.

By the time they reached the other side of the hamlet, Atreus was convinced that Tarch had found his way into the valley. He said nothing to Seema, thinking it wiser to let her decide this for herself. In many ways, they were growing closer every day, but there remained between them a certain uneasiness he did not want to aggravate by pushing her to a conclusion she would soon reach for herself. Without exception, the women of Langdarma were as beautiful as Seema was, and it could hardly be a coincidence that two of them had disappeared since she had escaped Tarch.

As they traveled along the terraced vegetable slopes, Atreus soon found himself looking out over the edge of the basin, to where it dropped away into greater Langdarma. The valley was even more vast than he remembered, so wide that the other side was obscured in haze, and so deep that he could see no bottom, only the far wall plunging ever downward. The impossibility of finding the Fountain of Infinite Grace in such a immense place struck him heavily. Yago and Rishi had spent nearly a tenday searching just the upper basin, and it could not have been a thousandth the size of the main valley.

Clearly, he would need Seema's help to find the fountain, but he did not dare ask. The secret loomed over their relationship as heavy and foreboding as the ice-blue sky, an unspoken conflict they both feared to address. Atreus had asked many times whether there was not some way to change his external appearance, and Seema had always sidestepped the question, invariably changing the subject to his perception of himself. He could feel her holding back, trying desperately to avoid lying to him as she had lied about Langdarma, yet determined to keep from him some confidence she held even more dear than the valley's existence. As for Atreus, he felt burdened with guilt, like a thief who insinuates himself into a rich man's house in order to rob him blind. He did not see how Langdarma would be harmed by taking a single vial of water from the Fountain of Infinite Grace, yet he did not dare broach the subject for fear that the mere asking would somehow make his task impossible.

The trail entered the woods again and continued forward over the brink of the basin, but Seema turned up a side path and began to lead them uphill. The slope grew steadily steeper as they went. Soon, they were zigzagging up a series of switchbacks, creeping across craggy outcroppings and stealing glimpses down into the main valley. In many ways, it was a larger version of the upper basin, with a little less forest, a lot more barley field, and a broad blue river snaking down the center. At the far end, the valley gradually narrowed to a shadowy black gorge and disappeared into a wall of ice-capped mountains.

They had just reached the steepest part of the hillside when they began to hear voices chattering ahead. Seema broke from a fast walk into a run, tugging Atreus's yak along behind her. From somewhere ahead came a loud crash, followed by the clatter of tumbling stone.

Atreus and Seema emerged from the forest onto a steep, jumbled talus slope. Twenty paces below, a circle of men were gathered around Yago's stooped form. Above the ogre stood an old man in a scarlet tabard, issuing commands in a thickly accented voice that Yago probably could not understand. By the woolen herb satchel hanging over the old man's shoulder, Atreus guessed that this was Kumara, the healer Timin had mentioned.

Seema tied the yak's lead to a bush. Atreus dismounted and followed her down to the crowd. They arrived to find the head and shoulders of a glassy-eyed man protruding from beneath a wagon-sized slab of granite. The poor fellow was lying on a blood-smeared boulder, babbling incoherently about yetis and devils. Yago stood over him, struggling alongside several villagers to keep the huge slab from dropping on his chest. Timin was kneeling next to the victim, presumably his father, stroking his hair and speaking gently while two other men pulled his arms. A third man had crawled under the stone so far that only the soles of his boots remained visible.

The victim shrieked in pain, and a muffled voice under the slab cried out, "Now!"

The men holding the victim's arms stepped back, pulling him from beneath the boulder. As his legs came free, one ankle began to spurt long arcs of blood. The other merely oozed from a smashed stump. Kumara instantly jumped down beside the injured man and pressed one hand to the spurting ankle, fishing through his woolen satchel with the other.

The brave man under the slab began to inch out, but Yago was having trouble holding the heavy stone. He groaned deeply, and gasped, "Fingers . . . slipping!"

The villagers frowned and began to jabber in confusion, and Atreus realized they had not understood the ogre's warning. He shouldered his way into the crowd, grabbed the ankles of the man under the stone, and jerked him out backward.

"In the name of the Five Kingdoms, take care!" the hero cried, twisting around to glare up at his handler.

"Rishi?" Atreus gasped, surprised to find himself staring

down at his sly guide. "What are you getting out of this?"

"Nothing," Rishi, flushed with embarrassment, answered. "I am as surprised as you are, but no one else believed Yago could hold the stone."

At that instant, Yago cried out in alarm and jumped back. The granite slab crashed down, shaking the whole talus slope, and Atreus thought for an instant that the rockslide would begin again.

Rishi's eyes widened at the near miss, and he spun to glare at Yago. The ogre merely shrugged and turned away, stooping over the other onlookers to peer down at Timin's father.

"Is he gonna live?"

The father's glassy eyes grew round, then he began to shake his head in fear.

"Yeti devil!"

Yago's heavy brow rose. "Me?"

The man tried to push himself away. "Thief of daughters!" He scraped his fingers across the rock, searching for something to throw, crying, "Where is my Lakya?"

Atreus stooped over the man. "Is that what happened to your daughter?" he asked. "Did a devil steal her?"

When the man's gaze shifted to Atreus, he screamed in terror and cried, "Devils everywhere!"

He struggled to escape, flailing around so hard that the old healer could no longer hold him.

"You must step away," ordered Kumara. His glower slid from Atreus to Yago. "Both of you."

Yago scowled. "You guys are the ones that asked me—"

"Please, my father means no offense," said Timin, moving to block the injured man's view of Yago. "He is delirious."

Atreus nodded and pulled the ogre away, but even that did not calm Timin's father.

"Return my Lakya!" the man screamed. "Give her back!"

Kumara reached into his satchel and removed a small,

clear vial. The liquid inside looked remarkably like water, save that it seemed to catch the light like a fine diamond and cast it back in a sparkling aura of radiance. When Atreus made the mistake of gasping, Kumara frowned and shifted around to hide the vial from view. There was a small popping noise, then the sound of liquid being poured. A silvery halo rose around both the healer and his patient, and Timin's father grew instantly quiet.

This time, it was the villagers who gasped.

Atreus's heart began to pound faster. He leaned over to Seema and, as casually as he could manage, whispered, "What was that?"

Seema hesitated, then said, "Water."

Atreus risked a doubtful frown. "Water?" he asked. "No water I've ever seen—"

"It comes from a special place!" Seema hissed. "Only healers may go there, and now you must ask no more."

"Why?"

Seema scowled at him. "Because it is the sannyasi's wish, that is why!" She moved away, kneeled down beside Kumara, and said, "Is there anything I can do to help, Old Uncle?"

The old man gave her a glare that could have melted granite. "Have you not done enough already?" he asked.

Seema recoiled as though struck.

"What do you mean?"

Kumara nodded toward Atreus and Yago. "It is you who brought this evil on us." He ground a leaf between his fingers, then pushed the dust into the spurting wound on his patient's ankle and added, "You angered Fate by trying to cheat her, and now we must all pay."

Atreus could not stand the sight of the tears that welled in Seema's eyes. He squatted down across from Kumara, his misshapen face taut with anger.

"Speak how you wish about my friends and me, but

231

Seema is not responsible for this," he said, gesturing at Timin's wounded father. "Nor is she responsible for the missing daughters. Only a coward would blame a woman for a devil's doing."

Kumara returned the threat with a black-eyed glare, then hissed three times. An invisible force as soft and powerful as the wind struck Atreus in the chest, knocking him to his haunches and leaving him gasping for breath.

The old healer narrowed his eyes. "In this place, *you* are a devil." He glanced at Seema and added, "Women who consort with devils are witches."

Seema gasped in outrage, then met Kumara's eyes and locked gazes. Atreus sensed that some contest neither he nor the villagers could quite perceive, much less understand, was taking place. The two healers glared at each other for what seemed an eternity, neither blinking nor seeming to breathe, until Seema finally began to tremble.

Kumara sneered, then raised his chin. "Do you hear it, Seema?" he asked.

Atreus heard nothing, but Seema's eyes darted toward the head of the basin.

"You see?" Kumara sneered. "Even Jalil's ghost knows what you are."

Seema's eyes flashed with fury, but she seemed unable to keep from turning her gaze in the direction of her own hamlet. She cocked her head as though listening. Her shoulders slumped and tears began to spill down her cheeks. She spun away and bounded up the boulder field, leaving Kumara to smirk at her back.

Atreus glared down at the old healer and said, "If Seema did bring evil to Langdarma, she is not the first. There is enough wickedness in your heart for ten devils."

Kumara did not even look up. He simply hissed, and Atreus felt an invisible hand pushing him away. Yago scowled and started to step toward the healer, drawing an alarmed murmur from the crowd of villagers. Atreus quickly raised his hand.

"Seema wouldn't want that."

He motioned Yago and Rishi to his side and led the way a short distance up the talus pile. He spent the next several minutes glaring down the slope while Kumara tended to Timin's father, until he finally felt calm enough to speak.

"That old terror is right about one thing," he said. "Tarch followed us."

Yago's eyes grew round with fear, though it would have shamed the ogre to admit this, and Rishi shook his head.

"Such a thing is impossible," the Mar insisted. "You were not conscious, so you do not know—"

"I know that two girls have disappeared since we've been here," Atreus said. "It was no coincidence that Timin's father was babbling about devils. He must have seen Tarch before the landslide."

Rishi closed his eyes and said, "And you want to capture him."

Atreus shook his head. "No, we've tried that," he said. "I want you two to track him down. We'll let the sannyasi take care of the rest."

"*Us* two?" Yago could not quite suppress a knowing smirk as he added, "You going after the girl?"

Atreus nodded. "I'd only slow you down . . . and besides, you're not to get into a fight." He started to limp off, then paused. "Be back by dark, even if you find nothing. We promised Seema no killing, and I suppose that includes you two."

"The good sir is most generous," said Rishi. "I am certain he will reward us well for this danger."

Atreus smiled, then waved his hand around the valley. "You're seeing Langdarma," he said. "What more do you want?"

By the time Atreus hobbled up the slope to his yak,

Seema had disappeared down the trail. He untied the lead and started after her, expecting to find her waiting a few switchbacks below.

When he reached the main trail without seeing any sign of her, he began to worry. Though he was no scout, he dismounted and sorted through the muddy tracks until he convinced himself that Seema had indeed turned toward home. This hope was confirmed as he passed through the hamlet, where the worried villagers stopped him to ask why she had seemed so troubled. Atreus assured them it had nothing to do with the condition of Timin's father, who would no doubt be returning soon under Kumara's care. He urged his yak toward Seema's hut.

He arrived to find the door wide open and Seema kneeling beside a wooden chest, holding a small yak hair cloak. Her eyes were red and swollen from crying, and she was still huffing from her long run. Atreus stopped just inside the door, reluctant to intrude, happy just to find her uninjured and at home.

Seema set the cloak aside, then removed a pair of brown trousers and a striped tunic. Finally, she withdrew a round hat of black felt and held it before her, running her finger along the brim. Though Atreus had not realized she knew he was there, after a time she placed the hat with the other clothes and turned to face him.

"I heard Jalil," she said. "He was crying and calling for me, but I was gone Outside. I did not answer, and then he just stopped calling."

Atreus limped into the room and kneeled across from her, picking up the hat. It was small, only a little larger than his fist. "Jalil was yours?" he asked. "Your son?"

"He was eight."

She took the cloak in her hands, rubbing the material as though she could bring the boy back by stroking his clothes.

"Kumara warned me not to go. He said I could bring Jalil

234

nothing but pain by trying to cheat Fate. And now look. I have brought evil to the whole valley."

"You were trying to save your child. How can that be wrong?"

Atreus wanted to take her in his arms, but he could not quite bring himself to reach out, to believe that she, or anyone, would be comforted by his embrace. "If there was any evil in that, it was only that *you* had to go instead of Kumara," he offered.

Seema looked up from her son's cloak and said, "You don't understand. Life in Langdarma brings with it sacred duties, even greater than that of a mother's love for her child."

Atreus thought of the terrible sacrifice his own mother had made to save his life and shook his head. "There is no duty greater than that of a mother to protect her child," he said.

"In Langdarma, there is. Langdarma is the birth home to Serene Abhirati, Mother of Peace and Beauty."

Atreus frowned, not seeing the connection. "And?"

"And Abhirati has been gone wandering the heavens for a hundred centuries. She left us to watch over her valley, and the sannyasi to watch over us, so that all would be the same when she returned." Seema lowered her gaze, her hands crumpling the hem of her son's cloak, and said, "Kumara is right to be angry with me. My selfishness has brought evil into her home."

"Kumara is a fool," Atreus said, taking Seema's hands and gently smoothing Jalil's cloak. "If Abhirati is truly the Mother of Peace and Beauty, then she will understand . . . as one mother to another."

Seema looked up. "Do you think so?"

"I know so," Atreus said. "Would Abhirati have left the sannyasi to protect you if she were not a good mother? If she is a good mother, how can she condemn you for doing all you could to save Jalil?"

Seema considered this, then said, "That does not change the evil I have brought on the valley. If you are right about Tarch being here, it is because of me."

Atreus shook his head. "If anyone is to blame for that," he told her, "it is Kumara."

Seema frowned and asked, "How can you say that?"

"No slaver wants old men like Kumara," said Atreus. "Had Kumara gone after the yellow man's beard instead of you, Tarch would not have bothered to kidnap him."

Atreus did not add that Kumara might also have returned in time to save Jalil's life, but he saw by Seema's furrowed brow that this had also occurred to her.

After a moment, she shook her head.

"This game makes no sense. We can say 'what if this' and 'what if that' all day long, and it changes nothing."

"Aren't you the one who said no mortal can understand the Wheel of Life? Perhaps Tarch has been fated to come here since the beginning of time, or maybe it was Kumara who cheated fate by refusing to help save Jalil. I don't know." Atreus squeezed Seema's hands more tightly and said, "The only thing I do know is that no matter what Kumara says, you aren't to blame. You did what you did out of love, and that is never wrong."

Seema considered this, then said, "Thank you for saying these things." She closed her eyes and embraced him. "Even if they are not the truth."

"They are." Atreus kissed her forehead without really realizing he had, adding, "You can trust me."

"I already do."

Seema looked up, and Atreus was instantly lost in her brown eyes. He pressed his lips lightly to hers, then pulled away.

"I'm sorry," he said as he tried to disengage himself. "I don't mean to take advantage . . ."

"Do not apologize." Seema pressed a finger to his lips,

refusing to let go, and said, "You are not taking advantage. I trust you, and you are a comfort to me."

Seema kissed him again, this time harder, and he could feel her need drawing him closer. She pressed her body against his. He wrapped her in his arms, felt the softness of her breasts against his hard chest, the heat of her belly warming his, the smooth curve of her hip beneath his fingers. She melted to the floor beneath him, drawing him down on top of her, holding him so close that it seemed she was trying to make him part of herself. He wanted to become part of her, to feel their bodies join as he had felt their spirits unite earlier, when she told him not to apologize—and then Atreus realized he was deceiving himself. Worse, he was deceiving Seema. He did not deserve the trust she had granted so freely, not while the secret of the fountain remained between them. Now that he had seen the sparkling waters in Kumara's hand, he knew Sune's quest was a literal one. He was to find the Fountain of Infinite Grace and return with a vial of its waters. He also knew that this was forbidden, that when he did as his goddess bade and filled his vial, he would betray Seema's trust in the cruelest manner.

Atreus's embraces grew weak and his kisses guilty. He began to feel the ungainliness of his body and recall his hideous looks. His desire for Seema became a sick, shameful thing that even his body would not abide. He drew his face away from hers, then could not bear the beauty of her brown eyes and looked away.

Seema continued to hold him. "Atreus?" she whispered. "Did you hurt yourself?"

"No. No, I'm fine." He could barely choke out the answer.

"Then why did you stop? Is love-making not a Devotion to your goddess?"

"Yes, it is," Atreus answered as he rolled off Seema, but stayed beside her and continued to hold her in his arm.

Even that felt like a lie. He could not tell her about the fountain any more than she could take him to it. "I'm feeling uneasy."

Seema propped herself on an elbow. "You are wondering about Jalil's father?"

Atreus nodded, breathing a silent sigh of relief, and even that made him feel guilty.

"There is no need to think of him," Seema said. "He is only a friend now, and I seldom see him."

"He doesn't live nearby?" Atreus asked.

"No, he is a healer down in the valley. No more needs to be said about him."

Seema pushed herself up and began to fold Jalil's cloak.

"Now I am a little bit sad again," she said. "I hope you will forgive me."

"There is no need," Atreus said, picking up the boy's hat. "I fear it's you who must forgive me."

Atreus waited alone on the balcony until well after dark, when Rishi and Yago returned exhausted and famished. They had spent most of the day scouring the area around the rockslide and found nothing, not even a footprint they could identify as Tarch's. The Mar had been ready to declare the hunt over and report to Atreus that he was mistaken, but Yago, knowing first hand the comforts of a good deep grotto, had insisted upon investigating the Caves of Blue.

The task had proven more difficult than they could imagine. The mouths of more than a thousand different caverns dotted the face of the Turquoise Cliff, some located nearly a mile above ground. After a cursory examination of some of the ground level caverns, many of which they happened across only after catching a whiff of musty air from behind a bush, they had given up and returned to Seema's for the night.

At Atreus's insistence, they abandoned the search for the Fountain of Infinite Grace in favor of investigating the

Caves of Blue. No more girls turned up missing, and Atreus was at first inclined to attribute the basin's good fortune to the vigilance of his friends. When they found no signs of Tarch after seven days, even Atreus began to think he had been wrong about the slave master following them into Langdarma. Yago and Rishi returned to looking for the fountain, though they often made a point of passing through Timin's village to inquire about signs of the devil.

It was after one such stop that Rishi returned with news of the fountain. Grateful for his father's life, Timin had finally responded to the Mar's discreet questioning. According to rumor, the twinkling water came from an ancient temple somewhere in the main valley. The news had, at first, disheartened Atreus, but Rishi had quickly hit on the idea of searching for the temple from above. They would simply climb the canyon walls and scan the valley floor, looking for any likely buildings or streams that sparkled more than they should.

By the third day, Yago and Rishi had spotted a likely looking building not far down the valley. Atreus decided to go along, telling Seema that he was going to start hiking with his friends to strengthen his leg. To his dismay, she insisted on coming, greatly adding to the already heavy pall of guilt weighing him down. They started at dawn, intending to pass through Timin's village and start the descent into the main valley before midmorning.

An hour into the journey, they stopped to drink from one of Langdarma's pristine streams. As Atreus kneeled on the mossy bank, the water grew cloudy and pink. He cried out and jerked his hands back, wondering if the valley somehow knew of his plan and was passing judgment on his deception.

Atreus's companions gathered along the bank behind him, staring and gasping as the water grew murkier and darker. Yago kneeled and brought a palmful to his mouth.

"Vaprak's veins!" he cursed. "Blood!"

"Blood?" Seema gasped.

Atreus stood and looked up through the thick undergrowth, searching for any sign of a predatory beast. The rhododendrons remained as still as stones. The water continued to grow darker and redder. To lose that much blood, an animal would have to be the size of a dragon, and even in this dense forest a predator animal large enough to down a dragon could hardly be missed.

"Seema, what's at the top of this stream?" Atreus asked.

She glanced up at the ice-blue sky, somehow estimating their position from its mottled surface. "A herder's shed."

"Please do not tell us this herder has a daughter," said Rishi.

Seema's face grew fearful. "I am afraid he does," she said. "Two of them."

Yago studied his companions, then said, "Can't be what you're thinking. Too much blood."

"I don't think it's blood," said Atreus, "at least not the way you think."

He pointed down the creek to where it was joined by a small rivulet from a side gully. The red stain was spreading *up* the side gulch.

"Think we found Tarch?" Yago asked.

Atreus's only response was to start up the stream bank.

They crept through the rhododendrons, moving as quietly and rapidly as four people could through such thick undergrowth. The water continued to grow redder and thicker until the stream took on the appearance of a vein filled with dark, clotty blood. A nauseating, copperlike stench began to hang in the air, and alarming little noises began to rise from Seema's throat. When they finally reached the terraces beneath the herder's shed, it grew apparent that there was no need for stealth. The grassy pastures were strewn with slaughtered yaks, and an old

woman was up near the shed, wailing and cradling her husband's smashed head.

"Seema, you'd better go first," said Atreus, recalling how
Timin's delirious father had initially reacted to him and
Yago. "We'll follow after you cover her eyes."

Seema nodded, then clambered over the terraces. She
kneeled beside the old woman and spoke to her softly, covering her head with a shawl. By the time Atreus and his
companions arrived, Seema had the story.

"She said a sharp-eared devil came for her daughters and
killed her husband when he tried to save them. The beast
left five minutes ago." Seema's face was hard and angry,
almost ugly. She pointed into the shed. "There are axes and
scythes inside."

Rishi's jaw fell and he asked, "Are you saying what I
think you're saying?"

Seema glanced at the destruction surrounding her and
said, "Do what you must. I want him stopped."

Atreus raised his brow. "We'll try," he said, "but it
wouldn't hurt to call the sannyasi."

Seema nodded, and Rishi rushed off to fetch the
weapons. Yago glanced at Atreus. Though the ogre had
managed to force a smile onto his jaw, Atreus could read
the doubt in his friend's eyes. Shieldbreaker or not, Yago
was afraid. As far as he was concerned, Tarch could not be
stopped.

Atreus clamped the ogre on his huge forearm and said,
"We'll manage."

"Don't we always?" Yago answered. "But if I get—"

"I know . . . don't let the crows get your eyes," said
Atreus.

Yago's behest was a standard Shieldbreaker request. They
believed crows to be spies of Skiggaret, the fear-loving god of
their bugbear enemies. Though the reminder betrayed
Yago's fear at facing Tarch again, Atreus said nothing to reas-

sure his friend. Among ogres, acknowledging another's fear was the worst kind of insult.

"You have nothing to worry about, Yago," said Seema. "There are no crows in Langdarma."

The ogre forced a smile and said, "So this *is* paradise."

Rishi returned with an armload of tools. He had a rope and the scythe for Yago, an iron kettle lid and a double-bladed tree axe for Atreus, and a pair of skinning knives and a net for himself. As he accepted the kettle lid, Atreus frowned in confusion.

"For the flames," Rishi explained, smiling. "I am always thinking of the good sir's safety, am I not?"

"What you're thinking is that I'll go in first," Atreus replied, "and you're right."

He started off at a trot and they had no trouble following Tarch's trail. The devil was tearing a broad swath through the rhododendrons, angling up the slope toward the cliffs at the mouth of the basin. The slave master appeared to be carrying one daughter under each arm, as the stalkers never saw any tracks but his. Even so, he was moving so rapidly they never seemed to catch a glimpse of him.

After a quarter hour of running, they climbed out of the forest, emerging onto one of the talus fields that tumbled down from the basin walls. Tarch was nowhere in sight. It was impossible to follow his trail across the field of jumbled boulders, but there was no question about where he was going. A mile ahead loomed the Turquoise Cliff, its face pocked by the dark mouths of the Caves of Blue.

"Got to catch him before he gets into them caves again," huffed Yago.

The ogre bounded up the talus field at an ungainly sprint, quickly drawing away from his companions. Atreus followed as best he could. His weak leg began to ache from the exertion, but he clenched his teeth and hobbled up the mountain, inspired by his friend's example. Yago soon vanished behind a jumbled crest of stone. Tarch's silhouette appeared farther up the hill, running along a flat boulder with a beautiful Langdarma girl tucked under each arm.

For the next few minutes, the chase continued with Yago and Tarch vanishing and reappearing at odd intervals, the ogre steadily closing the distance as the devil drew nearer to the Caves of Blue. Rishi hung back for a while, then finally cursed Langdarma for rubbing off on him and danced up the hill ahead of Atreus. Atreus tried to match the Mar's pace, but found it impossible and resigned himself to watching the first part of the battle from below.

Yago was still twenty paces behind when Tarch reached the Turquoise Cliff and, tucking both girls under one arm, began to scurry up the rocky face as easily as a spider. Yago grabbed a melon-sized rock and hurled it on the run.

The stone caught Tarch square between the shoulder blades. The devil grunted loudly, let his captives tumble free, and pushed off the cliff. He spun around in mid-air and landed facing his attacker. The battle was on, with Atreus still a hundred paces down the slope.

The fury of Yago's assault belied his dread of facing Tarch again. The ogre stepped in swinging, bringing the scythe around in a two-handed sweep that caught the devil in his midsection and launched him across the slope. Tarch landed a half dozen paces away, clattered down between the boulders, and disappeared. For one long moment, Atreus dared to hope Yago had ended the battle with a single bloody stroke.

As the ogre stomped over to finish what he had started, a goat-sized boulder came flying up at him. He raised his scythe to block. The rock smashed through the wooden handle and caught him full in the chest, bowling him over backward. He came down hard, a sharp crack echoing off the cliff as his head struck the flat of a stone.

Tarch clambered into view and staggered toward his

groaning foe, a flap of scaly hide dangling from the gruesome wound in his side. Rishi was a dozen paces behind
the devil, creeping across the boulder pile as silently as a
cloud. Atreus wanted to shout at him to hurry but did not
dare. The Mar's only advantage was surprise.

Tarch stopped a pace shy of the groaning ogre and lifted
a hand, preparing to incinerate him. Atreus opened his
mouth to shout. In the same instant Rishi braced himself
and flung his net, wrapping the devil's arm in a mesh of
coarse rope.

Rishi gave the draw line a terrific jerk and leaped down
behind a boulder. Tarch was spun around, his hand spraying a crescent of flame across the talus field.

"Filthy Mar!" The devil shook his arm free of the net's
charred remains, then started toward Rishi's hiding place.
"That's the last time you skrag me!"

"Then it's . . ." Yago paused, drawing in a breath so deep
Atreus heard it fifteen paces away, ". . . my turn!"

The ogre sat up, heaving the boulder on his chest toward
Tarch. The devil brought his arm up and spun around, but
the stone's momentum blasted through the block and sent
him tumbling headfirst down into the talus.

Yago was up in an instant, flinging himself across the
jumbled stones with scythe in hand. A scaly hand emerged
from between the boulders. The ogre stopped short, twisting aside just as a long gout of orange flame shot past.

Then Atreus was there, climbing over the talus from the
opposite side, holding the kettle lid in front of him like a
shield. Tarch lay down in a hollow between three boulders,
one leg trapped under the heavy stone he and Yago had
been hurling back and forth, struggling to twist around so
he could bring his crackling flames to bear on the ogre.
Though his side lay flayed open from sternum to spine, his
scaly face betrayed nothing but anger. Atreus leaped down,
turning the iron lid flat and lowering it over the devil's hand.

The flame stream reversed itself and roared back into the hollow and billowed up in a huge, orange halo. The acrid smell of scorched leather filled the air. Tarch howled in anguish. Atreus dropped the lid and leaped away, one arm raised to protect his face from the searing heat.

The roar died as abruptly as it had begun, as Tarch started to rise from his fiery grave.

Atreus jumped down to meet him, wielding his axe with both hands. Tarch, now a withered and blackened thing that seemed nothing but scorched claw and charred fang, lashed out with both claws. Atreus slipped the first attack and caught the second on his axe head, then brought the sharp blade around and buried it deep in the devil's shoulder.

Tarch bellowed and brought his uninjured arm up to unleash another of his conflagrations. Yago's scythe arced down from above, severing the scaly hand at the wrist. A gummy syrup of fire oozed from the stump, rolling back down the devil's arm and engulfing it in flame.

Tarch's blazing arm went limp and fell back toward his scorched chest. Atreus and Yago were on him with their flashing blades, hewing and chopping and slicing until the battered devil finally stopped struggling and lay in his hole charred and bleeding, barely conscious and clinging to life only by the thinnest strand of wicked will.

Atreus stepped over next to Tarch's mangled head and raised his axe, preparing to finish the battle. The devil glared up at him out of one blood-shot eye, his vicious stare expressing the hatred his tongue was too weak to speak. Atreus bent his knees, gathering the strength he would need to chop through the tough sinews and thick bone of Tarch's neck. Then a pair of small voices gasped from the edge of the hollow.

He looked up to see Tarch's kidnap victims standing on a boulder above him, staring down at him with two pairs of horrified brown eyes. They were as beautiful as all the children of Langdarma, and in their puzzled expressions he saw both the innocence and the peaceful repose that had first attracted him to Seema.

Rishi rushed up from behind the two girls. "What are you doing?" he said. "This is not for the eyes of little girls."

The Mar pulled the girls back from the edge of the hollow, but Atreus could not bring the axe down. Instead, he motioned Yago to his side.

"The sannyasi should be here soon." Atreus handed the axe to the ogre. "Until then, you're in charge."

The ogre frowned, then glanced in the direction of the retreating girls and seemed to understand. He hefted the axe over Tarch's throat, sneering down at his prisoner.

"I doubt you can move," he said. "But just so you know, I'd enjoy taking your head off if you try."

15

By the time Seema arrived at the Turquoise Cliffs, all the streams in the basin had turned the color of blood. The stain was creeping down into the main valley, lacing its way through the trees as though some huge spider was spinning a scarlet web over Langdarma itself. Atreus could see by the alarm in Seema's eyes that such a thing had never before happened, and that she blamed herself for this horror. Had she known what would come of bringing strangers into paradise, he wondered if she would still have saved his life.

As Seema came up beside him, Atreus gestured down into the hollow, where Yago still held the axe over Tarch's neck.

"He's pretty beaten up, but we didn't kill him," Atreus said, glancing out over the red-laced basin. "I don't know if that will mean anything for Langdarma."

"Who can say?" Seema sounded drained and numb. "It is good you spared him. A second murder does not undo the first. What of the girls? Are they injured?"

Atreus shook his head, then pointed toward the base of the cliff and said, "Rishi has them up in a cave. They're not hurt physically, but they're not saying much." He looked down at Tarch's mangled form. "They saw a pretty bloody fight."

When Seema glanced at the devil, her eyes grew hard and surprisingly ugly. "At least they did not see a vengeance murder," she said. "They will heal better for it, but I am not sure I will. I wanted him dead. I still do."

Atreus looked away, not knowing what to say. Had she

expressed such sentiments in Rivenshield he would have handed her Yago's axe and told her to take as many swings as she liked. But they were not in Rivenshield, and Atreus was as lost with his emotions as she was with hers. He had spared Tarch's life only because he did not want to corrupt the innocence of the two girls watching. Now that Seema had lost hers, he had no idea how to give it back.

Instead, he said, "Maybe you should check the girls. You'll be more comfort to them than Rishi."

The suggestion seemed to lighten Seema's burden. Her eyes grew brighter and she said, nodding, "Of course. They will need to know their mother is well, and perhaps I can explain to them how this happened." She squeezed his shoulder. "Thank you."

Seema started up the slope. Not long after, Atreus noticed a silver comet over the main valley. For a moment, it seemed to hang motionless near the far end, then it gradually began to swell and brighten. A faint sizzling echoed up the canyon, growing louder as the comet enlarged, and at last it became apparent that the shiny ball was actually moving, streaking through the air toward the Turquoise Cliffs.

The sizzle built to a roar, and the silver ball became a platinum blur arcing down toward the talus slope. Tarch's bloodshot eyes grew large and angry. He tried to roll to his feet, but Yago hammered his head with the flat of the axe blade and beat him back into submission.

The platinum blur resolved itself into a milky white oval supported by two shimmering wings. Seema and Rishi came down from the cave with the two sisters and stood next to Atreus. Together, they all waited respectfully as the figure slowed and took on the more humanlike form of the sannyasi, then circled overhead, creating a pearly halo over the hollow where Tarch lay trapped.

After this brief inspection, the sannyasi alighted on the boulder next to Atreus. He turned at once to the girls.

"Have no fear," he said, and touched his palms to their faces. "The devil will harm you no more."

"We are not afraid for ourselves," said the oldest sister. "We are thinking of our father."

"The devil bit him!" gasped the younger.

"I know," the sannyasi said grimacing. He continued to touch them, but even he could not erase their pain or explain to them why Tarch had done such a terrible thing. He merely nodded and said, "He is from Outside, and there are things Outside we can never understand. Do not worry on your father's account. He is with the Serene Ones now, and it makes no difference to them how he died. You were a blessing to him in life, and I have it on good authority that his only wish is for you live in peace and forget what you have seen today."

This drew some of the pain from the girls' faces, and only then did the sannyasi spread his feathery wings and glide down into the hollow. Tarch's scorched and battered body began to tremble and exude vile-smelling fumes, and he glared at the winged guardian in red-eyed hatred.

The sannyasi took the axe from Yago and motioned him out of the hollow. He looked down at Tarch.

"How dare you bring your evil into this place." The sannyasi's voice was filled with controlled fury. "Did you not see my wards?"

"Pike it . . . bubber!" Tarch barely managed to moan the words. "How long you think you can hold this little corner? This world's ours. We'll be coming for you soon enough. . . ."

"If that is so, you will not see it."

The sannyasi stepped on his prisoner's chest. A glowing white halo appeared beneath his foot and started to spread outward, slowly turning the devil's scaly hide pale and translucent. Tarch howled in pain and began to flail around, his thrashing fists pounding stones to powder. He struck at his captor time and again, clawed his leg, tried to drag

249

himself free, but he was no match for the sannyasi's strength. The white radiance continued to spread over the devil's body, turning him as clear as glass from head to toe, and when he became nothing more than a crystal ghost, he finally let out an agonized howl and stopped writhing.

The sannyasi glared down at the devil's still form, then brought the axe down. Tarch's body shattered like ice, and began to melt away and stream off in all directions.

"Water turns the wheel, the wheel turns time," said the sannyasi. "When the wheel brings your spirit around again, I pray you find a happier life."

Yago arched his bushy brows. "You killed him," he said. "After all we went through *not* to?"

"I did not kill him. I sent his spirit back to the endless river," the sannyasi said, then returned the axe to Yago. "You were right to spare his life. It will help you find happiness Outside."

"Outside?" Seema asked.

The sannyasi nodded. "It is not easy to subdue such a fiend without killing him," he said. "If your friends are strong enough to do this, they are strong enough to leave Langdarma."

Atreus's heart sank.

"How soon?"

The sannyasi looked from Seema to Atreus. "Three days," he said. "The fall storms are coming soon."

"And if we don't care about the storms?" Atreus asked. He glanced at the scowl on Yago's face, then added, "What if *I* don't care about the storms. What if I don't want to leave . . . ever?"

The sannyasi's eyes softened. "This is not your home," he said softly.

"I have never been happier in my home than I am here." Atreus took Seema's hand, then added, "I have found here what is forbidden me in Rivenshield."

"Perhaps that is so. But you are a child of Rivenshield. You have a violent heart, and we have already seen what comes of violent hearts in Langdarma." The sannyasi gestured at the web of scarlet streams spreading over the valley and said, "It cannot be."

"Violent hearts?" Rishi scoffed. "Did we not risk our own lives to spare Tarch's?"

"Tarch was here only because of you, and you are here only because of him." The sannyasi glanced up at the two young sisters, who were observing the exchange with blank, faraway eyes, and continued, "Violence clings to you like an aura. You carry it with you wherever you go. You may stay for three days . . . no more."

"Ungrateful squab!" Rishi hissed. "After all we have done for Langdarma, you dare insult us like this? You do not know who you are talking to."

"I do not need to," said the sannyasi. "You have proven my point with your own words."

"And if they don't leave?" Yago's tone was stubborn and menacing, but it did not escape Atreus's notice that the ogre had not included himself. He, at least, knew where he belonged, and it wasn't Langdarma. "You think you can force them?"

Seema gasped at the ogre's brazenness, but the sannyasi's silvery eyes remained calm and patient.

"They will leave. That is the only possible outcome." He looked away from the ogre and asked Atreus, "What of the other two missing women?"

It took Atreus a moment to swallow his disappointment and answer, for his stomach had grown so bitter and tight that he could barely speak.

"I imagine they're still alive," he said, gesturing at the cave mouth toward which Tarch had been climbing. "We'll find them somewhere in there."

"*I* will find them," said the sannyasi. "You must rest and

prepare yourself for your journey."

With that, he spread his wings and flew up to the cave, leaving Atreus and his companions alone with the two girls. Atreus watched the sannyasi disappear into the dark cavern and turned to stare out over Langdarma. The red web already stretched over as much of the valley as he could see.

"Maybe the sannyasi is right," Atreus said, shaking his head sadly. "I only hope we haven't destroyed this little world already."

"*Us?*" Rishi snorted. "This is not our fault. It was Tarch who killed, not us."

"Tarch wouldn't have found Langdarma if we hadn't been looking for it," said Atreus.

"And Seema would've been some devil's bed slave by now," Yago said, and smothered Atreus's shoulder beneath his heavy hand. "Don't go playing 'what if.' This is a big valley. If you want to stay, we can hide out until after the storms start. The sannyasi won't send us off till next summer, and maybe he'll change his mind by then."

"Thanks. I know what a sacrifice that would be for you," said Atreus, "but no good can come of defying the sannyasi. It would only harm Langdarma, and we'd still have to leave."

Seema raised her brow, then her eyes grew glassy. She turned to the girls Tarch had kidnapped and asked them, "Will it be okay for Rishi and Yago to take you back to your mother? They helped rescue you, and I believe you know you can trust them."

The oldest girl nodded, and the younger one said, "Rishi is nice."

"So is Yago," said Seema, "and very brave."

"And where will you be taking the good sir?" asked Rishi.

Seema turned to Atreus and said, "There is something I would like to show him before he leaves."

"And this is something we are not permitted to see?" Rishi leered, then gestured at himself and Yago.

"I fear not," Seema blushed. "Besides, you saw much of Langdarma while Atreus was recuperating. I think it only fair that he gets to see something special."

Atreus bit his lip, torn between his desire to spend his last few days with Seema and to continue his search for the Fountain of Infinite Grace. "How long will this take? Perhaps we could meet Rishi and Yago after they return the girls."

Seema winced, clearly stung by Atreus's suggestion.

"You do not wish to spend your remaining time with me?"

"Of course I do!" Atreus exclaimed, realizing what a mistake he had made. "It's just that . . . we all had our plans, and I didn't want to let the sannyasi's decision change them."

"Oh, you must not concern yourself with Yago and me," said Rishi, patting Atreus's side. "We will see to the girls and continue on as before, but I think you should go with Seema and see this special sight."

Atreus felt something small and light drop into his cloak pocket. Guessing that it was probably the empty vial Rishi had taken from Seema's kitchen, Atreus realized the Mar was right. Perhaps Seema had decided to show him the Fountain of Infinite Grace after all. Atreus turned to Seema and took her hands.

"I would enjoy nothing more than spending all my remaining time with you." Though he was speaking the absolute truth, he could not escape the hollow feeling in his stomach as he added, "I hope you'll forgive me for being as foolish as I am ugly."

"There is nothing to forgive." Seema smiled. "I am glad you find my company inviting. Besides, in the weeks to come, I am sure you will be seeing more of your friends than you like."

"Too much of *us*? He's the ugly one!" joked Yago. The ogre took the youngest girl's hand and turned down the mountain. "We'll see you back at the hut?"

"Yes." Seema smiled mischievously. "Sometime."

She led Atreus along the base of the Turquoise Cliff toward the brink of the upper basin. Soon, they drew close enough to the edge to see down to the mottled floor of the main valley. Along the crimson web of streams and rivers stood scattered clusters of tiny figures, gesturing excitedly and peering toward the upper basin. Only a single stream, cascading down from someplace hidden around the shoulder of the Turquoise Cliff, retained its natural silver.

Atreus stopped and looked down the length of the immense valley, his eyes silently tracing a dozen scarlet waterfalls into the mouths of a dozen hanging basins like this one.

"Will the stain ever fade?" Atreus asked. "Or now that Langdarma has seen bloodshed, will its waters run red forever?"

"There is bloodshed in many lands, and their streams are not red. I think it will not take long for the beauty of Langdarma to wash the stain away."

Seema guided Atreus to an immense fir growing along the cliff face. Beneath the crisp smell of sap hung the odor of musty stone, and there was a dampness to the air that suggested the cool breath of a cave. Seema ducked under the tree's low-hanging boughs and disappeared on her hands and knees. Atreus followed, his huge shoulders and humped back scraping the branch thickets somewhat clumsily. Soon, he found himself sliding down a muddy chute into the mouth of a small cavern.

Seema took his hand and led him into the dank-smelling darkness. The floor was sometimes soft and level and other times hard and steep, but it was always slick. Several times Atreus slipped and nearly fell, and once the ground completely disappeared beneath his boot. Seema always seemed to know exactly where she was, cautioning him to duck when the ceiling grew low, or warning him not to trip over some unseen boulder lying in the path. He was beginning to wonder if this was another mystical Passing when they finally rounded a corner and he saw a faint circle of light fifty paces ahead. When the passage grew bright enough to see clearly, Seema released his hand and led the way out onto a narrow ledge.

Atreus found himself standing many thousands of feet above the valley floor, staring down the length of the broad canyon at a hazy blue cloud he took to be the mountains at the far end. The tiny figures he had seen standing along the river banks earlier were mere specks, discernible from the boulders and trees around them only because they moved. The streams and creeks had become a mesh of red threads, and the main river was a scarlet rope snaking back and forth across the valley floor.

"You are not afraid of heights, are you?" asked Seema.

Atreus glanced down and found himself looking at a mottled carpet of green woods. He could discern nothing about the forest except its color—not the shape of the individual trees, nor whether their crowns were pointed or billowing, nor even whether they were conifers or deciduous.

"It's too far down to be afraid."

"Good," Seema laughed. "I would not like having to blindfold you on this trail."

She started along the rocky shelf. Atreus followed as quickly as he could, keeping one hand on the cliff and his eyes on his feet. The ledge had a disconcerting downward slope and an alarmingly smooth texture, and he had the constant feeling his boots were about to slide out from beneath him. If Seema felt the same way, she showed no sign, walking along as comfortably as on the balcony of her own stone hut.

At length, Atreus grew relaxed enough to tear his gaze away from his feet. He saw that they were curving along the valley wall toward the head of the canyon, where a glistening tail of water fell to the valley floor in a series of steplike cascades, plummeting from one pool to the next until it finally plunged into a small, gleaming lake. It was the out-flow of this lake that Atreus had glimpsed earlier, a single silver stream in the web of scarlet.

"That stream is the source of Langdarma's beauty," said Seema. "It will wash away the stain of Tarch's murderous heart."

"But those are the sparkling waters," Atreus said, pointing at the cascades. "I thought it was forbidden to bring me here."

"It is. Of all the forbidden things I have done, this is most forbidden. But I cannot let you leave without bringing you here. It is the reason you came to Langdarma."

She took his hand and led him along the curving wall to the end of the ledge, where a small slot canyon cut up through the cliff to a hanging meadow. Here, overlooking the entirety of the valley's beauty, sat an alabaster palace flanked on both sides by lotus ponds. The building had an ancient, guileless beauty, with the lower story painted in bright horizontal stripes and the upper decorated in swirling reliefs. A second-story balcony room commanded one end, while the other was dominated by an elaborate open rotunda skirted by two domed gazebos. Connecting the two was a long gallery of scalloped arches and slender columns, with two streams of twinkling silver water joining halfway down a Y-shaped staircase, then draining into a large oval reflecting pond.

"I've seen something like this before," Atreus gasped, "after the avalanche!"

Seema nodded and said, "Of course. Did you not say you had found Langdarma?"

"I did, but after—when I forgot—I thought it was a dream."

"Langdarma *is* a dream."

Seema took his hand and led the way across the meadow to the reflecting pool and knelt in the soft grass. Even with the tiny stream flowing into the upper end and draining out the lower, the edges of the pool were as still as glass. Its silvery surface reflected Atreus's hideous face in perfect detail—every lump, every blotch, every gruesome deformity. He turned his head aside.

"No, do not look away," said Seema. "Close your eyes and drink."

"Drink?" Atreus avoided his reflection as he swung his gaze back in her direction. "That is permitted?"

"Why not? Do you think we will run out?" Seema giggled. "Drink as much as you like."

Atreus closed his eyes and cupped his hands in the pool. The water was as cold as a glacier, but he could feel its sparkling magic in his hands. It was a sweet effervescence that tingled down to the bone. A smile crept across his face, then he heard himself chortle in delight.

Seema's palm touched his elbow, urging his hands toward his face. "What are you waiting for?"

Atreus saw the radiance of the water through his eyelids, silvery scintillations that popped inside his mind like bursting stars. He lowered his lips to his palms and drank, gulping the icy water down so fast it made his throat ache. The water filled him with an airy giddiness similar to the first time Seema kissed him, and he felt as if he would float into the air.

"Atreus, look," Seema whispered as she pulled his hands down.

The face in the water was as unbalanced and misshapen as his own, with the same beetling brow and sunken eyes, the same enormous nose and twisted mouth, but it was not him. All of the disparate parts of this face fit together in a natural way that was sincere and unpretentious, noble in its casual warmth. This face was handsome, rugged, happy, and utterly at peace with its own uncommon character.

Seema peered into the pool beside Atreus, her reflection a likeness of her customary loveliness. "This is the way I see you. It has always been the way I see you."

She turned to look at him, reached up behind his head, and drew his face down to hers. Her lips were warm and sweet and intoxicating, and now that she had given him freely what he had come to steal, he found it impossible not to respond. He slipped his hands under her cloak, felt the heavy softness of her breasts, and lifted the cloth over her head. She raised her arms, letting her silky hair cascade free as he undressed her, and pressed her nakedness to him, undoing his clothes as he had undone hers. She touched every part of him, running her warm hands over his burly shoulders and down his broad back, feeling the solidness of his stomach, the sinewy strength in his hips, the pent-up ardor of his loins, and Atreus thought he would explode.

What happened then became a blur. Seema pulled him on top and they melted together. They lay writhing in the meadow for an eternity, skin-to-skin, oblivious to the chill breeze or the gurgling water or the passing day, sometimes locked in embraces so tight Atreus could not tell where his body ended and Seema's began, sometimes merely resting in each other's arms, exhausted and content, their bodies drained and their hearts full. They lost themselves in each other, forgot the morning bloodshed and Tarch's evil and the sannyasi's verdict, and they became one. If only for a few hours, Atreus learned what it was to be beautiful.

At last, the afternoon light began to fade, and their strength with it. Seema curled into the crook of Atreus's arm and started to breathe in a deep, steady rhythm. He pulled her cloak over her and lay holding her until his arm fell asleep and his back ached from lying so still. Using his free hand, he folded her clothes into a pillow and gently slipped them under her head and withdrew his numb arm. She curled into a tighter ball and continued to sleep but otherwise did not stir.

Atreus stood and pulled on his own cloak, then looked out over Langdarma. Long curtains of afternoon drizzle were beginning to fall from the icy sky, cloaking most of the valley in haze as gray as the canyon walls. Through the mist, Atreus could see little more than a sweeping swath of mottled green with the outline of a broad river snaking down its center. With Seema sleeping behind him, it seemed the most beautiful landscape he had ever seen.

Atreus stood breathing in Langdarma's peace and serenity for a long time. Then he closed his eyes and kneeled beside the reflecting pool. At that moment, he was strong enough to accept whatever he saw, but he had to see it alone. If the image in the water was ugly, he wanted some time to swallow his disappointment, to put on a happy face so Seema would not think him ungrateful. Atreus leaned forward until he saw the water's radiance twinkling inside his eyelids and opened his eyes.

The reflection was as handsome as before.

Atreus breathed a sigh of relief, then glanced over his shoulder. Seema was still sleeping, her lips curled into a dreamy smile. Atreus reached into his cloak pocket and found the vial Rishi had slipped him earlier. He began to feel guilty and disloyal, though he could not understand why. Seema had told him he could drink as much as he liked, and the whole flask would not amount to a single gulp. Whatever Sune wanted with the twinkling water, he did not see how taking such a small amount could harm Langdarma.

Atreus plunged the vial into the icy water and watched the air bubble rise to the surface of the pool, then inserted the cork while it was still underwater. When he lifted the flask from the basin, it was gleaming and twinkling just like the one Kumara had used to calm Timin's delirious father. He checked his reflection one more time, just to be certain he had not broken the pond's magic, then slipped the flask into his cloak pocket.

A low hissing sounded from the alabaster palace. Atreus glanced toward the sound and saw—or thought he saw—a trio of dark eyes peering out from within the second-floor gallery. A ring of black tentacles seemed to be writhing around the three eyes, and between the eyes was something that looked vaguely like an ebony beak. Atreus gasped and rose.

"There is nothing to fear," said Seema.

Atreus glanced back to see her slipping her cloak over her shoulders. She pulled her silky black hair out of the collar and let it cascade down her back, then came to his side.

"It cannot escape the palace," she said.

"What is it?"

Seema shrugged. "Only the sannyasi knows," she replied, "and perhaps not even him."

"Every beauty hides a greater ugliness," Atreus said, recalling what Seema had said to him not so long ago.

Seema nodded.

"Every adage has its source."

Atreus gave an involuntary shiver and asked, "How long has it been watching?"

Seema blushed. "Not *that* long, I am sure," she said. "It has no interest in Devotions." Despite her assurance, she glanced up at the sky and grasped Atreus's hand. "Come along, now. It would not do for us to be on the ledge after dark."

They returned to Seema's house to find their friends fast asleep downstairs. Yago woke up long enough to mumble something about staying up half the night worrying, then rolled over and began to shake the entire hut with his snores. Seema giggled, then took Atreus's hand and led the way upstairs, where he discovered he was not quite as tired as he thought.

The next morning, Atreus awoke at the crack of dawn, roused from a sound sleep by an alarming hollow in the pit of his stomach. At first, he credited his anxiety to the loss of waking from a blissful dream, but when he felt Seema's warm body curled against his and looked over to find her smiling in her sleep, he knew this particular dream was not yet over.

Atreus lay there without moving for several minutes, trying to recover the peace he had experienced at the Fountain of Infinite Grace. Finally he realized that what he felt was guilt. As of yet, he had said nothing to Seema about the vial in his cloak, and he did not see how he could. To admit filling it was to admit that he had planned to deceive her all along. Even more than he wanted to be handsome, he did not want to lose her love. He slipped out from beneath the heavy blanket, collected his clothes, and crept downstairs to dress. Part of him wanted to empty the vial and return it to the cabinet, but another part whispered that Seema need never know what he had done, that if he could keep the vial hidden for just two days, he would have both Seema's love and Sune's gratitude.

On the bottom floor of the hut, his friends were already up, brewing a pot of the greasy buttered tea that Yago loved more than anything in Langdarma. Atreus stopped on the stairs to pull on his tunic, drawing a sly grin from Rishi.

"Yago, look at our master. Does he not look content this morning?"

Atreus could not help beaming, but his joy was quickly spoiled by the thought of what he had done to win the compliment. The smile vanished from his lips, and he said, "I wish I felt as content as I look."

Rishi frowned. "She did not take you to the Fountain of Infinite Grace?" the Mar asked.

"She took me." Atreus tied his trousers, then added, "I filled the vial."

"Then what's your grumbling about?" Yago continued to stir his tea. "That's what Sune sent you for."

"I didn't tell Seema about it."

Rishi's eyes widened in alarm. "And why would you want to do such a foolish thing?" he asked. "If she knew—"

"Seema would only object if it endangered Langdarma," Atreus said. He hung his cloak on a wall peg. "And if it endangers Langdarma, then I shouldn't do it. That would be the worst kind of betrayal."

Yago looked up from his stirring and said, "So you'd betray your goddess instead and go home empty-handed? After coming all this way, you expect me to believe that?"

Atreus hesitated, unsure of his answer and hating himself for it. "Maybe it won't come to that," he said.

"I do not think that is a chance you wish to take," said Rishi. "You saw the sannyasi's power. Now, are you going to let us look at this marvelous water? I did not see it when Kumara used it on Timin's father, and I am most curious about its glow."

Atreus withdrew the vial from his cloak pocket, then scowled. The only thing sparkling in the flask was the reflection of the flames under Yago's tea pot.

The ogre squinted at the glass. "Sure," he said, "I can see something sparkling in there."

"But not the way it should, I fear," said Rishi. He eyed Atreus nervously. "This is not how it looked when you filled it?"

Atreus shook his head. "No." He stared at the vial for several moments, then noticed his knuckles turning white from squeezing it so hard. He placed it on the table and said, "The sparkle is gone."

Yago frowned. "Did Sune say it—"

"The water must be sparkling," Atreus said. "She even reminded me."

Rishi picked up the vial and held it to his eye.

"Then there is clearly more to the task than we thought."

"Why doesn't that surprise me? This whole trip . . ." A terrible thought occurred to Atreus, and he turned to Yago. "What do I look like?"

"Same as usual. Like the loser of a bad fight," Yago said. He used his bare hands to lift the tea pot off the fire, then placed it in on the table to cool. "Why?"

Atreus turned to Rishi and asked, "What do you think? Am I handsome?"

The Mar's eyes shifted away.

"Certainly, Seema must think so. . . ."

Atreus's heart sank at the word "certainly."

"It's a simple question, Rishi. I look no better than before?"

The Mar dropped his gaze and said, "No."

"By Sune's red hair!" Atreus cursed.

He plucked the vial from Rishi's hand and hurled it against the wall, then heard a small gasp. He turned to see Seema standing on the stairs behind him, her hands to her face, her gaze fixed on the shattered remains of the vial.

Atreus's fury was instantly replaced by shame and remorse. "Seema! This isn't what you think." Realizing how insincere and deceitful that particular lie sounded, he began again, "Well, I can't imagine what you must think."

Seema pointed at the corked neck of the broken flask and said, "I think that you broke one of my vials."

Atreus nodded.

"What was in it?" she asked.

Atreus started to answer, but found his throat so dry he could not choke out the words.

"It was my doing," said Yago, ever the loyal guard. "I took one of your vials—"

Atreus waved the ogre off, then said, "But I am the one who filled it . . . from the pool of sparkling waters."

Seema frowned and said nothing.

"It's what we've been looking for all along," Atreus explained. "My goddess, Sune Firehair, promised to make me handsome if I brought her a vial of sparkling waters from the Fountain of Infinite Grace."

Seema studied him for a long time, her eyes growing harder and more angry as each moment passed. Finally, she came down the stairs and began to pick up the pieces of her

263

shattered vial.

"I do not know this Sune Firehair of yours, but I think you are a fool for worshiping her. To ask such a thing, she must be a heartless witch."

"Fickle as a game of knucklebones," agreed Yago.

"Fickle is not cruel," said Seema. She continued to avoid Atreus's gaze. "What Sune Firehair asks is impossible."

"I was afraid of that," Atreus sighed. "The last thing I want to do is harm Langdarma, but—"

Seema whirled on him and shouted, "Do not lie to me!" Her eyes were glassy with unshed tears. "If you feared for Langdarma, then you would have asked first."

"You said it was forbidden for anyone but healers to see the shining waters," Atreus explained. "We were—I was—afraid you wouldn't do it."

"I would do anything for you," Seema answered bitterly. She tossed the broken glass shards into the hut's fireplace. "Have I not proven that already?"

"You would not help him find Langdarma," Rishi reminded her.

Seema cringed, and her expression grew more sad than angry. She looked up at Atreus. "It seems we have both agonized over the wishes of our goddesses. I will fetch you all the sparkling water you wish, but that will change nothing. What your goddess asks is impossible. The pool's magic lasts only a few hours. By the time you return to her, the water in your vial will be as plain as the water from your own well."

Atreus was too stunned to reply. "What do you mean?" he finally asked. "It stops sparkling?"

Seema nodded. "Did you not see that for yourself?" She ran her fingers along the rough skin of his cheek. "I am sorry, but your goddess sent you for nothing."

"No!" Atreus collapsed onto a chair, shaking his head numbly. "All this way . . . why?"

Seema sat beside him and said, "I do not know. If she is not a cruel goddess, then perhaps she sent you looking for one thing knowing you would find something else."

"What?" Atreus demanded. "The knowledge that I'll always be a monster?"

"Perhaps it was me."

"You?" Atreus took a deep breath, reminding himself that he was not the only person who had been deceived here. He took Seema's hand and shook his head. "Perhaps Sune is fickle, but she is not cruel, not when it comes to love. She would never have sent me to find you, knowing I would only lose you a few weeks later."

"Perhaps you do not have to lose me," said Seema.

"Then you can convince the sannyasi to let us stay?" asked Rishi.

"That is not what I was thinking," said Seema. "The sannyasi never changes his mind, because nothing he decrees can ever be wrong."

"He is wrong this time!" snapped Rishi. "We are not going to bring any harm to Langdarma."

"Your anger is harming it now," said Seema. "And there is no sense in it. The sannyasi's will cannot be challenged."

"Then he is an ungrateful fool," Rishi said, his eyes burning with indignation. "I would not live in a place ruled by such a buffoon! But if he thinks we are leaving without our reward . . ."

"Reward?" asked Atreus. "What reward?"

"Our reward for saving the daughters of Langdarma," Rishi said. "I did not risk my life battling Tarch for free."

Atreus started to chastise the Mar for his greedy attitude, but Seema spoke first. "What is it you want, Rishi? You are welcome to take anything you like, but we have no gold or jewels in Langdarma, and yaks will not survive the Passing."

Seema's offer calmed Rishi as no argument of Atreus's could have. The Mar glanced around the hut with an appraising eye, then simply shook his head and muttered, "How can a people so poor be so happy?"

"Perhaps we are happy because we are poor." Seema smiled at the Mar's bewilderment, then turned to Atreus and said, "But as I wanted to say, I would be happy with you wherever we were. Could that be the reason Sune sent you here?"

"Not likely," scoffed Yago. "Seeing a beauty like you with a beast like him would only insult that prissy hag. He'd be lucky if she didn't strike him dead on the spot."

Atreus barely heard the ogre's appraisal of the situation, so astonished was he by Seema's offer.

"You would leave Langdarma for me?" he gasped.

"If that would make you happy."

"It would . . . it does." Atreus's heart was suddenly as light as a bird. He took her hands and said, "Just knowing that you would come with me makes me happier than I have ever been in my life."

"*Would*?" Seema echoed. "You do not want me to?"

"I want you to. . . ."

Atreus paused to gather his strength, imagining what Seema's life would be like in Erlkazar. Court ladies whispering that she loved Atreus's gold more than him, freshly slaughtered meat at every banquet, jousts, bloodbaths, and wars that sprang up on the whim of an angry king.

"I can't ask you to leave Langdarma," he continued. "My world would poison you, just as surely as Tarch poisoned Langdarma."

Seema squeezed his hand. "You are not asking me to leave," she countered. "I am asking you to let me come."

Atreus did not even hesitate in saying, "I can't. The sannyasi is right about the Outside. It ruins everything it touches, and I would hate myself for allowing that to happen to you."

"I am strong," Seema insisted. "You cannot know—"

"He's right." Yago came around the table and laid a big hand on Seema's shoulder. "I'd like nothing more than for you to come with us—for Atreus's sake—but it wouldn't be right. Sooner or later, you'd start missing this place more than you love him, and then you'd hate him for it."

Seema furrowed her brow and said, "I could never hate—"

"In Erlkazar, you could," said Atreus. "The Outside is full of hate. I love you more than my own life, but you are not the reason Sune sent me here."

"Then Sune is a cruel goddess," said Seema, "because I am going to miss you, and there was never any hope of finding what you came for."

"I found it for a time, and I will never forget that."

Atreus grew thoughtful, recalling how he looked in the reflecting pool, then thought of the beast he had glimpsed watching them.

"Perhaps she is not so cruel after all."

Seema scowled. "What are you saying?" she asked.

"That she told me to fill the vial from the Fountain of Infinite Grace, not the pool. . . ."

Seema looked more concerned than ever. "There are no fountains at the Palace of Serenity," she said.

"Not outside," said Atreus, "but that water must be coming from somewhere."

16

As Atreus and his companions splashed up the flooded
stairs into the alabaster palace, a scaled tentacle flicked out
from a second story archway and twined itself around one
of the gallery's slender support columns. The expedition
came to a stunned and breathless halt. The appendage was
as thick as Yago's forearm, coated in stringy gleet, and as
black as obsidian. It ended in a small scarlet mouth surrounded by a ring of fingerlike tendrils.

Rishi stopped at the top of the stairs and reached past
Atreus to catch Seema by the sleeve. "Good lady," he said,
"you are certain we need nothing but these stones?" He
hefted the bucket of pebbles in his hand. "Whatever awaits
us at the other end of that tentacle, I would feel much safer
meeting it with an axe in my hands."

"I do not care how you feel." Seema pulled her arm free,
then stepped onto the gallery with her own bucket of
pebbles and said, "If you are afraid, do not come."

Atreus winced at Seema's harsh tone. She had agreed
only hesitantly to help him find the source of the twinkling
stream, and even more hesitantly to bring his companions
along in case of trouble. He paused at the edge of the
gallery and turned to the nervous Mar.

"Rishi, there's no need for you inside. In fact, if something does happen, it might be better to have someone out
here."

"Are you saying I am a coward? I have every right to be
here. If you want to leave someone behind, leave Yago!"

The Mar stepped past Atreus and followed Seema onto

the gallery. Yago raised his brow and glanced back at the reflecting pool, clearly thinking it would be a fine place to wait.

"Sorry, Yago," said Atreus. "If we do run into trouble, you'll be our only advantage."

"I'd be more of an advantage with a club," grumbled the ogre. He shifted his hold on the heavy cask in his arms. "If that thing attacks us, what am I going to do with a bunch of pebbles?"

Atreus glanced at the huge tentacle stretched across the gallery, trying to imagine the size of the beast at the other end. "Probably the same thing you'd do with a club . . . not much."

Carrying his own bucket of pebbles, Atreus stepped onto the gallery behind Seema and Rishi. On the other side of the scaly black tentacle, the stream of shining water spilled out from the palace's central arch and split into two currents, one flowing toward Atreus and the other in the opposite direction. Though the water was only fingertip deep, Atreus could feel its magic prickling his feet through his boots.

Seema reached the tentacle and stopped to stare down at it. When the creature did not withdraw the scaly appendage, she shook her pebble bucket loudly, then squatted down and duck-walked underneath. When she stood on the other side, her chestnut skin had paled to the color of honey.

She waved Rishi under the tentacle. "Come along," she said. "The Dweller won't bother you."

"You are certain?" Rishi asked.

Atreus gave the Mar a gentle nudge and said, "Go on."

"Yeah . . . what you waiting for?" added Yago. "Ain't you got every right to be here?"

Rishi scowled over his shoulder, shook his pebble bucket as Seema had, and ducked under the Dweller's tentacle.

269

When he reached the other side, he stood quickly and turned to face Atreus and Yago. Before the Mar could repay their taunts, the tentacle slowly untwined itself.

Rishi dropped his pebble bucket and leaped back, reaching under his cloak. The tentacle merely rippled back into the murky archway, and the Dweller vanished into the darkness.

Atreus caught Rishi's wrist. "What have you got there?" he asked sternly. "Seema said no weapons."

"Most definitely, she did," Rishi admitted and drew up his cloak, displaying the yak-hair tunic underneath. "My reaction was only out of habit, as the good sir will certainly agree if he cares to examine my person."

Atreus studied the Mar's torso and the inside lining of his cloak. When he did not find the telltale bulge of a hidden knife, he motioned Rishi to lower his cloak.

"My apologies for doubting you."

"No apologies necessary," said Rishi. "The blame is mine, entirely and without sharing."

Atreus motioned the Mar forward, feeling somewhat guilty for his suspicions. He was hardly blind to Rishi's anger over the sannyasi's decision, but it seemed hypocritical to doubt the Mar when he himself resented having to leave Langdarma. Seema had accused Sune of being cruel, but it seemed to Atreus that the sannyasi was the heartless one. If Langdarma could abide someone as bitter and sharp-tongued as Kumara, surely the valley would not be ruined by the presence of a single ugly westerner.

Seema paused to wait at the central arch, and they all stepped into the murky palace together. A film of cool dew formed on their skin almost instantly, and the air smelled as dank and earthy as a cavern. The trickle of running water came from every direction, echoing through a ghostly forest of alabaster support columns. The only light came from the sparkling stream itself, leading like an arrow straight to a distant aura of silver radiance.

Atreus glanced into the murk alongside the stream and saw the Dweller lurking among the shadows, a nebulous black shape silhouetted against the alabaster columns beyond. The monster seemed as large as an elephant, with a sluglike tail and a formless body covered in dense black scales. Just looking at it filled Atreus with a cold, queasy fear. Seema led the way deeper into the palace. The monster slithered along beside them, laying a swath of white slime in its wake. As it moved, it emitted a low, constant rumble that might have been a gurgling belly or a threatening growl.

The thing swung its gruesome head around, locking gazes with Atreus. Suddenly, he could see nothing but an ebony beak and three scarlet eyes ringed by a mane of writhing black tentacles. He felt goose bumps prickling his skin, shivers running down his spine, and something oily and alien gliding into his mind. He experienced a sensation somewhere between thought and emotion, an instinct of pure, unbridled malevolence that might have been the Dweller's or his own.

Atreus wanted to look away but could not free himself from the monster's gaze. It was as though one of the creature's scaly tentacles had somehow slithered into his skull and wrapped its tiny fingers around his brain, holding his head motionless so that he could neither close his eyes nor look away. His thoughts and memories began to swirl through his mind in a wild cyclone, then he heard his pebble bucket crash to the floor and felt himself step forward.

As his foot came down, the monster blinked. Atreus found himself dangling above the ground, pinned to Yago's massive chest. His face was cold and wet and tingling with the magic of the shining water, and Seema was stooping down before him, cupping her hands in the stream. She stood and hurled another handful into his eyes, nearly

271

blinding him with brilliant flashes of silver.

"That's enough . . . I can't see it anymore!" Atreus said, shaking the water from his eyes. "I can't see anything."

"That will pass soon enough," said Seema. "But you must not allow the Dweller to lure you off. They are very unpredictable, and sometimes it is decades before they release their playmates."

"They?" Atreus demanded. "There's more than one?"

"So it is said," Seema replied. "I have only seen one."

"You told us it wasn't dangerous," growled Yago.

"I said you would not be harmed if you did exactly as I said," replied Seema. "Has Atreus been harmed?"

The ogre placed Atreus on the ground and rapped him between the shoulders. Atreus, still struggling to overcome the water's dazzling effects, stumbled two steps forward before catching his balance.

"I guess you're okay," said the ogre. "But I still don't like coming in here with nothing but rocks. She could be leading us into a trap."

"Seema wouldn't do that," said Atreus.

"Because you two did a fracas?" Yago mocked. Among ogres, it was not uncommon for an unhappy wife to arrange her mate's death. "Maybe that's the reason. It's not like you've had a lot of practice with the real thing."

"Seema's not a thing," Atreus said. "And humans don't treat their mates . . . er, lovers . . . that way."

"Why didn't she warn us about that Dweller?" Yago demanded.

"The Dwellers summon every person differently," Seema said. "I have heard of people being sung to or lured with sweet aromas—"

"And she didn't want us to come here in the first place," Yago continued, speaking over Seema. "She's trying to protect something—just like she was trying to protect Langdarma when she nearly got you killed."

"Yes, and I suspect now she's trying to protect us," said Atreus. He gestured into the shadows, which were empty of the Dweller. "Whatever that thing is, I don't think weapons would do us much good."

He gave Seema an apologetic shake of the head, picked up his pebble bucket, and gestured for her to lead the way. The Dweller did not show itself again, but they could hear it paralleling their course, its heavy body making wet sucking sounds as it slithered through the shadows alongside them.

After Atreus's nose grew accustomed to the cavernlike smell of the place, he began to notice the subtle stench of brimstone wafting through the alabaster forest. At first, he thought it might be some odor the creature was emitting. Then he started to glimpse the jagged throats of rough-hewn tunnels along the palace walls. They had passed into the mountain itself.

As they neared the back of the huge chamber, the forest of alabaster pillars gave way to a black granite wall. The aura of silver radiance continued to brighten, and they soon recognized it as the shining aura of a small pond, formed when an alabaster pillar toppled or was pushed across the stream. The falling column had brought with it a sizable heap of rubble that someone had shaped into a shallow dam. On one rim of this dam sat a small marble bench, and scattered across its surface were a dozen floating lotus blossoms.

Beyond the pond, barely visible through its cloudy aura of brilliance, an even brighter stream of twinkling water cascaded down a stairway from the unseen depths of the palace's inner sanctum. Atreus smiled. The water appeared to be growing more potent as they neared its source.

The Dweller emerged from the shadows beside the pond, its big belly scales hissing across the stone floor as it slithered up to the dam. Atreus's stomach turned cold and queasy again. Without really meaning to, he stopped and averted his gaze, watching from the corner of his eye as the monster stuck its tentacle-festooned head into the water.

The creature looked as though it were drinking, but then it began to stretch forward and twist its neck about, searching for something on the bottom of the pool. Seema continued forward until she could peer over the rubble dam down into the pond, and waved her companions forward.

"This is very special," she whispered. "You must see."

Rishi crept ahead without hesitation, but Atreus found himself lagging behind, struggling with his memory of how easily the monster had taken control of him. Only his bodyguard's looming presence, and the certain knowledge that the ogre would interpret any hesitation as further evidence of Seema's untrustworthiness, compelled Atreus forward at all.

When he reached Seema's side, he bit his cheeks to keep from crying out in wonder. The bottom of the pool was buried in diamonds, rubies, sapphires, every type of precious stone, all in their natural form and some as large as a man's thumb. The Dweller was rummaging through the jewel bed, pulling out the brightest stones and holding each one to an eye for a closer examination. It threw many stones back, usually those cloudier or less deeply colored than their fellows. It placed the other gems into the scarlet mouths at the end of its tentacles and sucked them up inside the scaly appendages.

"Seema, you are a hopeless liar!" cried Rishi. "Did you not tell me just this morning there was no treasure in Langdarma?"

"This is not Langdarma's treasure." Seema smirked at the Mar as though daring him to steal it. "It belongs to the Dwellers, and you must not touch it."

"Are you mad?" Rishi gasped. "Those are diamonds . . . and rubies. They are not meant to fill the gizzard of some overgrown snail!"

"They will not," said Seema. "The Dwellers take them down into the mountains and plant them beneath the far reaches of the Yehimals."

"Where they will not be found for centuries?" A larcenous gleam appeared in Rishi's eye, and he seemed unable to rip his gaze from pool bottom as he said, "What good does that do? It is better for me to take them now. I can carry them straight to the finest markets in the Five Kingdoms."

The Mar dropped his bucket and started forward without awaiting Seema's reply, but Atreus quickly caught him by the shoulder.

"Don't you think the Dweller will object to another pair of hands in its gem bed? Seema promised no harm would come to us as long as we did what she said. I intend to see to it that we honor our agreement."

Rishi's gaze ran along the pool bottom to one of the Dweller's scaly tentacles, then up the appendage to the shapeless bulk of the monster's huge body. The larcenous gleam faded from his eyes, and he seemed slowly to return to his senses.

"You are absolutely right. A thousand gratitudes. I was lost in the monster's fiendish grip and would certainly have brought a swift and terrible end to us all if not for your ready intervention."

"The Dweller calls to each of us in a different way," Seema agreed. "I am glad you have heard yours and returned to us whole."

"We will have to wait until after the monster is gone," the Mar said, then sat down on his pebble bucket, his gaze still fixed on the pool. "Surely, there will be a bucketful left for us."

Seema's face grew stern and she said, "Even if you had so many days, that is not why I brought you here." She jerked Rishi to his feet, snatched his bucket up, and thrust it into his hands. "Let us do what we came to do and be gone."

Seema cast an angry look at Atreus, clearly holding him responsible for the Mar's sacrilege, then climbed onto the dam and dumped her pebble bucket into the shining basin. A tentacle snaked over to inspect the stones and rose briefly out of the pool and slapped the surface, splashing Seema with a stream of shining water. It was impossible to guess whether the gesture was one of thanks or irritation.

Seema motioned the others over, gesturing for them to do as she had. After dumping their buckets, Atreus and Rishi each received a similar splash. When Yago dumped his cask, the Dweller rested its tentacle on his shoulder and rubbed his face, smearing the ogre's orange cheek with white slime.

"Hey!"

Yago knocked the tentacle away and the Dweller responded by flicking the appendage back toward him. When the ogre fell for the feint and brought his other arm across to block, the monster struck, slapping Yago alongside the head so hard that he tumbled backward off the dam. He landed with a deafening crash and sprang instantly to his feet, only to find the tentacle's fingerlike end tendrils waving in his face.

Keeping a cautious eye on the tendrils, Yago began to edge toward the marble bench.

"Yago!" Seema hissed, wrapping both hands around the ogre's wrist and pulling him toward the head of the pool. "What are you doing?"

"You saw," the ogre said as he backed away from the Dweller. "That thing went after me!"

"It was only playing," Atreus said, hoping he was right. "If that monster had been attacking, I doubt any of us would be here."

Seema nodded, her eyes as hard as ice. "I pray we are not about to discover the truth of that," she said, and began to edge along the dam toward the granite stairs. "I do not know what the Dweller will do when we pass the Pool of Gems. I have never been beyond here."

Rishi rolled his eyes, clearly believing this was just one more lie designed to protect Langdarma's secret treasures.

Atreus stepped to the head of the line. "In that case," he said, "let me go first . . . alone. If the Dweller objects, perhaps he will only attack me."

"I'm the bodyguard," objected Yago.

"But it's *my* quest," Atreus said, then made the small leap from the dam to the first step. "What does it mean if I don't go first?"

Yago frowned, and Atreus ascended the staircase while the ogre was still trying to puzzle out the question. The Dweller raised its tentacles and cocked its head, its dark scarlet eyes growing steadily dimmer as Atreus climbed out of the pool's brilliant aura. He averted his own glance and was careful not to lock gazes with the monster. When the trio of scarlet eyes finally faded to nothingness, the creature let out one of its low belly rumbles and splashed its tentacles back into the water.

Atreus found himself standing alone at the entrance to what appeared to be a narrow, vaulted temple. Down each side ran a low meditation platform covered in the moldering remains of folded carpets. On the walls hung tatters of silken tapestries whose patterns and colors had long ago vanished into dust and mildew. The shining stream ran straight up the aisle between the meditation platforms, narrowing in the distance until it finally vanished into the darkness.

"Atreus?" called Seema. For the first time since leaving her hut, there was genuine concern in her voice. "Is everything well?"

"It's fine. Come up."

His companions emerged from the cloudy aura one after

the other, each entering the strange vault in awestricken silence. Once they had gathered, Atreus quietly led the way up the aisle. A low murmur began to resonate in the back of his mind, growing more noticeable as they progressed. It was not a sound, but rather the perception of a sound, an echo that reverberated inside his head without passing through his ears.

The murmur became a rhythmic growl, then a deep, guttural chant, and finally an eerie pulsing roar as mesmerizing as it was maddening. Atreus looked back and found Yago and Rishi staring wide-eyed at the dark walls.

"You hear it too?"

Though Atreus had intended to speak only loud enough to make himself understood, his voice rang through the silent temple like a thunderclap.

Both Yago and Rishi nodded nervously.

"It says, 'Luck and Happiness to all creatures. May the Serene Ones spread their grace over the world,'" explained Seema. "The ancient monks filled the stones with their voices, and now the walls are ringing their chants back to us."

"The walls?" grumbled Yago. "It sounds like ghosts."

Seema whirled on the ogre. "You mustn't say such things," she said. "Not here!"

Yago's orange cheeks darkened. "Sorry," the ogre apologized. "I didn't know they was listening."

Atreus led the way down the aisle. The chanting continued to swell, but as they grew accustomed to it, it became almost calming. They soon found themselves droning along, "*Omna lo reng ge suun, song tse ngampo ge lung pa . . . omna lo reng ge suun, song tse ngampo ge lung pa . . .*"

The chant seemed to free their minds from all awareness of time and space, so they were all taken by surprise when the sparkling stream suddenly narrowed and became a fan-shaped cascade spilling down yet another stone stairway.

For a moment, Atreus just stood there, too mesmerized by the hypnotic rhythm inside his head to realize what he was seeing. His gaze began to rise, following the stream up a long series of steps to the summit of a pyramidal dais.

On top sat a pair of golden yaks, kneeling across from each other and facing a great alabaster altar inlaid with a thousand-spoked wheel of gleaming silver. At one end of the altar sat three elegant vessels: a bronze brazier with incense smoke still rising from its heart, a glass butter lamp with a tiny flame still flickering on its wick, and a jade vase with a single hibiscus blossom still rising from its mouth. At the other end sat three plain objects: a loaf of steaming rice-bread, a tin caster filled with fresh cinnamon, and a sandal-wood lute still resonating from the touch of its last player.

In the center of the altar, resting on its side between the two groups of sacred objects, lay what Atreus had come so far to find, a platinum cup rimmed in sapphires and rubies, from whose mouth spilled a perpetual stream of glittering silver water.

Rishi clutched Atreus's arm and whispered, "Good sir, your wisdom and faith are the measure of all men!" The Mar glanced over his shoulder. "If I may suggest a small precaution, we should see to Seema with every haste."

Atreus tore his eyes from the altar and scowled down at Rishi and said, "*See* to her?"

Rishi winced, then held a finger to his lips. "Quietly, good sir," he cautioned. "I am sure it will only take one scream, and then the Dweller will come running."

Atreus glanced back at Seema, who was standing at the base of the dais as awestruck as he. "Why would she do that?" he asked.

Rishi raised his brow, genuinely surprised. "Is it not obvi-ous?" he whispered. "Your goddess sent you here to *steal* the Fountain of Infinite Grace . . . that is how you are to return the shining water to Erlkazar."

279

The Mar's sly logic stunned Atreus. It was an elegant solution to an otherwise impossible problem, but for the one detail Rishi had overlooked.

"Sune would never want such a thing."

"Want what thing?" asked Seema, finally drawn out of her reverie.

Rishi glanced at Yago, then cocked his head meaningfully in her direction. Atreus scowled and shook his head.

Getting no answer to her question, Seema stepped to Atreus's side and asked, "What is all this whispering?"

"Nothing for you to worry about," Atreus replied.

He was careful not to look in the direction of the alabaster altar, but Seema's suspicions were already raised. She glanced at the toppled cup, her eyes lit in understanding, and she grabbed Atreus's arm with surprising strength.

"You would steal Langdarma's beauty?"

"No," Atreus said, and covered Seema's fingers with his hand. "Sune would not want me to. The last thing she would want is to spoil a place like Langdarma."

Yago rolled his eyes and quickly looked away, but his skepticism was not lost on Rishi.

"What do you think, my friend?" asked the Mar. "Is this Sune not a jealous goddess, who might very well resent this stream of beauty pouring forth from her ancient rival's temple?"

The ogre gave a grudging shrug. "She's fickle enough," he said. "I wouldn't put anything past her."

Seema paled, turning to call the Dweller.

Atreus pulled her back, clamping a hand over her mouth. "You have nothing to worry about," he assured her. "Even if Sune did want the fountain, how could we get it past the Dweller? I'm sure it would frown on us stealing the source of its shining pool."

"How would it know until it was too late to stop us?" asked Rishi, smiling.

FACES OF DECEPTION

The Mar bounded up the dais and snatched the cup off the altar, eliciting a muffled scream from Seema.

"Put that back!" Atreus ordered.

"Have no worry, I am not stealing the cup," said Rishi. "I am only demonstrating how such a thing might be possible, in case the good sir should in his own judgment consider it necessary."

"I won't."

Rishi paid Atreus no attention, began to descend the dais, and said, "You see?" The Mar stopped two steps above, holding the cup sideways so that the water continued to pour out at an even rate. "In this manner, we could advance all the way to the stairs above the Pool of Gems, where we might wait until the Dweller wandered away on its business. Or perhaps we would send someone to distract it while the others fled with the Fountain of Infinite Grace."

"How do we escape Langdarma before the sannyasi catches us?" Atreus asked, more to prove the impossibility of Rishi's plan than because he was really interested. Or so he told himself. "From what little I recall, the Passing was something of a challenge."

Rishi's smile grew confident. "Langdarma is difficult to enter, but easy to leave," he said. "Yago and I learned of many exits while we were searching for the fountain."

Seema's body stiffened. She began to struggle in Atreus's arms, going so far as to bite his palm. He winced, then pointed his chin at the altar.

"Put it back," Atreus said, feeling Seema's chin grow slick with his blood. "Sune didn't send me here to steal the fountain or anything else."

Rishi's eyes hardened and he demanded, "Do you never think of anyone beyond yourself?" He glanced back toward the alabaster altar. "I am sure that any two of those treasures would make me the wealthiest bahrana in the Five Kingdoms!"

281

"I'm tired of telling you." Atreus caught Yago's eye swung his chin toward the Mar, and said, "Feel free to break an arm if he doesn't give it to you."

Instead of rushing to obey, the ogre asked, "You sure about that?"

"What?" Atreus gasped, astonished by Yago's disobedience. "You can't be with him!"

Yago scowled, clearly insulted. " 'Course not!" he said. "I'm just trying to figure out why you want to stay ugly for the rest of your life." The ogre glanced at Rishi and added, "He's right about Sune. You know he is. I didn't come all this way to see you go home empty-handed."

Atreus fell silent, weighing the ogre's opinion and hating himself for it. To even consider the possibility that Sune had sent him after the cup was a betrayal of Seema's love, yet the way she continued to struggle in his arms made it clear that she believed he had already forsaken her. He glanced down and noticed his blood drops falling into the stream of sparkling water and turning into little beads of gold. Everyone but him, it seemed, knew exactly what the goddess expected.

"On my heart," Atreus growled. "How I wish I could stay."

"But the sannyasi will not permit it, and so he deserves what he shall receive." Rishi smirked, then started back up the dais. "Come along, Yago, and help me retrieve the rest of the treasure."

"No," Atreus said, closing his eyes. "Don't do it."

Seema stopped struggling, astonished, and Rishi spun on his heel, spraying her and Atreus with a stream of shining water.

"What?" the Mar demanded.

Atreus opened his eyes again. "We came to fill the vial." He pointed his chin toward the cup. "Put it back."

Rishi glared at Seema icily, clearly blaming her for the loss of his fortune. A crafty gleam came to his eye.

"You are very clever, good sir. If the water loses its sparkle again, we can always return for the cup in the morning. But how will you pay me with all your gold lost in the river? Even the clothes on your back are not your own."

Seema tensed at Rishi's words, but she did not resume her struggle. Though even Atreus could not say what he would do if the water lost its sparkle again, he sensed that Seema hoped as much as he that he would not have to make the choice. He glanced in Yago's direction and nodded.

"Give me that!" Yago's gangling arm lashed out, ripping the cup from Rishi's hands and inadvertently turning it upside down.

It was as though the ogre had punched a hole in the bottom of a lake. A raging torrent of water poured from the mouth of the chalice, instantly sweeping the legs out from under Atreus and Rishi and sweeping them down the aisle.

Fearing the Mar would take advantage of the situation, Atreus released Seema and grabbed Rishi instead. They tumbled a dozen paces down the aisle, before Yago finally thought to right the cup. The torrent ended as swiftly as it began, depositing Atreus and his captive among the moldy-smelling rugs on a meditation platform.

"There is no need to crush me," Rishi wheezed. "You are the ugly one. If you do not want to steal the fountain, then I am as willing as you to leave it behind."

"I'll believe that when we're back in the Five Kingdoms," Atreus said.

He glanced up and saw Seema across the aisle, wiping the moldy remnants of a carpet off her cloak. The flood itself had spent its fury washing onto the meditation platforms and was slowly draining back into its main channel. Yago stood near the bottom of the dais, holding the cup upright and staring at its gem-studded rim as though he were clutching a live cobra. In this position, the fountain looked much the same as any other chalice. There was no water spilling over its rim and only a faint aura shining up from its interior.

Atreus dragged Rishi over to Yago's side, exchanging the indignant Mar for the platinum cup.

"Keep an eye on our thieving friend."

"Why do you insist on insulting me, good sir?" Rishi protested. "Did I not give you my word? I have completely forgotten the Fountain of Infinite Grace. If you cannot see that Langdarma has nothing to fear from me, then you are certainly the fool they took you for in Queen Rosalind's court!"

"I've been called worse than a fool." Atreus glanced back at Seema, who was watching him with veiled emotions, and added, "Perhaps rightfully so."

Atreus climbed the dais and laid the cup on the alabaster altar, restarting the flow of shining water. Though he had reached the end of his quest, he experienced no exultation or relief, only a queasy sort of guilt that made him feel hollow and cold inside. He removed the empty vial from his cloak and held it beneath the falling water and, as the flow spilled over his fingers, took no joy in the sweet tickle of its magic.

When the vial was full, Atreus corked it, carefully wrapped it inside a cushioning rag, and began to descend the dais.

"Ain't you gonna take a drink?" asked Yago, oblivious to Atreus's remorseful mood. "I'd kinda like to see you handsome."

"Yes, drink," sneered Seema. "If the magic here is as potent as you hope, you will be handsome forever."

Stung by the sarcasm in her voice, Atreus started to decline, then realized she was right. Whether the magic lasted or not, he stood to lose nothing by drinking, and it just might be what Sune had intended all along. Anything was worth a try, if it meant avoiding the decision of whether or not to steal the fountain.

Atreus knelt beside the altar, then opened his mouth under the cup and let the shining water pour down his throat. He experienced the same airy giddiness as before, save that it was a hundred times as strong, so strong that he felt its radiance shining inside every part of his body, filling him from head to toe with a sweet burning he swore would turn him to smoke.

A terrible thought occurred to Atreus then, and he turned to see if he could read any sign of betrayal in Seema's face. She grimaced and looked away in disappointment, but Yago smiled broadly.

"Now, if that ain't a wonderful sight!" said the ogre. "I wish they could see you back in the Church of Beauty!"

"Yes, he is as handsome as a prince," drolled Rishi. The Mar twisted around to look up at Yago. "Now, perhaps we should turn our concerns to the real danger in our midst. Seema certainly knows whether or not the magic will last, and even as we speak, she is most likely plotting to set the Dweller upon us."

"Rishi, how can you say such a thing?" Seema asked. She appeared more amused than affronted. "Even if the Dweller were mine to control, to do such a thing would be to kill . . . and you know I would never kill, not even to protect Langdarma."

17

Atreus stood with his companions at the temple exit, staring down the granite stairs into the cloudy brilliance below. The Dweller was still down there, calmly sloshing through the Pool of Gems with its long tentacles. Though the dam had obviously survived Yago's flood, there was no telling what the monster had made of the change in flow or if it had noticed at all. Atreus suspected it had. As alien as the creature was, it struck him as anything but stupid.

"Are you worried the Dweller will sense your guilty conscience?" Seema asked.

"My conscience is clear," Atreus replied. "I have taken nothing but water."

"Today, but what of tomorrow?" Seema said as she stepped around Atreus and started down the stairs. "The Dweller knows me. I will go down first and watch how it behaves."

When Atreus made no move to stop her, Rishi cried, "Are you mad? She will run and sound the alarm and perhaps leave us trapped in here with the Dweller!"

Atreus caught Seema's shoulder and asked, "Is he right?"

"Why should that matter?" Seema asked. "If you are taking nothing but water, no one will try to stop you."

"Maybe I'll go first."

Atreus pulled her gently back up the stairs, then descended into the aura. The sloshing sounds ceased, and a few steps later he saw the monster's amorphous bulk silhouetted in the brilliance below. It swung its head in his direction, fixing its trio of red eyes on him and clacking its beak. Atreus averted his gaze and continued down the stairs, his heart hammering in his chest.

When he reached the edge of the pond, one of the scaly tentacles, swollen and lumpy with gems, rose to flit over his body. He waited and allowed it to inspect him. The finger-tendrils squeezed the pocket containing the vial, apparently trying to make out the shape of the container beneath his cloak. Atreus remained as still as a statue until he felt the tiny mouth nibbling at the cloth.

"Hold on!"

Very gently, he removed the vial and unwrapped it, displaying the shimmering contents within. The finger-tendrils danced over the glass briefly. Then the monster seemed to lose interest and returned to searching for its gems. Atreus finally exhaled and went to stand by the marble bench where they had left their empty pebble buckets.

"It's okay to come down," Atreus called, returning the vial to his pocket, "but don't be surprised if it inspects you."

As Seema descended the stairs, Atreus stood across from the Dweller, trying to keep an eye on the monster without meeting its gaze. Of them all she seemed the least likely to be attacked, but he did not want to take any chances with her safety. Even without getting her injured or killed, he felt vile enough. He still did not know what he would do if the water's sparkle faded, and he hated himself for being such a weak and wicked person.

The Dweller let Seema pass with only a cursory examination. She came to stand near Atreus on the dam, just out of arm's reach. He did not try to apologize or speak to her. There was nothing he could say she did not know already.

Yago and Rishi came next, the ogre clasping the Mar's shoulder and carefully sidestepping to fit his huge feet on the wet stairs. As they neared the bottom, the Dweller swung a tentacle over to inspect the pair as it had Atreus.

Rishi stared wide-eyed at the approaching appendage and forgot to watch his footing, missed a step, and tumbled screeching into the pool. Yago tripped over the fallen Mar and splashed down on top of him.

Atreus's first thought was of the Dweller. He snatched a bucket off the bench and raised his arm to throw, but the monster remained on its side of the pool, tentacles hovering above the frothing water as Yago and Rishi struggled to untangle themselves. Rishi seemed particularly confused, clutching at the ogre's heavy cloak while at the same time pushing him off. Yago simply tried not to crush his panicked companion, holding himself up over the Mar on splayed limbs.

Atreus stepped into the pond to help. The water was only waist deep, but the loose bottom made moving difficult. Though the distance was a mere two paces, it took several moments to catch the Mar's arm and haul him out from under Yago.

As soon as Rishi's head cleared the water, he cried, "A thousand blessings on you!" He glanced back at Yago's sprawled form. "Had you not rescued me, I would certainly have drowned beneath that great buffoon."

"Hardly," Atreus said, dragging Rishi toward the edge of the pool. "All you had to do was stop panicking."

Atreus demonstrated by standing the Mar on his feet.

As soon as his boots touched bottom, Rishi's face flushed with embarrassment.

"Oh, what an ox I am!" He turned to the ogre and said, "My apologies, as profuse as the luxuries that once filled this palace. First I trip you, and then I blame you for my own clumsiness."

As the Mar spoke, Seema's jaw dropped. "Yago!" she cried. "Watch your—"

A wet slap sounded behind Atreus, then Yago bellowed in pain and splashed into the water.

So astonished was Atreus that he did not instantly comprehend that the ogre was being attacked. By the time he spun around, the Dweller had turned the surface of the pool into a churning mass of froth, and he could see nothing but flailing arms and lashing tentacles. Rishi was already wading into battle, one hand thrust down under the water, struggling to pull something from his boot.

Atreus stepped toward the fight, demanding of no one in particular, "What happened?"

Yago bellowed and screamed, pummeling the Dweller's head with his boot heels. One arm was wedged down inside the tentacle, but the other was clutching the tip of the scaly appendage, struggling to keep its waving finger-tendrils away from his face.

Rishi's hand came up holding a long, thin knife. The Mar hurled himself into the attack, stabbing madly at the black coil wrapped around Yago's chest. On the third try, the blade finally slipped between two scales. A whistle trilled from the monster's beak, and the tentacle loosened. Atreus wrapped his arms around the appendage and began to pull, half blinded by the dazzling gleam of splashing water.

A second tentacle came up beneath the Mar, heaving him out of the pool. Rishi cried out and arced away over the dam, releasing his hold on the knife. There was a dull thud as he struck the wall, another as he fell to the floor, and after that only silence.

At last, Atreus opened enough space for Yago to free his trapped arm. The ogre lunged for shore, releasing his grasp on the tentacle to grab the marble bench. The scaly tip shot toward his face, its powerful finger-tendrils digging his eye from the socket. Yago howled in pain, but snatched the bench off the dam and smashed the edge down on the Dweller's head. The tentacle slackened, and Atreus stumbled backward, pulling the coils open as he moved. The ogre took advantage of the opening to twist around and slam his makeshift club into the Dweller's face.

The bench cracked in two, and the tentacle went limp. Atreus fell, landing up to his chin in water. The Dweller's body seemed to sag and spread, and for a moment the monster appeared unconscious. Yago dropped his broken weapon and raised a hand to his mangled eye, roaring in pain.

"No! You must not touch it," cried Seema. To Atreus's surprise, she was in the water beside him, reaching out to take the ogre's arm and guide him to the bank.

Then the Dweller lurched forward, heaving its bulk onto the dam and thrusting its head completely into the pool. The resulting wave washed over Atreus's face, filling his eyes with dazzling sparkles of silver light. He heard Yago bellow, then there came a tremendous splash and another surge of water. Atreus stood and reached toward the sound. Through his spotty vision, he could barely make out the ogre stretched across the water, surrounded by lashing tentacles, flailing his long arms in a mad attempt to keep his head above the surface.

Atreus wiped the water from his eyes and the image grew a little clearer. He saw that two of the monster's tentacles lay over Yago's shoulders, trying to pull him down under the water. A third tentacle lay floating just beneath the surface, the handle of Rishi's knife protruding from its flesh. The rest of the appendages, about half a dozen, were sticking up out of the water, ringing the ogre's wailing figure.

Seema dodged forward and grabbed Yago's head, holding it up so the ogre could breathe. A tentacle wrapped itself around her waist and tossed her against the dam. Atreus slipped forward and grabbed Rishi's knife, plucking it from its scaly sheath and unleashing a gush of brown blood. The murky syrup turned instantly to silver and dropped out of sight in the magic water.

A tentacle slithered around Atreus's waist. He hauled it out of the water and brought the knife down. Though hardly as powerful as Yago, he was much stronger than Rishi, and the blade shattered the thick scale, sinking deep into the Dweller's flesh. The monster flailed its other tentacles, but slipped one around Atreus's waist, and began to lift.

He brought the knife down again, burying it to the hilt. When the Dweller still did not release him, he twisted the blade, working it back and forth, slashing muscle and severing tendons. The tentacle fell limp, and Atreus stepped to Yago's side, grabbing another appendage and driving his weapon through the six inches of scale and sinew. The Dweller beat the water again and drew its bulk off the dam, pulling both Yago and its own head out of the shining pool.

What Atreus saw made him wish the monster had stayed in the water. The thing had caught Yago's leg in its beak and was frantically snapping its way up his thigh. Long sections of bone lay exposed to the open air, and the ogre's blood was pouring into the pool and sinking to the bottom in a steady cascade of golden nuggets. Atreus grabbed a handful of Yago's cloak, then swung around and slashed at one of the monster's red eyes.

The orb exploded in a gout of frothing bronze blood. Yago screamed as the beak clamped down on his leg. Atreus reached over to slash another eye, when a thick tentacle slapped his neck and began to tighten around his throat, fluttering its finger-tendrils before his eyes and pulling him away from the Dweller's face. Atreus lashed out at the monster's head but felt no telling cascade of hot blood.

He glimpsed Seema stepping in beneath him with a bucket of shining water. He tried to call her off but could not force the words past his throat. His vision began to darken, and the last thing he saw was Seema flinging the bucket at the monster's eyes.

"Strike, Atreus!" Seema's voice sounded tinny and weak, as though she were calling from a great distance. "Strike!"

Atreus swung blindly. The knife bounced off the Dweller's scaly face, and he struck again.

The blow never landed.

He felt himself arcing through the air until his legs slammed into an alabaster pillar. The impact whirled him around, and he hit the floor spinning like a top. Both knees erupted into aching pain. He clenched his teeth and scrambled to his feet. His head was reeling and the knife was still in his hand, but when he finally collected his bearings and found the pool, his heart sank.

It was already retreating through the alabaster forest, belly scales clattering on the floor and Yago screaming in its beak.

"No! Stop!"

Of course, the Dweller did not obey. Atreus lurched after the monster at his best sprint, but even without aching knees, he was no match for the thing's speed. The creature pulled steadily away, growing fainter and fainter until it finally disappeared into the murk.

"Atreus, wait!" called Seema. "The Dweller does not need light, but we do."

Atreus turned to find Seema approaching with two buckets, a small aura of silver radiance hovering above each. He took one and set off through the alabaster maze, following the Dweller's wet slime trail to the mouth of one of its dark tunnels. Yago's voice was echoing up from somewhere below, alternately cursing the beast and screaming in anguished incoherence.

Atreus turned to Seema and said, "You don't have to come. In fact, I'd rather you didn't."

Seema raised her brow. "Why?" she asked. "If you are thinking that you will slay the Dweller—"

"Not exactly, but I've caused you enough trouble without getting you killed."

"Getting me killed would be the least of the troubles you have caused me," Seema said. "Besides, if I do not come, who will rescue you?"

Atreus nodded, more in thanks than consent, then stepped over a small rim of loose rock into the tunnel. The passage sloped down at a steep angle, with rough-hewn sides and a vaguely circular profile just large enough for the Dweller. Innumerable passes of the monster's slimy body had coated the walls in a chalky white powder that glistened brightly in the watery light and enclosed Atreus and Seema in a small bubble of glimmering radiance. Yago's screams continued to grow increasingly faint as his captor carried him deeper into its lair, and it was not long before the tunnel split into two branches.

"I hope you have a good ear for echoes," said Seema.

"We'll have other hints." Atreus stooped down and traced a line in the wet slime on the floor.

The tunnel became a warren of tunnels, then a maze, and still the Dweller continued its descent. Yago's screams grew sporadic and weak, but the slime trail remained fresh. They had little trouble following their quarry. Atreus lost all track of time and direction, and eventually the ogre's cries vanished altogether. Seema said nothing, but Atreus knew she was wondering the same thing he was. Had Yago finally died, or had the monster simply carried him beyond their hearing?

They followed the slime trail down into a tunnel so steep they had to sit on their haunches and kick their heels into the floor to keep from sliding. About halfway down, Atreus heard a low moan coming from a side passage.

"Yago?"

More groans, then came the pained answer: "No." It was the ogre's voice, weak and languid with delirium. "Go 'way—"

A terrifying, incoherent scream followed, and Atreus's first thought was that his friend was trying to warn him of an ambush, but if that were so, Yago would have said something simple like, "Watch out for the ambush." Atreus slipped into the side passage, trying not to gag on the awful, bloody smell of the place, then advanced with Seema at his back. Yago continued to groan, but it was impossible to say whether he knew of their presence.

They passed yet another side passage angling down into the mountain. Low animal sounds began to fill the tunnel, then Atreus saw a pair of red eyes reflecting the light from his bucket.

He stopped and whispered, "It's the Dweller. Stay back."

This time, Seema did not argue. She ducked into the side passage and watched around the corner as Atreus crept forward, his eyes averted to avoid locking gazes with the monster. He had advanced only a few steps when the glow from his bucket illuminated Yago's mangled form.

The ogre was lying in a pool of blood, holding one hand over his good eye. His mangled eye was dangling out on his cheek, and his wounded leg lay stripped to the bone from the hip down. The Dweller was holding him down with two tentacles and shuffling through his cloak with four more. Able to stand the sight no longer, Atreus raised his knife and started forward.

The Dweller raised its head. Atreus braced himself for its attack, preparing a slash-and-dodge defense, but the monster simply opened its beak. There was a great whooshing of air, so powerful that a breeze cooled the back of his neck, then the beast raised all six of its uninjured tentacles.

Atreus dropped his bucket and fled, flinging himself into the side passage just as a tremendous *whumpf* rolled down the tunnel behind him. A terrific impact spun him half around, and his entire flank erupted into stinging pain. He bounced off the wall and began to roll down the chalky floor.

A few revolutions later, Seema caught his arm and hauled him to a stop. "Atreus!" she cried. "How badly are you hurt?"

He glanced down and discovered that his whole flank had turned wet and red from his ribcage to his knee. He found Rishi's knife and cut away the tattered remains of his cloak, revealing a mass of raw and bloody flesh pocked with dozens of tiny punctures. From the bottom of many holes shined the colorful reflections of small gemstones.

"The Dweller must be frightened of you indeed," gasped Seema. "To sacrifice its jewels. . . ."

"I'd rather it had kept them," said Atreus.

He allowed himself a moment to test the strength of his savaged flank, then scrambled back into the main passage and advanced by the weak light of his overturned bucket. The Dweller was again snuffling through Yago's cloak, but it stopped and raised its head as he drew near. Atreus lifted his dagger and charged, determined to engage the monster before it had time to hurl some other surprise at him.

Instead, the Dweller let out a long, plaintive whistle and retreated, halting a few paces beyond tentacle range. Atreus stopped, astonished, and cautiously kneeled at Yago's side. The ogre's chest continued to rise and fall, but he seemed unaware that anyone was with him. Atreus took his hand.

"Yago?"

The ogre turned his head slightly, but continued to hold his palm over his good eye, protecting it from the Dweller. His orange skin had paled to a sickly ivory.

"Atreus . . . don't look." His voice was a bare whisper. "Don't want you to . . . to see what I let happen."

"Okay, I won't look."

"Good." Yago squeezed his hand. "Atreus . . . it got . . . got one of my eyes."

"No, it didn't."

"The eye is here, on your cheek," Seema said. She kneeled beside Atreus, then gently laid the eye back in its swollen socket. "It just fell out."

The ogre sighed in relief, then seemed to realize that something was amiss. "Hey, how you'd know?" He uncovered his good eye and raised his head, scowling. "You cheated!"

Atreus nodded.

"You see? I ain't so dumb after all," the ogre said, letting his head drop back to the floor. "And Atreus, I . . . I didn't really forget your mom's name."

"I know."

"It was . . ." The ogre winced. "She told me not to tell . . . no one. But I didn't know if she meant you."

"It doesn't matter," Atreus said. "You kept her secret."

"Yeah . . . I did."

Yago smiled, then his hand opened and fell away.

"Yago?"

Atreus pressed his ear to the ogre's chest and heard nothing—no heartbeat, no breath, no final groan.

The strength left Atreus in a rush. He slumped forward and stretched his arms across Yago's massive torso, embracing him in death as he had never done in life. It was not the ogre way of grieving, but there were no handy trees to mangle or walls to smash down. Besides, Atreus was a man, and there was no ogre name for what Yago had been to him—less than a father, but so much more than a bodyguard: Protector, drill-master, dutiful servant, loyal comrade, only friend.

Tears began to well up in Atreus's eyes. Yago would have ridiculed crying as a mark of weakness, but even growing up among the Shieldbreakers had not made Atreus enough of an ogre to keep from weeping. He sat up and wiped his eyes, determined not to dampen Yago's body with tears the ogre would have scorned.

" *'Til them mountains crumble,*" Atreus whispered.

It was the last line of the Shieldbreaker requiem, spoken only in honor of faithful warriors whose memories the tribe promised to keep alive. Atreus ran his hand over Yago's face and closed the ogre's one good eye. He was overcome by such a profound sense of guilt that he broke into a sweat and had to turn away.

"I am so sorry, my friend," Atreus said grasping the ogre's cold arm. He could not look at the ogre.

"I should never have brought you here. This is my fault."

"I am not so certain," said Seema.

She kneeled next to Atreus and began to go through Yago's cloak. The Dweller let out a warning whistle and slithered closer, but she ignored the monster and continued her search.

"What are you doing?" Atreus asked.

"Was the Dweller not looking for something?" She pulled a handful of small stones from Yago's pocket, and her face fell in disappointment. "Gems," she said. "This is the reason he was attacked. But why did Yago not listen to me? I warned you all not to touch the Dweller's jewels."

"Yago *did* listen to you. He didn't steal those," Atreus said. He took the gems and tossed them in the Dweller's direction. "Back in Rivenshield, we have chests filled with jewels."

Seema frowned, confused. "How come the stones were in his pocket?" She had hardly asked the question before her jaw dropped. "Rishi!"

Atreus nodded and rolled Yago onto his face—a Shieldbreaker custom to protect the eyes of the dead from crows—then stood and started back up the passage at a hobbling trot.

Seema grabbed her bucket and followed close behind. "You don't think . . ."

"I do," Atreus said. "Rishi set this up so he could steal the

297

Fountain of Infinite Grace . . . and everything else."

"I saw him hit the wall," Seema said, her voice far from confident. "He did not even groan. He had to be dead or unconscious."

"Or a good actor," Atreus added. "And Rishi is a very good actor."

18

By the time they found their way out of the Dweller's
warren, Atreus's wounds ached as terribly as his heart. His
whole flank was sore and swollen, and every step sent a
fresh rush of agony surging through his joints. He did not
care, nor did he make any concession to his injuries, pushing his body through its torment as only a man raised by
ogres could. The question in his mind and Seema's was the
same: had Rishi planned Yago's death?

They knew the answer as soon as they climbed out of the
tunnel. Save for a faint aura of radiance still lingering over
the Pool of Gems, the alabaster palace was as dark as a crypt.
Even from the edge of the vast chamber, they could see that
the stairs into the temple were dry, as was the hallway
leading to the exit. Rishi had stolen the Fountain of Infinite
Grace, and no doubt everything else on the altar as well.

"I'll kill him!"

"You mustn't say such things, not even for what Rishi has
done," Seema told him in a voice as sad as it was gentle.
"Your anger will destroy you as surely as his greed has
destroyed him."

"It's Yago that his greed destroyed," Atreus countered.
His hand ached from clutching the knife so hard. "And
Langdarma."

"I do not see how that makes him different from you.
Had you awakened ugly tomorrow, would you have left the
cup in its place?"

Atreus answered in a bitter voice, "Now I'll never know, will I?"

He set off toward the exit, not looking at Seema. She was

at least half right. The results for Langdarma would have been the same whether Rishi stole the cup or he did. Perhaps it was a blessing to have escaped the temptation. Had he yielded, Atreus had no illusions about how he would have felt about himself.

Atreus reached the exit and stepped out onto the gallery, then heard Seema gasp as she followed him through the door. The reflecting pool below had turned as brown as the Dweller's blood, and the meadow beside it had faded to the dead gold of parched grass. Even the vast valley of Langdarma itself was fading from emerald to amber.

At the edge of the meadow stood the milky-winged figure of the sannyasi, weeping tears of silver. Atreus's rage turned instantly to remorse. Had Seema not been standing behind him, he would have retreated into the palace and gone to lose himself in the Dweller's warren.

The sannyasi's silver eyes rose and lingered on him, looking less angry than shocked. Atreus could not bring himself to move or speak. It required all his strength simply not to look away.

After a time, Seema took Atreus's hand and led him down the stairs. "Have no fear. The sannyasi would never harm us, no matter what we have done."

This seemed a small consolation to Atreus, whose own guilt was eating away at his insides. He would almost rather have been stricken dead on the spot, but there was still the matter of Rishi to deal with.

The sannyasi watched them descend the stairs and cross the meadow, then turned his silver gaze on Seema alone.

"You brought this man here?"

Seema stared at the ground and said, "Him, and his friends Rishi and Yago."

Something inside the sannyasi appeared to collapse. His wings drooped, he seemed suddenly smaller, and his eyes grew old.

Seema continued, "There was a fight. The Dweller killed Yago. Rishi stole the cup of shining waters and probably six other sacred items as well."

The sannyasi only nodded and turned to look out over the valley. He remained silent for a long time, then spoke without looking at Seema.

"You have done the unpardonable. Langdarma will suffer terribly for it. I doubt your healing magic will return."

Seema squeezed her eyes shut, but could not quite keep the tears from flowing down her cheeks. "I understand," she managed to say.

"There is more." The sannyasi still did not look at her as he said, "I will go and organize a search for this Rishi and the Seven Sacred Gifts. If they are not recovered, I fear you must leave Langdarma and never return."

Seema started to nod, but this was more than Atreus could bear.

"You're not being fair," he said. "Seema isn't to blame. I forced her—"

"That is not so," interrupted Seema. She grasped Atreus's arm. "My reasons for bringing you here were as selfish as yours for wanting to come. To claim otherwise is to cheapen what there was between us."

The word "was" hit Atreus like a hammer. Though he had already guessed the price of his betrayal, this was the first time Seema had confirmed the loss.

The sannyasi studied Atreus for a moment and said, "I am sorry. This pain I cannot bear for you."

"And what of his wounds?" Seema gestured at Atreus's mangled side. "Will you heal them?"

The sannyasi glanced down at Atreus's knife, still brown and crusted with the Dweller's blood. "The wounds will heal in time, but for now it is better to let pain temper his violent heart."

"Temper my violent heart?" Atreus's anger returned in a

301

flood. "You don't know violence until you've traveled with Rishi Saubhari. He's a murdering thief who won't hesitate to kill everyone you send after him. Help me catch him, and you'll save a dozen lives."

"And take one." The sannyasi's eyes grew stern and he continued, "You are as much a killer as your friend, and I will not help in your wickedness. To slay a man over the shining waters would be an evil beyond redemption. It would draw a cloak of darkness over Langdarma so black that the Serene Ones would never find us again."

The sannyasi paused to calm himself, then spread his wings and turned toward the edge of the meadow.

"You will not defy me in this."

He stepped off the cliff and dropped into the valley. A moment later his silver wake was curving around the Turquoise Cliffs into the basin where Seema lived.

As soon as the gleaming trail had faded from the sky, Atreus turned to Seema and said, "I have no right to ask you for anything, and I'm not asking for myself, but your sannyasi doesn't know Rishi."

"He knows you."

Seema's eyes dropped to the knife in Atreus's hand.

Atreus thrust the weapon into his belt. "You must understand what I'm saying. Rishi has a plan . . . just like he did when he tricked the Dweller into attacking Yago. He wouldn't have risked that without knowing that he could escape me. If he can escape me, no one from Langdarma is going to stop him. He'll kill anyone who tries."

Seema remained silent for several moments, then looked away. "I can't defy the sannyasi," she said. "Not in this."

"You'd rather let Rishi steal the cup?"

"Than let you kill him over it? Yes."

Seema stepped back, met Atreus's gaze, and shook her head.

"You are a good man, Atreus, but a weak one," she said.

"You are no match for your passions, and if I help you again, you will only end up killing Rishi or stealing the cup for yourself . . . or both, which would be as bad for you as for Langdarma."

"I am also a man of my word," said Atreus. "I swear on my life—no, on Yago's memory—I swear to return the cup."

Seema glanced out over the browning valley and considered his words for a long time, then finally pointed to the knife in his belt.

"What of Rishi?"

Atreus closed his eyes and slowly exhaled, letting go of his anger, or trying to. Certainly, Yago would have expected a fellow Shieldbreaker to avenge his death, and in his heart Atreus longed to do his friend this honor. But he could see for himself the harm that killing had already brought to Langdarma, and he knew that the sannyasi had not been exaggerating when he claimed that Rishi's death would destroy it forever. For now, at least, Atreus would have to put aside the ogre part of his nature.

"I doubt I can ever forgive what Rishi has done." Atreus opened his eyes again and held out the knife. "But," he continued, "I think I can find the strength not kill him."

"Good. You will be a happier man for it." Seema took the knife, then said, "I remember Rishi talking about the ways to leave Langdarma. If he and Yago investigated this as carefully as he claimed, he will know he can escape only by the Roaring Way."

"The Roaring Way?"

"The great gorge at the end of Langdarma," Seema said as she turned and pointed toward the haze-shrouded cliffs at the far end of the valley. "It is the only route the sannyasi will not block. There is no return, and no one knows where it goes, so no man has ever been brave enough to enter it."

"Then that's exactly what Rishi will try," Atreus agreed.

Seema glanced up at the afternoon's graying sky. "Let us go." She started across the meadow, then added, "Even Rishi will not run the gorge in the dark. If we hurry, we can be there waiting at dawn."

Seema led the way back along the ledge and through the cave, then they spent the rest of the day descending a long, steep trail into the main valley below. By the time they reached a tiny hamlet on the river, dusk was already falling over the little shanties perched on the shore. Even at this late hour, the townspeople were gathered in the village circle, murmuring in their strange language and lamenting the brown tide sweeping their valley.

As soon as Seema heard their angry voices, she took Atreus's hand and circled around the outskirts of the village. On the other side, they found a dozen flat-bottomed boats beached on the muddy shore, half hidden beneath a copse of drooping willow trees. She selected a pair of huge oars from an assortment leaning against a low-hanging limb, slipped the nearest boat into the water, and quietly guided them into the current.

The river was one of those flat giants that swept along spinning off huge eddies and churning up water-heads the size of elephants, and it was not long before the swift current had carried Seema and Atreus hundreds of paces downstream.

Once they were safely beyond earshot of the village, Atreus asked, "Isn't stealing frowned on in Langdarma?"

Seema shrugged. "Our need is great," she said, "and I do not think the villagers would have been very kind to you had we asked."

"I wouldn't have expected them to be."

Atreus glanced around at the deepening gloom. Already the light had grown so dim that the trees along shore were mere silhouettes. With no moon to brighten the sky, night would bring darkness as black as a cave. "How are we going to see?"

"With our ears," Seema answered. "But now you must tend your wounds and rest. Whatever tomorrow brings, you will need all the strength you can gather."

Atreus washed his mangled flank, pitching the gems from his wounds into the water, but rest proved difficult. As quiet as the river was, it produced an alarming array of gurgles and bubbles. He spent the entire night staring into the inky darkness, expecting to be overturned at any moment by some unseen log or sandbar. Once they actually struck the shore, but the broad-beamed boat was as steady as a barge and simply spun off, then hung idle in an eddy until Seema could collect her bearings. The few rocks they encountered came almost as a relief, as the stones caused such a loud rushing that it was easy to steer around them.

After many hours of tense darkness, the river seemed to grow slow and quiet. Atreus began to feel a soft, almost imperceptible thunder in the pit of his stomach, and Seema started to row. When he offered to take her place, she only laughed and said she would rather trust her life to her own ears.

The subtle rumbling built to an audible roar, and soon the roar started to reverberate inside Atreus's chest. A series of rhythmic booms echoed up the river, the sound of huge waves hurling themselves one after another against the granite walls of the Roaring Gorge. He could almost feel the river gathering itself beneath him, filling him with the water's mad energy. He imagined being drawn down the canyon and sucked into the crashing cataracts in utter darkness, being hurled against an unseen cliff and splashing into the black water amidst the splinters of their boat, being swept to a watery grave in the unexplored vastness beyond.

Oblivious to Atreus's growing concern, Seema merely continued to row. When the current finally began to draw them onward again, she abruptly changed directions and worked madly to maneuver upstream into the still shelter of a shore eddy.

"Now we wait," she said. "Sleep, and I will watch for the dawn."

"Sleep may be difficult," Atreus said, settling down in the bow of the boat. "This isn't the quietest place in Langdarma, and I've got a lot on my mind."

But the pulsing crash of the Roaring Way proved surprisingly soothing. Atreus soon fell into a deep, rejuvenating sleep, and it seemed only moments later when Seema began to shake him, one hand covering his mouth to keep him from crying out.

"Wake up," she whispered. "Rishi is coming."

Atreus opened his eyes and found himself staring up into a huge willow tree, its drooping boughs silhouetted against the dim gray sky. Beyond the stern of the boat, less than a thousand yards downriver, loomed the soaring black throat of the Roaring Way. It was a narrow crashing slot of froth and foam, cut straight down the face of the towering granite cliff that shielded Langdarma from the unknown wilderness.

Seema was looking in the opposite direction, her gaze fixed on something well upriver. Atreus sat up and turned, then hissed in anguish as he tore open a dozen scabs. His flank was instantly coated in ooze, and his whole body felt achy and hot. Daggers of pain lanced outward from his swollen hip, shooting down his leg into his foot and up under his ribs as high as his shoulder.

Seema frowned and said, "Atreus, you are not up to this."

"I'll be fine," he groaned. "I'm a lot bigger than he is."

Seema looked doubtful, and said, "Getting killed for the Seven Gifts would be as bad as doing the killing."

"That's not going to happen." Atreus reached into his cloak for the vial of shining waters, which was still swaddled in its protective rags and said, "As I recall, this can be almost as good as a healing spell."

"What of your quest?" Seema asked. "I doubt an empty vial will please your goddess."

"Don't let it trouble you," Atreus replied, then looked across the gray waters to the center of the river, where a lone boatman, completely oblivious to his hidden audience, was gazing into the throat of the Roaring Way. "I know where to get a refill."

Atreus pulled the vial from its protective swaddling, and his heart sank. The water within looked no different from that in the river, save perhaps that it was a little clearer.

Seema touched his arm. "Atreus, I am so sorry."

Atreus shrugged, forcing himself to swallow his disappointment. "It looks like Rishi was right after all." He uncorked the vial and dumped the water into the river, then looked toward the Mar's boat and said, "I guess I'll have to do this the hard way."

Seema studied him warily, making no move to take the oars. "Do what?" she asked.

Atreus winced inwardly, but tried not to show his disappointment. She had every reason to be suspicious.

"Well, I won't be needing this for it." Atreus tossed the vial into the river, motioned at the oars, and said, "Now, will you start rowing or do I have to do everything myself?"

Seema smiled, took up the oars, and rowed out of their hiding place. Rishi was so intent on the Roaring Way that he did not notice them until their boat left the shore eddy, and even then he was so astonished that he wasted many valuable seconds standing frozen at his oars. Seema nosed into the main flow and began to row across the current, moving them into a perfect position to cut the Mar off downstream. Rishi began to row madly, aiming his prow at their midsection.

"He's going to ram us!" Atreus said.

"He is going to try," Seema sneered. "Stay in front and be ready. Do not worry about me or the boat."

Atreus crouched on his haunches, bracing himself to jump. Though Rishi was rowing like a galley slave, it seemed to take the Mar's boat forever to close the distance. Atreus glanced downstream. The Roaring Way was less than seven hundred paces distant, its dark throat growing wider and more ferocious-looking every moment. Whether there would be enough time to recover the fountain was anyone's guess. The nearer they drew to the canyon, the faster the current seemed to flow.

Atreus looked back to find the Mar's boat almost upon them, its sharp prow aimed just behind Seema's oarlocks. He stood, gathering himself for a long leap.

"Wait," Seema said.

She reversed her downstream oar and began to row in two different directions at once. The craft pivoted on its center, executing a graceful pirouette that brought it alongside Rishi's boat so close that Atreus simply stepped across into the bow.

The Mar's eyes grew wide. He dropped his oars and reached for something behind him. Atreus sprang toward the middle of the boat and cursed when his sore hip buckled and left him lurching into the oars. Rishi came up with a hatchet in one hand and the Fountain of Infinite Grace in the other.

"Put the hatchet down!" Atreus demanded, sinking into a defensive stance, ready to dodge or block. "The cup, too. I won't hurt you."

Rishi looked doubtful. "Indeed," the Mar said. "You will only deprive me of all I have worked so hard for."

The Mar raised the hatchet as though to attack, then turned and leaped into the stern of Seema's boat as it passed by. Atreus scrambled after him, but by the time he had clambered past the rowing thwart, Seema's craft was several paces upstream. He grabbed the oars and struggled to maneuver after her but could not reverse the boat's momentum quickly enough to prevent the distance from opening even farther. Seema spun her boat around to meet him, but Rishi was on her in an instant, his hatchet poised to strike if she closed the distance.

Atreus's boat began to tremble with the crash of the Roaring Way. He looked back to find the gorge less than four hundred paces away, its craggy mouth looming dark and wide. The current was picking up speed even faster than he had feared.

"You are as stubborn as a water buffalo!" Rishi called. He hefted the platinum cup in his hand. "But there is no reason we cannot strike a bargain. I will give you the fountain, and you will give me everything else."

"What about Seema?" Atreus asked. He glanced down into the back of his boat and saw the other six Sacred Gifts lying among the Mar's stolen supplies. "She must not come to any harm."

"Do not worry about me," she called.

"You said there could be no killing over the Sacred Gifts," Atreus replied. He picked up the jade vase and displayed it, praying that Seema would understand he was trying to show her where the other gifts were. "I suppose that applies to you as well."

Seema arched her brow. "I suppose it does," she said.

Rishi smiled in relief and said, "Good."

The Mar nodded to Seema and as she maneuvered their boat toward Atreus's, Rishi called, "I cannot say how pleased I am to discover that you are a reasonable man who does not hold grudges for what could not be helped."

"If you're talking about Yago, thank Seema."

The effort of rowing against the current made Atreus weak and feverish, but he did not slacken his pace. He could feel the power of the Roaring Way coursing through the boat, a constant reminder that every second was carrying them all that much closer to the canyon of no return.

"She made me promise not to kill you," Atreus added.

Rishi's smug smile vanished. "How unfortunate, then,"

he said, "that we will not be traveling together."

Seema drew her boat up alongside, and Atreus said, "Just leave the cup with Seema and come over. Everything's here."

"I am begging your pardon, good sir, but I fear that would be most foolish of me." Rishi backed toward the stern of his boat. "I will stay in my boat while you come over here, and then when I am safe—"

"Now!"

As Atreus spoke, he raised his oar out of the water and swung it into Rishi's arm. The hatchet fell free and clattered into the bottom of the boat, and Seema hurled herself from between the oarlocks, lunging for the fountain in Rishi's hand.

The Mar pivoted away, at once drawing the cup out of reach and cuffing her behind the ear. Seema did not even have a chance to cry out; she simply flew over the side and splashed into the water.

Atreus dropped his oars and kneeled, grabbing a handful of long hair and pulling her over to his boat.

"Do not worry about me," Seema sputtered, grabbing hold of the boat. She thrust a hand behind her, where Rishi's boat was beginning to drift away. The Mar himself was stooping down in the bottom of the craft, no doubt retrieving his dropped hatchet. "The cup . . . we are almost too late. . . ."

Atreus glanced downstream and saw the gorge rushing up fast. He could not even guess at the remaining distance. There was nothing ahead but a short stretch of shore eddy and the dark abyss of the granite canyon. Leaving Seema to pull herself aboard, he gathered his feet beneath him and hurled himself across the growing distance between the two boats.

He was still in the air when Rishi came up with the hatchet.

310

Atreus raised both arms, blocking with one and reaching for the Fountain of Infinite Grace with the other. His hand closed around the cup, but he was sore and feverish and too slow to stop the hatchet. The blade arced over his arm and bit into his back. He bellowed and lashed out, catching Rishi in the chest and sending him tumbling; only then did Atreus realize that he had crashed down on the side of the boat. He was hanging half in the river and half out, huffing like an exhausted carp and clutching the fountain in one bloody hand.

Rishi appeared in the stern, sitting up and trying to shake his head clear. Atreus heaved himself aboard, nearly capsizing the boat, and turned to Seema. She was standing at the oars, nosing her craft out of the current into the last little section of shore eddy. He could feel the thunder of the Roaring Way reverberating behind him, filling his body with the mad energy of wild water and the unknown beyond.

Seema yelled something he lost in the thunder and waved for him to jump, but Rishi hurled himself out of the back of the boat. Atreus brought his arm around underhand and sent the platinum chalice arcing toward Seema's boat.

Rishi screamed madly and raised his hatchet. Atreus spun on his aching sore leg and glimpsed the fountain trailing silver water as it dropped into Seema's boat, then brought a foot up for a stomp kick. Rishi flung himself into the air, stretching for Atreus's head. Atreus thrust out his leg and planted his heel square in the Mar's chest. The hatchet flew one way, Rishi the other, and they both disappeared into the river.

Atreus felt the first gentle cataracts rocking the boat. He dropped into the bottom, leaned over the side, and saw Rishi flailing about in the water. He caught the Mar by the shoulder and hauled him aboard, then glanced down the canyon. There was nothing ahead now but walls of white thundering water and the dark, looming gorge.

Atreus shoved Rishi toward the oars and glanced upstream. Seema was standing in her own boat, safe in the calm waters of the shore eddy, looking toward him holding the Fountain of Infinite Grace. She extended her arm and inverted the cup, pouring its silver waters into the river. Atreus's boat passed into the mouth of the gorge and the canyon wall loomed up beside him. It was a dark, craggy thing soaring up to the ice-blue sky itself, and Seema vanished from sight.

There was no time to wave.

NOVELS

Ed Greenwood's
The Temptation of
Elminster

The third book in the epic history of the greatest mage in the history of Faerûn.

The glory that was Cormanthyr is no more. The mighty city of Myth Drannor lies in ruin, and the still young Elminster finds himself an apprentice to a new, human mistress. A mistress with her own plans for her young student. Tempted by power, magic, and arcane knowledge, Elminster fights wizard duels, and a battle with his own conscience. Available in hardcover, December 1998!

Evermeet
Island of Elves

Elaine Cunningham

The millennia-old history of the center of elven culture. What draw does this tranquil island have on Faerûn's elves? What does the future hold for this ancient and elegant race? From the long-forgotten struggles of the elven gods to the abandonment of the forest kingdoms of Faerûn, *Evermeet* is a sweeping tale of history, destiny, and fate. Available now in hardcover.

NOVELS

CRUCIBLE:
THE TRIAL of CYRIC the MAD
Troy Denning

The time has come for the gods of Toril to bring the mad god into line for the good of the world and all its people. But on this world, the gods are far from infallible. . . . The eagerly awaited sequel to *Prince of Lies*, by the *New York Times* best-selling author of *Waterdeep*. The legacy of the Avatar continues!

Edited by Philip Athans

An anthology of all new FORGOTTEN REALMS stories by **Ed Greenwood, Elaine Cunningham, Jeff Grubb, James Lowder, Mary H. Herbert, J. Robert King**, and a host of other talented authors that bring you tales of murder, intrigue, and suspense in the strange world of Faerûn. A world where detectives can Speak with Dead, and villains can animate a victim's corpse and have it cover the clues to its own murder. A world where the mystery story takes on a whole new dimension. . . .

Richard Baker

A young apprentice wizard is confronted by the corrupting influence of power gone mad. Now, against all odds, he must stop his teachers from ripping the world apart with their unquenchable thirst for evil.